COURTNEY MILAN

the Duchess War

The Duchess War: © 2012 by Courtney Milan.
Cover design © Courtney Milan.
Cover photographs © Anna Furman | istockphoto.com.

Print Edition 1.1

For Carey
who prefers beagles over bagels

Chapter One

Leicester, November, 1863

ROBERT BLAISDELL, THE NINTH DUKE OF CLERMONT, was not hiding.

True, he'd retreated to the upstairs library of the old Guildhall, far enough from the crowd below that the noise of the ensemble had faded to a distant rumble. True, nobody else was about. Also true: He stood behind thick curtains of blue-gray velvet, which shielded him from view. And he'd had to move the heavy davenport of brown-buttoned leather to get there.

But he'd done all that not to hide himself, but because—and this was a key point in his rather specious train of logic—in this centuries-old structure of plaster and timberwork, only one of the panes in the windows opened, and that happened to be the one secreted behind the sofa.

So here he stood, cigarillo in hand, the smoke trailing out into the chilly autumn air. He wasn't hiding; it was simply a matter of preserving the aging books from fumes.

He might even have believed himself, if only he smoked.

Still, through the wavy panes of aging glass, he could make out the darkened stone of the church directly across the way. Lamplight cast unmoving shadows on the pavement below. A pile of handbills had once been stacked against the doors, but an autumn breeze had picked them up and scattered them down the street, driving them into puddles.

He was making a mess. A goddamned glorious mess. He smiled and tapped the end of his untouched cigarillo against the window opening, sending ashes twirling to the paving stones below.

The quiet creak of a door opening startled him. He turned from the window at the corresponding scritch of floorboards. Someone had come up the stairs and entered the adjoining room. The footsteps were light—a woman's, perhaps, or a child's. They were also curiously hesitant. Most people who made their way to the library in the midst of a musicale had a reason to do so. A clandestine meeting, perhaps, or a search for a missing family member.

From his vantage point behind the curtains, Robert could only see a small slice of the library. Whoever it was drew closer, walking hesitantly.

She was out of sight—somehow he was sure that she was a woman—but he could hear the soft, prowling fall of her feet, pausing every so often as if to examine the surroundings.

She didn't call out a name or make a determined search. It didn't sound as if she were looking for a hidden lover. Instead, her footsteps circled the perimeter of the room.

It took Robert half a minute to realize that he'd waited too long to announce himself. "Aha!" he could imagine himself proclaiming, springing out from behind the curtains. "I was admiring the plaster. Very evenly laid back there, did you know?"

She would think he was mad. And so far, nobody yet had come to that conclusion. So instead of speaking, he dropped his cigarillo out the window. It tumbled end over end, orange tip glowing, until it landed in a puddle and extinguished itself.

All he could see of the room was a half-shelf of books, the back of the sofa, and a table next to it on which a chess set had been laid out. The game was in progress; from what little he remembered of the rules, black was winning. Whoever it was drew nearer, and Robert shrank back against the window.

She crossed into his field of vision.

She wasn't one of the young ladies he'd met in the crowded hall earlier. Those had all been beauties, hoping to catch his eye. And she— whoever she was—was not a beauty. Her dark hair was swept into a no-nonsense knot at the back of her neck. Her lips were thin and her nose was sharp and a bit on the long side. She was dressed in a dark blue gown trimmed in ivory—no lace, no ribbons, just simple fabric. Even the cut of her gown bordered on the severe side: waist pulled in so tightly he wondered how she could breathe, sleeves marching from her shoulders to her wrists without an inch of excess fabric to soften the picture.

She didn't see Robert standing behind the curtain. She had set her head to one side and was eyeing the chess set the way a member of the Temperance League might look at a cask of brandy: as if it were an evil to be stamped out with prayer and song—and failing that, with martial law.

She took one halting step forward, then another. Then, she reached into the silk bag that hung around her wrist and retrieved a pair of spectacles.

Glasses should have made her look more severe. But as soon as she put them on, her gaze softened.

He'd read her wrongly. Her eyes hadn't been narrowed in scorn; she'd been squinting. It hadn't been severity he saw in her gaze but something else entirely—something he couldn't quite make out. She reached out and picked up a black knight, turning it around, over and over. He could see nothing about the pieces that would merit such careful attention. They were solid wood, carved with indifferent skill. Still, she studied it, her eyes wide and luminous.

Then, inexplicably, she raised it to her lips and kissed it.

Robert watched in frozen silence. It almost felt as if he were interrupting a tryst between a woman and her lover. This was a lady who had secrets, and she didn't want to share them.

The door in the far room creaked as it opened once more.

The woman's eyes grew wide and wild. She looked about frantically and dove over the davenport in her haste to hide, landing in an ignominious heap two feet away from him. She didn't see Robert even then; she curled into a ball, yanking her skirts behind the leather barrier of the sofa, breathing in shallow little gulps.

Good thing he'd moved the davenport back half a foot earlier. She never would have fit the great mass of her skirts behind it otherwise.

Her fist was still clenched around the chess piece; she shoved the knight violently under the sofa.

This time, a heavier pair of footfalls entered the room.

"Minnie?" said a man's voice. "Miss Pursling? Are you here?"

Her nose scrunched and she pushed back against the wall. She made no answer.

"Gad, man." Another voice that Robert didn't recognize—young and slightly slurred with drink. "I don't envy you that one."

"Don't speak ill of my almost-betrothed," the first voice said. "You know she's perfect for me."

"That timid little rodent?"

"She'll keep a good home. She'll see to my comfort. She'll manage the children, and she won't complain about my mistresses." There was a creak of hinges—the unmistakable sound of someone opening one of the glass doors that protected the bookshelves.

"What are you doing, Gardley?" the drunk man asked. "Looking for her among the German volumes? I don't think she'd fit." That came with an ugly laugh.

Gardley. That couldn't be the elder Mr. Gardley, owner of a distillery—not by the youth in that voice. This must be Mr. Gardley the younger. Robert had seen him from afar—an unremarkable fellow of medium height, medium-brown hair, and features that reminded him faintly of five other people.

"On the contrary," young Gardley said. "I think she'll fit quite well. As wives go, Miss Pursling will be just like these books. When I wish to take her down and read her, she'll be there. When I don't, she'll wait patiently, precisely where she was left. She'll make me a comfortable wife, Ames. Besides, my mother likes her."

Robert didn't believe he'd met an Ames. He shrugged and glanced down at—he was guessing—Miss Pursling to see how she took this revelation.

She didn't look surprised or shocked at her almost-fiancé's unromantic utterance. Instead, she looked resigned.

"You'll have to take her to bed, you know," Ames said.

"True. But not, thank God, very often."

"She's a rodent. Like all rodents, I imagine she'll squeal when she's poked."

There was a mild thump.

"What?" yelped Ames.

"That," said Gardley, "is my future wife you are talking about."

Maybe the fellow wasn't so bad after all.

Then Gardley continued. "I'm the only one who gets to think about poking *that* rodent."

Miss Pursling pressed her lips together and looked up, as if imploring the heavens. But inside the library, there were no heavens to implore. And when she looked up, through the gap in the curtains…

Her gaze met Robert's. Her eyes grew big and round. She didn't scream; she didn't gasp. She didn't twitch so much as an inch. She simply fixed him with a look that bristled with silent, venomous accusation. Her nostrils flared.

There was nothing Robert could do but lift his hand and give her a little wave.

She took off her spectacles and turned away in a gesture so regally dismissive that he had to look twice to remind himself that she was, in fact, sitting in a heap of skirts at his feet. That from this awkward angle above her, he could see straight down the neckline of her gown—right at the one part of her figure that didn't strike him as severe, but soft—

Save that for later, he admonished himself, and adjusted his gaze up a few inches. Because she'd turned away, he saw for the first time a faint scar on her left cheek, a tangled white spider web of crisscrossed lines.

"Wherever your mouse has wandered off to, it's not here," Ames was saying. "Likely she's in the lady's retiring room. I say we go back to the fun. You can always tell your mother you had words with her in the library."

"True enough," Gardley said. "And I don't need to mention that she wasn't present for them—it's not as if she would have said anything in response, even if she had been here."

Footsteps receded; the door creaked once more, and the men walked out.

Miss Pursling didn't look at Robert once they'd left, not even to acknowledge his existence with a glare. Instead, she pushed herself to her knees, made a fist, and slammed it into the hard back of the sofa—once, then twice, hitting it so hard that it moved forward with the force of her blow—all one hundred pounds of it.

He caught her wrist before she landed a third strike. "There now," he said. "You don't want to hurt yourself over him. He doesn't deserve it."

She stared up at him, her eyes wide.

He didn't see how any man could call this woman timid. She positively crackled with defiance. He let go of her arm before the fury in her could travel up his hand and consume him. He had enough anger of his own.

"Never mind me," she said. "Apparently I'm not capable of helping myself."

He almost jumped. He wasn't sure how he'd expected her voice to sound—sharp and severe, like her appearance suggested? Perhaps he'd imagined her talking in a high squeak, as if she were the rodent she'd been labeled. But her voice was low, warm, and deeply sensual. It was the kind of voice that made him suddenly aware that she was on her knees before him, her head almost level with his crotch.

Save that for later, too.

"I'm a rodent. All rodents squeal when poked." She punched the sofa once again. She was going to bruise her knuckles if she kept that up. "Are you planning to poke me, too?"

"No." Stray thoughts didn't count, thank God; if they did, all men would burn in hell forever.

"Do you always skulk behind curtains, hoping to overhear intimate conversations?"

Robert felt the tips of his ears burn. "Do you always leap behind sofas when you hear your fiancé coming?"

"Yes," she said defiantly. "Didn't you hear? I'm like a book that has been mislaid. One day, one of his servants will find me covered in dust in the middle of spring-cleaning. 'Ah,' the butler will say. 'That's where Miss Wilhelmina has ended up. I had forgotten all about her.'"

Wilhelmina Pursling? What a dreadful appellation.

She took a deep breath. "Please don't tell anyone. Not about any of this." She shut her eyes and pressed her fingers to her eyes. "Please just go away, whoever you are."

He brushed the curtains to one side and made his way around the sofa. From a few feet away, he couldn't even see her. He could only imagine her curled on the floor, furious to the point of tears.

"Minnie," he said. It wasn't polite to call her by so intimate a name. And yet he wanted to hear it on his tongue.

She didn't respond.

"I'll give you twenty minutes," he said. "If I don't see you downstairs by then, I'll come up for you."

For a few moments, there was no answer. Then: "The beautiful thing about marriage is the right it gives me to monogamy. One man intent on dictating my whereabouts is enough, wouldn't you think?"

He stared at the sofa in confusion before he realized that she thought he'd been threatening to drag her out.

Robert was good at many things. Communicating with women was not one of them.

"That's not what I meant," he muttered. "It's just…" He walked back to the sofa and peered over the leather top. "If a woman I cared about was hiding behind a sofa, I would hope that someone would take the time to make sure she was well."

There was a long pause. Then fabric rustled and she looked up at him. Her hair had begun to slip out of that severe bun; it hung around her face, softening her features, highlighting the pale whiteness of her scar. Not pretty, but…interesting. And he could have listened to her talk all night.

She stared at him in puzzlement. "Oh," she said flatly. "You're attempting to be kind." She sounded as if the possibility had never occurred to her before. She let out a sigh, and gave him a shake of her head. "But your kindness is misplaced. You see, *that*—" she pointed toward the doorway where her near-fiancé had disappeared "—that is the best possible outcome I can hope for. I have wanted just such a thing for years. As soon as I can stomach the thought, I'll be marrying him."

There was no trace of sarcasm in her voice. She stood. With a practiced hand, she smoothed her hair back under the pins and straightened her skirts until she was restored to complete propriety.

Only then did she stoop, patting under the sofa to find where she'd tossed the knight. She examined the chessboard, cocked her head, and then very, very carefully, set the piece back into place.

While he was standing there, watching her, trying to make sense of her words, she walked out the door.

❧ ❧ ❧

MINNIE DESCENDED THE STAIRS that led from the library into the darkened courtyard just outside the Great Hall, her pulse still beating heavily. For a moment, she'd thought he was going to start interrogating her. But no, she'd escaped without any questions asked. Everything was precisely as it always was: quiet and stupefyingly dull. Just as she needed it. Nothing to fear, here.

The faint strains of the concerto, poorly rendered by the indifferent skills of the local string quartet, were scarcely audible in the courtyard. Darkness painted the open yard in a palette of gray. Not that there would have been so many colors to see in daylight, either: just the blue-gray slate making up the courtyard and the aging plaster of the timber-framed walls. A few persistent weeds had sprung up in the cracks between the paving stones, but they'd withered to sepia wisps. They had scarcely any color in the harsh navy of the night. A few dark figures stood by the hall door, punch glasses in hand. Everything was muted out here—sight, sound, and all of Minnie's roiling emotions.

The musicale had drawn an astonishing number of people. Enough that the main room was mobbed, all the seats taken and still more people skirting the edges. Odd that the weak strains of badly played Beethoven would draw so many, but the crowd had come out in force. One look at that throng and Minnie had retreated, her stomach clenching in tight knots. She couldn't go into that room.

Maybe she could feign illness.

In truth, she wouldn't even have to pretend.

But—

A door opened behind her. "Miss Pursling. There you are."

Minnie jumped at the voice and swiftly turned around.

Leicester's Guildhall was an ancient building—one of the few timberwork structures from medieval times that hadn't perished in one fire or another. Over the centuries, it had acquired a hodgepodge collection of uses. It was a gathering hall for events like this, a hearing room for the mayor and his aldermen, storage for the town's few ceremonial items. They'd even converted one of the rooms into holding cells for prisoners; one side of the courtyard was brick rather than plaster, and made a home for the chief constable.

Tonight, though, the Great Hall was in use—which was why she hadn't expected anyone from the mayor's parlor.

A stocky figure approached in quick, sure strides. "Lydia has been looking for you this last half hour. As have I."

Minnie let out a breath of relief. George Stevens was a decent fellow. Better than the two louts that she'd just escaped. He was the captain of the town's militia, and her best friend's fiancé.

"Captain Stevens. It's so crowded in there. I simply had to get some air."

"Did you, now." He came toward her. At first, he was nothing more than a shadow. Then he drew close enough for her to make out details without her spectacles, and he resolved into familiar features: jovial mustache, puffed-up sideburns.

"You don't like crowds, do you?" His tone was solicitous.

"No."

"Why not?"

"I just never have." But she had, once. She had a dim memory of a swarm of men surrounding her, calling out her name, wanting to speak with her. There'd been no possibility of coquetry at the time—she'd been eight years old and dressed as a boy to boot—but there had once been a time when the energy of a crowd had buoyed her up, instead of tying her stomach in knots.

Captain Stevens came to stand beside her.

"I don't like raspberries, either," Minnie confessed. "They make my throat tingle."

But he was looking down at her, the ends of his mustache dipping with the weight of his frown. He rubbed his eyes, as if he wasn't sure what he was seeing.

"Come," Minnie said with a smile. "You've known me all these years, and in all that time I've never liked large gatherings."

"No," he said thoughtfully. "But you see, Miss Pursling, I happened to be in Manchester last week on business."

Don't react. The instinct was deeply ingrained; Minnie made sure her smile was just as easy, that she continued to smooth her skirts without freezing in fear. But there was a great roaring in her ears, and her heart began to thump all too swiftly.

"Oh," she heard herself say. Her voice sounded overly bright to her ears, and entirely too brittle. "My old home. It's been so long. How did you find it?"

"I found it strange." He took another step toward her. "I visited your Great-Aunt Caroline's old neighborhood. I intended to merely make polite conversation, convey news of you to those who might recall you as a child. But nobody remembered Caroline's sister marrying. And when I looked, there was no record of your birth in the parish register."

"How odd." Minnie stared at the cobblestones. "I don't know where my birth was registered. You'll have to ask Great-Aunt Caroline."

"Nobody had heard of you. You *did* reside in the same neighborhood as the one where she was raised, did you not?"

The wind whipped through the courtyard with a mournful two-toned whistle. Minnie's heart pounded out a little accompanying rhythm. *Not now. Not now. Please don't fall to pieces now.*

"I have never liked crowds," she heard herself say. "Not even then. I was not well-known as a child."

"Hmm."

"I was really so young when I left that I'm afraid I can be of no help. I scarcely remember Manchester at all. Great-Aunt Caro, on the other hand—"

"But it is not your great-aunt who worries me," he said slowly. "You know that keeping the peace forms a part of my duty."

Stevens had always been a serious fellow. Even though the militia had been called on only once in the last year—and then to assist in fighting a fire—he took his task quite seriously.

She no longer needed to pretend to confusion. "I don't understand. What does any of this have to do with the peace?"

"These are dangerous times," he intoned. "Why, I was part of the militia that put down the Chartist demonstrations in '42, and I've never forgotten how they started."

"This still has nothing to do with—"

"I remember the days before violence broke out," he continued coldly. "I know how it starts. It starts when someone tells the workers that they should have a voice of their own, instead of doing what they've been told. Meetings. Talks. Handbills. I've heard what you said as part of the Workers' Hygiene Commission, Miss Pursling. And I don't like it. I don't like it one bit."

His voice had gone very cold indeed, and a little shiver ran up Minnie's arms. "But all I said was—"

"I know what you said. At the time, I put it down to mere naïveté. But now I know the truth. You're not who you say you are. You're lying."

Her heart began to beat faster. She glanced to her left, at the small group ten feet away. One of the girls was drinking punch and giggling. Surely, if she screamed—

But screaming wouldn't do any good. As impossible as it seemed, someone had discovered the truth.

"I cannot be certain," he said, "but I feel in my bones that something is amiss. You are a part of *this.*" So saying, he thrust a piece of paper at her, jabbing it almost into her breastbone.

She took it from him reflexively and held it up to catch the light emanating from the windows. For a second, she wondered what she was looking at—a newspaper article? There had been enough of them, but the paper didn't have the feel of newsprint. Or perhaps it was her birth record. That would be bad enough. She retrieved her glasses from her pocket.

When she could finally read it, she almost burst into relieved laughter. Of all the accusations he could have leveled at her—of all the lies she'd told, starting with her own name—he thought she was involved with *this?* Stevens had given her a handbill, the kind that appeared on the walls of factories and was left in untidy heaps outside church doors.

WORKERS, read the top line in massive capital letters. And then, beneath it: *ORGANIZE, ORGANIZE, ORGANIZE!!!!!*

"Oh, no," she protested. "I've never seen this before. And it's really *not* my sort of thing." For one thing, she was fairly certain that any sentence that used more exclamation points than words was an abomination.

"They're all over town," he growled. "Someone is responsible for them." He held up one finger. "You volunteered to make up the handbills for the Workers' Hygiene Commission. That gives you an excuse to visit every printer in town."

"But—"

He held up a second finger. "You suggested that the workers be involved in the Commission in the first place."

"I only said it made sense to ask workers about their access to pump water! If we didn't ask, we would have done all that work only to find their health unchanged. It's a long way from there to suggesting that they organize."

A third finger. "Your great-aunts are involved in that dreadful food cooperative, and I happen to know you were instrumental in arranging it."

"A business transaction! What does it matter where we sell our cabbages?"

Stevens pointed those three fingers at her. "It's all of a pattern. You're sympathetic to the workers, and you're not who you claim to be. *Someone* is helping them print handbills. You must think I'm stupid, to sign them like *that.*" He gestured at the bottom of the handbill. There was a name at the end. She squinted at it through her glasses.

Not a name. A pseudonym.

De minimis, she read. She'd never learned Latin, but she knew a little Italian and a good amount of French, and she thought it meant something like "trifles." A little thing.

"I don't understand." She shook her head blankly. "What has that to do with me?"

"De. Minnie. Mis." He spoke the syllables separately, giving her name a savage twist. "You must think me a fool, *Miss Minnie.*"

It made a horrible kind of logic, so twisted that she might have laughed outright. Except that the consequence of this joke was not amusing.

"I have no proof," he said, "and as your friendship with my future wife is known, I have no wish to see you publicly humiliated and charged with criminal sedition."

"Criminal sedition!" she echoed in disbelief.

"So consider this a warning. If you keep on with *this*—" he flicked the paper in her hands "—I will find out the truth of your origins. I will prove that you are the one behind this. And I will ruin you."

"I have nothing to do with it!" she protested, but it was futile. He was already turning away.

She clenched the handbill in her fist. What a damnable turn of events. Stevens was starting from a false premise, but it didn't matter how he found the trail. If he followed it, he'd discover everything. Minnie's past. Her real name. And most of all, her sins—long-buried, but not dead.

De minimis.

The difference between ruin and safety *was* a little thing. A very little thing, but she wasn't going to lose it.

Chapter Two

"MINNIE!"

This time, when the voice came across the courtyard, Minnie didn't startle. Her heart didn't race. Instead, she found herself growing calmer, and a real smile took over her face. She turned to the speaker, holding out her hands. "Lydia," she said warmly. "I am so glad to see you."

"Where have you been?" Lydia asked. "I looked all over for you."

She might have lied to anyone else. But Lydia... "Hiding," Minnie returned. "Behind the davenport in the library."

Anyone else would have taken that amiss. Lydia, however, knew Minnie as well as anyone ever could. She snorted and shook her head. "That's so...so..."

"Ridiculous?"

"So unsurprising," her friend answered. "I'm glad I found you, though. It's time."

"Time? Time for what?" There was nothing playing beside Beethoven today.

But her friend didn't say anything. She simply took hold of Minnie's elbow and walked her to the door of the mayor's parlor.

Minnie planted her feet. "Lydia, I meant it. What time is it?"

"I knew you'd never suffer the introduction in the Great Hall with all those people about," Lydia said with a smile. "So I asked Papa to keep watch in the parlor. It's time for you to be introduced."

"Introduced?" The courtyard was almost empty behind them. "To whom am I being introduced?"

Her friend wagged a finger at her. "You need to stay abreast of gossip. How is it possible that you do not *know*? He's only twenty-eight years old, you know, and he has a reputation as a statesman—he's widely credited with the Importation Compromise of 1860."

Lydia said this as if she knew what that was—as if everyone knew about the Importation Compromise of 1860. Minnie had never heard of it before, and was fairly certain that Lydia hadn't, either.

Lydia let out a blissful sigh. "And he's *here.*"

"Yes, but who is he?" She cast another look at her friend. "And what do you mean by that sigh? You're engaged."

"Yes," Lydia said, "And very, very happily so."

One too many *verys* for believability, but as Minnie had never successfully argued the point before, there was no point in starting now.

"But *you're* not engaged." Lydia tugged on her hand. "Not yet. And in any event, what does reality have to do with imagination? Can you not once dream about yourself dressed in a gorgeous red silk, descending into a crowd of adoring masses with a handsome man at your side?"

Minnie *could* imagine it, but the masses in her imagination were never adoring. They shouted. They threw things. They called her names, and she had only to wait for a nightmare to experience it again.

"I'm not saying you must lay out funds for a wedding breakfast on the instant. Just dream. A little." So saying, Lydia wrenched open the door.

There were only a handful of people in the room beyond. Mr. Charingford stood nearest the door, waiting for them. He greeted his daughter with a nod. The room was small, but the walls had been paneled in wood, the windows were stained glass, and the fireplace was adorned with carving. The Leicester coat of arms took pride of place on the far wall, and the heavy mayor's chair stood at the front of the room.

That was where the few people had congregated—the mayor, his wife, Stevens, a man she didn't recognize and... Minnie's breath caught.

It was him. That blond-haired, blue-eyed man who'd spoken to her in the library. He'd looked far too young to be anyone important. More to the point, he'd seemed far too nice for it. To see the mayor dance attendance on him...

"You see?" Lydia said in a low voice. "I think even *you* could dream about him."

Handsome and kind and important. The tug of her imagination was an almost visceral thing, leading her along paths paved with moonlit fantasies.

"Sometimes," Minnie said, "if you believe in the impossible..."

She had been so young, when her father had been liked well enough that he was invited everywhere. Vienna. Paris. Rome. He'd had little to his credit aside from an old family name, an easy style of conversation, and a talent for chess-playing that was almost unsurpassed. He'd dreamed of the impossible, and he'd infected her with his madness.

All you have to do is believe, he'd told her from the time she was five. *We don't need wealth. We don't need riches. We Lanes just believe harder than everyone else, and good things come to us.*

And so she'd believed. She'd believed him so hard that there had been nothing to her but hollow belief when all his schemes had broken apart.

"If you believe in the impossible," Lydia said, jerking her back to the present, "it might come true."

"If you believe in the impossible," Minnie said tartly, "you let go of what you have."

There were no moonlit paths that led to this man. There was only a gentleman who had spoken kindly to her. That was it. No dreams. No fantasies.

"And you have so much to lose." Lydia's voice was mocking.

"I have a great deal to lose. Nobody points at me and whispers when I go down the street. Enraged mobs do not follow me seeking vengeance. Nobody throws stones."

And strange men were still kind to her. He was unfairly handsome—no doubt that explained the gleam in Lydia's eye. From what Lydia had said about importation, he was involved in politics. A Member of Parliament, perhaps? He seemed too young for that.

"So serious," Lydia said, pulling a face. "Yes, you're right. You could be spit upon and hailed as a complete monster. And perhaps you might be eaten by dragons. Be reasonable. Nothing of that ilk is even remotely possible. Since you can't envision it for yourself, I'll do it for you. For the next minute, I'm going to imagine that he'll turn around and take one look at you..."

There was no need to imagine. He, whoever he was, turned at that moment. He looked at Lydia, who was bristling with excitement. She sank into a deep curtsey. Then his eyes rested on Minnie.

There you are, his gaze seemed to say. Or something like. Because a spark of recognition traveled through her. It wasn't something as simple as seeing his face and finding it familiar. It was the sense that they knew one another, that their acquaintance ran deeper than a few moments spent together behind a davenport.

The man's eyes traveled right, lighting on Lydia's father standing by them. He took a few steps forward, abandoning the people around him. "Mr. Charingford, isn't it?" he asked.

As he came closer, he caught Minnie's eye once more and he gave her a slightly pained smile—one that tugged at some long-hidden memory.

If Mr. Charingford's agitation hadn't given her a hint, that smile would have convinced her. This man was someone important. It took her a moment to place that curious expression on his face—that small smile, paired with eyes that crinkled in something close to chagrin.

She'd seen it eight years ago on Willy Jenkins's face. Willy Jenkins had been bigger than all the other boys his age—alarmingly so. At just fifteen years of age, he'd been six feet tall and almost thirteen stone in weight. He had the strength to fit his size, too. She'd seen him lift his two younger brothers, once, one in each hand.

Willy Jenkins was big and strong, and the other boys would have been frightened of him were it not for his smile.

Mr. Charingford gave an obsequious bow, so low that he almost doubled over. He scarcely choked the words out. "Might I present...?"

Mr. Charingford didn't even assume that this man would *allow* the introduction—seemed to think that it would be perfectly good manners if he said no.

"By all means," the man said. He met Minnie's gaze; she looked away swiftly. "My circle of acquaintance is never so large that it cannot include more young ladies." That apologetic smile again—Willy's smile. It was the one Willy gave when he won at arm wrestling—and he had always won at arm wrestling. It was one that said: *I'm sorry that I am bigger than you and stronger than you. I'm always going to win, but I'll try not to hurt you when I do.* It was the smile of a man who knew he possessed considerable strength, and found it faintly embarrassing.

"So considerate," Mr. Charingford said. "This is my daughter, Miss Lydia Charingford, and her friend, Miss Wilhelmina Pursling."

The blond man bowed over Lydia's hand—a faint inclination of his head—and reached to take Minnie's fingers.

"Young ladies," Mr. Charingford said, "this is Robert Alan Graydon Blaisdell."

His eyes—a blue so lacking in color that it put her in mind of a lake in winter—met hers. That smile curled up at the corners, more chagrined than ever. His fingers touched hers, and even through their gloves his hand felt overly warm. Despite every ounce of good sense, Minnie could feel herself respond to him. Her smile peeked out to match his. In her imagination, for just that one moment, there *were* moonlit paths. And that silver light painted every bleak facet of her life in magic.

Beside her, Mr. Charingford swallowed, the sound audible at this distance. "He is, of course, His Grace, the Duke of Clermont."

Minnie almost yanked her fingers back. A duke? A bloody *duke* had found her behind the sofa? No. No. Impossible.

Charingford indicated the other man by his side. "And his, uh, his man of business—"

"My friend," the duke interrupted.

"Yes." Charingford swallowed. "Of course. His friend, Mr. Oliver Marshall."

"Miss Charingford. Miss Pursling," the duke said, nodding to Lydia over Minnie's shoulder. "All the pleasure in the introduction is surely mine."

Minnie tipped her head slightly. "Your Grace," she choked out.

The entire night was conspiring to destroy her. Her best friend's fiancé thought she was engaging in sedition, and the Duke of Bloody Clermont could ruin her with a single word. That for her treacherous imagination. That for moonlit paths. That for even a moment's contemplation of romance. Dreams failed, and when they fled, they left reality all the colder.

His Grace met her eyes just before Minnie took her leave. And once again, he gave her that sheepish smile. This time, she knew what it meant.

She was nothing. He had everything. And for what little it was worth, he was embarrassed by his own strength.

⌘ ⌘ ⌘

THE CARRIAGE SWAYED, NOT SMOOTHLY, but in harsh back-and-forth jerks. Once, Minnie supposed, the springs had been new, and every bump in the road back to her great-aunts' farm would not have been magnified into teeth-jarring jolts. But funds were scarce, and repairs were a luxury, one that her great-aunts could ill afford.

Her Great-Aunt Caroline sat on the bench across from Minnie, her cane poised over her knee. Next to her sat Elizabeth, less stooped but far more gray. They could not have looked more different if they had been picked from a crowd. Caro was tall and plump, while Eliza was short and angular. Caro's hair was sleek and dark, with only a few gray strands; Eliza's once-blond hair had become white and frizzled.

At their age, they should have been resting at home by the fire on a cold November night, not gallivanting out to attend musical evenings. But they had come with her, and now they wore twin expressions of grim dissatisfaction.

In the dark of night, shielded from the view of the man who drove the carriage, they'd joined hands for comfort.

And, as she always did, Minnie was about to make everything worse.

"Great-Aunt Caro. Great-Aunt Eliza." Her voice was quiet in the velvet night, almost overwhelmed by the rattle of the wheels. "There's something I have to tell you. It's about Captain Stevens."

The two women exchanged a long, lingering glance. "We know," Great-Aunt Caro said. "We were wondering whether to mention it to you."

"He's looking into my past."

The two women exchanged another slow look. But Caro was the one who eventually spoke. "It's a setback, to be sure, but we've weathered worse setbacks before."

Minnie shook her head. "He knows. Or he will. Soon. I don't know what to do."

Eliza reached over and patted Minnie on the knee. "You're panicking," she said softly. "Never panic; it tells others that something is wrong. Just remember, the truth is too outlandish to be considered. Nobody will ever guess."

Minnie took a deep gulp of air, and then another.

"But—"

"In order to uncover the truth," Eliza said, "he'd have to ask the right questions. And trust me, my dear. Nobody, but *nobody,* is ever going to ask whether your father passed you off as a boy for the first twelve years of your life."

"Still, he only needs to suspect—"

"Stop. Minnie. Breathe. Working yourself into a state won't accomplish anything."

Easy for them to say. With her eyes shut, she could almost see the mob closing around her, harsh discordant shouts emanating from faces twisted by anger…

"It's nothing," Eliza said, awkwardly rearranging herself in the carriage so that she sat next to Minnie. She put her hand on Minnie's shoulder. "It's nothing. It's nothing." With each repetition, she smoothed Minnie's hair. Each whisper brought greater calm, until Minnie could curb her rising panic. She locked that memory back in the past where it belonged, held it there until her vision stopped swimming and her breath returned to a regular cadence.

"That's better," Eliza said. "We'll handle this. Stevens spoke to me as well. He thinks you're lying to us—he suggested, in fact, that you might not be who you claimed, that you were taking advantage of our kindness."

"Oh, God." Minnie put her head in her hands.

"No, no," Caro said. "This story is easier to combat, because it is so clearly false. There's no need for us to even lie. I said that I'd been there the day you were born, that I promised your mother on her deathbed that I would see to your wellbeing, and that I didn't appreciate his poking his nose in where it didn't belong. When I told him that there was no way that

you were some cuckoo thrust into our nest unawares, he believed me."
Caro gave a sharp nod. "He knows you're my great-niece—no question
about that. He suspects that something is not quite right, but I've made
him very uncertain. He won't do anything."

"But I'm not." Minnie gulped for air. "I'm not your great-niece. I'm—"

Caro reached out her cane and rapped Minnie smartly on the leg.
"Don't you speak like that. You know how it is."

She did. For as long as Minnie could remember, she'd called both
Caro and Eliza great-aunt, even though Eliza was her only blood relation.
Almost fifty years ago, the two women had gone to finishing school
together. They'd come out in London society at the same time. And when
they failed to find men that they loved after a handful of Seasons, they had
refused to marry for convenience. Instead, they'd retired together to the
small farm that Caro owned just outside of Leicester—friends and
spinsters for the remainder of their lives. They were as close as sisters.
Closer, Minnie suspected.

"Don't you worry," Eliza said. "I did promise your mother. We *both*
did." Her voice shook. "I failed her once, to my great shame. Never
again."

Minnie reached up and touched the scar on her cheek. When she was
a child, she'd thought herself invulnerable. Other people might falter and
fail, but she could not. The very brazenness of what she'd achieved was
matched only by how far she'd fallen after. She could still remember lying
in the dark, not knowing if she'd have the use of her eye again. That was
when her great-aunts had come for her.

"If you come with us," Caro had told her, "you'll have a chance."

They had offered not the glittering, glamorous life that most young
girls dreamed about. If she came with her great-aunts, she could expect a
frugal life. An assumed name. She'd have a few years of childhood,
followed by a little time to meet the local men in town. She might marry
and have children. There would be no fame, no adulation. They could
provide her only one benefit: a future without angry mobs.

Her great-aunts had sacrificed so much to give her that bare, gray
chance. They'd scraped pennies so that she could have a respectable
wardrobe once she was old enough to go out in mixed company. They
never complained, but Minnie knew why there was no sugar in their tea.
She knew why they'd—regretfully—let their subscription to the lending
library lapse. They'd sacrificed every comfort of their old age for Minnie.

And she didn't even have the grace to want what they had so
generously won for her.

"Maybe," she suggested, "maybe if we tell Captain Stevens the truth…"

Her great-aunts stared at her in dismay. "Minnie," Eliza said slowly. "Darling. After all this time! You know you must never do that."

Caro picked up where Eliza had left off. "These rules we made for you—they're not intended to be strictures. Or punishments. We made them because we love you. Because we want you to have a future. Isn't Walter Gardley sweet on you? Because if you could catch him, and marry him quickly…that might be a good idea."

"Yes," Caro echoed, nodding. "That would be a very good idea. All Stevens's wild imaginings will lose force once you're married to a distiller's son. Then it would be your own livelihood at stake should the workers organize. Marriage would secure not only your future, but your credentials."

Nothing she hadn't thought to herself before.

She'd known what a coup it was to get even that. For a girl with no dowry and only middling looks, *any* man was a catch. Even if he wanted her because he thought she would suffer his boorish behavior in silence. And yet she couldn't muster even the smallest iota of enthusiasm over the prospect.

"I heard him talking," Minnie choked out. "He said I was a mouse— that I'd keep my peace while he took a mistress."

Caro and Eliza looked at one another.

"You don't have to marry him," Eliza said slowly. "Of course you don't, if it will make you unhappy. But before you refuse, please consider what your other choices would be. I *might* counsel you to wait." That was said with a dubious frown, one that said a second, preferable proposal was unlikely to come as Minnie aged. "If there's the smallest chance that Stevens might hit on the truth…" She trailed off.

She didn't need to voice the words. If the truth came out, there wouldn't be another offer.

Minnie hadn't lied to the Duke of Clermont. Gardley *was* the best she could hope for—a man who knew only that she grew quiet in crowds. A man who preferred her quiet. He hadn't bothered to discover a single thing about her: her favorite color, her favorite food. But then, it would be safer to marry a man who wanted to know nothing of her.

Miss Wilhelmina Pursling would be pathetically grateful to Gardley for an offer of marriage. But Minerva Lane, on the other hand…

"He doesn't even know who I am," she said. "He called me a little rodent. Minerva Lane was *never* a rodent."

"Don't say that name." Eliza's voice was quiet but alarmed. Her hand pressed against Minnie's knees, clutching.

"Keep quiet," Caro said. "It never does to speak the truth."

Keep quiet. Don't panic. Never tell anyone the truth. She'd lived with their rules for twelve years, and for what? So that she might one day be so lucky as to be forgotten entirely.

The memory of Minerva Lane—of who she'd been, what she'd done—felt like a hot coal covered in cold ashes. It smoldered on long after the fire had been doused. Sometimes, all that heat rose up in her until she felt the need to shriek like a teapot. Until she wanted to burn the mousy shreds of her tattered personality.

It rose up in her now, that fiery rebellion.

The part of her that was still Minerva—the part that hadn't been ground to smoothness—whispered temptation in her ear. *You don't need to keep quiet. You need a strategy.*

No strategies. Her great-aunts really *would* protest, if they knew that she contemplated taking action. It had been years since she'd allowed herself to do so.

Stevens thinks you're writing the pamphlets. You know you're not. So find out who's doing it.

Stupid. Foolish. Idiotic. Impossible.

But it didn't matter how she browbeat herself; the insidious thought wouldn't leave. How could she find out who'd done it? It could be anyone.

No, it can't. You know it's not Captain Stevens. Not your great-aunts. Not yourself. If she could figure out who couldn't have done it, only the guilty would remain. By process of elimination…

No, you fool. There are hundreds that could be to blame. Thousands.

But having given herself a task, it was nearly impossible to shut down her thoughts. There were those block-letter capitals, the exclamation points. Paragraphs of text, describing the factory owners and their offspring. Something *was* odd there.

And then, for some reason, she thought about something else entirely. Minnie knew why she had been hiding behind the davenport. She'd been avoiding the crowds and Gardley's proposal.

But why on earth had the Duke of Clermont been there?

ORGANIZE, ORGANIZE, ORGANIZE!!!!

And how strange was that smile of his—that friendly smile, slightly abashed? When would a duke ever have learned to apologize for being what he was?

No, there was definitely something odd there. Something…

The realization hit her with a force so blinding that the carriage almost seemed to disappear in a flash of light.

Moments like these were one of the reasons it had been so lovely to be Minerva Lane. There were times when it felt like words were mere threads, completely inadequate to contain the enormity of her thoughts. The landscape in her head rearranged with tectonic vigor, coming together with a certainty that was larger than her ability to explain.

And like that, even though she knew she shouldn't—even though she knew how dangerous it was to strategize—Minnie knew what she needed to do. The plan fell into her lap with full force.

It was not the kind of thing that the rodent-like Miss Pursling would consider. But Minerva Lane, now—*she* knew what to do.

And thank God, she *wasn't* going to have to marry Walter Gardley immediately.

Maybe one day she would. But if she could keep Stevens from suspecting her, she might be able to put him off for months. And maybe—just maybe—something better would come along.

Chapter Three

IT WAS ALMOST UNFAIR, MINNIE THOUGHT as the Duke of Clermont entered his front parlor, how handsome he was. The morning sunlight streaming in through the windows bounced off light blond hair that would have been too long, had it not had a bit of an unruly curl to it. He stopped on the threshold and rubbed his hand through his hair as he contemplated her, mussing it even further. But whatever softness the disarray of his hair might have imparted to his appearance was countered by his eyes. They were sharp and cold, a piercing blue, like a creek flooded with icy spring waters. Those eyes landed on her and rested for a few seconds, and then darted to Lydia, who stood by her side.

Lydia had giggled when she heard that Minnie intended to call on the Duke of Clermont—and she hadn't batted an eyelash when Minnie had explained that she needed to talk to him privately.

It was only in Minnie's imagination that the duke's gaze sliced through the façade that she presented to the rest of the world. He only *looked* as if he knew everything.

He couldn't have known anything, because as he looked at her, he smiled in something like pleasure. Just a little curl to his mouth, but there was also a subtle change to his eyes—a shift from the pale blue of ice-water to the slightly-less-pale blue of a light summer sky.

There was something boyish about his good looks: a hint of shyness in his smile, a leanness to his frame. Or maybe it was the way that he looked away from her so quickly and then glanced back.

If she hadn't heard Packerly, the MP, talking last night, extolling the young duke's efforts in Parliament, she'd have believed him a fraud. Handsome, young, and unassuming? Far too good to be true. Dukes in reality were paunchy, old, and demanding.

"Miss Pursling," he said. "This is an unexpected pleasure."

Unexpected, she believed. Pleasure…well, he'd recant that before they were done.

"Your Grace," Minnie said.

He briefly took her hand in his—through their gloves, she had a sensation of warmth—and inclined his head to her.

"Miss Charingford." Clermont bowed over her friend's hand as if she were the grandest lady. As he did, Lydia cast a sidelong look at Minnie and pressed her lips together as if suppressing the urge to giggle.

"What brings you ladies here?" he asked.

Lydia cast a speaking glance at Minnie, waiting to have all revealed.

"If anyone asks," Minnie said, "we've come to solicit donations for the Workers' Hygiene Commission." She held her breath, wondering how astute he was.

The duke pondered this for a few moments. "I consider myself solicited," he said. "I'll be sure to make an appropriate donation, if you'll leave the particulars. As for the rest... If this is about last night, you can rest assured that I am the soul of discretion."

Astute enough.

Lydia raised an eyebrow at the implication that they'd talked before and Minnie shook her head. "No, Your Grace. There's something else I must discuss with you. I'm afraid that Miss Charingford has come along as chaperone, but what I must say is not for her ears."

"True," Lydia said cheerfully. "I have no idea what any of this is about."

"I see." His smile faded to guarded coolness. No doubt he was imagining something lurid and scandalous—some plot to entrap him into marriage. He was a good-looking duke with a reasonable fortune; he likely encountered such plots on a regular basis. But he didn't throw her out. Instead, he rubbed his chin and looked about the room.

"Well. If you're capable of conversing quietly, Miss Charingford can sit here." He gestured to a chair by the door. "We'll leave the door open, and we can arrange ourselves by the window. She'll be able to see everything, ensure propriety, and hear nothing."

He held out the chair for Lydia. He acted the perfect gentleman, his manners so uncontrived that she almost doubted her own instincts. He rang a bell—tea on two trays, he said, when a servant ducked her head in. While they were waiting, he set one hand in the small of Minnie's back and walked her to the window. It was the tiniest point of contact—just the warmth of his hand against her spine, muted by layers of fabric—yet still she felt it all the way to the pulse that jumped at her throat.

It was so unfair she could scream. He was rich, handsome, and able to set her heart beating with a mere tap of his finger. She was here to blackmail the man, not to flirt with him. Out the front window, she could see the square outside.

Squares were less common in Leicester than London. This one was badly kept. There was one tree, so spindly it was scarcely fit to be called by the name. The grass had long since perished, giving way to gray gravel. But then, this was one of the few neighborhoods in Leicester where there *were* squares.

The most successful tradesmen made their homes a short ways down the London road in Stoneygate. The gentry lived on great tracts of land on estates in the surrounding countryside. Everyone with real wealth and position made their homes outside the town.

But the duke had not. Minnie fingered the paper in her pocket and added that to the list of strange things about the man. When dukes came to the region, they situated themselves in Quorn or Melton-Mowbray for the fox hunts. He, however, had leased a residence that stood mere blocks from the factories.

"How may I be of assistance?" he asked.

There was too much that didn't fit. He *was* lying. He had to be. She just didn't know why. A chessboard was set up on the side table. She tried not to look at it, tried not to feel the inevitable tug. But...

White was winning. It was six moves to checkmate, maybe only three. She could see the end, the pincer made by rook and bishop, the line of three white pawns slicing the board in two.

"You play chess?" she asked.

"No." He waved a hand. "I lose at chess. Badly. But my—that is to say, one of the men here with me plays chess by correspondence with his father. This is where he keeps the board. You're not going to challenge me to a game, are you?" He smiled at that.

Minnie shook her head. "No. An idle question."

The maids came with the tea. Minnie waited until they left. Then she reached into her skirt pocket and removed the handbill that Stevens had shoved at her on the previous evening. The edges, wetted by last night's rain, had curled and yellowed as they dried, but she held it out to him anyway.

He didn't take it. He glanced at the paper curiously—long enough to read the block-letter title that took up the first quarter of the page—and then looked back at her. "Am I supposed to take an interest in radical handbills?"

"No, Your Grace." She could scarcely believe her audacity. "You don't take an interest in radical handbills. You write them."

He looked at the paper. Slowly, he looked at her and arched his eyebrow. Minnie looked away, her innards twisting under his intense perusal. Finally, he picked up a bun and broke it in half. Steam rose, but the heat didn't seem to bother his hands.

He didn't even need to respond. Her accusation was laughably absurd. He sat in his comfortable chair surrounded by furniture that was waxed and polished on a daily basis by servants who had nothing to do but leap on motes of dust as soon as they dared to appear. The Duke of Clermont had taken a house and hired twelve servants for the space of two months. He had estates scattered across England, and a fortune that the gossip papers could only breathlessly speak of as tens, if not hundreds, of thousands. A man like him had no reason to publish radical political circulars.

But then, she already knew he wasn't what he seemed.

As if to underscore all that, he casually ate a bite of bun and gestured to her to do the same.

No chance of that. Her stomach cramped when she even thought of sipping tea. Just when she thought he was simply going to freeze her accusation into oblivion by refusing to address it, he reached out and adjusted the paper.

"Workers," he read. "Organize, organize, organize, followed by a great many exclamation points." He made a dismissive noise. "I abhor exclamation points, for one thing. Why do you suppose I have anything to do with this?"

She had no real proof to offer, only the feel of the way the pieces fit together. But still she was sure of it. The worst case was that she was wrong. Then she would embarrass herself in front of a man she would never see again. She folded her hands in her lap and waited. If he could make her uncomfortable with silence, she could do the same.

And indeed, he spoke first.

"Is it because I've just arrived in town, and you don't want any of your friends blamed?"

She held her tongue.

"Because I look like a rabble-rouser?" There was a wry tone to his voice. He looked—and sounded—like anything but. His voice was smooth and fluid, drawling out syllables in the queen's best English. He had a faint smile on his face, a condescending expression that said he was humoring her.

"Or is it because you've heard stories of my radical proclivities?"

There were no such stories. His reputation was that of a statesman, a man who was both shrewd and soft-spoken.

"Why are you here?" Minnie asked instead. "I've heard what's said, but a man of your stature who was thinking of investing in Leicester industry would send a man of business, instead of arriving himself and overawing everyone."

"I have friends in the vicinity."

"If they were such good friends as to necessitate a visit, you would be staying with them."

He shrugged. "I hate imposing on others."

"You're a duke. You're *always* imposing."

He grimaced, looking faintly embarrassed. "That, Miss Pursling, is why I hate doing it. Have you any substance to your accusations?"

She picked up the paper. "If you must know, there are two paragraphs in this circular that convince me it was written by you."

"By all means." He held out his hand, palm up. "Read them, and expose me."

Minnie took her spectacles from her pocket and found the right place. "'What do the masters do to earn the lion's share of the pay? They supervise. They own. And for that task—one that takes no thought, no labor—they are paid sums so large that they need not even lift a finger to dress themselves. Their daughters, instead of toiling from the age of fourteen, are free to do as they wish; their sons need worry only about the degree of their dissipation.'"

No reaction whatsoever from the duke. He simply sat in his chair and looked at her with those ice-blue eyes, tapping his fingers lightly against the arm. "You think a duke wrote that?" he finally asked, a note of humor in his voice.

"It wasn't a worker."

"You'd be surprised at the literacy that many—"

"I *am* involved in the Workers' Hygiene Commission," Minnie interrupted. "I don't underestimate any of them. There's a fellow with a memory like an encyclopedia, who reads the latest Dickens serial by night and recites it back to the others during the day. It's not merely the first paragraph that gives you away. It's the first taken in concert with the second."

"Oh," he said, still smiling. "There's a second, much more damning paragraph. Of course, the flyer is only two paragraphs long. So by all means, read away."

"I can't do that." Minnie set the paper down and removed her spectacles. "The second paragraph, Your Grace, is the one you failed to write. You wrote all about what the masters *didn't* do. You never once mentioned what the workers *did* do. A laborer would have been focused on how he spends his day—what he did, who it benefited—not how someone else spends his. This was written by someone who, whatever his intentions, was thinking like a master."

Clermont paused and tilted his head. Then he reached out, picked up the paper, and read it through. When he started, his lips were set in a frown. He read quickly, his eyes scanning down the page. But she could watch his expression alter—running from disbelief, to the quirk of an eyebrow in surprise. Slowly, his mouth curled in a smile. When he looked up, his eyes—so stark and cold before—were sparkling.

"Well," he finally said. "I'll be damned. You're right."

"Knowing that, it's a matter of simple logic." Minnie folded her hands. "A master wouldn't write that—he has too much at stake. And once I subtract the workers and the masters, my choices are few. You *were* hiding behind the curtain last night. You're not what you seem. You are the only possibility that makes sense of the available evidence."

She expected him to deny authorship once more. What she presented was the feeblest pretense of proof.

But he didn't argue with her. He glanced across the room at Lydia—who was sipping her tea and casting glances laden with curiosity in their direction. Then he lowered his voice even further. "If you intended to denounce me publicly, you would have told the magistrate, who would have come here with a handful of angry masters in tow, all demanding that I stop riling the workers. You didn't. In fact"—he inclined his head toward Lydia—"you've taken pains to hide the true purpose of your visit from everyone. What is it you want from me?" His hand rested over his waistcoat pocket, where a man might keep a coin purse.

"I want you to stop."

His eyes bored into her.

"Please." She swallowed. "You see, these sheets put everyone at each others' throats. Everyone is watching each other. And I am involved with distributing handbills for the workers' charity—there's nothing radical about those; they're all about cholera. Still, suspicion might fall on me."

"Surely, even if you came under scrutiny, you would be quickly vindicated." He paused. "Unless you have something else to hide. Perhaps you don't want anyone asking why a young lady on the verge of matrimony leaps behind a davenport when her suitor appears." He raised an eyebrow.

Minnie couldn't meet his eyes any longer. "That's the way of it," she whispered, looking into her teacup.

"What a surprise," he said, his voice low and teasing. "Never say that *you* have something in your past you wish to hide."

She stared into the brown liquid in her cup. "Easy for you to find this all so amusing. But my future is no game. I have worked hard to get where I am, and I will fight to keep what little comfort I've earned, small though it may be. I don't wish to have my actions examined too closely. Neither, I suspect, do you. If you stop, we'll both be safe."

"Safe." He drew out the syllable, as if savoring the word. "I don't much care for *safe,* myself. And I'd be doing you a favor if I separated you from your suitor."

She could hardly argue with that. But she shook her head. "It's no favor if you make it impossible for me to find another. I live on fate, Your Grace. When my great-aunt passes away, the farm will go to her cousin. My Great-Aunt Elizabeth and I will have nowhere to go. I *must* marry." She lifted her head now, and looked him full in the eyes. "I haven't any choice."

His gaze softened. "Your past… It's so bad that you're worrying that someone *might* poke into it because of a handbill?"

For one mad moment, she considered laying the whole story at his feet. He looked so open, with his head tilted in that welcome, beguiling manner. Surely, she could…

Even the thought of confession brought a chill to the air, a cramp to her lungs.

She looked back at her tea. "Do you know what it is like to be a woman in these modern times? Gentlemen marry less and less these days. I read that thirty-four percent of genteel young ladies reach the age of twenty-seven without marrying. I don't need anything shameful in my past. Anything outside the ordinary, no matter how harmless it might seem, is a catastrophe."

He sat back in his chair and considered this. "Then I see an alternate solution to our mutual problem. I, apparently, need a more believable reason to stay in town. If you didn't believe what I said, others won't either. You need to be in the top sixty-six percent of marriageable women, such as it is." He shrugged. "So I'll set up a flirtation with you while I'm here. You can reject me; I'll moon about morosely. The whole thing will do wonders for your reputation. I keep writing; you get your husband."

He said it so matter-of-factly, but the image that brought up—of *him* dancing attendance on *her,* of his hand resting over hers in a waltz—made her stomach flutter uncertainly. She gave her head a fierce shake. "That's a terrible idea. Nobody would ever believe that you had any interest in me."

"I could make them believe. Not one in ten thousand would have figured out what you just did. Not one. I could make everyone believe in the woman who saw that—quiet, yes, and perhaps a little shy in company—"

Minnie made a rude noise, but he waved her quiet.

"You have steel for your backbone and a rare talent for seeing what is plainly in front of your face. I could make everyone see that." His eyes were intense, boring into her. There was no escaping him, it seemed. He dropped his voice. "I could make everyone see *you.*"

Was it just her stomach fluttering? No. Her whole body seemed on the verge of trembling. It had been years since anyone pretended to have an interest in her. To have his attention fall upon her in such concentrated fashion… It was too much.

But he wasn't finished. "Then there's your hair. Hair shouldn't change color, just by curling, but the edges seem to catch the light, and I can't be sure if it's brown or blond or even red when it does. I could watch that for hours, to try and figure it out."

Her heart was thudding in her chest. It wasn't beating any faster; just more heavily, as if her blood required more work to move.

But this was an exercise in hypotheticals, and Minnie was too desperate to be anything other than practical.

"Go on with you." She'd intended the words to be dismissive, but her voice trembled. "What would you say when it was just men about? When they were asking you what the devil you saw in that mousy Miss Pursling? I daresay you'd never tell them that you were entranced by the curl of my hair. That's the sort of thing a man says to convince a woman, but men don't talk that way amongst themselves."

He'd obviously expected her to swallow that codswallop about her hair, because he paused, slightly taken aback. And then, he gave her a shake of his head and a grin. "Come, Miss Pursling," he said. "Men wouldn't ask any such thing. They'd already know what caught my eye." He leaned forward and whispered in conspiratorial fashion. "It's your tits."

Her mouth dropped open. She was suddenly very aware of said tits— warm and tingling in anticipation, even though he wasn't anywhere near them.

He murmured, "They're magnificent."

He wasn't even looking at them, but Minnie's hands itched to cover herself—not to block out his sight, but to explore her own curves. To see if, perhaps, her bosom *was* magnificent—if it had been magnificent all these years, and she had simply never noticed.

If another man had said that her tits were magnificent, it might have been in a leering, lustful way—one that would have made her skin crawl. But the Duke of Clermont was smiling and cheerful, and he'd thrown it out there as if it were merely one more fact to be recounted. *The weather is lovely. The streets are paved with cobblestone. Your tits are magnificent.*

"Don't protest," he said. "You did ask, and after furthering our acquaintance over a spot of blackmail, we've no need to encumber ourselves with false modesty."

Minnie squared her shoulders, all too aware that the act of doing so brought her bosom up a notch.

"Look in a mirror sometime," he suggested. "Look beyond *this.*" He touched his cheekbone, mirroring the spot on her face where her scar spread. "Look at yourself sometime the way you are now, all fire and anger, ready to do battle with me. If you'd ever once looked at yourself that way, you wouldn't question whether I'd want a flirtation with you. You'd *know* I would."

Her whole body felt on fire—a cold, shimmering, sparking flame. She'd never been so aware of her own flesh—every inch of it, from the tips of her breasts, which might or might not have been magnificent, to the heels of her feet. His eyes were boring into her.

She swallowed. "It's not well done of you, to try to turn my head before I've agreed to your plan." And if she'd contemplated it at all, that little display decided it. A man who could flirt like *that* had no business flirting with her.

He frowned, and then scrubbed his forehead. "Come, Miss Pursling." He gave her a little grin. "You're the most interesting person I've met since I arrived. It would be a pleasure to spend more time in your company."

For him, that would mean that he could waltz off to other cities. For her... For her it would mean a short spell of having this man dance attendance on her. A month of his compliments, a few weeks of melting smiles. It would mean day after blissful day where she might fall under his spell. And just look what he'd done to her in ten minutes.

Minnie shook her head, clearing away the cobwebs that he'd so artfully strewn about. It would mean everyone looking at her at every assembly. She couldn't stand for that kind of scrutiny.

"There's no benefit for me in that plan, Your Grace. If I help you and we are discovered, you'll be excused as wealthy and eccentric and powerful. I'll be the woman—the traitor!—who gave up everything for you. And if you've set me up as a flirt, everyone will believe I've been your lover. I'll be ruined. And when—" A wave of sadness passed through her; she couldn't finish that sentence. She didn't want to think of Great-Aunt Caroline gone. Instead, she took a deep breath. "At the end of it all, I'll be destitute, and you'll be a duke."

"I treat my lovers better than that. Even my pretend ones."

She raised her chin and gave him a flat look. "My future is not a joke, Your Grace."

He winced. "I'm going about this all wrong. Look, Miss Pursling." He sighed. "I'm not trying to make light of your situation. But I'm not here to dabble in Leicester on a whim. I'm here because of a promise I made. My father put some things wrong, and I must set them right. I don't *wish* to cause you any harm, but I won't cease simply because you ask it. There's no need for us to be at odds."

"I don't *wish* to have to slowly drop hints and build up a store of proof that would inevitably point you out as the culprit," she said. "But I will if I have to. If I do it my way, when it's all said and done, people will say, 'Well, Minnie really kept her head, even when a duke was about.'"

"And men will marry you because of that?" he asked dubiously.

"I only need one man to do so," Minnie shot back. "More would be illegal."

The smile popped back on his face. "You don't miss much, do you? I can't believe Gardley called you a rodent. You're the most formidable mouse I've ever met."

He placed his index finger atop her hand. It wasn't a caress. It couldn't be a caress. Still, her entire being seemed to freeze in place, fixed by that solitary point of contact. "My dear," he said. "I give you my word that you'll have an offer of marriage before I leave. Even if I have to do the job myself."

She jumped to her feet, pushing away from him. "That's not funny," she said, not even bothering to moderate her tone. "It's not a joke, no matter what you might think, and I'll thank you to stop treating it as one."

She'd knocked her teacup off the table and onto her foot in her attempt to escape from him and his horrible proposition. She could feel the wet liquid seeping into her stockings. But he made no comment; he simply straightened the tray on the table. Behind them, Lydia's brows had drawn down; she watched them uneasily.

"Well, then," he said, keeping his voice low. "I'll do it my way, and you try it yours—and we'll see who wins out."

"That's impossible," she said flatly. "You can't flirt with me. I'm going to be at war with you."

"No, you won't," he said politely. "Try going to war with an unwilling combatant. I don't think even you can manage that."

"You don't know what I can manage."

"No." He gave her a broad grin, one that started sparks flying in her belly.

And then he stood up and took her hand. This time, he bowed over it—bowed so low that his lips brushed the curve of her palm. She'd removed her gloves, and she felt the light kiss he brushed against her hand from head to toe.

"I don't know," he said. "But I'm looking forward to finding out."

Chapter Four

RAIN DOTTED THE WINDOWPANES of Robert's upstairs study, dissolving the world outside into murky swirls. The two women on the street below appeared as receding blobs of fluttering skirts under dark umbrellas. Pale blue—that was Miss Charingford—and dark brown—that was the inimitable Miss Pursling. From above, nothing set Miss Pursling apart from any other umbrella on the street. If he hadn't seen her gown just a few minutes ago, he'd not even have realized who it was.

He felt as if he'd woken up, weak and confused, only to be told that he'd spent the last three weeks in bed with a fever—and that during his illness, Queen Victoria had abdicated the throne and run off with a lion-tamer from Birmingham. The world seemed an entirely different place. And yet there stood Miss Pursling, pausing to stand under an awning on the corner, turning to her friend and twirling her umbrella as if nothing had happened.

As if she hadn't just upended his every expectation.

The door opened quietly behind him and footsteps approached. He didn't need to look to see who was coming; the servants in this household were still too much in awe of him to approach without begging for permission. That left only one possibility—Mr. Oliver Marshall.

"So," Oliver said from behind him. "Was it as bad as you feared?"

Robert drummed his fingers against the windowsill and pondered how to respond. "Two young ladies came to solicit a contribution for the Workers'… Oh, Devil take it. I can't remember—oh yes. The Workers' Hygiene Commission."

There were very few secrets that Robert kept from Oliver. He'd not mentioned Miss Pursling last night. For one, it hadn't seemed important, and for another, if there was a secret there, it belonged to her, not him. This, though… This touched on one of the few secrets he had no choice but to keep from Oliver.

"I see. They came to gawk at you." There was a hint of humor in the other man's voice, and he came to stand next to him. He peered out the window too, frowning when he saw nothing of interest.

"No, actually." Across the way, Miss Pursling and her friend passed under the awning, heads tilted toward one another, shoulders touching. The rain spilled off the metal overhang that shielded them, splashing to the ground in dirty waves of dishwater. Oliver thought they were only here to talk to the residents of town about the prospect of voting reform. Miss Pursling had threatened to reveal the truth about Robert's other activities here, and that was substantially more annoying than gawking. On the other hand…

Robert turned to the man standing beside him. "Oliver," he said, "how did you ever come to the conclusion that I was a worthwhile human being?"

Oliver took off his glasses and cleaned them with a handkerchief. "What makes you think I did?"

"I'm being serious. Until I met you, nobody who looked at me saw an actual person. Just a duke's son." Nobody since Oliver had seen an actual person, either. They'd seen a vote in the House of Lords, a fortune inherited from his grandfather. They'd seen the possibilities he represented.

Miss Pursling disappeared around the corner, and Robert shook his head. She was a problem—and a pleasure—to be dealt with on some other occasion.

Oliver gave his spectacles one last swipe and then looked over at him. "Well," he said. "Perhaps it was because I knew precisely how much it is worth to be a duke's son. You weren't the only one."

"But when I met you, I was a complete ass."

"True," Oliver said.

Their friendship—or whatever it was they shared—hadn't come easily. When he'd first met Oliver, he'd made an enemy of him, encouraging the other boys to rile him up. Not as if Oliver had needed much encouragement on that score.

One day, Oliver had told him—quietly, matter-of-factly—that they were brothers. And Robert's entire world had turned upside down.

"Why all this introspection?" Oliver asked. "It was simple. We fought; brothers often do. We took a little time to get to know one another. Then…" A shrug.

"Your memory is terrible. We didn't 'take a little time to get to know one another,'" Robert said. "I egged the other boys on, encouraging them to pick on you. And even once we declared peace, I had the devil of a time coming to terms with what you told me."

He'd spent months pondering the inevitable, awful arithmetic—one that subtracted nine months from his brother's age and came up with a date two months after Robert's parents' had married. His mind kept trying to manufacture some perfectly good reason why his father had sired a son out of wedlock and then abandoned him with no financial support. Robert built elaborate explanations based on messages that went astray, lies that were told, servants who happened to go on leave...

"I only stopped making excuses for my father's behavior because I asked him what happened."

I don't care what she says, his father had growled. *She wanted it. They always do.*

This reflexive denial of a crime he'd not been accused of had made everything painfully clear. Robert had found Oliver directly after the holidays.

I'm not my father, he'd said, his voice shaking. *I'm not my father, no matter what anyone says.*

And Oliver had simply grinned at him. *I know that,* he'd replied cheekily. *I've been waiting for you to figure it out.*

I know you're not your father. Over the years, those words had meant more to him than any of the flattery that so often came his way. A don at Cambridge had looked him in the eyes, and said, "My God, you're the spitting image of him." When he reached his majority, men slapped him on the back and told him how much he looked like the old Duke of Clermont. Every time they complimented him on his heritage, he heard his father's plaintive lament. *She wanted it. They always do.*

Robert was taller than his brother by two inches. He was the elder by three months. And—the only thing that really counted—he was the legitimate child, the one who'd inherited a dukedom from his father and a vast fortune by way of his mother. Nobody would have blinked if he had put his brother in his place—somewhere far, far behind him.

Which was why Robert never would. *I won the first toss, therefore I win everything from here on out* did not make a satisfying battle cry. Especially when he'd only won that first round because his father had cheated.

Since that day, every reminder of his privilege—of his father's wealth, his father's station—had rankled. It reminded him of the moment when he'd discovered what it meant that his father was a duke. It meant that nobody questioned him, no matter how wrong his actions were. It meant that he would not be held to account for his crimes, no matter who paid the price. It meant that if Robert followed in his father's footsteps, nobody would blink an eye.

Men, after all, had their needs. And women wanted it. They always did.

In all his life, only one person had ever looked at him and said, "You don't have to be your father."

One, and… Robert's gaze slid out the window once more. One and a half.

Because Miss Pursling had just walked into his home, given him that handbill, and told him that he'd written it. It had taken all of his power not to glow with pride and ask her what she thought. *Was it persuasive? Did you like it?*

Instead, he simply wrinkled his nose. "Our father was an ass."

Oliver grimaced. "*Your* father," he said sharply. "The Duke of Clermont didn't raise me. He didn't take me fishing. He's my *sire*, not my father. He was never my father."

By that standard, Robert had been raised by teaspoons and blades of grass.

"I wasn't speaking as a matter of history," Robert said stiffly. "Just biology."

Oliver shook his head. "Family isn't a matter of history. Or biology," he said softly. "It's a matter of choice. And don't look so grim. You know what I meant. Just because I refuse to let that man be my father doesn't mean you can't be my brother."

"If only everything were that easy." Robert put his hands in his pockets and looked away. "I had a message from my mother this morning."

"Ah." Oliver reached over and touched his shoulder. "Indeed."

"I know," Robert said, with a hint of what he hoped came out as wry amusement. "And I saw her in London only two months past."

His brother glanced over at that—a swift look out of the corner of his eye, one that had rather too much pity in it. Robert waved him away.

"Don't," he muttered brusquely. "She's coming here."

Clermont, she had written. *I will be taking rooms in Leicester's Three Crowns Hotel for a space of time. As I believe you are in the vicinity, we shall dine together on the nineteenth of November.*

"She didn't say why, and I can't think what would draw her." Robert carefully avoided looking at his brother. "If family is a matter of choice, she chose everyone other than me a long time ago. Why she'd bother with me now, when she's never noticed me in the past…"

"Maybe," Oliver said, "maybe she wants…"

"She doesn't want," Robert snapped. "She never does."

Oliver and Robert had known each other more than half their lives. They'd attended Eton together, followed by Cambridge. During that time, Oliver had been showered with constant letters from his family. He couldn't have helped but notice that Robert received almost no correspondence from his parents.

Oliver's eyes moved up and to the right, as if he were choosing his next words carefully. "So what are you going to do?"

"I already wrote back and told her I'd be gone on that date—that I'd promised to accompany Sebastian up."

"Ah," Oliver said blankly.

"And then I wrote to Sebastian and begged him to come," Robert admitted. "Whatever she wants can't be of much importance. Besides, the three of us haven't been in one spot together for almost a year. If the Brothers Sinister in all our villainy isn't enough to drive her away…"

Oliver smiled. "They only called us that at Eton because we're all left-handed. I'm practically respectable these days. You're a duke. And Sebastian is…" He frowned. "Well thought of, among intelligent people. Some of them."

Robert laughed. "A valiant attempt, but it won't wash. My mother thinks that your existence is a personal insult. She is certain that Sebastian is an apostate—and ever since he flirted with her last year, a lecher."

Oliver sputtered. "He *what?*"

"I asked him to save me at a gathering. He did." Robert shook his head. "His way."

Oliver winced.

"He didn't mean anything by it," Robert said. "But it all comes down to the same thing. If she insists on seeing me despite the change in date and the presence of two people she hates, the situation is dire."

At one time, Robert might have lost himself in a daydream, one in which his mother fled to his side in tears, desperate for his help. He'd save her through a combination of wit and good sense. And she would tearfully apologize for having avoided him.

In his youth, when he'd imagined her heartfelt regrets, he'd always told her not to cry.

"Don't worry," he'd imagined himself saying. "We have years left ahead of us."

He hadn't run out of time, but hopes could be dashed only so many times before one gave up out of weariness. It had been more than a decade since he let himself dream of a world in which his mother gave a single solitary damn about him, and he wasn't about to start up again now. As unlikely as it seemed, she probably had business in Leicester—business that would take her away before he arrived. They'd both be happier if they didn't try.

"And what will you do," Oliver said, "if the situation *is* dire?"

Robert shook his head. "I'll do what I've always done. Whatever I must, Oliver. Whatever I must."

⌘　⌘　⌘

THE QUESTION OF WHAT TO DO ABOUT MISS PURSLING naturally waited until Robert saw her again. That happened three days later, at the Charingford residence where Robert and Oliver had been invited for dinner.

He'd thought about her in those intervening days, of course. Something about her caught his fancy. Her quick wit, her intrepid style—they appealed to him. He woke one night from a dream in which she was gratifyingly brazen.

But nighttime fantasies rarely translated into reality. He doubted that she intended to bring him pleasure of any sort. In reality, he suspected that he was about to be subjected to a barrage of amateur sleuthing. Bad disguises, ham-handed questions, attempts to go through his rubbish in search of clues… Miss Pursling was undoubtedly the sort of hotheaded young lady who would throw herself into the chase with abandon.

So he wasn't surprised to see her at the dinner. She'd already made herself comfortable when he arrived, but it was only a matter of time until she sought him out. He watched her out of the corner of his eye before they sat down to the meal, waiting for her to listen in on his conversation.

Instead, she ignored him.

She ignored him so well that just before they were called in for the meal, he found himself angling to overhear *her* discussion with three other young ladies. He was sure that she'd be asking about him.

She wasn't.

She scarcely spoke at all. And when she did, her voice was so quiet that he had to strain to overhear her words.

He remembered a sensual lilt to her speech, a martial light that had brightened her features, rendering her pretty. Now, there was no hint of that.

She wore a high-necked gown of stiff brown, adorned only with a plain, military braid along her cuffs and neckline. Her spectacles must have been hidden away in the plain bag she wore at her wrist. She kept her distance from him, and she didn't say anything clever. She scarcely said anything at all.

He had almost pointed her out to Oliver as a wit; when they sat down to dine, she was seated just down the table from his brother. She engaged Oliver in no conversation. She didn't even raise her eyes from her dinner plate, except to glance occasionally at the level of watered wine in her glass. She did murmur something to Oliver once—but as he responded by passing her the saltcellar, Robert suspected it was entirely innocuous.

This woman had threatened to prove him responsible for the handbills? Unbelievable.

Oliver directed a few inquiries at her over the course of the meal. In response, she mumbled something unintelligible in the direction of her meat. Gradually, his brother gave up his attempts at conversation.

All trace of the woman he had seen had vanished, leaving behind a shadow with perfect posture and no conversation. She was right. Everyone *would* wonder if he flirted with her. He wouldn't even know how to manage it. One couldn't flirt with a lump.

Still, after the gentlemen rejoined the ladies, he did his duty—pausing to talk to everyone present, learning their names, asking after their health. He would have done it no matter what—no point being a duke if you couldn't use your station to make people smile—but this time he had an added incentive. He made his circuitous way about the room, winding inevitably to her. She was seated on a chair at the side of the room, gazing out at the other speakers. If she looked at any particular person overlong, he couldn't detect it.

"Miss Pursling. How good to see you again."

She looked up, but not at him. Instead, she looked just beyond his shoulder. "Your Grace," she said.

Her voice was quiet, but it was still as he remembered it, a low, husky velvet. At least he hadn't imagined that.

"May I sit next to you for a spell?"

She still didn't look at him. She glanced down at the carpet and then, with a twitch of her hand, indicated a chair to her side. Robert lowered himself into it and waited for her to speak.

After a full minute ticked by in silence, Robert realized she wasn't going to say anything.

He leaned back in the chair. "I see how it's going to be. Leave all the work of moving the conversation along to Robert—he's a duke, so he must be good at it."

"Oh, no." The corner of her mouth twitched. "I wouldn't assume you had any particular talent in that direction."

It was the first hint that she'd given that there was anything to her but an excess of shyness. He'd begun to actually doubt his own memory. Surely this woman hadn't come to his house and attempted blackmail. Had she?

"Tell me," he persisted, "how does one get *Minnie* from Wilhelmina? *Minnie* makes me think of miniature—and nothing about you seems diminutive."

She examined her gloves closely. "It comes from the third syllable, Your Grace."

Back to being a cipher once more. *Had* he imagined the conversation? Maybe he was going mad.

"What's wrong with the first syllable?" he tried. "Or the second?"

She glanced up. For the first time all evening, she looked in his eyes. He would have sworn there would have to be some kind of spark in her— some indication of the intelligence that had blazed at their last meeting. But if eyes were windows to the soul, hers had been bricked up to avoid taxation. He could see nothing in them at all.

"Surely," she said pleasantly, "you can ascertain the problems for yourself. *Willy* wouldn't do. It's too masculine."

"There is that," he murmured.

"As for the second syllable…" She looked over his shoulder again, avoiding his gaze. Her eyes were a mask, but her mouth twitched once more. "Just think of it, Your Grace. What am I to say? 'My name is Wilhelmina Pursling, but you can call me Hell.'"

He laughed, almost in sheer amazement. She *still* looked like a lump, shyly twiddling her fingers, refusing to meet his eyes. But there was that voice. Her voice made him think of woodsmoke on an autumn evening, of silks laid out atop lush bedding. Of her hair, rid of those confining pins and spread over a pillow, the honey-colored ends spilling over her breasts.

He swallowed and cleared his throat. "This isn't what I expected when you said you'd go to war with me."

"Let me guess." She fingered her glove carefully, and he noticed that she was worrying at a tiny hole in the tip. "You thought I would simper if you smiled at me. You supposed that when I said I would prove what you were doing to everyone, that I planned to engage in a bumbling, graceless investigation into your surface activities."

"I—no. Of course not." But Robert felt his cheeks heat. Because that was precisely what he had thought.

She bit her lip, the picture of shyness. But her words were the opposite of shy. "Now," she whispered, "you're surprised to find that I overmatch you."

"I am?" he echoed, looking at her. "You do?"

Her eyes were fixed over his shoulder, no hint in her posture of what she said so quietly.

"Of course I overmatch you," she said. She spoke as if the matter were beyond question. "You're a well-educated duke—one of the most powerful men in England. Your staff likely numbers in the hundreds across your many estates. If needed, you could draw on resources in the tens of thousands of pounds."

The corner of her mouth lifted now, dispelling the illusion of a simple, quiet girl. A dimple emerged on her cheek. She glanced up at him—once—and he almost couldn't breathe.

This, *this* was the woman who had threatened him.

"You have all those things," she said. "But then, I have one thing you do not."

He leaned in, not wanting to miss a word.

"I," she said, "have a sense of tactics."

He had just that one glimmer of a smile from her, a small moment when he caught his breath—and then it all disappeared. Her face smoothed; she looked down once more, and Miss Pursling looked utterly plain.

Another man might have been surprised into compliance. But Robert couldn't imagine backing down now—not when she ducked her head and stared at the floor. No; he wanted to bring her out again.

"You haven't done anything," he said.

Her expression didn't change.

"I'm winning," he announced. "You can't bore me into a surrender."

"You probably think battles are won with cannons and brave speeches and fearless charges." She smoothed her skirts as she spoke. "They're not. Wars are won by dint of having adequate shoe leather. They're won by boys who make shells in munitions factories, by supply trains shielded from enemy eyes. Wars are won by careful attendance to boring detail. If you wait to see the cavalry charge, Your Grace, you'll have already lost."

He blinked. "You're trying to make me back down. It won't work."

"That's the beauty of strategy. Everything I do contains a double threat. If you don't back down from spoken words, you reveal your character. Everything you say, everything you do, every charming smile and sweet protestation—the most you can hope for is to change the manner of my victory. The fact of it, though, is a foregone conclusion."

She looked so small sitting in her chair, so fragile. It was only when he shut his eyes and erased that jarring image of a diffident spinster that he could comprehend the evidence of his ears. Miss Pursling wouldn't even look him in the eyes. But her voice seemed indomitable.

"So," he said, "you think that I'm charming. You didn't list that among my assets before."

"Of course you're charming." She didn't look up. "I'm charmed. I'm charmed to my teeth."

There was a note in her voice that sounded so bitter that it almost tasted sweet.

"You're a force of nature, Your Grace," she said. "But so am I. So am I."

She hadn't said that *she* was charming…and, in point of fact, she wasn't. Not in the usual sense. But there was something utterly compelling about her. He had no idea who she was any longer. He'd thought at first that she was a high-spirited, clever woman. He'd wondered next if she were a wallflower. But at the moment, she seemed beyond any category, larger and far more complex than anyone he'd encountered thus far.

"If you want me to back down," he said softly, "you shouldn't be so interesting."

Her lips compressed.

But before she could answer, a noise sounded on the other side of the room. Robert turned his head in time to see a woman—Miss Charingford, the daughter of the house, and if he recalled correctly, the friend that Miss Pursling had brought with her the other day—standing so abruptly that her seat overturned.

"Come now, Lydia," the man who had been sitting next to her said. "You can't really mean—"

"I do," Miss Charingford snapped. So saying, she took a glass of punch from the table next to her. Before anyone could intervene, she dashed it into the fellow's face. Red dripped down his nose, his chin, staining his cravat. Gasps arose around them.

"You can't do this!" he said, standing from his chair.

The man was George Stevens. Robert had spoken with him twice now, enough to remember that he had charge over the militia. An important man, as things were judged in these parts.

"I can't?" Miss Charingford snapped. "Just watch."

She snatched a second glass of punch from her neighbor's fingers and threw this one in his face as well. "You see? Apparently, I *can.*"

So saying, she put her nose in the air and stormed out the door.

Robert turned back to Miss Pursling.

"Is she—"

But Miss Pursling was no longer there. She was already halfway across the room. She hadn't apologized to him or made her excuses. She had simply left, dashing after her friend. The door closed on her moments later.

He'd been amazed that her posture, the expression on her face, had remained so smooth throughout their conversation. But she had been hiding from him, too. She'd gestured him to the chair that would allow him to talk with her while she could still keep one eye on her friend. He had thought she had looked away from him to feign shyness. Instead, she'd been watching Stevens.

Everything I do contains a double threat. That had been no braggadocio, there. She'd been fending off his attempts at conversation with half her attention, lecturing him on strategy, and pretending to be a shy lump for anyone who was watching. And while she'd done that, she'd also been tracking her friend's escalating drama from across the room.

My God. His head hurt just thinking about all the threads she must have been keeping straight in her mind.

"Your Grace."

Robert turned from his reverie to see a man beside him. It was George Stevens, standing with a grim look on his face and a disapproving set to his jaw. He'd wiped most of the punch off, but his cravat was still stained pink, and his forehead had a sheen to it that sent Robert's own skin itching in sticky sympathy.

"Captain Stevens," Robert said.

"If I might intrude a moment?"

Robert glanced once again at the door through which Miss Pursling had vanished. "Of course."

Stevens gave him a stiff bow, and then just as stiffly took the seat that Miss Pursling had so recently vacated. "It is admirable," he said, "in every way admirable, for a man in your position to condescend to speak to everyone deserving at a gathering such as this." He rubbed his hands together. "But...ah, how do I say this?" He lowered his voice. "Not all women are equally deserving. And Miss Pursling is not what she seems."

"Oh?" Robert was still too taken aback to do more than take this in. "In what way does the reality of Miss Pursling differ from her appearance?"

Stevens seemed to relax at that. "I have reason to believe she is not who she claims to be."

"Reason? What reason?"

The other man blinked, as if unused to having such questions asked. "Well. I, uh, I talked to someone who was intimately familiar with her great-aunt. That woman had no knowledge of Miss Pursling's existence."

"*Was* intimately familiar, you say?" Robert kept his tone mild. "How long ago did this individual know her great-aunt?"

Stevens was beginning to squirm like a schoolboy caught out in a lie. "Technically, she knew her before she moved to Leicester. That is to say—"

"Technically?" Robert raised an eyebrow. "Forgive me if I do not know the families in the area as well as you do. But did not Miss Pursling's great-aunt move to the area fifty years ago?"

"Yes." Stevens hunkered down in his seat. "But she knew the whole family, da—ah, dash it." Stevens stopped, took a deep breath. "She would have known if the young Miss Elvira Pursling had married—the woman who is purported to be Miss Wilhelmina's mother. People talk, Your Grace, particularly about happy events. But there is no such record. I have reason to believe that Miss Pursling may not be legitimate."

It might be true. If so, it would explain her insistence that she didn't want anyone looking into her past. *A little different,* indeed.

If there were any truth to Stevens's claim at all, Robert could settle this for good. One little threat, when she'd already put blackmail in play…

But no. He was a gentleman and one of the most powerful men in the country. Powerful men who used their prerogatives to hurt women—they were scum.

Robert let his expression freeze to ice. He didn't glower. He simply watched the other man, unblinking, until the captain of the militia dropped his gaze and winced.

"Stevens," Robert said, not bothering with the honorific, "is there perhaps something you have heard about me that made you think I would want to hear such aspersions?"

"But, Your Grace. Miss Pursling is an unknown to you. I only wished—"

"You thought I would be amenable to baseless gossip simply because it was not aimed at someone I knew?"

Stevens's jaw worked. "I only meant—"

"I'm done with your speculation. If I hear you've indulged it any further, I'll see that Leicester receives another captain of the militia."

Stevens turned white. "You couldn't."

But the man no doubt knew all too well that Robert *could.* Not directly, no, but he only needed to drop a word in the right ear… Robert wouldn't use that influence without good reason, and given what he expected to find here, he needed to conserve that power as best as he could. Still, threats were free.

The man bowed his head. "Forgive me, Your Grace. The woman is nothing. I erred. I never thought you would take an interest in one so much beneath you."

"What's the point in being a duke if I *don't?*" The query was out of his mouth before he could call it back—but he wouldn't have, even if he could.

Stevens blinked in confusion and Robert shook his head. It was madness to give a man so much power and to have no expectations as to how he'd use it. He could crush Miss Pursling with one sentence. He might have crushed her with silence. But that would have been wrong.

"Your Grace," Stevens finally said, "your concern does you justice."

The man's toad-eating did him none.

Robert met Stevens's eyes. "No, it doesn't. It's called basic human decency, and I deserve no credit for doing what every man should."

Stevens flinched again, and set his hand to his forehead—his sticky forehead, if the fingerprints he left were any guide.

"Now," Robert said, standing, "if you'll excuse me, I have other people I must speak with."

He was aware of the man's eyes boring into his back as he crossed the room. Robert made a note: This man bore watching.

Chapter Five

"LYDIA," MINNIE SAID, DASHING DOWN THE CORRIDOR. "Lydia, wait! What are you doing?"

Lydia stopped in the corridor, her arms held straight at her sides, terminating in tight fists. "Going upstairs." She didn't turn around. "What does it look like?"

Minnie came abreast of her. "It's not too late. Go back in there and apologize—Stevens will forgive you. I know he will."

"Well, I won't forgive him," Lydia said. "He related the most vile rumor about you—that you were not legitimate. The *cad,* saying such things to me!"

Minnie took hold of her shoulders. "Lydia, listen to me. Go back. Apologize. Say you're sorry. Say you were mistaken. Say you were drunk on punch, and I'm sure he'll take you back."

"Well, I won't have him." Lydia stamped her foot. "I won't. I won't have a man who could talk about my dearest friend that way. I won't marry someone who could laugh about it and expect me to nod my head. I won't do it."

"You know what will happen when your father dies. Your brother gets the mill, and you…"

"I'll have my portion." Lydia raised her chin.

Scarcely enough to live on, Minnie knew. And having severed her relationship with Stevens in so uncivil a fashion, Lydia would be unlikely to find anyone else. Besides…

"What if next time, the rumor is about you?" Minnie persisted.

She didn't have to say that it might be. Too many people knew Lydia's secret. The doctor who had diagnosed her. Anyone who had seen her in Cornwall during those dreadful months. Lydia lived with the possibility of public ruination every bit as much as Minnie did.

"What does it matter who knows?" Lydia said, looking away. "Apparently, truth is no bar to rumor. After all, Stevens is spreading that vile rumor about you."

Explaining the source of the rumor would raise questions—questions that Minnie couldn't answer. Questions like, why was there no record of the birth of one Wilhelmina Pursling? What had her name once been, and why was it necessary to change it?

Minnie shook her head. "My parents were married. I can assure you of that." That, and nothing more. "But Lydia, you must not be so neglectful of your future. Throwing away a fiancé, simply because he said one thing you did not like? Nobody is perfect."

Lydia simply wrapped her arms around herself and shook her head. "How can you ask? How could I stay silent?"

"But he was..." She stumbled. "You said..."

Lydia had said Stevens would make her happy. She'd said it over and over, as if trying to believe it herself. It was the way Lydia was. She believed the best. She wished everyone happy. She could have found the bright side of a solar eclipse.

Lydia turned to Minnie now. "Sometimes," she said slowly, "one is faced with choices. When something seems inevitable—when, for instance, marriage to a man would do my father good—when he's a decent man who likes me... Well, it didn't seem that I would find a better match. It makes sense." She frowned fiercely. "It *made* sense."

"So go back and apologize."

Lydia's features hardened. "After what he said about you? He told me I should have nothing more to do with you. I cannot believe this world is so cruel as to require me to sacrifice my dearest friend in order to make a good marriage."

Oh, Lydia. Minnie's heart hurt for her. Even with all that had happened to her friend, she still believed that.

"It might be that cruel," Minnie whispered. And then, because she knew how cruel it could be, she added: "It *is.*"

"It is not." Lydia unfolded her arms, but only long enough to put them around Minnie, to draw her close. "I won't let it be."

Minnie could almost let the warmth of that embrace fool her. Almost. Someday...

Someday, Lydia would discover all that Minnie had withheld from her. Their friendship couldn't survive it. It wasn't the truth of what had happened that would destroy their intimacy, but the fact that she had held it back all those years. That she'd been the repository for her friend's darkest secrets, while holding her own selfishly close to her chest.

It wasn't a matter of *if* they would stop being friends. It was a question of *when*. And yet Minnie had been unable to give her up. Lydia was warm and hopeful and happy, and sometimes, despite Minnie's logical bent, Lydia managed to infect her with sheer optimism.

Sometimes, she believed they would be happy. There would be no more fears for the future. It would all come out right, and they would be friends forever.

Of all the fool fantasies that Minnie could have indulged in, *that* was the one that hooked deep under her skin, the one that she could never let go. And so she simply held her friend and prayed that she would not be proven right too quickly.

"So," Lydia said. "The Duke of Clermont spoke to you for a long while there. What did he say?"

"Nothing." But Minnie smiled despite herself. "Nothing at all."

⌘ ⌘ ⌘

THE DWELLING—IF YOU COULD CALL IT THAT, and Robert was uncertain it deserved the title—was the worst kind of slum. What plaster remained on the wall of the single room was cracked and streaked with soot. The single room smelt of sour vinegar and old cabbage. The chair he sat in was uncomfortably close to the ground, as if one leg had broken and they'd cut the rest down to match. If he leaned too far to either side, the chair squeaked and swayed. This squalid tenement represented everything that Robert's father had put wrong in Leicester, and he'd come to fix it all.

It had taken Robert far too long to try to make amends. But in his defense, he'd only recently discovered what had gone wrong.

In front of him, the resident—a thin, coughing man by the name of Finney—pulled his coat around him.

"Graydon Boots." Finney pushed back in his seat and stared at the ceiling. "Now *that* is a name I've not let myself think in years. I last worked for them back in…'58, was it?"

"That is what the records say," Robert told him.

The man pointed his pipe at Robert. "And you're telling me that after all these years, after Graydon Boots has been gone for over a decade, that some high Muck-a-Muck wants to award me a pension. *Me.*"

Robert nodded.

"Mr. Blaisdell, I spent four months in prison. It ruined my health, but my mind still works. I'll not be believing that, I won't. There's some kind of trick."

There wasn't a trick. Robert's grandfather had given the factory to his father as part of a devil's bargain. His father—who had known nothing of industry—had handed the factory over to an overseer and ordered him to extract as much profit from it as he could get. Robert had only discovered the place while looking over his grandfather's records from decades before. His father's books, incomplete as they generally were, hadn't even mentioned it.

"Mr. Finney," Robert said, "I am not telling you that Graydon Boots is awarding you a pension. That would be absurd. The charity I represent has been looking into the events of that year. They've decided you were unfairly imprisoned."

"*I've* been saying that for years."

"In fact, Leicester has a curious history in that regard," Robert said. "Did you know that more people have been convicted of criminal sedition in Leicester in the last decade than in the entirety of England?"

Another thing his father's overseer had started, as best as Robert could tell, and that hadn't ended when the factory went under.

"We speak our minds here, we do."

Robert set the papers on the table. "Speaking your mind is only illegal if your words are intended to create disaffection with the government. Not with your masters; with the government." At first, Robert had only wanted to try to make right what his father had destroyed. But the closer he'd looked, the more he'd found. He'd eventually gone through the records of those trials, and it was clear that the jury had not been correctly charged with the law. "You should never have been convicted simply for organizing a union."

Finney looked at him, shaking his head. "As you say. But the masters get what the masters want. I don't want to be involved any longer. I've my hands full with the Cooperative, I do."

As if to emphasize this, the door to the tiny room opened. Two women stood in the doorframe. One, a thin elderly woman in a sagging brown gown had a sack of groceries. She shoved at a yellowing cap that was slipping from her head, and gestured to her companion. "I just don't think it will work, is all I'm saying."

Her companion was Miss Pursling. She seemed a picture of severity, her honey-brown hair pulled tightly up, with only a few tamed curls at her neck.

The two women were focused totally on one another.

"Mrs. Finney," Miss Pursling was saying, "I've talked to every chemist in town. You're my last hope."

Mrs. Finney unwrapped her shovel. "But the Cooperative sells food. Not any of that other nonsense."

"But the advertisement—"

"Miss Pursling, I do like you, but how can I bring this before the Board?"

Miss Pursling looked down. "You have no idea how the rest of the Commission will scold if I come back a failure." She did meek well, her head bowed, her hands clasped in front of her. "Please."

"Well." Mrs. Finney set her shawl on the entry table. "I suppose. Maybe. I might say something."

"Thank you," Miss Pursling said. "Thank you."

That was the moment when her husband intervened. "Mrs. Finney," he called. "We have a guest. You'll never believe what he is saying."

The two women turned to Mr. Finney. Miss Pursling's gaze fell on Robert. Her eyes widened and she took a step back.

"It's a gentleman from London," Mr. Finney said. "Mr. Blaisdell, my wife. And Miss Pursling. He's a solicitor, I believe."

Miss Pursling didn't bat an eye at that. "A solicitor," she repeated. "How curious, Mr. Blaisdell."

"Merely a representative," Robert returned.

"Mr. Blaisdell here is saying that there's a fund that has established pensions for men who have devoted themselves to unions, who find themselves in poor straits for it." Mr. Finney laughed.

Mrs. Finney simply frowned. "Well, then what could they want with us?" She looked around. "There's only the two of this in this wide, big room, and we have meat on the table three times a week. We're not poorly off."

Robert blinked at this and looked around the room, trying to see it with her eyes. Not poorly off?

"They've offered me a pension!" Finney laughed. "Me! When the only service I did for Graydon Boots was to get everyone to turn out after Jimmy died of poisoning."

Robert looked away. One of the overseer's first cost-cutting mechanisms had been to replace the original boot-blacking with a formula that was less expensive—but far more dangerous for those who had to stand with their hands immersed in it on a daily basis. Money couldn't make up for that, but he'd had to try.

"Yes," Robert said. "And I've explained this isn't for your work at Graydon Boots, but for your experience in organization."

Finney simply shook his head sadly. "You're a young lad. You wouldn't understand. I learned my lesson, then, about keeping to my place. No more turning out. No more association with that sort of thing. Especially not now. I hear the Duke of Clermont's in town."

"He is," Miss Pursling put in.

Finney spat on the ground. "It all started when *he* acquired Graydon Boots." His hands, liver-spotted with age, trembled. "More hours worked for less pay. Then came the strike-breakers, the convictions. He's a beast of a man, and I'll never—"

"Nathan Finney," Mrs. Finney interrupted, "that's dangerous talk. You were taken from me once. Did you not learn to think before you speak?"

"No, no," Robert said. "You needn't hold your tongue on my account. I am quite in agreement."

Miss Pursling took two steps into the room. "You are, sir?"

She clearly thought he was here on a whim.

He turned to her. "I've gone through the records of what Clermont did," he said softly. "Is it so wrong to want to make matters right again?"

She turned her head away. "I question only your methods." A trace of a frown flicked across her face. "Your motive...I do not yet understand."

"But my motive is simple. I think privileges are wasted on the peers," Robert replied. "They have the right to be tried in the House of Lords. Think, Mr. Finney, what that would have meant for you. The Lords would never have heard a case of criminal sedition based on the evidence presented against you. The law is too clear; they'd protect their own."

"Too true, too true," Finney echoed.

"I think," Robert said, turning to Miss Pursling, "that if the Duke of Clermont, for instance, were to write handbills saying what Finney here had said back in '58—now, *he* could speak the truth and nobody could stop him with threats of imprisonment based on a perversion of the law."

Miss Pursling had tilted her head at him. "Could he?" she asked.

Finney nodded. "All too right, Mr. Blaisdell."

"But peers use that privilege not to speak truth, but to suppress it. Think, Mr. Finney, what could you do with a seat in the House of Lords?"

"Me, sitting in the Lords?" Finney laughed. "I should like to see *that.*"

"So should I," Robert said. "If *I* had a chance to be a part of this nation's governance, I'd not waste it protecting my prerogatives and interests. No. I'd find every last way that the deck was stacked to allow people like Clermont to poison his workers, and to punish them for voicing complaint when he did so. And I'd eradicate them all."

He was surprised by the vehemence in his voice.

"Now that," said Mrs. Finney, "that *is* sedition, and best not to say those words no matter how safe you think you are. You're young, Mr. Blaisdell. We were all once young. But take a deep breath and put such talk away. It'll do nobody any good." She glanced warily at Miss Pursling.

"Besides, Miss Pursling, have you not *met* the Duke of Clermont? You do travel in those circles. Sometimes."

Mr. Finney subsided in his chair, somewhat embarrassed.

Miss Pursling looked away from Robert. "I have."

"And how is the old bugger?" Finney asked. "One can only hope—"

"Shush, Mr. Finney."

"I believe," Miss Pursling, "that this is the other man's son."

Finney brushed this off. "Seen one duke, seen 'em all. Am I right, Mr. Blaisdell, am I right?"

Robert didn't answer. He simply watched Miss Pursling. She'd scarcely shown any emotion at all as he spoke, not even a furrow of concentration on her brow.

She shook her head now. "He's tall. He's wealthy. He's handsome, and those things rarely bode well for a man's character."

Robert winced.

But she wasn't done. "I very much doubt he understands what it means to be a working man, and I suspect that all his life he's had anything he wanted handed to him, just for the wishing."

It was a harsh judgment, made harsher still because it was the truth. Robert burned in his seat.

"Men who have only known easy times often cannot comprehend hard ones," Miss Pursling said.

Amazing how deeply facts could cut. Robert couldn't even be angry with her. It was no more than he'd told himself of an evening.

"And yet..." She trailed off, shaking her head, and Robert leaned forward, desperate to hear what she might say of him.

Her voice was so quiet, and yet the room seemed quieter still, waiting for her to fill the silence.

"And yet," she said, without once looking Robert's way, "I think he is not at all like his father. I don't know what to make of him."

He felt rooted in place, unable to move. She hadn't glanced his way once as she spoke. She hadn't raised her voice. And yet those words, spoken in a near-whisper, seemed like a benediction whispered over his head.

Not at all like his father.

He let out a shaky breath. "So will you tell the magistrates about this conversation, Miss Pursling?"

"And involve the Finneys? I think not." She bit her lip. "Tell me, Mr. Blaisdell. This charity you represent. Are you offering pensions to *everyone* who worked at Graydon Boots?"

Not everyone. They wouldn't believe that, for one. Half of them were dead; more had left town.

"Those who were wronged," he said tightly, looking away.

"Mrs. Finney," Miss Pursling said, "I am most grateful for your agreement to present the proposal to the board of the Cooperative."

"Of course," the other woman answered.

"Mr. Finney. Mr. Blaisdell." Miss Pursling inclined her head, touched her skirts in a mild curtsey, and withdrew.

He'd thought her unattractive in this mode, head turned down, voice so quiet. Not any longer. Some women blazed with light and energy. Miss Pursling reminded him of the pearlescent hint of dawn that crept under the door after a long, long night. There was a quiet grace to her, like a tiger pacing in its cage. There was a majesty in claws unused, in muscles poised for action that never came. There was a somber beauty to a caged beast.

He wanted to see her break free of that melancholy. He wanted her to turn those knowing eyes on him and tell him that he wasn't his father, that he *wouldn't* be him.

What stood between them had become infinitely simple and entirely too complicated all at once.

Not at all like his father.

He wanted her to say that again, and he wanted her to mean it.

Chapter Six

ROBERT'S DREAM THAT NIGHT—as so many of his dreams were these days—was charged with sexual longing.

In this dream, he had Minnie where he'd first met her: behind the davenport in the Guildhall library, the curtains shielding them from all eyes. This time, though, instead of listening to someone else's conversation, they heard the gentle murmur of ocean waves. Neither remarked on the oddity of the sea in a library. Instead of being fully clothed, Robert wore nothing at all—and she was stripped to the waist. The dream version of Minnie smiled up at him with inviting allure. Her honey-brown hair was down and it curled over her shoulders, framing naked breasts tipped with deep rose. Those breasts brushed his knees as she knelt before him and took the length of his cock in her mouth.

The details of his dreams were always frustratingly vague. He couldn't feel the wet heat of her mouth or the pressure of her tongue. There was only the fire of his own burning lust and a dulled sensation of want. But at least in dreams, one needn't worry about morality or consequences. In dreams, there was nothing but the physical truth of desire, and that had him firmly in its grip.

In his dream, she was very, very good. He knew it, even though he could not quite feel it. No matter how he pivoted, no matter how he held her, he couldn't really touch her. Just the force of his own red-hot desire growing with every stroke. He could only lust, and lust, and lust again.

"God, Minnie," he begged in his dream. "Give me what I want."

But instead of taking him harder—or shifting herself so that he could plunge inside her—the dream Minnie simply looked up at him and sat back on her heels. "If you insist," she said with a coquettish smile. She leaned in, and suddenly, as these things were in dreams, she was whispering in his ear. "I know who you are."

The shock was so great that it woke him. He blinked, blearily. It was the middle of the night, and silence reigned. His bedchamber was dark. Even though he'd tossed off most of the covers in his sleep, he felt as if he were burning with fever. His cock was rock-hard, his body shuddering with tension, demanding relief. And he couldn't dispel the image from his dream. Miss Pursling, unclothed, her hair down to her shoulders, looking up at him with that brilliant smile.

God.

He'd thought that it would have been hard to explain what he saw in her to his friends. She wasn't classically pretty; she wasn't even striking. And while her figure had much to recommend itself, he was aware that there were better.

Maybe it was simply this: When first she'd seen him, she hadn't seen a duke, but a man who wrote radical handbills.

I know who you are.

His left hand slid around his erection.

Robert believed in restraint. He made it a point *not* to emulate his father. He refused to be the kind of man who took a woman just because he fancied her. But, damn it, sometimes he wished he were. He wished he were with every part of his being.

He threw off the sheets that still covered him and let the cold air wash over him. It did no good.

It never did any good, not by itself. Instead, he slid his palm down his cock, ever so slowly, letting himself fall into that familiar rhythm. He let the dream play back in his mind—Minnie on her knees, Minnie smiling up at him as her lips closed around his member. He stroked himself in short, sharp jerks, letting them come faster and more urgent until the moment of climax came.

And in that moment, he imagined Minnie giving him that smile—a smile that held nothing back—and saying that she knew who he was. He bit his lip against the savage pleasure that filled him.

It took a few moments for reason to find him afterward, for him to admit that he found himself in a state that was unusually fixed on one person. This was not the first time he'd dreamed of her. It wasn't the first time he'd awoken in a fit of wanton lust and indulged himself, either. In his mind, he'd had her against walls and in beds. The beauty of masturbation was that he always got what he wanted, how he wanted it. Nobody was hurt, and it left no lasting effects.

I know who you are.

He stared into the darkness of the night. It had just been a dream, of course. Things happened in dreams that had no bearing whatsoever on reality. If his dreams had any relation to the truth, he'd have been exiled from decent company years before. Still, dreams often served as a lever for his lust. He'd wake in a fever, would think about the images from his dream as he brought himself to climax, and the combination of the dream and his own efforts alleviated the worst of his frustrations.

But there weren't enough orgasms in the world to give him relief from the want that coiled about him now. Up until this point, he'd had the good sense to indulge in desires that he could easily satisfy. No reason to change that now.

I know who you are.

He stared into the darkness and wished those words away. Instead, they hung about him, unsaid and yet still ringing in his ears.

She didn't think he was his father. He wanted her to know who he was. And he wanted to know her back.

⌘ ⌘ ⌘

DESPITE ROBERT'S BEST EFFORTS, it was a week before he saw Miss Pursling again—and that was a meeting he had to engineer.

He'd made a donation of one hundred pounds to the Workers' Hygiene Commission. That made him one of their patrons—and wouldn't it make sense to see how his money would be spent?

The Commission, however, didn't meet in a respectable private room at the Three Crowns Hotel, or in the front room of the Bell. It met instead on the outskirts of the old town, at a run-down place called the Nag's Head Hostelry.

Robert arrived ten minutes after the appointed time and drew no eyes at all when he slipped into the room behind a barmaid. She bustled about the room in swift competence, filling the ladies' cups with what looked like barley water, pouring weak beer for the gentlemen, swiping up the inevitable spills with a wide, dirty towel that hung from her apron strings.

Nobody paid any attention, they were already so intent on their argument.

He made his way to a chair in the back and sat down.

Not only was this particular commission held in an odd location, but the composition was surprising. He'd sat on enough charitable boards to know what to expect—a few wealthy people, who'd been asked for their money and their connections, rather than their knowledge, interspersed with a few professional folks. But here, there was a man he remembered as a doctor. There was Captain Stevens. Miss Pursling, of course, seated next to a wealthy-looking older woman. Those formed the usual sort that made up these charity boards. But across the table, there sat a young woman, maybe Miss Pursling's age, dressed in a serviceable shirtwaist. Next to her was an older, grizzled man dressed in well-patched tweed. One seat over was a plump woman in a high-necked black wool gown, complete with a round, black collar—the kind of uniform that shouted that she was in service. Half the participants had the look of working people.

That made it like no charity that Robert had ever seen. He leaned forward in interest.

Stevens was shaking his head. "Well," he muttered, "we'll worry about that later. Miss Pursling, you have your report on the disinfectant?"

Miss Pursling nodded. Her back was to him, and he could see her curls dip against her neck. They were interesting, those curls of hers, not the fat sausage curls that were carefully constructed by maids with irons. These curls were a masquerade—a little too corkscrewed, too wild. He rather suspected her hair had a natural curl to it, one that no iron could tame into regular twists of hair.

"The board of the Cooperative met last evening." He had to strain to hear her talk. Her voice was clear, but so quiet. "They agreed to sell the disinfecting solution at their cost—provided that we mention the Cooperative in the handbill. They were eventually convinced that the advertisement was compensation enough."

A strange way to say it—*they were eventually convinced.* Another person would have said *I convinced them,* thus claiming the credit. Robert steepled his fingers.

All he could see of her was the back of her head, the lovely flare of her waist, that small hint of hip before her bustle and crinolines obscured all her natural curves. As she spoke, she turned her head. She was still faced three-quarters away from him. He couldn't see her eyes—just her cheek and that faint web of a scar. But she was wearing her spectacles and reading from the papers in front of her.

Oh, yes. He'd thought of her in the intervening week. He'd thought of her so much that he was no longer put off by her quiet speech, her downcast eyes. No matter how unlikely it seemed, Miss Pursling had convinced everyone here that she was next to nothing. The truth of her competence seemed an intimate secret between them.

"What'll be the cost of the solution, then?" one of the working girls asked. Her voice was normal, but next to Miss Pursling's quiet tones, she sounded almost loud.

"A shilling per bottle. If used sparingly, that amount ought to last a household of six or seven a full month. Miss Peters, is that a reasonable sum to expect of a working family, or must we find a way to further subsidize the cost?" Miss Pursling tilted her head toward the youngest of the working girls.

The other girl bent down to a notebook and flipped through it. "Mm," she said. "That…should be sufficient."

"Foolishness," Stevens interrupted. "It's all foolishness, as I've said— the instructions on disinfection, the solution, the handbills." He cast a hard look at Miss Pursling. It was a look that said that he'd not taken Robert's last warning to heart—that he still thought ill of her.

"Surely not *all* foolishness," Miss Peters put in. "After all—"

Robert leaned forward.

Stevens slammed his hand on the table. "There'd be no need for disinfection if those infernal monkey workers would just vaccinate their children as required by law."

The man in patched tweed shot to his feet. "Blast me if I let some vaccinator stick my children with pins made of some disease!"

"My mum, she was inoculated and died the next week!"

The plump woman leaned across the table. "Well, I had my Jess get the vaccine, and he still took sick of the smallpox and lost his sight. Turned out the vaccinator had run out when we came, so he just used spirits and charged the same anyway!"

Half the people at the table had come to their feet; they glowered uniformly at the captain. One wrong word, and the whole thing might explode into violence.

In that tense atmosphere, Miss Pursling slid back in her seat, her back utterly straight. Her hand rose to touch the scar on her face, fingering it as if it were a talisman against future harm.

"Stevens," said a man with a low drawl, "surely I have as much interest in vaccinations as you do."

That came from a dark-haired man sitting near the foot of the table— Doctor Grantham, a young man who had a practice on Belvoir Street. His words cut through the gathering tension, and Miss Pursling let out a little sigh, leaning against the back of her seat.

Grantham toyed idly with his fountain pen. "But in my practice, I've learned that I must treat the patients I have, not the ones I *wish* I had."

Stevens glowered. "What is that supposed to mean?"

Grantham shrugged. "I wish I had patients who had meat and vegetables at every meal, clean water to wash with, and windows in every room. I wish I had patients who didn't need to stoop to work." His pen tapped against his knuckles as he spoke. "Hard on the spine and the internal organs, stooping." He shrugged. "I wish I had patients who made twice as much in the factories, too. But alas, I take the patients I have."

"You tell him, Doctor," murmured the plump woman.

"Letting them make such decisions on their own leads to thoughts of self-governance," Stevens hissed. "Talk of making their own rules. Next you know, we'll have another episode of the Chartists to put down. Already people are talking about the vote. This town is a powder-keg of unrest, and you lot are waving a torch." By his gesture, Stevens implicated not only Grantham, but Miss Pursling as well. "All this talk is giving them *ideas.*"

Grantham smiled and leaned forward. "In the course of my medical training, did you know that I learned that all people use brains? Even paupers and working men. They don't need a wealthy person to give them ideas. They get them all on their own."

"Gentlemen." Miss Pursling rapped the table with her knuckles, the first loud sound she'd made. "The question of vaccination is one we must put off for later. The topic for the moment is *disinfectant*—and might I remind you both that disinfectant helps prevent cholera and influenza, two diseases we cannot inoculate against in any event."

"Ah, Miss Pursling," Grantham said softly. "Using facts to settle disputes. How bold of you."

Miss Pursling didn't blink in response, but Robert rather thought she was discomfited by even that much recognition.

"It's settled then," she said. "Marybeth Peters and I will post the handbills—"

"Two women, wandering the streets alone?" Stevens said. "I should think not."

"If it comes to that," Grantham put in, "I'll come along. And Miss Pursling, perhaps you could bring your friend—Miss Charingford, is it not?"

That would be the woman who had so recently baptized Stevens with her drink. At that jab, Stevens's face mottled almost as red as the punch that had been tossed in his face more than a week ago.

"The three of you posting leaflets about the Cooperative?" he sneered. "I won't allow such a gathering of radicals in my town. Not under my nose. No, *I'll* accompany them—and tell Miss Charingford to stay home where she belongs."

"As you're afraid of a solitary woman," Grantham said silkily, "I doubt you'll be able to provide the protection that the ladies require. I'll do it."

"To h—Hades with you," Stevens snarled. "In fact, to Hades with this entire—"

"I'll do it," Robert said.

At the sound of his voice, they all turned to look at him. Miss Pursling's eyes widened; Doctor Grantham looked at him quizzically. But Stevens turned utterly pale.

"Surely," Robert said, "you don't suspect *me* of radical tendencies, do you, Stevens?"

"Your Grace!" Stevens shot to his feet. "Of course not, Your Grace. But we wouldn't dream of discommoding you. And…and, what are you doing here?"

Robert waved the question away. "No inconvenience. It will give me a chance to see the town on foot."

Miss Pursling shot him a repressive look.

"Miss Pursling has gone to all the trouble of convincing the Cooperative to sell this solution at a good price," Robert said. "It would be my pleasure to see all her hard work vindicated."

If anything, Miss Pursling looked vexed at having credit so clearly assigned to her.

But—"Agreed," said Doctor Grantham.

"Agreed," growled Stevens.

And that left only the details to sort out with Miss Pursling. She gave him only the one venomous look before looking off into the distance and folding her hands. She didn't glance his way again through the remainder of the discussion—not even to glare at him. She didn't acknowledge him as they stood. Instead, she started to gather up her things.

He came up to her before she had a chance to disappear.

"Shall I send a note, then, to determine an appropriate time to distribute the handbills?"

She didn't look at him, putting papers and a pencil into a slim satchel. "If it suits you, Your Grace."

"We could decide it now."

"If that is your wish, Your Grace."

She was pointedly giving him her profile—the side with the scar again. Objectively, he knew that the scar was the kind of failure in perfect symmetry that would have most men looking away from her, unwilling to even glance at the mark. But it didn't bother him. She wore it like a mask at a ball, as if she could use it to push him away.

"I am going to be out of town for the next few days," he told her. "I've agreed to accompany my cousin…well, never mind."

Miss Pursling ducked her head. "As you require, Your Grace. The corrected handbills won't be printed for a few days in any event."

"Shall we say Thursday, then?"

"Whatever is easiest for you."

"Then let's meet at two in the morning," he suggested. "When the bears come out to play."

She finally glanced up at that, a quick flashing look of anger that was just as quickly suppressed. Robert sighed. She did her best not to draw attention to herself—that quiet voice, that understated way of discussing her accomplishments. He wondered if there was any connection between that mark on her cheek and her reticence. Hers was not the quiet of the naturally shy, after all, but a silence of a different quality altogether.

"Come, Miss Pursling," he said. "You can do better than all of this. I didn't think you were the sort to make idle threats."

"I don't know what you mean." She turned away from him slightly. And was that a *lift* to her nose?

It was. She'd actually turned her nose up at him.

Robert suppressed a grin.

"We had a deal," he said. He spoke low—so quietly that Doctor Grantham, now standing at the door and adjusting his coat, would not hear. "I flirt with you, and you try to destroy my reputation. You're not upholding your end of the bargain. You haven't done anything to me at all. I never took you for a welcher."

She tilted her head to look at him sidelong. "A thousand pardons, Your Grace." She sounded anything but sorry. "Were you actually expecting me to give you progress reports?" As she spoke she did up the buckles on her satchel.

"I figured you'd get a few preliminary jabs in, yes."

She gave him a frosty look. "Clearly you hold yourself to low standards. Whatever your faults may be, *I* do not jab prematurely."

He choked on a sputtering, outraged laugh and looked about. But there was no longer anyone around to hear that little remark.

She folded up the sample handbill that she'd brought with her, now marked up with the Commission's notes, and put it in her skirt pocket. "I surely don't parade my strategy before my enemies. That would be idiotic."

"What you mean is that you've not yet discovered any kind of proof."

She gave him a level look and a shake of her head. "What I mean is that I'm not so foolishly prideful that I'll disclose everything I've learned just because of a little inept needling on your part."

"Ouch," he said ruefully. "You accuse me first of jabbing prematurely, and then of inept needling. Take pity on a man's pride."

She smiled a little at that and leaned over and patted his hand.

"I'm sorry," she said sweetly. "I had no notion that you would be so susceptible to the wilting of your…pride." Said in a low, certain tone, that much innuendo sent a flash of heat through him. *Wilting* was the opposite of what he was doing. She hefted the satchel on her shoulder and headed for the door. She'd taken two steps before she turned around and gave him a low smile, one that seemed to stab straight through his gut. "I'm sure your prick is as massive as your head is thick."

There was no way he was going to let her walk out on that condescending, sexually-charged note, leaving him stewing in lust.

He took three steps after her, setting his hand on her sleeve. "Wait."

But she didn't, and so he found himself following after her, keeping silent as they made their way through the hostelry out onto the street. When they came out into the daylight, when they'd walked far enough that nobody was close enough to hear them, Robert spoke again.

"What I meant to say was—I *know* you've discovered nothing. Under the guise of obtaining bids for that little handbill of yours, you've been to every printer in town, looking for evidence that they're working with me. And you haven't found a thing."

She paused at that, her head cocking, and turned to him. "You've been watching me," she finally said.

"Not as such. That would be rather sordid, having you followed about. But I have asked a few business acquaintances to let me know what you ask about." He smiled at her. "As I didn't precisely expect you to give me progress reports."

She shrugged. "It would be sordid if you had a lover followed about in a fit of jealous suspicion. But we're enemies, recall. Keeping me under watch is merely prudent. I applaud it."

She started walking away again. Robert stared after her in bemusement.

He tried to be honest with himself. He had to be, as so few others were. His friend, Sebastian, could charm the bloomers off even the most upright dragons of the *ton*—and had, on occasion. His brother had a razor-sharp wit on the one hand, and a way of making others comfortable on the other. Oliver could make ladies laugh.

For himself... He could rarely think of how to respond when immersed in that heady back-and-forth. Sometimes he thought of clever things to say...hours later. Usually, he committed the worst sin possible: He said what he was really thinking. That was why he came out with gems like, *I like your tits.* Not one of his finest moments, that.

"No," he said, with a shake of his head, falling in step beside her. "Why do we have to be enemies? We could be...allies."

She squinted at him suspiciously. "Why? Because you need more half-blind near-spinsters on your side?"

He winced.

Her lips twitched. "Never mind. I saw you at the Finneys'. Clearly, you do."

He ignored this. "Because when you set out to prove that I was the author of the handbills, you first made a list of every printer in town, and then systematically visited them. You have a sense of…tactics. I appreciate that."

She tapped a gloved finger against her lips. "You keep saying that I found nothing," she mused. "You're wrong. I discovered that the handbills weren't being printed in Leicester. As there's only one possible suspect who is not a native, I think I've made quite an advance."

He blinked. He had the sense that he was lost in those quiet gray eyes, unable to look away from her. He was a duke. She was a—what had she called herself? A half-blind near-spinster. It shouldn't even have been a fair fight.

"You think," she said, "because you've identified one purpose of mine, that you know what I'm doing. But this inquiry among the printers was something of a discovered attack."

Standing this close to her, he could begin to see the difference. She was still looking down, still acting shy and quiet so that anyone more than three paces away would have no idea what she was saying. But there was a little more excitement in her hands. Her lips twitched, on the verge of smiling.

"What do you mean, a *discovered attack?*"

"A tactical term." She touched her fingertips together. "When you make a move, you do two things. First, you move forward—and the space you now occupy has value. But you also vacate the spot where you once were, exposing your enemy's flank to longer-ranged attacks. Be aware of where you are, and the space you'll leave behind."

"That's not a sense of tactics you have," he said, blinking down at her. "That sounds like actual tactical training. Where would a half-blind near-spinster acquire that?"

Where would *any* woman get that, for that matter? But Miss Pursling didn't seem to be rattled.

"I have collected a stack of papers that *will* show you to be the culprit. What have you accomplished, Your Grace? You've pretended to flirt with me."

He blinked, utterly startled. She wasn't looking at him. Of course she wasn't looking at him. She studied the pavement beneath her feet as if she were just another pale, downtrodden woman, unable to look him in the eyes.

"Pretending?" He felt almost dangerous. "You don't meet my eyes. You whisper your clever responses. You shy away from any hint that you're an intelligent woman. You're the one who pretends, my dear."

Her eyes widened slightly. "That—that is just conformity to the pressures of society—"

"Is it? Look up, Minnie. Look in my eyes. Let everyone on this street see what we both know is true. You're not deferring to me. You're challenging me. Look *up.*"

She didn't. Her head remained stubbornly bowed before him. He wanted to grab her and shake her. He wanted to tilt her chin up and force her to gaze in his eyes. He wanted—

He wanted a great many things after that, none of which he was going to get from her by force.

"I'm not *pretending* to flirt with you," he said instead. "There's no pretense in it. I want you. God, I want you."

She let out a little gasp and then—almost involuntarily—she looked up.

For just one moment, he saw something he thought was not pretense—a hopeless yearning in the way her face tilted toward his, a flutter in her ragged exhalation. Her lips parted, and she seemed suddenly, devastatingly beautiful.

But she shut her eyes and looked down again. Her breaths came a little louder; her fists clenched at her side. She shook her head. "Lucky you," she said bitterly. "Lucky you that you can plan and think and plot without pretense. That you can want openly, that you don't have to stuff it all inside yourself to molder. Lucky you that you can lift your eyes to the sky without singeing your wings. Lucky you that you can consider the future without terror."

Her hands were beginning to shake.

"I have looked high." Her voice was an urgent whisper. "And I have fallen farther than you can imagine. So don't *you* lecture me. All I want is to pretend that this is enough—that I can be satisfied by the scraps that remain to me. "

He had that sense again, of a great beast pacing in its cage. He wanted to touch her cheek, to turn her face up to his. He wanted to whisper that all would be well.

"Minnie," he said instead.

She winced. "Don't say my name like that. Please, Your Grace. If you have any care for me at all—*pretend* to flirt. But don't actually do it."

"Minnie," he repeated instead. "Who would you be if you didn't devote three-quarters of your attention to hiding what you could accomplish?"

She shook her head. "Don't tell me to look up. Don't ask me to want. If I do, I'll never survive." Her voice was shaking. He would have thought her on the verge of tears, by the sound of her. But her eyes were dry and clear and fixed on the pavement.

In that moment, he longed to take her in his arms and hold her close, to make her safe from whatever it was she feared. If she'd looked up at him again for even one second, he would have kissed her, and to hell with everyone around them.

She didn't. Instead, she seemed to gather in that unnatural, graceful calm with every breath.

"Marybeth Peters is waiting for me by the pump," she said, her voice smooth once more. "If I might withdraw, Your Grace?"

It wasn't a question. He didn't have a choice.

And so he watched her walk away, letting her return to pacing the confines of her cage.

Chapter Seven

WHEN MINNIE ARRIVED HOME, her great-aunts met her at the door, all aflutter. The reason for their excitement quickly became apparent when they told her that Walter Gardley was waiting in the front room. Alone.

Gardley. At this, of all times!

Minnie set her hand over her abdomen. It felt as if a fire raged inside her, as if she'd gorged herself on all the things the duke had said.

You're an intelligent, brilliant woman.

Look up.

I want you. God, I want you.

She couldn't go to Gardley feeling this way. But she had little enough choice in the matter. If she sent him away, he'd only return. And if he didn't...

She smoothed her skirt and went in to see him.

He stood as she entered the room. "There you are," he said—precisely as if he had mislaid her, and only now discovered her amidst the dust balls under the divan.

She tried to tell herself that he wasn't so bad. He was handsome enough, as these things went. He was only a few years older than she, and didn't look as if he would lose his hair.

You're the one that's pretending, she could hear the duke whisper behind her back.

"Mr. Gardley," she made herself say, with all the warmth she could muster. "How can I help you?"

He fixed her with a nonchalant look. "Well, Minnie," he said. "My mother's pushing me to settle things. I've done what's pretty. I'll call the banns this Sunday for a December wedding."

He was so sure of her that he didn't even wait for a response. He adjusted his coat and sat down again, before she could take a seat.

"Middle of the month, I think, would be best for us."

Who would you be if you didn't devote three-quarters of your attention to hiding what you could accomplish?

It was stupid to compare the ever-possible Walter Gardley to the unattainable Duke of Clermont. Still, Minnie couldn't help doing it. Gardley paled in every way. There was that hint of a paunch just above his belt, the lazy way he'd thrown himself back in his chair without waiting for Minnie to sit down first. There was what he'd said about her. He thought her a quiet little mouse who would stay where she was put. Who wouldn't complain about his mistresses.

And then there were the things he *didn't* do.

He didn't make her belly flutter. He didn't make her catch her breath. He'd never even pretended to flirt with her.

That's not just a sense of tactics. That sounds like actual tactical training.

It was her entire future at stake. She couldn't afford to be irrational. Every woman in her position would have to put up with imperfections in a mate. A bit of a paunch, a few women on the side—these were not things to trouble herself over. He wanted her because he believed she would be pathetically grateful. And he wasn't wrong. She *was* grateful. She *was* pathetic. Wasn't she?

"No," Minnie heard herself say.

Gardley shrugged. "After Christmas, then—I assume you want to spend the holidays with your great-aunts? I suppose I can allow that much."

She had spoken aloud in answer to her own question—*No, she wasn't pathetic.* But speaking those words aloud brought clarity to the endeavor. He wanted her because he believed she was pathetic. And if she married him, she would be.

"You'll allow me to choose the date of my own wedding?" she muttered. "How permissive of you."

His head came up at that. "Permissive? Don't think that because I grant you this that I will be an easy husband. I won't, not in the least. If you try any tricks once we're married, Minnie, I'll toss you out. And we both know you have nowhere to go."

She couldn't breathe.

God, she couldn't breathe.

Nothing he said came as a surprise. But she'd imagined that marriage—even to a man who made her skin crawl—would bring safety and security. In her own mind, marriage lasted forever. It had never occurred to her that someone else would see it differently.

If she married him, she would only become *more* desperate, not less. If the truth about her ever came out, he would turn her out, and never mind the marriage.

Minnie smoothed her hands on her skirt. "Mr. Gardley, that was a no to your entire proposal, not just to the wedding date. Thank you, but no."

He frowned and rubbed his forehead. "Why would you say no?"

After that little speech of his? "You think I am quiet, meek, and biddable." Even now, her voice was low, scarcely enough to fill on corner of the room. He moved; his seat creaked loudly. She could feel herself drowning in the noise of him.

He let out a forced little laugh. "Your womanly character, Miss Pursling, is your highest recommendation." He leaned in. "Never think yourself weak because you are bendable."

"Mr. Gardley, you are not listening to me."

"The woman bends like a reed in the storm," he continued, talking over her. "The man breaks like an oak." He frowned. "Or is it supposed to be a beech tree? Yes, that's it. In a strong wind, a man breaks like a beech." He reached for her hand. "I chose you because you would understand my requirements, and because I believe you have the ability to execute them."

Look up? No, the Duke of Clermont had it all wrong. She needed to look down. She'd allowed herself to believe that this man offered her some measure of safety. She suffered from too much optimism, not too little. Gardley had made it perfectly clear that he felt no loyalty to her. Where was the safety in that?

"That's ridiculous," Minnie said. "Women break like beeches, too. Why on earth do you imagine that I am so flexible, when I am refusing to marry you?"

"You're...you're refusing?" He frowned. "You can't refuse. That was the whole point—" He coughed, grimacing.

"That was the whole point of telling your mother that you were courting me?" Minnie finished for him. "That you'd pick someone she approved of, someone so desperate she could not say no, even if you never bothered to exert yourself to win me over?"

He was silent. He wasn't even man enough to look her in the eye and admit it. Finally, he shrugged sullenly. "What do you want? Should I take you driving a few times?"

Stevens still suspected her. The threat of exposure was as great as ever. But if she married Gardley, she'd never be safe. That realization terrified her more than ever. For so long, marriage had seemed a talisman. But it wasn't enough. She wasn't sure what was enough any longer.

She reached out and turned Walter Gardley's face to hers. He wouldn't look her in the eyes, and since his gaze kept shying away from her scar, it left him staring at the corner of her right cheek.

"No," she said quietly. "I will not marry you."

He looked utterly flummoxed. "But…but…what will you do?" he asked.

⌘ ⌘ ⌘

"BUT WHAT WILL YOU DO?" AUNT ELIZA ASKED, not quite thirty minutes later.

Minnie sat in the front parlor, her great-aunts seated on the sofa across from her. Eliza's needles clacked as she carefully darned a stocking. Caro simply watched her with folded arms.

Always know the path ahead. That had been one of her father's rules. Why she would cling to those now, after everything he'd done to her, she didn't know. Maybe because forgetting them would make her childhood not just a result of lies, but false through and through. Still, Minnie shook her head.

"We want you to be happy," Caro said. "And I would never tell you to have no ambition. But the trick is to want only an *appropriate* amount. If I yearned to be Queen of England, you see, I'd never be satisfied."

"I don't want to be Queen of England." Minnie folded her arms around herself.

"No, no." Caro smiled sadly at her. "All I'm saying is, you should want just enough to make you stretch your arms a little bit. More than that, and you'll do yourself an injury."

Minnie stood. "I didn't refuse Gardley because I wanted too much. It wasn't that I thought I could do better. It was simply that I couldn't do worse."

Caro tried to suppress a sigh, but she didn't quite manage it.

"Think of this logically," Minnie said. "Because I should have before. If I marry someone who wants a quiet, dutiful wife, he will put me away if he discovers my past."

Eliza's needles came to a standstill.

It was dangerous talk, that, and they all knew it.

Look up. But she wouldn't. If she were looking up, she'd think of a man standing next to her, the sun glinting off his blond hair while he told her how clever she was.

"You *are* quiet, Minnie," Eliza finally said. "I wouldn't want you to go against your nature."

Quiet, yes. Her voice wasn't made to carry. She didn't like to draw attention to herself. She could never be happy anywhere but at the edges of a gathering. Dutiful, however…

She could almost see Clermont from the corners of her vision, as if he were still standing next to her. He had brilliant blue eyes and a smile that curled up at the corners when he saw her. She thought of his hand, wrapping around her wrist before she could punch the davenport again. Of the rich timbre of his voice as he stood next to her and said...

I want you.

She shook her head. Reach that high, and she'd be burned for certain. All she wanted was a little security.

"Men look for many kinds of wives," Eliza finally said. "Pretty, vivacious wives. Wealthy, indulgent ones. Highborn, prideful ladies." She bit her lip. "I don't want you hurt, Minnie. But it is my duty to make you face the truth. Nobody is looking for a shy, clever girl whose father died halfway through his sentence of hard labor."

Minnie put her fingers against the bridge of her nose, pressing to try and drive the pain away. It didn't help. The boundaries of her life pressed in on her like prison walls. Look up? With rough rocks under her feet, to look up was to stumble.

"List the things you are," Eliza said, "and ask yourself what man would want them."

I want you. But Clermont didn't know her, either.

"Your choices are yours," Eliza intoned. "We won't steal them from you."

No. They never *stole* her choices. They only pointed out—kindly, sweetly, implacably—that she had few to begin with. Minnie's hands shook. The only thing they had done wrong was to allow her to believe that she had *one* choice, instead of zero.

Minnie didn't see any way forward. She couldn't see a future at all. She felt chokingly blind.

There was really only one thing she could do, and that was to keep on going in the direction she'd started. To avoid ruin for another week, to pray for shelter where there had been none thus far. And that meant she needed to find proof of what Clermont had done. She had to take care of the next step, and hope for the future.

And that meant... "I'm going to London tomorrow," she announced.

Their eyes widened, blinking. Eliza sat up straight. "But—"

"Have you—"

"Is this about a position?" Her great-aunts spoke atop one another. Their hands had met on the sofa between them.

"Be careful," Caro said. "I've read of those schemes in the newspaper—faithless madams who advertise good jobs at excellent wages, only to—"

"I am not taking a position," Minnie said. "You're right. I can't look up. I can't dream. I don't dare to. All I can do is take the next step forward."

Caro frowned. "And the next step forward is...London?"

"The next step forward," she said, "is to win the game I'm playing. And that means I must talk to some paper sellers. I'll be back in three days."

Her great-aunts exchanged glances—wary glances, ones that tugged at her chest. But she couldn't explain and she couldn't back down. And while it was not quite the done thing for a young woman of her age to travel alone on the train, she wasn't a debutante who would have to account for every waking hour of her day.

"Well," Caro said finally. "If that's what you believe you must do. You...you have the means?"

"I do."

She had her egg money. Even that was a misnomer. When she'd reached her majority, her great-aunts had given her responsibility for the chickens—and allotted her all the income from them. A gift, that, since they could have kept it all. But it hadn't just been a gift of money they'd given her, but a present of independence. It was one they could ill afford.

They let Minnie go back to her room to get her things ready. But instead of packing, she found herself drawn to the chess set that had been left to molder in the trunk in her room. Twelve years since she'd last looked at it, and still she approached it with a grim wariness. She knelt before the wooden trunk, folded back the cloth that covered it, and undid the buckles. The metal resisted moving; she had to jam her palm against it and shove.

The chess set was at the bottom, hidden under old clothing and a smattering of brittle newspaper clippings. *There.* The pieces were ebony and ivory, both oddly familiar and curiously strange. Her first memories were of this board—lifting pieces that had seemed large and heavy. Now, she could curl her hands around the pawns and hide them entirely.

She took out the board and removed the pieces from their velvet bag. She set them atop her writing desk. Even after all these years, she didn't have to think about what went where. Queen, king, and a host of pawns all fell into place. If she were a piece in a chess game, she'd be... No, she wouldn't even be a pawn. She had become too small even for that.

Setting up the pieces had once given her spirits a lift. The beginning of every game was awash in possibility. Anything could happen. Every choice was open. Today, she felt nothing at all. She stared at the pieces and realized that she wasn't at the beginning of this game, but near the end.

Now there were entire swathes of the board that were unreachable, pieces that had been stolen away, moves she could never make.

There was almost nothing left on her board. Still, she drew out her spectacles, donned them, and studied it.

"There is a point in almost every game," her father had once said, "when a win is inevitable. When your every move forces your opponent to react, and by reacting, to dig his own grave."

How strange. She could no longer recall what he looked like, but she could see the board precisely as it had been laid out at that moment. She brushed pieces off her board, leaving only the ones that had been there at the time. Her bishop and knight, holding down his rook; her queen arrayed against two pawns that served as his only fragile protection against her offense.

"Have we reached that point yet?" he asked her. "Plan it out. Always know the path ahead."

She'd stared at the board, squinting—and then she'd seen it for the first time. She could force those protecting pawns away. They'd be picked off by knight and queen until her rook swept in and hammered the king against the anvil of her bishop.

"Yes," she'd said in wonder. "We're there."

"Then on the next move, when you pick up your piece—give it a kiss. Like that, love."

She reached for her bishop. In her memory, the piece was large, her hands chubby. She couldn't have been much older than six at the time.

"Why?" she'd asked.

"Lane family tradition." Her father smiled. "When you've backed the other fellow into a corner, you give him a kiss to show there's no hard feelings."

After that, whenever they'd played—when one of them came close to a checkmate—he'd laughed and said there was a kiss just around the corner. She wanted to remember her father like that—warm and smiling, instructing her in everything he knew. Laughing, saying that she was the center of his existence. She had to remember her father like that, because the alternative was to think of him as he'd been at the end.

Look up? Her father hadn't just told her to look up. He'd taught her to fly. And then, when she'd reached the top of the world, he'd ripped her from the sky.

Chapter Eight

IN THE END, IT TOOK DAYS for Robert to bring Sebastian in—in large part because Violet, the newly widowed Countess of Cambury, insisted on coming along.

"First," Violet had said, spearing Robert with her gaze, "I am tired of sitting on an estate in Cambridgeshire with nothing to do. Second, you'll need someone to keep Sebastian on a leash." She'd nodded at Sebastian, who had attempted to look innocent.

There had been some truth to that. Violet *could* get Sebastian to behave—nominally—when she wished. Violet was two years older than Robert and Sebastian. She'd grown up on the estate next door to Sebastian's, and until Violet had been deemed too old to play with boys, she'd accompanied them during the summers.

But Robert had far more memories of Violet tweaking Sebastian and sending him climbing trees for hawks' eggs in a fit of rage, than he did of Violet getting Sebastian to behave.

"Finally," Violet said, "your mother actually likes me, and if we wish to distract her, a two-pronged approach will work best. Sebastian can drive her off, and I'll lure her away from you."

But it had been Sebastian who provided the final impetus, after Violet had disappeared that first evening. "Look," he'd told Robert, "she's in mourning for a man she hated. Give her a chance to get out."

So Robert had relented—and thus brought upon himself an entourage of servants and maids and dressers, of messages sent to reserve rooms in a hotel, as Violet could not stay in Robert's bachelor establishment. It was more than forty-eight hours before Robert found himself, his cousin, the Countess of Cambury, nine separate servants, two cats, and one owl on the platform at Euston Square in London.

The servants were engaged in wrestling the luggage into the proper compartment, and Robert took the time to walk with his cousin. There was a bit of a breeze, enough to keep the air along the platform crisp and pleasant. The tang of burning tobacco—that was Robert's excuse for not sitting in the station proper alongside Violet—made an acrid counterpoint to the smell of autumn leaves.

He walked beside his cousin, and all his myriad worries seemed to grow smaller.

"So," he said to Sebastian, "they're actually taking steps to make some sort of position for you at Cambridge. Given what they said of you when you were a student there, I would imagine that was the last thing you'd expect. Are you dying of shock yet?"

Sebastian gave him a long look. "I'm not a student any longer, you know."

"Don't pretend you've grown up."

That got him an impish smile. "Wait until I turn it down," his cousin said. "That will shock everyone."

Robert blinked and looked at the man more closely. Sebastian was a known prankster, but he took the work he did now very seriously. "You're going to turn it down?"

"I'm afraid I have to." Sebastian put his hands in his pockets. "Even Newton had to get a dispensation from Charles II because he didn't believe in the Trinity. Oxford has become more liberal, but Cambridge…" He shrugged. "Still the Dark Ages there. They insist on adherence to Church of England doctrine. Half the natural scientists want me because they think I'm doing interesting work. The other half believe that appointing me a Fellow will force me to shut up."

"Would it?" Robert glanced at him. "I've never known you to shut up, not about anything. And *are* you an unbeliever? I've read all your papers, even the ones that are well over my head, and I don't recall you taking a position."

Sebastian shrugged. "Haven't you heard? I'm a godless scientist, an apostate follower of Darwin."

"Even Mr. Darwin isn't an unbeliever."

Sebastian didn't answer the question. Instead he gave a resigned shrug. "I not only think that the species evolved, I can prove that characteristics are transmitted from parent to offspring in a dependable, scientific manner. Not by the grace of any divine being. By the operation of simple, natural principles." He gave Robert a look. "That makes me an unbeliever in half of society's eyes. Who am I to argue with them?"

"I take it that's a rhetorical question, as you argue with them at every opportunity."

Sebastian smiled in pleasure and shook his head.

"I think you just like being an outcast."

"That must be it." Sebastian shrugged.

"And you've managed to distract me. You never did answer my question. *Do* you believe in God?"

"I've given you as much an answer as I'll give anyone. I think it's a shame that Mr. Darwin must account for his religion on the basis of the work that he does. A man's beliefs should be between himself and whatever deity he does—or does not—worship. Nobody asks a cooper whether he believes in God. Why should I have to answer? Why should anyone care?"

It had come on so quickly, Sebastian's fame. So much that it was still rather a shock to discover that Sebastian—quick-minded, foul-mouthed Sebastian Malheur, his cousin and onetime coconspirator—had become a famous scientist. Not that Sebastian didn't have the brains for it; he'd always been quick and clever. It was just easier to see his cousin as the prankster he'd been as a child, rather than an actual serious-minded adult.

"Besides," Sebastian said, "it's loads more fun tweaking everyone. Refusing to answer the question has all the old biddies hem-hemming and striking me from their guest lists."

Possibly this was because Sebastian had not become an actual serious-minded adult. Robert had missed him.

The conductor sounded his whistle, and people began to board. Robert and Sebastian waited at the end of the platform for the first crowds to dissipate, and then walked back. They passed the luggage cars, then the second-class cabins, on their way to their seats.

But as they walked past one car, Robert blinked. He couldn't have seen... He quickly turned and walked back.

"Oy!" Sebastian called. "You're going the wrong way."

Robert waved him off. He'd had the strangest illusion when he'd walked by—that the woman he'd seen out of the corner of his eye was none other than Miss Pursling.

It couldn't be.

When he came abreast of the window, he saw his eyes had not deceived him. The woman lifted her head from contemplation of her book to stare out the window on the other side. The sun spangled through the dust collected on the window, illuminating that nose he knew so well—and those lips.

Miss Pursling was sitting in that compartment. She'd be sitting there the entire way to Leicester—several hours with nobody to talk to. Nobody, unless...

Violet had come out of the station as well. She was tossing orders to the porter.

Robert tapped her on the shoulder.

"Violet," he said, "might I borrow your maid?"

Violet's eyes narrowed in suspicion. "Borrow my maid? No, you may not borrow Matilda. Whatever do you need her for?"

"I—" He tried not to look in Miss Pursling's direction. "Ah."

"It's a woman," Sebastian put in. "You can tell by the look of nervous anticipation on his face—it's a woman."

"Oh?" Violet looked around demurely. "Is it… No. Don't tell me who. Let me guess."

Violet was capable of a demure little glance about. But Sebastian craned his neck, looking from side to side with exaggerated motions.

Robert winced. "Stop. Stop. Do you have to be so obvious?"

"I knew it was a woman!" Sebastian said triumphantly. "We're embarrassing him—it has to be a woman."

Just a moment before, Robert had been thinking how lovely it was to be around people who understood him. No longer. His cheeks flushed. "If I admit it's a woman, will you stop gawking and pretend to be normal people?"

Violet sniffed. "I still don't see what a woman has to do with your needing Matilda."

"She's riding in one of the second-class compartments alone," Robert admitted. "I want to sit with her."

This pronouncement was met with a rigid silence. Sebastian looked at Violet; Violet looked at Sebastian. The two of them might as well have waggled their eyebrows in accusation.

"*You're* interested in a woman who is riding second-class," Sebastian finally said.

Violet gave him an almost identical look. "You're interested in a woman who is riding second-class, and your interest is such that you care about the effect on her reputation."

Sebastian rubbed his hands together. "Oh," he said with glee, "your mother is going to *love* this."

"I hate it when you two do that," Robert groused, which was a lie. He usually loved it when they spoke like that, Violet's thoughts piling on top of Sebastian's, making an ungainly heap of the conversation. Now, though, it was going to prove inconvenient. He had to get rid of them before they said something dreadful.

Violet looked up. "Well, I'm sorry, Robert. You may not borrow my maid."

"But—"

"But," she said, brushing her hands together briskly, "I will be happy to accompany you myself."

Robert swallowed. He tried to imagine carrying on a conversation with Miss Pursling while the Countess of Cambury looked on with avid interest.

"Second class," Sebastian said. "I've never ridden second-class. This is going to be fun."

Robert coughed heavily into his hand. "No, not both of you. Definitely not both of you."

"You need both of us," Sebastian said. "There are four seats. If you take Violet on her own, someone else might come and sit in the car with you. There are four seats. Surely you wouldn't want all opportunity for conversation quashed."

"But—"

"You know me," Sebastian said. "I'm the soul of discretion."

"No, you're not. You are exactly the opposite."

Sebastian grinned. "I'm the soul of only teasing you about things when nobody else is around to hear me. And besides, if *you* don't sit with this mysterious woman, I'll go join her myself. I believe I saw where she was."

He was doomed. It would almost be better to simply walk away and not speak to her at all. But...

He glanced back at her car. She was staring out the window away from the station, her fingers pressed to the glass. She wasn't contemplating anyone; she was looking into the distance, away from the high columns of the station, as if what she yearned for was far off.

"Don't say anything embarrassing," he said.

"Me?" Sebastian said. "It would be counterproductive to do so. I'm no student of human behavior, but as a scientific matter, noninterference is necessary in order to properly observe the primitive mating rituals of—"

Oh, God. This was going to be *awful*. He should never have said a word.

"I mean it," Robert said. "If you two come, I don't want to hear a peep out of you. Not one word the entire trip."

"Really," Violet said, "you know you can trust me to be circumspect."

"I'm not worried about you," Robert said, which was true in the relative sense. "Sebastian?"

"You can rest assured that I will not break my vow of silence until you have given me leave to do so, lest I lose my immortal soul."

A less grandiloquent promise would have inspired more trust. Particularly since Sebastian refused to admit whether he believed in an immortal soul. Still, Robert bowed his head and hoped—fervently—that this would not turn out as badly as he feared.

❋ ❋ ❋

THE CONDUCTOR WAS CALLING FOR ALL TO BOARD the train leaving out
of Euston Square, and Minnie had hidden herself in the second-class car.
The cars were almost empty, and she had her cloak drawn up to her cover
her face. A look of firm disapproval usually sent any would-be traveling
companions scampering for the next compartment over.

So when the door handle rattled, she fixed a grim, uninviting
expression on her face. The hinges squeaked; the door swung in, and a
woman stepped into the compartment.

Not just a woman; a *lady*. She was dressed in the dark gray of half-
mourning, ribbons and bows flirting with a lavender so pale it was almost
colorless. Minnie didn't need to see the seed pearls lining her cuffs to
know that this woman was wealthy and important. She'd have guessed it
from the careful tucks and frills of the gown, the fabric that billowed out
in careless excess, the fit of a gown that could only have been perfected
through countless visits from a *modiste*.

What was a woman like that doing back here in the second-class cars?

Her eyebrows were drawn down; she rapped the bench across from
Minnie lightly, as if to ascertain that it was indeed as hard as it appeared.
Then she shrugged prosaically.

Before she could look at Minnie, a man—a gentleman, by the look of
him, trousers pressed and creased, red waistcoat covered by a long
traveling coat—ducked his head in. "Cobber's lost the truck again," he
said. "And Matilda says the porter insists on loading your second crate on
bottom, no matter what the markings say."

"Oh, hell," the woman said.

The man didn't blink at the profanity. He simply stood aside and let
her sweep out the door.

Oddly enough, that gentleman—dark-haired and dark-eyed—looked
at Minnie. It was probably too late to drive these people away, whoever
they were, but she glared at him anyway.

In return, he winked at her.

"The first-class cars are there." She gestured.

He shrugged, tossed his heavy coat on another seat, and then
followed after the woman.

So she was to have companions after all—and odd ones, at that.

The door rattled again. She looked up, expecting to see her strange
companions—but no. Her heart dropped. Her hands burst into flame.

"Miss Pursling," the Duke of Clermont said. "How absolutely lovely
to see you."

The last time she'd seen him, he'd told her to look up. She'd *wanted* to do it. And then… Then, she'd discovered that she had even fewer choices than she supposed. Looking at him made her want to forget all that. She'd hoped to put that longing out of her mind for good, but at the sight of him, the memory returned unbidden, waiting on the surface of her skin, reviving with every breath that passed through her lips.

I want you.

Those words had taken hold of her imagination, and even though her mind knew that nothing had ever happened between them, her flesh seemed unconvinced. She broke out in prickles of awareness at his presence. She looked down.

"Are you having a nice journey?" He placed a satchel in the rack overhead and then sat across from her.

"Yes," she said, somewhat stiffly. "I visited a papermaker in London so I could discover where you were getting your materials."

She tossed it out so he would know where they stood—as far apart as she could push them.

His nose twitched. "A progress report," he said happily. "I see I *have* advanced in your standing. How lovely." And he smiled at her.

There was no place for him and his wants in her life. No place at all. Luckily, the door opened again to admit the lady in the impressive traveling habit.

"Robert," she said, "we cannot leave yet. They have misplaced Herman and the conductor is threatening to go anyway. What can it matter if the train is delayed? You must stop them, because my stratagems will not last much longer."

"Your stratagems?" The Duke of Clermont sat up straight, and his voice grew darker. "What have you done?"

The woman held up a silver-plated whistle. "The conductor's," she said simply.

The duke stared at her, then groaned and rubbed his forehead. "Oh, God." He touched his hat and turned to Minnie. "Wait. I'll be right back."

The door closed again, and she was once more left alone. Minnie briefly considered moving compartments. But if she did, he would only find her again. Besides, the conductor had marked off her ticket in this seat, and she wasn't certain he'd remember her if she moved to another compartment.

The next temptation struck in a moment. He'd thrown his bag on the seat next to her. Only a single metal buckle separated her from his papers. His potentially damning papers.

He had to be importing the handbills from somewhere. Maybe he had a bill of sale or a note in that satchel.

But…it would be a tremendous breach of privacy.

And what would she do even if she found something? His word against hers would still leave her ruined. She argued with herself back and forth, until the passage of time made her decision for her.

The door to the car opened. It was the duke. He glanced at his satchel overhead and then shook his head. "Really," he said, "you didn't go through it?"

"Really." Minnie gritted her teeth. "I didn't go through it."

"Am I not your enemy? Are we not at war?"

"I don't know what you are. I certainly don't know what we are doing." Her nose wrinkled. "But I would have the devil of a time proving the provenance. Even if I did find a stack of radical handbills in your satchel, what would I do? Take them out and show the magistrate? I'd have no proof you once owned them."

He took the satchel down and looked over at her. "You are constantly surprising me. I have to remind myself that whatever it is you are planning, it is going to be thought through more thoroughly than anything I have ever contemplated." He undid the leather strap and reached in, taking out a handful of papers. "Here," he said. "If you had gone through my satchel, you'd have found this. I wrote it for you anyway."

He held out a piece of paper.

Minnie didn't take it.

"You said you were terrified of the future, when last we spoke. I want a truce. This is my best offer." He smiled at her, and oh God, she *felt* it, felt the force of his smile all the way to her toes.

She reached out and gingerly removed it from his hand. He was right; the letter had her name scrawled on the front.

"Pax for the journey?"

"I—I don't know."

"A few hours, Miss Pursling. That's all I'm asking for." His smile tilted. "And incidentally, about the other two passengers—"

The door opened, and he grimaced, folding his arms over his chest. The two people who had come in earlier entered once more.

The woman's eyes rested on Minnie…and narrowed just long enough for Minnie to realize that this calm, impressive woman had likely heard something about her from the duke. Enough that she took in Minnie's plain gown, the scar on her cheek, and tilted her head. Behind her stood the gentleman who'd winked at her, his hair dark, his cravat white.

The Duke of Clermont gave a rueful smile. "Heh," he said. "Well, as to that." He bit his lip. "Yes. Violet, Sebastian, may I introduce you to Miss Pursling? Miss Pursling, this is Violet Waterfield, the Countess of Cambury."

"Charmed, I'm sure," the countess said, in a voice that suggested she was anything but.

"And behind her is Mr. Sebastian Malheur."

Minnie forgot to be quiet. Her mouth fell open. "*The* Sebastian Malheur?" she found herself exclaiming. "The one who wrote that impassioned defense of Mr. Darwin?"

Goodness. If the stories about him were even remotely true, he was an absolute reprobate. He was wildly rumored to be not only a religious dissenter, but an actual atheist. A womanizer. A rake. But Mr. Malheur simply shrugged and set two fingers to his lips in an exaggerated gesture.

"Yes," the duke said after a slightly stilted pause. "He's that self-same benighted fellow. All the rumors you've heard are true. Also, he's my cousin." He let out a sigh. "Well, you two might as well come in and sit down," he finally said. "It's not as if you could make things any worse."

She had no idea what he meant by that, if he was talking to them or to her. But the two of them trooped into the car. Without saying a word, or even once glancing at Minnie, they took their seats.

Chapter Nine

OUTSIDE, A WHISTLE BLEW.

The train shuddered as doors rattled shut all along its length. And Robert waited in misery for what he knew would come.

For a moment, all seemed well. Violet reached into her bag and took out some yarn and knitting needles; Sebastian sat, looking straight ahead at absolutely nothing.

Miss Pursling kept her gaze on the wooden slats that made up the floor. She'd put his letter in her pocket and didn't even touch the fabric. The train began to move, swaying from side to side, and still she didn't speak.

It shouldn't have surprised Robert—she did this every single time he saw her—but Violet glanced up and over at him, then over at Miss Pursling. Her brows drew down in something like confusion. She exchanged a worried glance with Sebastian.

"So," Robert said. "Miss Pursling, are you coming from London?"

Miss Pursling glanced at him and then looked away. "Yes, Your Grace," she said meekly.

"What brought you there?"

She tilted her head forward so that there was no chance she might meet his eyes. "I had business, Your Grace. Business of a personal nature."

If this was pax... Robert sighed.

He couldn't very well talk about the handbills. Neither Sebastian nor Violet knew about those, as they didn't have the protection Robert did, and he preferred to keep it that way. Silence stretched in the car, and it occurred to Robert that banning Violet and Sebastian from speaking had not been the best idea. What felt like a companionable silence among two seemed devilishly awkward with four people staring at one another, mouths clamped shut. This had the potential to be the most painful train ride ever.

"So," he tried again, "the Workers' Hygiene Commission. Why did you take an interest in it?"

She tilted her head and looked up at him. Her lips flattened as if she were suppressing a smile. "Because," she said, "hygiene is important. Don't you think so, Your Grace?"

"Of course, but many things are important. We've all made different choices as to how to spend our time. Violet here volunteers her time at the Botanic Garden in Cambridge, presumably because she likes plants. Sebastian…"

Sebastian looked up, a look of interest on his face.

"Yes," Miss Pursling said, "I would very much like to hear how Mr. Malheur spends his time."

"Ah…" Even a clinical description of Sebastian's work was suspect in mixed company.

"Because *I* heard," Miss Pursling said, "that he threatened to institute a program for human breeding amongst the Cambridge faculty in order to prove his theories on the sexual inheritance of traits."

Yes. That was why it was difficult to talk about what Sebastian did. Because in order to do so, one had to say "sexual inheritance" without blushing—something Miss Pursling managed abnormally well.

Sebastian fixed her with his most earnest gaze, and Robert recalled, rather belatedly, that his cousin had something of a talent for mesmerizing women. What had he been thinking, bringing the man into close proximity with Miss Pursling? By the end of the ride, she'd be smitten.

In fact, she probably already was.

But Sebastian simply shrugged once more, placed his hand over his mouth in an exaggerated motion, and then bowed, gesturing to Robert. Robert translated this as *I'm deeply sorry, but having promised my cousin that I wouldn't say a word, I must now embarrass him as best as I can with gestures.*

"Oh, for God's sake," Robert muttered, pressing his fingers into his forehead. The train squeaked as it went around a bend.

Sebastian shook his finger at him in an invocation of shame and then made a gentle back-and-forth gesture with his hand, not clearly invoking anything at all.

"Are you…injured? Ill?" Miss Pursling guessed. "Unable to talk for some reason?"

Sebastian's face lit up, and he pointed one finger at her.

"Have you tried tea?" she asked. "With honey—it's quite soothing on the throat."

Another meaningless gesture from Sebastian—this one, his arms thrown up to the heavens and then quickly lowered.

"At least make an attempt not to strike me in the face, Sebastian," Violet said. "And for God's sake, we both know Robert didn't mean it literally. He wanted us not to embarrass him—but you're managing that perfectly well without words."

Miss Pursling's eyes darted between the two of them. If ever there was a woman to pick up on what had not been spoken, it was Miss Pursling. He could imagine her reconstructing what he must have told the two of them.

He felt his cheeks warm. "You might as well speak," he muttered gruffly.

"I knew perfectly well what you meant," Sebastian said. "But I've always found that the quickest way to make someone relent in his foolish edicts is to take every command literally and to perform it with flagrant obedience."

"It is not too late to toss you from this car," Robert said. The train was shifting back and forth, scuttling along the tracks. It hadn't yet come up to full speed—they were still barely out of London, after all.

"You see," Sebastian said to Miss Pursling, "my cousin's true nature revealed: unforgiving, cruel, and violent."

Robert did his best not to whimper and was mostly certain that he succeeded.

"And incidentally," Sebastian told her, "I did *not* threaten to create a human breeding program at Cambridge to prove my theory. For one thing, one does not *prove* a theory in that sense of the word. One tests it by considering the next most likely explanation. For another, that story has been much exaggerated in the retelling. I simply noted that one could use simple principles to determine, after the fact, the probability that a certain don's wife had—"

"Ha. Yes." Robert jumped into the conversation before it could run further afield. "So maybe there are some things we'd all be happier not discussing."

"Forgive my cousin," Sebastian said with a slow shrug, "for he is a bit of a prude. But my apologies; I was intruding into your very delightful conversation. Please, continue with whatever it was you weren't saying to each other." He leaned back.

"Indeed," Violet said. "Don't mind us. We're scarcely even here. And rest assured, if you'd like to talk of secrets, I'll never repeat a one. I'm known for my trustworthiness."

"This is true," Sebastian said. "The Countess of Cambury is like a deep, dark hole—secrets go in, but none of them ever come out."

"Sebastian," Violet replied, calmly looping the yarn about one of her needles, "it is neither proper nor respectful to let a woman know that you think of her as nothing more than a hole."

Miss Pursling choked, and then coughed, and Robert sank an inch lower in his seat, wishing that he had not set his hat on the rack above his head. He needed something to cover the violent flush in his cheeks. He should never have let either one of them anywhere near her, and if they kept on in this fashion, he was never going to forgive them.

Violet's face was unruffled; she continued on with her knitting.

Sebastian waved a hand. "My apologies; the countess is, of course, a sweet flower of womanhood."

Shut up. Shut up.

Thankfully, Sebastian did not take his apology any further.

Violet seemed to accept this without comment. "Don't mind me," she said. "In fact, don't mind any of us." She blinked and held up her needles before her as if constructing a wall.

"I think we may have started this conversation off on the wrong foot," Robert said finally. In fact, if the conversation had been animate, the merciful thing to do would have been to take it out behind the barn and shoot it.

"Is that so?" Miss Pursling looked out the window.

"I just thought that perhaps if we dealt with one another fairly for one afternoon, that we might—"

"Oh, never believe him when he talks that way!" Violet interrupted, still pretending to be engrossed in her needlework. "He may rattle on for as long as he wishes about fairness and equality, but he is the only one who refused to play princess."

Robert's smile felt a little sickly. This was precisely the sort of thing he had most feared. *Shoot* the conversation? He wanted to beat it over the head and dump it in an unknown grave.

Miss Pursling looked over at the other woman, her eyebrows furrowing in confusion. "Play princess?"

"Yes," Violet answered. "We did when we were children. Over the summers, his father would go off visiting, and he'd leave Robert with his sister—Sebastian's mother. Robert, Sebastian, and I used to play a game that they called 'Knights and Dragons,' and that I called 'Extremely Boring.' They got to be knights, but *I* had to sit around as the princess and wait for them to rescue me."

"I see."

"So one day," the countess continued serenely, "while they were charging about pretending to attack the dragon, I wrote a note saying that I had run away to tread the boards."

Sebastian snorted. "I believe you added that you meant to give your virtue to an entire group of bandits first."

The countess didn't seem the least bit offended by this. "At the time I had no notion what that entailed, but my governess was constantly warning me to protect my virtue with my life. It seemed the worst threat I could muster."

Miss Pursling leaned forward with a slight smile on her face. She lifted her eyes to Violet's. "What did your valiant knights do when your defection was discovered?"

"They decided it was their duty to hunt me down and feed me to the dragon as punishment." Violet frowned at the mess she'd made of her knitting and then calmly began to pick out the last row. "They were not successful. In any event, it made for a far more amusing game."

"Mud was involved," Sebastian supplied.

"Thereafter," Violet continued equably, "it was agreed that it was patently unfair for me to play princess every time. So we tossed a coin for it. But Robert never would play princess—not even when it was his turn." The countess frowned at Robert, and he looked about.

"A coin only has two sides," he said. "There was no way to assign a side to me."

"Except by—"

Robert raised a hand. "And now is not the time to get into methods for making coin tosses balance amongst three. Suffice to say, I would have made a very bad princess."

"I see," Minnie said slowly.

"You don't," Sebastian threw in. "You're thinking that Violet might make a reasonable princess. But she was exactly like this when she was a child—all prim and proper on the outside, but a hellion when no adults were looking. She only looks respectable. I don't know how she did it, but Robert and I would return from our outings covered head to toe in mud, and Violet would look fresh as a spring day."

"There is this lovely thing called water," Violet put in. "Boys seem to be unaware of its existence." She cast a look at Minnie over her knitting. "Hygiene is important."

Miss Pursling smiled and looked down.

"Incidentally," Sebastian added, "for the sake of my dignity, Miss Pursling, I must inform you that when I played the role, it was called 'prince.' Not princess."

"Called prince by you," Robert put in. "The rest of us called you 'princess.' It doesn't make sense otherwise. Dragons want to devour princesses. They don't care about princes."

"You have a great deal to learn about dragons. Think about it: We get more beef from steers than cows. It's well known that the male of the species produces finer flesh."

"I thought," Miss Pursling said, "that we didn't eat female cows because we preferred to save them for their milk."

Not this argument. Down this road there could only lie doom. Robert hunkered back in his chair and waited for the inevitable time in which Sebastian would send Miss Pursling screaming.

Mr. Malheur winked at Miss Pursling. "Dragons like cheese."

"But dragons cannot milk princesses," Miss Pursling responded. "They do not have opposable thumbs."

Sebastian looked upward. "Very clever, and you'd almost be right. But dragons have *minions*. In any event, it's quite clear that the female of the human species has inferior meat. They are saddled with those unfortunate fatty deposits round the front. Whereas flank of manflesh is lean, tender, and succulent." He emphasized this by standing up and setting one hand against the seat of his trousers.

Violet rolled her eyes. "The least said about flank of manflesh, the happier we all will be. Besides, I thought you rather liked those unfortunate fatty deposits round the front. You spend enough time—"

Robert coughed loudly.

"My preferences are irrelevant," Sebastian managed, with a great deal of haughty grandness. "*I* am not a dragon."

"True," Robert put in. "You're a peacock—flaunting your feathers for the female of the species."

"If it works…" Sebastian smiled, and then turned his head, peering at imaginary tail feathers on his behind. "And yes, that *is* one of my better features, thank you."

The countess let out a loud, defeated sigh. "Are we talking about Sebastian's buttocks again? Has he no other body parts?"

That was the point when Robert realized that Miss Pursling wasn't staring at the floor and hadn't been for some time. She had a small smile on her face, and she was looking between the two of them, her eyes round in fascination, her cheeks flushed pink.

Robert pointed a finger at Sebastian. "You see?" he said accusingly. "I knew you would do it. You baited me into that, you did. I will never believe a word you say again."

"You're welcome." Sebastian bowed low and then sat once more. "All that unrequited awkwardness…" He gave a mock shiver. "I will collect my thanks later."

"Gah. I hate you both."

Normally he'd have loved passing time like this—listening to his friends bat the ball of conversation back and forth between them like deranged cats. But Miss Pursling was going to think he was insane, spending time with these two. Hell; he was related to Sebastian. First cousins. He might as well have announced that he had an entire branch of his family in Bedlam.

"Oh, dear," Sebastian said. "Were we not supposed to have said any of that?"

"Of course we could," said Violet. "We specifically mentioned that he never played princess. That makes him manly. You still think him manly, Miss Pursling, do you not?"

"I feel it important to make no comment." Miss Pursling looked down, but her eyes sparkled.

"You know," Sebastian said, "I must object to that line of reasoning. It takes supreme confidence in one's manliness to play princess. Maybe we've only made him appear insecure."

"Maybe," Violet said all too loudly, "if we don't mention that, she won't notice."

Miss Pursling smiled. "Don't mind me," she said, dropping her eyes. "I never notice a thing."

"Well, then." Violet was using her *all's-well-that-ends-well* voice. "I don't see what there is to be upset about. Robert, stop sulking."

Robert shut his eyes in defeat.

When the train stopped, he waited until Sebastian gathered his things and left, until Violet followed after to see to her owl. Then, and only then, did he turn to Miss Pursling.

She was standing at the door of the car, wrapping a scarf around her neck.

He turned his hat in his hands. "Look," he said. "About that conversation…" But what excuse was he to make?

They're not usually like that.

That was a lie.

You have to understand. Sebastian's jokes brought me through many a hard time. I love him more than I want to kill him.

But the truth was too much. He was struggling to find some way to apologize—and he wasn't sure whether he should even be apologizing. But she adjusted her gloves, glancing down, before looking at him again.

"Your Grace."

"Miss Pursling."

Her eyes were gray, light and clear, and they seemed to see straight through his not-quite-apologetic hand-wringing.

"I always thought you could judge a man by the company he kept."

"Ouch." He winced. "Sebastian," he finally said, "he's always been excessive. He can be a little much to take in, all at once. But he's a good man." He was. Sort of.

Miss Pursling frowned. "What are you talking about? I like your friends."

"I—you…" He sucked in a breath. "That almost sounds like you like *me.*"

She gave him a nod. "Logic," she said, "is a lovely thing, Your Grace. That is precisely what I said. I only wish it weren't true." She turned the handle and stepped out the door.

"Wait," he said, reaching after her.

But the door had already slammed behind her. He was still staring at the space she'd occupied when the conductor blew the whistle. He grabbed his bag and ran.

She liked his friends. She *liked* his friends? It was odd, to have all that embarrassment turned around. He found himself grinning madly, gleefully, as he caught up with Violet and Sebastian and the rest of their entourage. They were crowded around Violet's notebook, peering at the pages.

"What are you two giggling about?" he asked suspiciously.

Violet snapped her notebook shut. "I was keeping score," she said. "I hate to inform you of this, but your Miss Pursling won the conversation."

He still had that stupid grin on his face, and it wasn't going away. "Yes," he agreed. "Isn't it marvelous?"

Chapter Ten

THE OMNIBUS DROPPED MINNIE a half mile from her great-aunts' farm. She pulled her valise under one arm and began to walk the rest of the way home.

When she'd left the few clustered houses behind her, she pulled out the letter in her skirt pocket and awkwardly—she had only one free hand, after all—broke the wax seal.

The letter was dated two days past.

My dear Miss Pursling, he had written. *I want to make clear what I meant the other day when we encountered one another at the Finneys' residence. Writing handbills is not some sort of a whim on my part.*

You told me the other day that you had looked high, and that you had been battered down. You're not alone. It is the nature of English society to do precisely that: to keep the lower classes low and raise the upper classes even higher. It is lucky of me indeed to be able to look where I wish.

My most ardent wish is that you, and everyone like you, will look up. That you'll do so and never be beaten into the ground again. I write handbills because I can write those words without fear of reprisal—because if I am discovered, the House of Lords will never prosecute me. I write because those words must be written. I write because to not write, to not speak, would be to waste what I have been given. I keep it secret because otherwise, anyone who associated with me would become the target for an investigation.

You are undoubtedly my superior in the matter of tactics. As proof, here you have a letter in my own hand, admitting what I have done. Use it to expose me, if that's what you think will get you your good marriage to an ordinary man who wishes nothing more than to have a quiet wife. Use it, if you must, or keep it and say nothing. You told me the future terrified you. I can't change the whole of it, but I can change this much.

Or you could look up. You could put that superior mind of yours to real use and fashion a different place for yourself entirely. You could be more. You could be much, much more.

Anything else would be a criminal waste of your talents.

Your servant,

Robert Alan Graydon Blaisdell.

No title. But then, the only title he'd chosen for himself in his writings was *De minimis*—a small thing. Not so small a thing, though. Minnie could feel the tide of his hope lifting her up with every step.

You could be more.

She'd tasted more once—just the tiniest nibble, but enough to make her life now seem dreary indeed. It was like eating nothing but unsalted gruel every meal, but smelling sausage and pastries all day. After all this time spent choking down tasteless glop, someone was offering her meat.

She couldn't think logically. She couldn't analyze. She could think of nothing but her hunger.

I could be more.

She had no idea what her future contained, but even the little hint of relief she'd felt at his admission—one less thing to fear, one worry put off after these last days of worry—seemed to ease her burden.

That feeling of false comfort stayed with her through the walk home. It buoyed up every step, elevated every breath. It buzzed through her as she greeted her great-aunts, as she went and washed and prepared herself for the evening meal. And it changed nothing. It only made the burden of reality feel all the heavier when its full weight descended on her shoulders.

By the time dinner came, Minnie found she couldn't taste the soup.

Her great-aunts sat before her, eating steadily, conversing as two good friends who had spent decades in one another's company were wont to do. The conversation ranged from the production of turnips to the uses for the far field come spring.

They chattered on as if nothing had changed, and she hated them because nothing *had.* Because on that fateful day when her life had upended itself, they had been the ones to come get her from London. They'd pointed her down this path.

If you come with us, Great-Aunt Caro had said, *Minerva Lane will die forever. You will never say that name. The person who you are today? She will simply vanish.*

Gruel. Nothing but gruel—and the fear that one day, there'd not even be that.

"Did you know that Billy is courting?" Great-Aunt Caro said.

"No! He cannot possibly be old enough."

"He's eighteen," Caro said. "And heaven help me if I know when that happened. Why, it seems as if it were just last month that he was born…"

She couldn't attend to the conversation. Minnie hadn't just taken on a new name when her great-aunts took her away; she'd taken on a new personality. She hadn't even known how to *walk* like a girl at first. For that initial year, her great-aunts had constantly corrected her behavior. *Don't contradict. Don't speak up. Don't step forward.* Anything that drew attention was absolutely forbidden; she'd found herself shrinking smaller and smaller until a walnut could have encompassed her personality—and left room for it to rattle around.

She'd been small and quiet. Having known so much more, her frustrated, pent-up ambition had chafed. She'd seized on what little charity work was allowed to women, but it wasn't enough. And now she faced a lifetime of this affliction—of being forced to make her soul as small and as tasteless as possible, in hopes that it would fit into the confines of her life.

You have steel for your backbone and a rare talent for seeing what is plainly in front of your face. I could make everyone see that.

Damn his eyes. Damn his letter. Damn that smile, the one that made her want to kiss him back, just so she could know that she'd put that light inside him.

Anything else would be a criminal waste.

Damn him, because even if he didn't mean it—even if it was all a way to try to fog her mind and lead her astray—he had made her believe that she could change things. And that this time, when she did...

It struck her, that want, like a sharp fist to her solar plexus—painful and paralyzing. She didn't just want. She hoped. She needed. She dreamed that this time, when she was revealed to the crowd for what she really was, they wouldn't mob around her and throw stones. This time, they wouldn't call her a beast or the spawn of the devil. This time, instead of stripping her of everything, someone would love her for who she was.

A yearning like that was too big for the person she had to be.

Damn the Duke of Clermont, for giving her that hope. Damn him for his admonition to look up. Damn him for making her believe.

Her eyes stung. She aimed her fork at her plate and stabbed blindly.

"Minnie," Eliza said, her eyebrows drawing down in worry, "are you well?"

"I am—" *Perfectly well.*

She was supposed to say those words. Ask for nothing, admit to no discomfort. That was the way of a lady.

But the lie could not pass her lips. She was full to bursting with emotion. And somehow, instead of murmuring her excuses and leaving the room as she ought to have done, she felt her fork fly from her hand—clear across the dining table, striking the far wall with a metallic clang.

"No," she said. "No, I am not well."

"Minnie!"

"I am not well," she repeated. "I am not well. How could you do this to me?"

Eliza shoved to her feet and took one step toward her. "Minnie, what is the matter?"

"You did this to me," she repeated, her voice quivering with all those years of unshed tears. "You both did this to me. You made me into this—this—"

She found her spoon next to her plate, and flung that bit of pewter across the room, too.

"—this nothing!" she finished. "And now I am stuck in it and I cannot find my way out."

Eliza and Caro exchanged a stricken glance.

"I have all of this inside of me—all these thoughts, these wants, these ambitions."

Caro winced at that last word.

"And they are nothing," she said. "Nothing, nothing, nothing! Just like me."

"Oh, Minnie," Eliza said, gently—as gently as a stable-hand to a rearing horse. "I'm so sorry. I promised your mother I would look after you when she passed away. Had I kept that promise, you would not feel that way now. You would never have known…"

It wasn't the words that worked, but the tone—cool and calming. She could feel her anger ebbing away in response. In another few minutes she would be placid again, with nothing to show for the evening but a few nicks in the wallpaper where the tines of her fork had left their impression.

But she could still hear his voice. She could still see his eyes, so brilliantly blue, the intensity of his expression. That letter might have been a nothing-gesture for a man who could indulge in such things. But there had been just enough truth in what he said that she could not help but cling to it.

You could have had this, the memory taunted, *if only you were someone else. You could have had him if you were yourself. But you aren't. You aren't.*

Eliza crossed the distance to her and set her hand on her shoulder. "You should never have known," she repeated.

And that memory of herself—of that brash confidence, of that youthful excitement—seemed so distant that Minnie could feel herself nodding.

You're nothing. Nothing doesn't feel.

Eliza pressed on her shoulder, and Minnie collapsed back into her chair.

"There, there," her great-aunt whispered. "It's nothing. It's nothing."

"Of course it's nothing," Minnie whispered. "That's all I have ever been."

After that, there was no holding back the flood of ugly tears. She cried until she'd expunged all the want from her heart—her wistful longing for the past she'd lost, entwined with the future she could not contemplate.

"Maybe," her great-aunt said, when her tears tailed off, "maybe you need to take some time away from the whole…marriage…thing. Just stay here on the farm. A few weeks. What do you think?"

She didn't have a few weeks. She had his letter, though—the proof that she needed. She could end the suspicion Stevens held toward her tomorrow.

So why wasn't she doing it?

Minnie shook her head. "It won't help," she said. "It never helps. Nothing helps any longer."

✿ ✿ ✿

THE TABLE AT THE HOTEL could have been laid for eight, had it been necessary. Today, it accommodated Robert's mother at one end, and at the other, separated from her by six feet of polished mahogany, himself. It seemed as if every silver fork that the hotel owned had been laid out for them, and most of their spoons beside. He could have constructed an entire clock tower out of the assembled cutlery.

From across the length of the table, Robert's mother laid her fork down gently.

This was his mother's way of sending a signal. She'd changed the date. She'd agreed to the meeting, knowing Sebastian and Oliver were both in town. That meant that this was not just a meal, but a palaver—two independent, faintly hostile parties meeting to come to an agreement on the tariffs between their nations.

As always, she had not a single hair out of place. She dressed in what he supposed was the height of fashion, if he'd bothered to follow it. Her gown was a dark blue, the hems embroidered in a white-and-gold pattern two inches thick. Her waist was slim, but not too tightly laced; a shawl of black lace looped over her shoulders.

She had always seemed imposing, like some faraway castle tower looming on the horizon. Even when she'd visited him when he was a child, she had been distant.

Now, the two yards between them could have been a furlong. In the years since he'd gained his majority, they'd come to a comfortable accommodation. When they were both in town, they had dinner together—no more than once—and talked of nothing. Her charitable work, his work in Parliament. Everything they said at those meals, they might have found out about one another through the society pages. He had no expectations of her and she no longer disappointed him.

But her coming to see him…this was new.

"Well, Clermont." She set her spoon down as a servant removed her soup bowl. Her gaze was fixed on him—affable, polite, and unexceptionable. "You must know why I have come."

"No," Robert said. "I don't."

She raised an eyebrow. "You don't recall? The last time we spoke, you mentioned that you were planning on taking a wife."

The last time they had talked had been two months ago. He had, in fact, agreed when she'd said that as a man approached his thirties, he ought to consider marrying. It had seemed an innocuous enough statement at the time. It had been talk that was not just small, but miniscule.

"You agreed to do your duty," she said calmly.

"I said I would marry," he said carefully. "I don't believe I spoke a word about duty."

Her nose twitched and her lips flattened, as if the idea that marriage could be more than a duty made her want to sneeze. Still, she didn't say anything until the next course had been laid in front of them. Then, she waited until Robert had taken a bite—and couldn't protest—before speaking.

"If we are to approach the matter properly, it might well take years. Such a thing cannot be taken on cavalierly. There are backgrounds to inquire into, information to obtain." She picked up her fork. "We must make lists. I've started three already."

Robert swallowed the bite of fish even though his throat had just dried. For all that the woman sitting before him was his mother, she was a stranger. He'd scarcely seen her when he'd been a child. There had been a time when he'd wanted her to care for him. He'd wanted it desperately; he'd made excuse after excuse for her absence. But she'd made it painfully clear that his excuses were just that, and that she wanted nothing to do with him.

"Your pardon," he said, realizing that the room had been cloaked in silence since she'd spoken. "What do you mean, *we* must make lists? Who is *we?*"

"No need for you to worry about it." She gave an elegant wave of her hand. "I can show you what I have thus far. I've organized the names I've gathered so far into three categories: peers' daughters, heiresses, and other." She sniffed. "With a little work on my part, I should be able to obviate the need to consider any women in the *other* category."

Twenty-eight years of near-indifference from the woman, and then *this?*

"So when you say *we*," Robert said slowly, "you are really referring to yourself."

"Well…" She looked startled at the question. "You needn't sound so put out, Clermont. Of course your wishes are to be considered."

"My wishes are to be considered," he repeated. "Such generosity. And such curious phrasing, absent any actors at all. Might I inquire after the name of the person who so kindly volunteers to consider my wishes? It is only *my* marriage, after all."

His mother licked her lips and fell silent. Her gaze fell to her plate, but her fingers curled around her fork.

"Thank you, Duchess," Robert said. "But your assistance will not be needed in this matter."

"Clermont." Now a hint of exasperation touched her voice. "It may be your marriage, but your choice will affect me." Her head tilted up, wide-eyed. "If your marriage is the subject of gossip, why, everyone connected with you will suffer. I have decades of experience with the *ton*. It would be foolish of you not to draw on it."

She had drawn herself up stiffly. Little blooms of pink touched her cheeks. No doubt she'd realized that once he married, she'd become the dowager Duchess of Clermont, and she was loath to give up her place in society to some chit who didn't respect her as she wanted.

"No offense, Mama," Robert drawled, "but I do not consider you an expert on marriage. Expertise, I think, would require you to actually *stay* in one."

Her lips pinched together. "Insults." She sniffed. "You become more like your father every day. Do think my offer over, Clermont, and talk to me when you are less emotional. You cannot simply bumble around London until you see a candidate whose looks you like. This is one of the most important decisions of your life. Your wife will share your life for the remainder of your days."

"She needn't," Robert contradicted. "She can always move out." He looked across the table at her. "In the event that she needs to do so, I'll point her in your direction. You have some qualifications on that front, I believe."

Her nostrils flared; he almost thought she might stamp her foot and paw the ground, like an angry bull. But she simply turned her head away and took another bite of her meal.

There was a reason they'd kept their conversations to inane niceties up until this point. There was no way to talk about anything else without bitterness. They had no common past to draw on, almost no shared acquaintances. His mother had spent more time visiting Sebastian's mother—her husband's sister—than she had lived in Robert's household as a child.

And she'd chosen to do it. He might have forgiven her at one time. At one time, he would have forgiven her anything. Knowing what he did of his father, it seemed unfair to hold her to account for leaving the man. But when she'd left her husband, she'd never looked back at her son. No matter how he asked, she'd never looked back.

"At least," she finally said, a little stiffly, "at least you might make use of my lists."

"No, Your Grace." Robert felt as cold as ice as he spoke. "I don't believe we will be needing your lists."

She blinked. She looked down in contemplation of her food. "We," she finally said. "Who is this that is encompassed by your *we?*"

"Why, didn't I say? Sebastian Malheur." Robert gave her a smile. "Why do you think I asked him down?"

Her eyes widened. "That man!" she hissed. "He has already called on me, and..." She hissed in displeasure. "He wouldn't know propriety if it came up and shook his hand. It is all very well for you to associate with him out of some sense of familial loyalty, but to actually treat him as an intimate—"

"Don't worry, Your Grace," Robert cut in. "Oliver Marshall is here, too, and he'll lend—"

"*That* is the company you keep? A reprobate and a bastard?"

Robert nearly sprang to his feet, his temper rising at that. But shouting had never got him anywhere. Slowly, he exhaled his anger, letting it flow from him until the serenity of ice returned.

"Ah," he finally said. "Insults."

She snorted.

"It appears that I take after you, despite everything. I hope you're not too horrified by the discovery."

But she didn't look upset. Instead a faint smile appeared on her lips— the first he'd seen from her since her arrival.

"I knew that already," she said. "Why else do you suppose I am here?"

Chapter Eleven

"WHERE HAVE YOU BEEN THESE LAST DAYS?" Lydia asked. "I sent a note over two nights ago, but your great-aunts returned that you were ill."

Minnie glanced at her friend. Lydia was smiling; she didn't look worried. Instead, she'd linked her arm through Minnie's and was conducting her to the back of the Charingford house.

"I wasn't ill."

"I know that, silly." Lydia patted her hand. "If it had been serious, you'd have insisted I be told. And if it wasn't serious, you'd have written yourself. Now, what was it?"

Minnie looked about. There were no servants nearby, nobody to hear what they said. Just the wood-paneled wall of the hallway. "I really can't tell you everything. But I'm involved in another strategy right now."

Lydia's face went utterly blank.

"Not like that," Minnie hastened to add. "Never like that."

"Oh, God. You scared me. Look at my hands." She held them out; they trembled.

"If it had involved you," Minnie said, "I'd have told you first thing. This one…" She grimaced. "It's someone else's secret." Lydia accepted this with a small shrug, and opened the door to the back sitting room. It was, to Minnie's surprise, occupied. Occupied and very, very warm.

Three servants sat at the hearth, which blazed a cheery orange, flames licking high enough to tickle the chimney. The servants were balling up papers and feeding them into the fire one by one, so as to keep the blaze under control. The air was heavy with the scent of burning fibers.

"What is this?" Minnie asked.

"Oh, didn't you hear?" Lydia said. "Some group of radicals is leaving handbills all over town. They left a huge stack outside Papa's hosiery. He had to rip them from the workers' hands himself. He spent the entire morning trying to round them all up."

Minnie looked at her friend. "They're that dreadful?"

Lydia gave her a cheeky smile and stepped into the room, rescuing one crumpled sheet from a servant's hands before the flames could take it. "See for yourself."

Minnie glanced at the page her friend held out. She took it, scanned it—

And ran into a paragraph that brought her hand to her mouth.

…Stopping work is something of a discovered attack. First, you give your concerns a real voice, one shouted out with a volume lent by a thousand throats. Second, you vacate the factories in which you labor—thus leaving the shrinking pocketbooks of your masters as a vehement counterpoint. Be aware of where you are, and the space you'll leave behind.

"It's talking about a strike," Lydia said, "is it not?"

Stopping work is something of a discovered attack.

Minnie felt all the blood in her turn to ice. "Perhaps." She was actually a little dizzy. "There's still a long way between talk and organization, and between organization and turning out." She put a hand against the wall for support.

Be aware of where you are, and the space you'll leave behind.

Those words were familiar—too familiar. That last sentence was almost a direct quote from Tappitt's *On Chess,* an obscure volume. She'd quoted it to the Duke of Clermont thinking nothing of the words. He'd confessed to ignorance of the game, after all.

She'd used those words before, too. She'd said something almost identical to Stevens just a few months ago when they were talking about the Harley street pump. Small surprise; the words of chess strategy had been part of her lexicon ever since she could remember. Her first memory was sitting at a chessboard, her father before her.

This, he'd said, *is a discovered attack. See? One move, two threats. Can you show me them?*

"If it weren't true," Lydia said, "Father wouldn't have been so furious. But he can't afford to have the hosiery stand idle."

"I see," Minnie said.

Lydia waved her hand at the servants. "We can finish these off," she said. "Leave us." The maids stood and vacated the room. Lydia sat before the fire and began feeding the pamphlets in at regular intervals.

Good. Burn them all. Maybe nobody had seen them. He'd used *her words.*

"Lydia, have you seen Stevens?"

"Just today. After this was distributed, he and my father were closeted together for hours. If there is a strike, after all, Stevens will be the one to put it down. They were arguing about something. And then Stevens left—

father told me he was going to Manchester to look into something. Although what he could learn from Manchester about our workers, I don't know. Perhaps the workers are communicating with one another?"

No. Stevens had read the handbill. He'd remembered that Minnie had once mentioned a discovered attack. And—true to his word—he'd gone to Manchester to look into her background because he believed she was involved. Minnie felt dizzy.

"Do you think my father pays his workers enough? Stevens says if he gives in to their demands once, they'll just prove all the more unreasonable. But I'd be willing to bet you could think of a way to prevent that. Like what you did with the W.H.C."

There wasn't anything she could do about that now. Minnie shook her head, clearing it of her racing fears. "I don't know," she said. "But Stevens and your father…"

Lydia rolled her eyes. "I don't want to talk of Stevens." She lowered her voice, and then in direct contradiction to her last statement, looked at her. "Do you think Stevens has figured out what happened all those years ago? That these rumors about your background have come about because someone talked about *me*? We both went to Cornwall. Maybe—maybe he's found something out there."

"He hasn't," Minnie said.

"But how—"

"I know because he confronted me with his proof," Minnie said. "There's nothing about you. It's all nonsense—something about my mother not being married, some rumor he heard from some silly goose at the end of her life who is losing her memory."

Lydia let out a whoosh of a sigh.

But it was no comfort to Minnie. Stevens had gone to search out news of Minnie. The room seemed wrapped in cotton batting, swathes and swathes of it surrounding her. Shouts sounded in the distance; muffled shouts. The sound of a great crowd, the blink, as bright sun swallowed her vision—

"Minnie, is everything all right?"

Lydia's worried voice brought her firmly back to the present. No shouts. No riot. No crowd.

Not yet, at any rate. And maybe…

"I'm well," she said slowly. "Just…thinking."

It would take Stevens at least a week to uncover the truth—if he even recognized what he was looking at when he saw it. And Minnie had the duke's letter. That, along with everything else she had come up with, would prove that she hadn't been involved.

Lydia watched her carefully. "What was it you wanted to talk with me about?"

Minnie sighed, and looked over at her friend. "At the W.H.C. the other day, Doctor Grantham asked to see you."

Lydia's nose went up a notch. "So?"

"So...he wanted to see you." Although he might have only said it to tweak Stevens. "He's handsome and young. I rather like him."

"I don't," Lydia said flatly. "He was working with Doctor Parwine when *it* happened. And ever since then he's looked at me in the most *knowing* way."

"He looks at everyone that way," Minnie said. "I think he can't help it."

"And he's so sarcastic."

"He's sarcastic with everyone."

Lydia looked away. "I don't like to remember, and he makes me remember. Every time I laugh, he looks at me, judging me for my frivolity. I can't stand being around him."

"I had no notion," Minnie said, moving over to sit beside her friend.

"I work so hard for my frivolity." Lydia's hands were shaking. "How dare he judge me for it!"

Only Minnie knew the truth of that.

"I know sometimes you think I'm not serious enough. That I dream too much. That I should be more rational." Lydia sniffed.

"I don't think that."

"Only the tragedies are great," Lydia said. "Melancholy is wisdom. Suffering is strength."

"Lydia..."

"Some people would think me weak, because I was seduced by an older man."

Minnie looked around—but the room was clear, and her friend spoke in a low voice.

"Because I didn't know he was married. Because I didn't truly understand what was happening. Some people would think that I was weak because I asked you for help."

"I don't." Lydia had come to Minnie, and Minnie had figured everything out—how to get Lydia away from the public eye for the term of her pregnancy, how to make the journey seem respectable so that nobody talked. It had required only a little strategizing—and at that point, Minnie had been happy to have something to do.

Lydia threw a stack of handbills on the fire and waited until they caught in flames. "Some people would think I was weak because I cried when I miscarried. And they would think you foolish for holding me and saying it would be all right. But most of all, they would think I was foolish because I learned to smile again. They think you are useless because you do not wear silks and ribbons, because one has to listen carefully to catch what you say. And those people don't know *anything.*"

Does nobody see you, Miss Pursling? The Duke of Clermont's words drifted back to her.

Yes, Minnie wanted to answer. *Yes. Someone does.*

"Just once," Lydia said, "I want everyone to see you as I do."

Minnie shook her head, folding her arms around her. "No. No. I don't want them to look. I can't bear it if they look."

"Well, maybe not everyone." Lydia gave her a sly smile. "But what about—"

Minnie let out a breath. "Don't say his name."

"—the Duke of Clermont," Lydia finished. "And that's his *title,* not his name, so don't glare at me so. He's involved in your latest strategy, isn't he?"

"Of course he isn't," Minnie said, but her friend just grinned.

"I want you to have a chance," Lydia said. "I want everyone here to know how badly they've misjudged you, imagining you as quiet and biddable. I want them to understand what I know so well. That you have a loving heart and a clever mind."

Minnie sniffed, looking away. "That only happens in fairy stories. Real girls do better with large dowries and flaxen hair."

"And what I hate most is that we can never tell anyone my proof of how wonderful you are. But I still believe that the truth of you will come out. That one day, everyone will know you as I do."

"And you think they would like what they saw?"

Lydia nodded firmly. "I know they would."

There was nothing naïve about Lydia's optimism. She'd won it fair and square, and even Minnie couldn't rob her of it. Odd, that Lydia could be so firm in her vision of the future, and Minnie could see nothing.

She turned her head. "As it turns out, I do have something else on that front I should tell you. Doctor Grantham wanted me to invite you to come along and put up handbills with me and Marybeth Peters."

Lydia's eyes drifted to the crumpled piece of paper she'd just thrown on the fire.

"Not those kinds of handbills," Minnie said with a smile she didn't quite feel. "Boring ones—about smallpox and disinfectant."

"And Doctor Grantham will be there?"

"No." Minnie gave her another smile she didn't feel. "That's the part you'll find so interesting. Someone else volunteered in his stead, and you'll never guess who."

"Fool." Lydia squeezed her hand. "I already know. Was it like a fairy tale? Minnie, pining in distress—wait, you'd never do that. Minnie, pinching the bridge of her nose while the idiotic men argued, wondering how she was going to get them all to do what she wished." Lydia smiled. "And then, the Prince of Wales stepped into the room!"

Minnie burst into laughter.

"Oh, very well," Lydia said. "That would be unlikely, I suppose. Besides, he's married, and I'd hate to imagine him unfaithful to Princess Alexandra. So instead, I'm going to guess it was the Duke of Clermont. He swept in, took one look at your bosom, and claimed you for his own."

"Well…"

Lydia pointed at her. "I knew it. You should *see* the way he looks at you."

Minnie tried not to, but she could call it to mind without any reminder whatsoever. Her cheeks warmed.

"Don't get any ideas," Minnie warned.

So he looked at her. It didn't mean anything. He spoke without thinking, didn't consider the consequences of the things he did. He likely looked without intending anything by it, too.

"He was just being…" She trailed off, not knowing how to finish. Gentlemanly? Annoying?

She was leaning toward the latter, given that he'd used her words directly in his handbills. But she could remember him looking at her after the Workers' Hygiene Commission had let out, his eyes so intense. And that surprised smile, when she'd said she liked his friends. It had felt as welcome as a sunrise.

"He sent a note around," she finally said. "He suggested we meet tomorrow afternoon. It will be me, Marybeth Peters…"

"And the Duke of Clermont." Lydia smiled. "I have such a feeling about this, Minnie."

Look up.

Minnie put her arms around herself. "Don't. Don't feel. I can't let myself."

Lydia simply shook her head. "Of course you can't. That's why I have to feel for you."

Chapter Twelve

I<small>T TOOK</small> M<small>INNIE NO EFFORT</small> on the next day to maneuver the Duke of Clermont into a nearly private conversation. After all, handbills were best put up in pairs—and once that had been established, Lydia latched herself on to Marybeth Peters and marched across the road, paste and paper in hand, leaving Minnie alone with the duke.

Not truly alone. They were on a public thoroughfare, for one, and Lydia and Marybeth were within shouting distance on the other side of Haymarket. People drifted down the streets. A man was selling chestnuts on the corner; some boys had made a fire on the pavement, one that they carefully fed with bits of rubbish.

And Minnie didn't know what to say to him. What was he up to? He'd given her that letter. He'd told her he wanted her, and she still felt shivers down her spine when she remembered the look in his eyes as he said those words. And then he'd used her words in a pamphlet, darkening the cloud of suspicion that followed her.

Instead of trying to sort all that out, she handed him the pot of paste. "What do you know of manual labor?"

"Um…" His eyes twinkled at her. "I've read about it. I toured the factories I inherited from my grandfather. I've made it a point to talk with workers when I have the chance."

"But you've never done it."

"Not…as such."

Minnie handed the duke a wooden stick. "Congratulations," she said. "You are about to lower yourself to new depths."

"I can hardly wait." He took the clay pot in bemusement and followed her down the pavement. She stopped at the first corner and held up a handbill.

"What do I do?" he asked.

"You take the paste," she explained, "and you put it on the handbill. Then I put the handbill on the wall."

"Just like that?" He unscrewed the top from the pot, dipped the stick in, and clumsily glopped the white mess onto the handbill Minnie was holding.

"You are an untidy paster." She turned from him, slapped the paper against the brick, and marched on.

She didn't think he'd meant to cause her problems. He looked at her as if nothing had happened. And for him, nothing had changed. They'd smiled at each other on the train, and she'd told him she liked him.

When she turned away, she caught his smile at her words. His smiles were like flashes of lightning come at night, swift and fleeting, lighting up the entire landscape for a few moments before vanishing once again. Smiles like that, she reminded herself grimly, might look pretty, but they could still leave heaps of smoking rubble behind.

"Well," he said, just behind her, his voice low and amused. "You know what they say. 'Paste not, want not.'"

She blinked. "Puns," she said, without turning around, "are the lowest form of humor."

"Not when a duke utters them."

She held up a handbill for him to paste and then slapped it against the wall, holding it for a moment to be sure that it would adhere. "Are you a duke?" she asked. "I had thought you were a dead man."

His Grace, the Duke of Clermont, showed no sign that he'd heard her. Instead, he held the paste pot in his hand and smiled. "Shall we proceed to the next corner? Miss Peters and Miss Charingford are already outpacing us." His eyes slid to hers. "Outpasting us," he corrected.

She was not—absolutely *not*—going to be seduced into laughing with him and making inappropriate jokes about paste. Minnie compressed her lips and stalked down the street.

He followed. "Is something...wrong? Did you read my letter?"

"Yes," she said. "I read *everything* you wrote. And I'm furious with you."

"Now, now," he admonished, "don't be pasty." He gave a chuckle— one that terminated as she turned to him and he caught sight of her expression. The smile slid off his face. "Oh. You really are angry. Did I do something wrong?"

Did he do something wrong? She wanted to punch him. "Your latest masterpiece. I cannot believe what you said."

His nose wrinkled. "Why? Because a strike would hurt your friends? Because you don't care about the conditions under which workers labor? Or do you think I shouldn't have written them? That I should keep silent, stew in my own thoughts—"

"Oh, for God's sake," she said in exasperation. "If I thought you shouldn't be writing those damned handbills, I would already have shown your letter to the town magistrates. Sometimes, I want to scream, too— scream as loudly as I can, and never mind who hears me. I'm angry because you used *my words* in your latest endeavor! *My words.*"

He blinked. "Oh." He bit his lip. "That. Well, in a manner of speaking, I suppose I did. Why wouldn't I? They were good words."

"Don't split hairs. Did you not hear Stevens talk? He has already accused me of radical sentiment. Why would you use a phrase you heard from *me?* Don't you understand how impossible my life will be if suspicion falls on me?"

With the workers in the factories until the evening whistle sounded, the streets were calm. A few women were out, trudging to the greengrocer; a harried laundress marched by with a sack on her shoulder. The rhythmic rumble of the machinery a few streets distant somehow made the streets seem quiet, blanketing all other noises.

"I'm terrified," she said, "and you have nothing to fear. It's not fair."

Across the cobblestones and ten yards up, Lydia and Marybeth were placing handbills in a methodical way.

"Well?" she demanded, shaking a handbill at him. "Don't waste time. I need paste."

"Miss Pursling," he said formally, "I do apologize."

He'd worn darker, rougher clothing for this outing—trousers of gray wool and a matching coat, the fabric coarse but the cut still perfect. Around his neck, he'd wound a soft, maroon scarf. His garb made him look not like a duke, but like some towheaded scoundrel—roguish, and maybe a little wicked. The kind of man who'd tempt a girl to walk outside with him at night, and who'd sneak her sips of heady spirits from a flask. It would be all too easy to become tipsy around him.

He sounded sincere and she wanted to believe him. "You're sorry for endangering me?"

He looked sincere, too, with that slightly embarrassed smile. Then he looked up at her. He swirled the stick in the pot, then brought up the wooden stick, a big glob of paste stuck to the end.

"No." His words were mournful, but there was a twinkle in his eye. "Not for that. For *this.*"

So saying, he flicked the stick at her midsection. She barely had the chance to lower the handbill in defense. The edge caught the glob of flying paste, breaking it in midair, spattering paste all over.

She stared at him in disbelief. "I had not realized," she said frostily, "that we were allowing twelve-year-old boys to take seats in the House of Lords."

He winked at her, then turned to the women on the other side of the street and waved. "We'll be at the pump through the alley there," he called out. "We've had a bit of a paste emergency over here."

"A paste emergency!" she huffed. "A paste assault, that's what we had."

But he was already taking her arm, leading her down a narrow gap between two buildings, into a dingy courtyard where a pump stood. He took off his jacket before working the pump handle; she could see the form of his muscles through his shirtsleeves. She was terrified, and he was showing off.

"For the record," he said, as he worked the pump, "I am twenty-eight, not twelve."

"Congratulations."

"Indeed. I've got you all alone after all."

He smiled at her again, and she felt speared by lightning. Minnie looked away. The pump let out a hollow whistle, signifying that the water had almost arrived.

"It's a messy business, flirting with you."

As he spoke, water gushed out of the pump head. He caught it in the bucket that was chained to the pump.

"Well?" He raised an eyebrow. "You wanted to yell at me. I figured I would give you a solid chance at doing so without causing a scene. Go ahead."

"Why did you use my words? Were you trying to endanger my reputation on purpose? Did you think that if I were blamed for it, you might escape all censure?"

He simply shook his head. "I should have known you wouldn't shriek." He shrugged and unwound his scarf from his neck and dipped it in the bucket. "To answer your question, no, I didn't intend any of that. I might have been a little thoughtless, but not malicious." To her surprise, he knelt in front of her, and dabbed at a spot of paste on her skirt with his scarf. "It was simply this," he said, his attention seemingly fixed on the paste. "You've made an impression on me. If you could recognize your words in what I said, it was because my thoughts have been on you." He looked up at her. "Often."

It wasn't fair that he could rob her heart of anger and her lungs of air with just one word. His gaze held hers overlong.

It wasn't fair. It wasn't right. Here he was, on his knees before her, and yet she was the one slipping under his spell.

Minnie looked away. "That doesn't change anything. It's still put me in an untenable position. I don't know what to do. You can't just apologize and expect me to smile at you."

He dropped his eyes from hers—not in surrender, but with a nonchalant air, as if to say he couldn't be bothered—and dabbed at another spot of paste.

She couldn't even feel his hands through her skirt. And yet she could imagine them, imagine that the slight pressure he exerted on her skirts transmitted itself to her petticoats, and from there to her drawers, her stockings, her legs. She shut her eyes as he worked his way upward.

The higher he got, the more she could feel it. When he got to the last bit of paste, there was nothing but the truth. He was touching her stomach. Through layers of cloth and corset, yes—but that was his hand against her belly. She sucked in a breath.

"I can't believe you threw paste at me," she muttered. "That has to be the stupidest thing—"

"Of course it was stupid." He looked at the damp end of his scarf and then shrugged and tossed it over his shoulder. "That's just the way these things go." He stood as he spoke, leaving Minnie looking down—directly at the buttons on his vest.

"That's the way things go?" she echoed dubiously. "Are you claiming to be a fool, Your Grace?"

"Under certain circumstances." His voice dropped to a low murmur, and he leaned down so that he was almost whispering in her ear. "You see, there's this woman."

She wasn't going to look at him. She wasn't.

"Normally, one might say that there was a beautiful woman—but I don't think she qualifies as a classical beauty. Still, I find that when she's around, I'd rather look at her than anyone else."

He set two fingers against her cheek, and Minnie sucked in a breath. She was *not* going to look at him. He'd see the longing in her eyes, and then…

"There's something about her that draws my eye. Something that defies words. Maybe it's her hair, but I tried to tell her that, and she told me I was being ridiculous. I suppose I was. Maybe it's her lips. Maybe it's her eyes, although she so rarely looks at me."

Those fingers on her cheek trailed down to her jaw. Minnie felt frozen in place.

"She's clever," he murmured. "Every time I see her I discover that I've underestimated her prowess. She ties me in knots."

They were just words—words that any man would say if he wanted to turn a lady's head. Just words. They didn't mean anything, not really.

But they were *not* just words. Nobody had ever said them to her; she hadn't even known she wanted to hear them until he uttered them. Now they lodged like a knife between her ribs. She longed for them to be true— yearned for it so much that each breath hurt.

"What are you trying to say?" Minnie said to his waistcoat buttons. Her voice didn't waver. It didn't falter. "That you're overmatched? We had already established that."

"Of course I'm overmatched." He was lightly stroking her cheek. "The male of the human species has a fundamental flaw. At the moment when we most want to say something clever and impressive, all the blood rushes from our brains."

"It does?"

"Physiological fact," His Grace said. "Arousal makes me stupid. It makes me say idiotic things like 'I like your tits' and, 'Help, we've had a paste emergency over here.' It makes me want to stay around you even though I know I'm overmatched, even though I'm sure you're going to win." His voice lowered. "You see, I want to watch you do it."

She swallowed. And for that moment, she believed him. That she *would* win, somehow, win through to some future so impossibly bright it blinded her even to think of it.

"Even though I know I'm going to say foolish things," he said. "And, apparently, throw paste at you." There was a pause. "Sorry about that," he finally said. "God, that was dumb."

"I thought there were…things…that the male of the human species could do about this physiological shortcoming."

He was still touching her, those two fingers lightly pressed against her jaw. She really couldn't look at him as she spoke. Her whole face heated just thinking about what would be entailed in those things.

"Not right here," he said, sounding amused. "Not right now."

His thumb whispered against her lip, faintly recalling a kiss.

"Not," he said, very quietly, "with you. Alas."

Oh, she burned at that. Her skin seemed to catch flame. She felt herself grow damp beneath her skirts. But that wash of liquid want only made her sad.

They'd both read the moment aright. Minnie was too genteel for him to bed in so casual a fashion, and yet not high enough for him to marry. That left her as nothing to him, a nonentity in skirts. Whatever this was between them, it was both heartbreakingly real—and impossibly nonexistent.

His voice was rough when he spoke again. "So beat me to flinders," he said. "Win. Overmatch me, Minnie. And when we're alone…"

His fingers touched her chin lightly.

"When we're alone," he whispered, "look up."

He could have tilted her chin, forcing her to do so. But his forefinger remained warm and steady on her face. He waited, and in the end, Minnie couldn't help herself. She looked up.

His eyes met hers with a warm greeting.

"Hullo, Minnie." He didn't smile. He didn't lean down to her. But when he whispered, "I wish you'd call me Robert," his voice was almost a caress.

"Robert."

"This," he whispered, in a solemn tone of voice, "is where I would say something exceedingly clever, had my brains not been turned to paste."

"How do you seduce anyone if you can't talk at this stage?" she asked.

"I—" He stopped, shook his head, and flung his hands out in frustration.

It's a Lane family tradition. When you've backed the other fellow into a corner, you give him a kiss to show there's no hard feelings.

"I see how it is," she said softly.

"You do?"

She didn't. She couldn't see anything at all. She didn't know what to do about Stevens, what to do with the future that appeared to be crumbling before her eyes. This was the exact opposite of the moment when she would have kissed a chess piece.

But looking into his eyes, she saw not endings, not the finality of marriage to a man who didn't know her, not the gray certainty of some future workhouse. She saw beginnings.

It was utterly impossible, this attraction between them.

"I do see," Minnie said. "You don't seduce women."

He gave her a half smile. "Heh. Well. About that…"

"*They* seduce *you.*" And then, before she could think it through—before she could outline the *shouldn'ts* and the *nevers*—she popped up on her toes. There were only inches between them, and Minnie closed the distance without thinking.

He made a soft exhalation of surprise. His lips were warm on hers, and after that first moment of shock, his arms closed around her.

"Like this," he murmured, and then his lips were not just pressed to hers, but moving along her mouth, coaxing the kiss from her.

His kiss was not an end, either, but a vibrant new thing, brilliant with possibility. His lips met hers, captured hers, over and over. When their tongues met, his hands came to either side of her face, holding her close, bringing her to him so roughly she feared she might break.

He kissed her and she pressed against him, her hands against his chest, his waistcoat buttons digging into her. Her fingers slid under his scarf, pulling him close.

And then he stepped away. Minnie opened her eyes to the courtyard, to the pump.

He smiled. "I believe that is the first time I've ever commanded your full attention."

"Robert." She swallowed awkwardly.

"In answer to what you said… You're right. I don't just owe you an apology. I can only repeat what I have told you before. I won't leave you worse off than I met you. I know you're worried. I know I can be thoughtless. But I don't *stay* thoughtless, Miss Pursling. There's a great deal I can do, and I won't let anyone hurt you. My word on it."

She shouldn't believe him. It was impossible for him to simply assert that. He'd already ruined her inside, made her question the bleak landscape of her life. He'd made her hope. She felt as if she were floating in the clouds, now. And that meant the ground was such a long, long way down.

"I shouldn't believe you." She ran her hands over her face. "I should go give your letter to Mr. Charingford right now."

"You should have done it two days ago."

She felt a shy smile take over her face. "I know."

She handed him back his paste pot. Their fingers met as she did, and her whole body sang in response. And for the first time, Minnie realized that he was too clever by half. She hadn't overmatched him. He'd handed her the key to his downfall…and made it nearly impossible for her to use it.

Chapter Thirteen

BY THE TIME MINNIE SNUFFED HER CANDLE that night and slipped between her covers, all the emotion of the day had passed from her. She felt as if she were standing in the aftermath of a wildfire, the terrain around her blackened and burned as far as the eye could see. She could almost smell the smoke, could feel the hidden embers inside her that had not yet burned to cold ash.

"Don't fall in love with him, Minnie," she warned herself. But the room was dark, and her bedsheets had not yet warmed from her body heat.

If only he'd been less handsome, less wealthy…and not at all a duke. A blacksmith. A bookseller. Someone else with that keen mind, those piercing eyes, that brilliant smile that seemed to be made for her alone.

Instead, he was one of the highest peers of the realm. He could have his pick of thousands of women. In fact, he was probably picking a woman right now—that *was* the sort of thing dukes did, was it not? Dukes entertained women as mistresses, choosing from blond and brown and black hair, depending on the whim of the evening, taking whatever they wanted and leaving a handful of coin as memory. Being a duke meant that one had a perpetual harem at one's fingertips. All one had to do was ask for it.

The thought should have disgusted her, but for some reason she imagined Robert—no, she had to think of him as the *duke,* not as a name, not as a person—looking over a passel of girls offered by a thin-faced proprietress. She imagined his gaze settling on some girl with honey-brown hair and a larger-than-usual bosom.

"Her," he would say. "I want her tonight."

I want you.

Stupid, stupid, stupid, to imagine that his desire—whatever inkling of it he had—would persist long enough for him to purchase a substitute. She writhed in her bed. But she couldn't get the notion out of her mind.

He might be in bed with her at this very moment. His hands would brush her breasts, like so. His lips would find not the palm of her hand, but her neck, her lips. There would be no hesitation, no holding back. There would be nothing but his rock-hard want.

His body would cover hers, and she would surrender to him. She would spread her legs, wrapping them around him…

Those thoughts were enough to warm her bed, but once she'd started the imagery, she could not shut it off. It was her own fingers between her legs, her own hand against her nipple. But she imagined him wanting her as much as she wanted him, taking her in her imagination the way she could never allow in real life. He plunged into her, hard; she shook as she brought herself to the brink. And when she came, biting her lip to keep herself from screaming, it was his face that she saw.

The bed was too hot after that, so hot that she threw back the blanket and let the cold air wash over her, honing her nipples to hard points once more. But the cold didn't bring the clarity she so desperately needed.

She stood, crossed the room to the washbasin, and poured from the pitcher. The water was ice-cold; the washcloth rough against her skin.

Maybe he had picked a woman tonight who looked like her. Maybe he hadn't even picked a woman, but had sat in his chamber and done to himself what she had just done. The thought left her with a deep wistfulness.

If only…

"There are no ifs," she told herself sharply. "Only what is."

This was the reality that she had to accept: What had just happened— that was the closest she would ever come to making love with the Duke of Clermont. One night, she might think of him, and if she were very lucky, he might spare a thought for her in response. Her throat tightened with yearning.

It didn't matter.

She'd learned long ago that her own emotions never mattered. Things were what they were, no matter how she felt about them. And this particular emotion… This one had sent her reeling far enough off course.

Still, she fumbled open her curtains. On another night, she might have looked down—down at the cabbage fields, down at the half ring of crushed gravel in front of her great-aunts' cottage.

Tonight, for the space of time it took her heartbeat to return to normal, she looked up. Up at the quarter moon, gleaming through the fringe of clouds, up at stars that twinkled for queen and peasant alike. She looked up until the clouds covered the moon and cut out all the light.

⌘ ⌘ ⌘

IT WAS MUCH LATER THAT EVENING when Robert walked the streets of Leicester again—this time with Oliver beside him. The fog had descended, mixing with the coal smoke to form an unholy pea soup, one that clung to his coat. Somewhere, a church bell to his right began to chime the nine o'clock hour; it was joined shortly by its neighbors to the left, and then those behind him, before him—a chorus of bells that seemed all the more eerie within the quiet grip of the mist.

"What is it?" Oliver finally asked. They'd been walking since the church had rung the half hour without saying a word.

Robert clenched his fist in his pocket.

"I am trying to do the right thing," he finally said.

The town was quiet. Strange, how sharply the factory whistle divided the days here. One moment, you could not escape the rattle of machinery; the next, it fell still and silent, like some noisome behemoth collapsing in its tracks. It left a curious silence in its wake, one louder than the quiet of a countryside. He could almost feel his teeth rattle with the sound the machinery did not make.

"Is something going awry?" Oliver glanced at him.

"There's this woman…" Robert let out the words on a great whoosh of air, and his brother cackled aloud.

"God, I've been waiting for you to tell me. Sebastian mentioned her and was shocked when I had no idea what he meant. Who is it?"

Robert told him. Not everything—he couldn't tell his brother about the handbills, as that was a risk that he insisted on taking alone. But about Minnie—how she seemed so quiet until she spoke to him. How she turned him upside down.

"I kissed her. I can't forget it," he said. "I can't do it again. I know how these things are done, and this isn't right."

"It's not right?" Oliver asked mildly.

The silence seemed to hold an edge now. They rarely talked about the circumstances of their brotherhood, but it stood between them. Oliver's mother had been a governess when the Duke of Clermont had visited her household. What choice did a governess have when a duke pursued? If she said yes, he would have her. If she said no, he would have her.

"I don't know what right is," he finally said. "I'm a duke. She's the great-niece of a woman who has a mere pretension to gentility. If I do something wrong here, you're the only one I trust to punch me in the stomach."

Oliver shook his head. "It wouldn't come to that."

The last of the bells faded in the distance. Robert could still feel her kiss, could still feel the want rise in his blood. "It might. You know who my father is. The sort of man he was." His voice dropped. "And I want her."

There it was, said aloud. He wanted. He didn't just want her body. So few people knew who he was, what he desired. And yet Minnie had accepted him at his word. She hadn't bowed or scraped to him; instead, she'd told him that she overmatched him.

More than that. He'd spent so long hiding how he felt, what he wanted. He had to work in Parliament to pass every bill that remotely advanced his goals, even while he gnashed his teeth at the slow pace of progress. The House of Lords bickered over the correct threshold for property ownership in voting while Robert chafed at the notion of any property threshold at all. They muttered about the privileges of peerage, when he wanted them all removed. But stating something so radical would have alienated them all. And so he kept it in. He argued minutiae. He voted for bills that made life a little more bearable when he wanted to scream at everyone.

Minnie, now... There was a woman who knew what it was to hide what she felt. And he wanted her so badly, so damned badly.

"I don't trust myself," he finally said.

Oliver shrugged. "Why would you trust me, then? I have as much of Clermont in me as you do."

"You..." Robert stopped, turned to his brother. "That's different."

"Same blood." His brother took off his spectacles. "Same eyes. Same nose."

"But you...your..." He stumbled for an explanation. "I can be a right bloody bastard. You of all people should know that. And why you gave me a chance, I will never know."

"That's easy." Oliver shrugged and looked at the pavement. "If you didn't take after the duke, I wouldn't have to, either."

Robert stopped walking.

"I'm not a prize, myself. I can be a right bloody bastard, too. I have a temper worse than anyone else in my family. Sometimes, when I was a child, I scared myself with my temper. I know I scared my mother." Oliver shook his head. "I'm not your conscience, Robert. I'm not a man who will show you what's right. My mother's suffering didn't wash me clean of Clermont's blood."

"That's not why I'm asking you." The fog seemed to eat his words. "I'm asking you because..."

When they'd been at Eton together, Oliver had spent hours fashioning cunning boxes from sheets of paper or whittling a little flock of sheep, complete with shepherdess, for his sisters. His mother had received sketches of the buildings, carefully made. And for his father...nothing was ever good enough for his father. One year, he'd been set on getting his father a pair of cufflinks. And so for months before November—because Mr. Marshall's birthday was in November—Oliver had worked, whittling carvings for the other boys for pennies apiece, just so he could have the money for a gift.

Robert had always watched in bemusement.

"You're asking me because..." his brother prompted.

"Because I have nobody else to ask," he said.

Robert had always hoped for a family of his own—first imagining his father more caring than he was, then hoping that his mother would love him. When he'd realized how futile his daydreams were, his wants had shifted outward. It had started so subtly that he couldn't pinpoint the moment.

He'd had daydreams in which he accompanied Oliver home during the summer holidays. He'd imagined spending entire days together, talking and playing and boxing and fishing and doing whatever it was that brothers did.

But even though that hadn't happened—his father, and then his guardian, would never have allowed him to spend his holiday with mere tradespeople—he'd gone one step further. It wasn't just a brother he coveted; it was an entire family.

And, as it turned out, Oliver had one ready-made.

In his daydreams, Oliver's parents would grow to know him. Mr. Marshall would give Robert sage advice and occasional clouts on the shoulder, while Mrs. Marshall would slide him slices of gingerbread, or whatever it was that mothers were supposed to do. Those details had always been frustratingly vague, but it hadn't mattered. In his wild fantasies, he'd imagined himself becoming something of a favored friend, an almost-son to these people who loved Oliver with no limitations.

By the time he was sixteen, he'd invented an elaborate dream world—one in which he would fall in love with Oliver's eldest sister (no relation; he'd made a point to convince himself on that score), and their difference in station be damned, he'd marry her anyway.

Of course, he'd never met Oliver's eldest sister. For that matter, he'd not met Mr. and Mrs. Marshall. But reality had no bearing on the substance of his dreams. Every time Oliver got a letter from home—or sent back another carving for a younger sister—Robert fell a little more in love with all of them. It didn't matter who they were, what they were like. If they would only love him back, then he would finally belong.

"Huh," Oliver said, and punched him on the shoulder. A veritable love tap, that. "Well, *I* believe that you have nothing of your father in you."

Robert shrugged. "If you say."

But he'd had it proven otherwise—and by nobody so much as Oliver's own family.

It had gone like this. On the day that Oliver's parents were finally to visit, Robert had dressed with painstaking care. He'd brushed his hair and his teeth twice over and had tied his cravat three times in an attempt to make himself look earnest and respectable. He found himself pacing the room with a restless, desperate energy while Oliver gave him odd glances.

He knew that his daydreams were just daydreams. They were so idiotic, he had never mentioned them to his brother. But even if it was all bosh, even if they never loved him...they might still like him a little. Mightn't they?

The door opened. Robert turned.

Mr. and Mrs. Marshall had to have been the most beautiful sight that he had seen. So utterly normal. They'd rushed forward, arms outstretched, and grabbed up Oliver. Who had scowled and made noises of complaint, the ungrateful wretch—noises like "Stop, Ma, not my hair," and, "Don't kiss me in front of the fellows!" All that fuss, just because they hadn't seen him in a handful of months. Robert had watched from the other side of the room, a lump in his throat.

And then the moment had come. After the affectionate greetings had been given, Oliver had turned. "Mother," he'd said, "Father, this is—"

But Mrs. Marshall had looked over just as her son did. Her gaze landed on Robert. And as it did, she went very still—so still that it felt as if the whole room came to a stop alongside her. Her eyes grew wide, and all the color washed from her face. She stared at him.

And then, without saying a word, without even lifting a hand in a pretense of a greeting, she straightened to her feet, turned, and left the room.

Robert's lungs seemed to fill with shards of glass. Every breath he took hurt. He took one halting step after her—only to have Mr. Marshall intervene.

"You must be the Duke of Clermont," Mr. Marshall said, putting himself in Robert's way.

He'd been going to say *Call me Robert* after the introductions. But those words—that request for intimacy—would have only made him look all the more desperate. He managed a firm jerk of his head.

Mr. Marshall's voice was quiet, but it couldn't soften the harshness of the blow. "You look like your father. Very like." He paused. "So much like, I think, that when my wife saw you just now, she saw him."

He had nodded in a haze of pain.

"Perhaps," Mr. Marshall said gently, "this is not the best moment to perform introductions."

"Yes," he'd said. "Sir."

And he'd understood that there would never be a moment for introductions. There would be no lazy family summers, no man-to-man talks, no gingerbread on plates for him.

It didn't matter what he did. He looked like his father; his father had forced himself on Mrs. Marshall.

In a way, everything he'd made of himself stemmed from that moment—that desperation to prove himself to be more than his face.

It was stupid to say that his heart had been broken by a pair of people he'd never met. It was even more idiotic that it was true. But for months after, every time he thought of that moment, he felt a sharp sense of loss. As if they really *had* been his family, and he'd lost them all at once under tragic circumstances.

He'd mourned the loss of those dreams more than he had the death of his childhood nurse.

"I don't have to be your conscience," Oliver said, breaking him out of his memories. His brother leaned into him ever so slightly as they walked, enough to convey a wealth of affection. "You have one of your own. And I trust you, even if you can't trust yourself."

He didn't have much, but what he had, that he would hold on to. And never let go.

He gave his brother a playful nudge, but his throat was tight. "I always knew you were the gullible sort," he said. "Lucky me."

Chapter Fourteen

MINNIE DIDN'T SEE THE DUKE AT ALL in the days that followed.

But it was impossible not to think of him. She examined his paper under a borrowed jeweler's lens, poked at the ink used in his handbills, cataloged the vagaries of the type used to create it. There was a lowercase *e* that had a hairline crack in the lower stem; she'd seen it on four separate handbills, now. A *b* that was a bit misshapen.

All of the proof that she'd found added up.

Details, all of that. Now that she had his letter, it was all rendered superfluous.

More importantly, when she imagined herself on the streets of Leicester, she no longer saw herself industriously collecting paper samples, but striding arm in arm with the Duke of Clermont.

Stupid. She was so stupid.

She told herself that all too often, and yet found that she could not make herself stop thinking of him. She remembered the feel of his lips, the look in his eyes. She remembered his hands, warm on her body. She remembered everything he'd told her, and she didn't feel stupid.

She looked at her reflection in the mirror one afternoon. "You," she told herself, "are an idiot."

Her gray eyes looked back at her solemnly.

He had sent over a message. His cousin was delivering a penny reading that evening for the Leicester Mechanical Society and he'd asked her to come.

Minnie suspected that she shouldn't go. The stupidity of what she wanted was evident just from her own mirror. She wore a plain blue gown, one he'd seen twice already. It was severe and high-necked, the sleeves long but unadorned. There was scarcely a hint of a bustle, and her skirt sported no flounces, no cunning knots. Fabric was dear, ribbons dearer. It was simple logic to dress like this when there was so little extra money. Garbed like this, nobody would look at her. She didn't *want* people to look at her.

But she wanted to make him smile.

"Oh, Minnie," she said in despair. "Really. Him? Could you be any more hopeless?"

He was a duke. She was...

"Look, damn you," she said. And she forced herself to look in the mirror. Not to focus on the pleasant parts—the curve of her bosom, or her waist—but to really look at who she was. To look at that scar on her cheek. That wasn't just skin-deep. It was etched on her soul. Wilhelmina Pursling was dried-up, severe, quiet, *mousy*.

"Miss Pursling," Minnie enunciated very slowly, "is a nobody. By design."

But those were still her eyes looking out at her. And no matter what she told herself, no matter how many times she named herself a fool, that wild, untamed want welled up in her.

"You," she repeated, stabbing her finger at the mirror, "are an idiot."

Still, if she was going to be an idiot, she might as well be one in style. And so she went downstairs and out into the fallow fields. She tromped up one hill and down another, searching the sheltered south sides until she found what she was looking for—a patch of late yellow pansies, hidden in the cornstalks.

And she harvested them all.

⌘　⌘　⌘

IF ANY STARS SHONE BEHIND THE THICK BLANKET OF FOG AND SMOKE, Robert couldn't see them. He descended from the carriage and then turned to help Violet out. The streetlamps let out a dull and heavy illumination, enough to show a gathered mass of people waiting on the front steps of New Hall. In the night, all the clothing looked black, and the effect was almost funereal. It would have been, had they not been chanting.

"Ah, good," Sebastian said at his side. "There's a crowd."

"A mob," Robert said.

Sebastian simply rubbed his hands together in glee. "When I speak, it's usually the same thing. Are those things *goats?*"

They were. In the market square outside the hall, someone had set up two temporary enclosures. There were placards tied to both, but he couldn't read them in the dark. Still, one of those pens was filled with goats—nearly a dozen of the beasts, milling about and bleating.

The other enclosure, oddly enough, was filled with children. Small children, more of them than there were goats. Robert frowned as he drew closer. The tallest of the children would scarcely have reached his waist;

the youngest was barely walking, stumbling after the others in grim determination. None of the shouts came from the children; all that tumultuous yelling came from the surrounding adults.

As they came abreast of the enclosures, Robert could finally read the signs.

THESE ARE ANIMALS, proclaimed one grim placard that graced the goat enclosure. The sign over the pen that held the children read: *THESE ARE NOT.*

Robert glanced at Sebastian. His cousin was still smiling—he'd always enjoyed stirring matters to boiling—but there was an edge to his smile. Sebastian took a few steps forward until he faced the children.

The children were far more confused than the goats. One small boy had his hands on the middle rail of the fence. He wore only a light coat and thin gloves. If he'd had a cap, it had fallen off. His eyes seemed luminous in the cold of the night; his breath made puffs of cold air.

Sebastian bent down, and the shouts redoubled. "We are not animals!" a woman was saying. "We are not animals!"

They weren't shouting at Sebastian; nobody chanting recognized him. To their eye, he was just another gentleman taking in the spectacle. Just another reason to hear their own voices. Slowly, Sebastian unwound his scarf from his neck. Without saying a word, he set it around the small boy's neck. The addition of the oversized scarf made the child look even smaller. Sebastian nodded wordlessly and then turned to go.

"What do you think you're doing?" a nearby woman screeched. "That's my son. We don't need your charity."

Sebastian kept walking.

"If you listen to that madman lecturing tonight," the woman yelled at his retreating back, "you stand to lose your immortal soul. We want none of the devil's teachings here."

Sebastian didn't look back; the woman watched him leave, setting her hands on her hips. Her lips pursed; her fingers tapped in impatience. Finally, she turned to her son. "What were you doing, sitting there like a lump, then?" She took hold of one end of Sebastian's scarf and gave it a yank. "I told you to chant. I want to hear you chant. Try it now: 'I'm not—'" She stopped mid-sentence, on the verge of pulling off Sebastian's scarf, as Robert came to stand by her. She looked at his boots, then followed them up his trousers, his waistcoat, until she saw his face.

"Madam," Robert said, "do you by any chance know the temperature this evening?"

She seemed somewhat startled. "Why, no. But I believe there's a thermometer mounted at—"

"It's thirty-five degrees out. Almost freezing and likely to get colder."

She gave him a sullen look. "If you knew already, why bother asking?"

He took another look at the boy before him. The child's nose was red and dripping with cold. "You have no right to lecture anyone on the care of animals," Robert said bitterly. "My cousin least of all."

She frowned in confusion, and he left, his fists clenched. Behind him, the chants continued. *We're not animals. We're not animals.*

Sebastian was a tease. He could tweak a man to the verge of annoyance and beyond. But he'd never been so thoughtlessly, callously cruel as the woman was with her own child. It chafed at Robert that his cousin was judged in danger of losing his immortal soul, when *he* wasn't the one rounding up children, treating them like cattle in order to score points.

He was thankful to leave the crowd behind him. The interior was warmer and drier. When the doors closed behind him, they cut off most of the noise from outside. He found Miss Pursling in one of the back rows, seated next to the aisle alongside her friend. Her hands were clamped around the edge of her seat. He paused next to her.

"Miss Pursling," he said. "We've seats up front, if you and Miss Charingford wish to join us."

"No, thank you." Her voice was cool. "I…I do not care for crowds. If I'd known it would be this bad, I wouldn't have come. If there were any way to leave…"

Her lips pressed together. It was hard to judge the pallor of her skin in the faint light at the back of the room, but he thought she looked a little wan.

"Are you well?" he asked.

"It's nothing." She swallowed. "It's nothing. It's nothing. I'm nothing."

"Your pardon?"

She glanced up and then swiftly away. "It's nothing," she repeated. "Please stop looking at me."

He sat down in the row behind her. "There. I'm not looking. You have flowers on your gown." She did. Real ones at that. Little yellow ones edging her hem, her cuffs.

"They seemed appropriate, in light of Mr. Malheur's work. He discusses plants, does he not?"

"He does. And yet I seem to recall that he started with snapdragons, not…what are those? Pansies. There's a missed opportunity on your part." He glanced sidelong at her and caught a soft smile on her face. "They're lovely."

"Ah." She stared straight ahead.

"There," he said in satisfaction. "Now you're breathing properly. You just needed a bit of a distraction for a moment."

He started to stand.

"Your Grace."

"Yes?"

"Thank you." She was still staring ahead of her. She no longer clutched the seat as if it were the only thing keeping her erect. "I didn't really wear the flowers in honor of Mr. Malheur, Your Grace."

He smiled. "I know. I know precisely who you wore them for."

"You...do?"

"You wore them because you knew that color would soften the angles of your gown. That touch at the neckline makes your eyes look like storm clouds. It's a lovely effect, Minnie. I know who you wore them for."

She held perfectly still.

"You wore them for *you*," he said. "Good for you."

She let out a breath. "You're a very dangerous man."

He stood. "The hall is almost full. I'm sorry you'd rather stay here. I must go to the front and see to my cousin. Shall I see you after?"

"I—the crowd..." She looked around. "I may leave early, Your Grace, so as not to be caught in the throng." She looked into her lap as she spoke, but her face had begun to grow pale again.

"You really aren't well."

"It's nothing." She spoke more sharply this time, and a gentleman up front had stood and looked on the verge of introducing Sebastian. Robert had little choice but to leave her. By the time he found his seat, the man was running through Sebastian's history.

"...After a distinguished beginning at Cambridge," the man said, "Mr. Sebastian Malheur made a name for himself by..."

Distinguished beginning? Ha. He'd scarcely made it through the first part of his Tripos examinations. He'd always been on the verge of being sent down, pulling prank after college-boy prank. Nobody had been more shocked by Sebastian's sudden success than the old men who'd once administered his exams.

In some ways, Sebastian's subsequent success—the nature of it, as well as the manner—was Sebastian's biggest prank of all. And he knew it. He came to the podium in front with a bit of a swagger and a smirk.

"Thank you, thank you all," he said, "for your very kind welcome." The quirk of his mouth was the only thing that acknowledged that half his welcomers had come to call him names. "I stand here to tell you about the science of inherited traits—the subject of years of study on my part. Over the course of my studies, I have come to several conclusions. One, that traits—like eye color, height, the number of petals on a flower, or the shape of a radish—are inherited from progenitors according to strict, inviolable rules. Second, that the rules of inheritance appear to be constant from animal to plant, from vegetable to tree, from cats and sheep to goats and, of course, the human animal."

Oh, he was enjoying himself. There was a gleam in his eye as he spoke, a faint smile that spread at the indrawn gasps scattered around the hall.

"Third, I shall explain how the rules of inheritance walk hand in hand with Mr. Darwin's discoveries on the origin of species. I know that many of you are particularly waiting for this portion, and so I shall explain the connection and the means by which I came to my conclusions, using—"

"Using the tools of the devil!" someone shouted in the back.

Sebastian paused only briefly. "Using facts, logic, and reproducible experiments," he said gently. "All those may seem dull to many of you. But my colleagues usually raise objection to proof by diabolical influence." There was another flicker of a smile and then he swept his arms wide, striding to an easel he'd set up at the front.

"I start with the color of the snapdragon."

He set his hand on the fabric covering the easel. At that moment, though, the back door of the hall flew open. Heads turned. For a moment, there was only darkness.

Then: "Get on!" someone shouted, and the goats that had once been in the square ambled into the hall. They looked about, mildly puzzled.

"As you think there's no distinction between humans and animals," someone yelled, "here's some for your audience!"

Titters arose.

Sheep, Robert thought aimlessly, would have been a better choice. Sheep were skittish things that bolted away at the flutter of a cloak. They would have panicked in an instant. Goats, on the other hand... Goats saw a gathering of this many people as an opportunity. They walked down the aisle, heads bobbing.

"I welcome all creatures intelligent enough to understand," Sebastian said grandly. "Never fear, my good man. I'm sure that after I'm finished, your animals will be able to explain the principles to you using very small words, the sort that even you might comprehend."

Another wave of laughter arose at that.

The head goat took another lazy step forward. Then it stopped. It turned its head in contemplation...and reached out to take a bite from the flowers at Minnie's hem.

Robert came half out of his seat, reaching back, even though she was yards away. She shoved at its head. He could see her lips move, see her slap it on the shoulder, but he couldn't hear what she said.

"Here now," the driver shouted behind her. "Don't touch that animal! You heard the man—she's one of us. I'll have you up for assault if you lay hands on her again." He gave another belly laugh.

Another one of the goats came up to her, stealthily reaching out its neck. Miss Pursling took a parasol from a nearby woman and whacked it.

"Assault! Assault and battery!"

Waves of laughter grew. Another whack with the parasol; yet another goat joined the fray. This one reached in and chomped at her hem. The blue fabric ripped, showing a hint of creamy petticoat.

And that was when Robert realized what was wrong. Nobody had moved to help her. They all surrounded her, watching, *laughing*. He found himself standing up, running down the aisle toward her.

"Animal or human?" the goat owner was shouting. "Ah, you see—we *can* tell the difference after all!"

The people around her were laughing at that fool—holding back, while Miss Pursling beat off the assault on her own. Robert shoved through the crowd, making his way up to the man.

"You think that's assault?" he growled.

The man didn't look behind him to see who was speaking. "What?"

Robert set his hand on one shoulder and forcibly turned the fellow around. "This," he said. "This is what a bloody assault looks like." So saying, he punched the man square in the jaw. The fellow's eyes widened in surprise. He seemed to teeter in place for a bare moment. Then his eyes rolled up and he toppled over.

Robert turned away. "For shame," he snapped to the gathered crowd. "Shame on all of you. Get those goats off that woman. *Now.*"

Minnie looked up at that. She'd been so busy fending off the goats that she hadn't noticed the crowd closing in on her. But instead of looking relieved at the men who advanced on the goats, her head whipped from side to side. She went absolutely white. Robert saw her eyes roll up in her head.

If anyone had asked him before this night, he would have wagered good money that she had nerves of steel. He started through the crowd, but he was too late.

She fainted in a crumpled heap before he could reach her.

Chapter Fifteen

THE WORLD WAS MADE OF VINEGAR, and Minnie's sinuses were on fire. She coughed and became aware that she rested on an uncomfortable surface—hard and lumpy and warm, all at the same time.

She opened her eyes.

Lydia was staring at her, waving a vial of *sal volatile* underneath her nose. Minnie coughed heavily and batted the smelling salts away.

"There," her best friend said brightly. "That's done the trick. Do you have a dreadful headache?"

It all came back to her. The flowers. The goats. The *crowd.* "Oh, God," she moaned. "Lydia, please tell me I did not just faint in front of everyone."

"You did."

She wanted to close her eyes again. Robert had been there. What he would think of her?

"Did the goats eat *all* of my gown?"

"None of the good bits," another voice said, this one directly above her.

And that was when Minnie realized her head wasn't resting on a pillow. Those uncomfortable lumps were thighs; her head was cradled on the Duke of Clermont's lap. She jerked upright, ignoring the pounding behind her eyelids, and pushed away from him. She had been laid out on a hard wooden bench. There was a desk at the front and a few chairs off to the side. She was in one of the upstairs merchants' meeting rooms in New Hall, she supposed.

Along with the Duke of Clermont.

"Lydia," she moaned, "how could you?"

But Lydia didn't answer right away. She glanced at the duke and then colored and looked away.

"Someone had to carry you," he said finally, "and, as it turns out, I was first to volunteer."

She felt sick just imagining it. They'd all have looked at her when she fainted. To have the Duke of Clermont wade in, though—that would make everyone pay attention. No doubt the gossip was running the rounds.

"Now," Lydia said, enunciating very carefully, "I am going to go fetch a glass of water—"

"Don't you dare leave me alone with—"

But Lydia was already withdrawing.

"Lydia!"

The door closed behind her.

Minnie shot to her feet with no thought but to put space between them. If he didn't touch her…

He stood along with her; when she wobbled, he caught her arm. "Sit down, Minnie."

"People must know we are in here together," she said frantically. "They'll see her. They'll think us alone. Everyone will think—"

"Everyone," he said distinctly, "is already thinking. Your friend left me alone with you because she knew what I was going to say. Please sit down and listen to me."

She looked into his eyes. He seemed quite forbidding, and her head was still spinning. She sat again.

"When those goats surrounded you," he said, "I punched the man who was driving them. In front of everyone. And then, when you collapsed, I picked you off the floor and carried you out of the room. Whatever gossip you imagine you might forestall by walking out now— believe me, someone is already saying it."

Oh, God. It had happened. It had really happened. Her head felt light. She was ruined; Stevens would come back with his proof, and it wouldn't matter. Minnie took a breath.

"I'm sorry," he said. "I didn't think. I told you I can be stupid. When I saw you out there, *thinking* was the last thing on my mind. I just wanted to be by your side."

Minnie shook her head, which made her feel all the more dizzy. "As much my fault as yours." If this was disaster, it was a disaster she'd courted. She'd known there was an attraction between them. He'd as good as told her nothing could come of it. And she'd kissed him anyway— kissed him and wanted him to look at her. That's what came of putting herself forward. "I'll take care of this somehow."

There had to be some explanation she could give, some way that this could all come right. Maybe if someone else fainted, and he grabbed her, too? Then it might be seen as mere chivalry on his part.

But that didn't feel right to her. Too forced. Unnatural. Minnie scrubbed her forehead in distress.

He sat down next to her and took her hand. "Minnie," he said gently. "Do you recall the time you came to my house and threatened me?"

"How could I forget?" She frowned. "I suppose I could use that. Expose you now and explain that you were just trying to keep me quiet. It still doesn't feel right. I don't think it will work."

"At the time, I said that if anything happened, I'd make sure you had a proposal of marriage. I believe my precise words were that I'd make sure of it, even if I had to make one myself."

All her plans came to a halt. Minnie looked up into his eyes. It would have been a vicious thing to joke about, and he'd never been cruel before. Still, it was easier to imagine him callous than the universe kind.

"You didn't mean it," she said. "It was said in jest."

He shrugged. "It was said in stupidity, not jest. I say a lot of stupid things when you're about." He scrubbed his hand through his hair and then sighed. "But stupid as it might have been, it was also true. I meant it, Minnie. I wish you would marry me." He glanced over at her. "Even without this, I would have asked. I've been thinking of nothing else for days. Marry me."

She couldn't comprehend that. Instead, she stood and walked over to the narrow window. From here, she had a view of the square in front of them. The last remnants of the crowd had dispersed, taking their goats with them. No, what he was saying didn't seem possible. "That makes no sense, Your Grace," she said. "That is madness talking. You cannot marry someone like me."

He didn't pretend to know what she meant. "That's what everyone says." He regarded her. "And I admit, I hadn't considered the possibility until I met you. But once I started thinking about it, you began to make all kinds of sense. Do you know why I haven't married yet?"

"You're not even thirty. You've years ahead of you…"

She trailed off, suddenly uneasy. His eyes had fixed on her in a way that started her heart beating in a way that had nothing to do with his age. Her hands grew clammy.

"Minnie," he said, "do you have any idea what I hope to accomplish? You must have gathered that my father took ownership of a factory here and ran it into the ground—that I hope to make up for that. I have a half brother who matters more to me than anyone in the entire world, who is looked down on for his birth. I don't stand on my prerogatives."

Minnie could scarcely breathe.

"But that is only part of what I hope to see in my life. If I had my way, I would abolish the hereditary peerage in its entirety."

She gasped.

"Every aspect of it," he said fiercely. "Lords should be indicted like commoners and tried by juries. We should not have the right to reject laws that Commons proposes. In fact, I don't think the House of Lords should exist at all. I wish to hell I was simple Mr. Blaisdell. My father—you have no idea how dreadful he was."

His hands clenched at his side; his eyes blazed with a light she hadn't seen since he talked to Finney.

"I could apologize for the benefits I inherited from him," Robert said. "But I learned long ago that an apology changes nothing. So I plan instead to use them—use them to make sure that what my father did, no lord will ever be allowed to do again."

This couldn't be happening. He couldn't be saying those things.

But telling herself that did no good. Minnie was just as certain that she was seeing the heart of him now.

"Of all the benefits I plan to relinquish, the chance to wed some peer's daughter will be the first to go. Think about what it would mean if I did offer for one for those girls. What would she think when she discovered that my life's goal was to divest her father, her brother, of their prerogatives? My parents fought every moment they were around one another. I won't have that kind of marriage. I won't."

She had nothing to say to that.

"Second," he said. "I've never expected love from a marriage. At best, I'd hoped to find an ally. Someone who would support me in what will come." He looked over at her. "You're better than I at tactics. You'd be a terrible wife for a duke, but for a man who doesn't want to be a duke any longer? I can't imagine anyone better."

She couldn't imagine anyone *worse*. He didn't know about her. He didn't *know*.

"Third," he said. "I want you. I want you very badly. I want you so much that when you fall down half a hall away from me, I'm by your side before anyone else can move. I want you so much that there are nights that I think of nothing but having you."

She felt those words, felt them in the inner core of her, in a flash of heat and longing that encompassed every lonely night she'd spent. In that, they were well matched. But…

"What of fidelity?" she asked. "I should like to know what to expect. Are you to have mistresses? Am I allowed to take lovers?"

He looked her over. "The last thing I'm thinking of right now is other women," he muttered.

"Answer the question, if you please." Her voice shook.

"Is that what you want? For us to take lovers at whim?"

"You've said you don't love me." Her voice was surprisingly steady. "If I had my preferences, I would want my vows to mean something. I was thinking more of your needs. I don't want to be unprepared."

He exhaled and gave her a glimmer of a smile. "Ah."

She crossed over to him. "You said that we'd be allies, that we'd think of each other. I can imagine what it's like to be a duke. Thus far, you've had your choice of women." And many of them, she didn't doubt. "Don't make a promise that will only chafe at you later. I'd rather have flat honesty than fidelity and flattery at this point."

"Flat honesty?"

She nodded.

"Then, my dear, you'll have it. I'm not so desperate for sexual relations as you might imagine. I don't need to wrangle women into my bed to obtain regular release. God gave me a strong left hand, and there have been many nights when I've preferred it to a woman." He wasn't looking in her direction. He couldn't be embarrassed by that admission, could he?

But his confession sent another flash of molten heat through her— the idea of him naked and hard, of his hand on his member. What would he look like when he stroked himself? Would he like long, hard strokes, or soft, gentle ones?

"I can't ruin my hand's reputation," he said, "or hurt its feelings, or get it with child. It has proved by far the safest option available to me. So you tell me, Minnie. Do you think you need to take lovers?"

"I have never given the matter any thought." It was true; she'd never considered being unfaithful in marriage. Not even if she'd married a man who took mistresses.

"Because I very much believe in making things clear," he said. "I don't want any misunderstandings between us. And—if it comes down to it—I promise that if you take a disgust of me, I will let you leave. No little stratagems to try to get you to return. No withholding of pin money. None of that." He swallowed. "I know things change. There is nothing worse in a marriage than a husband using his power to force his wife. I won't do it."

"Robert." Minnie turned to him. "There is no danger of my becoming disgusted by you."

She wasn't sure who moved first. Maybe she took a step toward him. Maybe he leaned toward her. Maybe it was mutual, a shift in the air that brought them together at last. Her hands wrapped around his shoulders; his arms came hard around her.

They were fully clothed, and still his kiss seemed carnal in a way that their last kiss had not. This one was a prelude to what might come if she said yes. His hands roamed, sliding down her, cupping her breasts, clasping her hips. This was a precursor to lovemaking.

He broke off the kiss, half-smiling. "There's one thing I need to say." He sounded almost out of breath. "When my parents married, my father swore that he loved my mother. It was a lie, and it did more damage than the truth. I won't marry under false expectations." His fingers flexed, and she looked up to meet his eyes. "I understand perfectly well what we mean to each other. I don't expect you to love me."

"What do we mean to each other?" she asked.

"I want children. As many as we can manage and maintain your health."

"Your Grace," she said, emphasizing his title deliberately. "That's not an answer."

He shrugged and looked away. "I don't know how to explain it. You looked at me and instead of seeing a duke, you saw a man who could write radical handbills. You know who I am."

And that brought reality crashing in on Minnie's head. He'd painted a lovely picture. If all she had to do was sit behind him in Parliament and whisper advice in his ear, figuratively speaking, she'd have said yes.

But this...

Duchesses went to parties—great big crushes with hundreds of people present. When they went walking in parks, people pointed them out and watched. And Minnie...Minnie began to panic if more than a handful of people looked her way. She'd fainted when twenty people surrounded her.

"Oh God," she said, moving away from him, pulling her arms about herself. "This really isn't going to work."

"Minnie?"

She turned back to him. "What do you suppose happened out there?"

He blinked. "Out there? There is an out there?"

"Why do you think I fainted?"

"Um." He scrubbed his hair through his hands. "The goats?"

"I live on a farm, Robert. I'm used to goats."

He frowned. "You're right. It was after the goats had been driven off. Everyone was crowded around you."

She usually tried *not* to remember those moments that sent her into spiraling terror; she'd put it out of her mind as soon as she'd woken. But she could see them now, a wall of faces and fabric, all jeering at her. Her stomach cramped just recalling it. Her heart pounded with a cold intensity.

"I'm afraid of crowds." The words squeaked out, but she'd said them. "No, not afraid—terrified."

He took hold of her hand.

"Especially crowds where everyone looks at me. I was caught in a mob once when I was twelve." She touched her cheek. "That's where this came from. They were throwing rocks."

He raised his hand to her face. His gloves were black leather; she could smell them, so close to her. He set his fingertips against her scar, traced it down her face, first lightly, and then with a little more force.

She had left off the last two words of her sentence. They hadn't just been throwing rocks. They were throwing rocks *at her.*

"That was a vicious throw."

She nodded.

He traced her scar again, this time pressing.

"I can actually feel a fracture in your skull. So close to your eye..."

"For the first few days, when I was all bruised all over, there was some question over whether I would be able to see out of that eye when it healed."

He hadn't moved his hand from her cheek.

"And so now I can't abide large groups of people. If they're all looking at me, it becomes impossible. I can't think. I can't breathe. I want only to escape."

"So you stay quiet. You hide every good thing about you and hope that nobody looks."

Minnie stared at her skirts. "Yes." The word was anguished. She curled up smaller.

For the longest time, he didn't say anything. Then, slowly, he tilted her head up. "Too bad," he murmured. "I've already seen you."

His lips brushed hers. It wasn't a kiss. Not really. Kisses would be more than just a light meeting of mouths, an exchange of scents. If it were a kiss, he wouldn't have pulled away so quickly.

She found herself looking up at him. His hand cupped her cheek.

"What was that?" she asked.

"If you couldn't tell, I must have done it wrong." And then, more slowly, more deliberately, he leaned in. This time, his lips didn't just brush hers; they met hers. His mouth was warm and dry; instead of a brief pressure, he nibbled at her. His hand cupped her cheek, pulling her closer, and that kiss...

Minnie turned away, but that only brought her forehead in contact with his shoulder. She leaned against him, learning how to breathe once more.

"I can't marry you," she said. "How could I be a duchess?"

"It's easy," he said. "You say yes. I get my lawyers to draw up the settlements. That will take three or four days, and by then, the special license will have arrived."

Oh, God. His version of marriage started with attorneys. If she'd needed proof of how far apart they stood, how different were the worlds in which they lived…

His hand rested on hers, and every muscle in her body came to a standstill—her lungs ceased to draw air; her mouth froze half-open. And her fingers—well, she didn't dare move her fingers, not one inch. Only her heart continued to pound in her chest, one staccato beat after another.

"After that," he said, "I get to take you to bed."

That, at least, was the same. Despite herself, Minnie smiled.

He drew his thumb along the side of her hand in a caress. "What am I going to do with you, Minnie?" he asked idly.

She jerked her hand away, her heart stinging with some emotion she couldn't identify. "Stop. Stop doing anything."

He tilted his head toward her. His profile was crisp and perfect. The lamplight kissed the tip of his nose, and Minnie felt an irrational surge of jealousy—that the light could touch him so indiscriminately, and she could hardly withstand the pressure of his fingertips.

"Your Grace," she said distinctly, "I must be more clear. I told you there was something in my past. Something I didn't want to come to light."

He didn't stop toying with her hand. "I can guess what you're about to say," he said mildly. "And I really don't give a fig about that."

Minnie's palms had begun to sweat. She was beginning to feel the first stirrings of nausea. It had been so long since she told anyone, so long since she'd said the words aloud.

"Until I was twelve years old—" She was beginning to tremble, and he sat up and looked at her with concern. There was nothing for it but to get it out quickly. "Until I was twelve years old," she said in a rush, "my father dressed me in trousers and introduced me to everyone as a boy."

He blinked, his eyes widening in surprise. "I was…definitely not going to guess that."

"It came out, of course," she said. "It came out badly." She rubbed her hands together, trying to stop them from shaking. "All of London knew. It was in the papers. That mob I told you about? They were after me. Wanting to punish me for daring to pretend so much. For being so unnatural."

"Huh." He had a small frown on his face as he looked at her. His eyes traveled over her, as if seeing her again, this time as a thing that had not come out right. Maybe he had read about the scandal at the time. Maybe he was trying to recall details. Maybe he'd been part of the crowd, part of the group throwing rocks.

No. Not that. He hadn't let go of her hand, and she couldn't imagine him hurling stones at anyone, let alone a child.

"It was so bad that I had to give up my life entirely. I changed my name. I was born Minerva Lane. When I was…when I was pretending, my father called me Maximilian."

"Huh," he repeated. His jaw moved, but he didn't speak.

"Say something," she said. "Say anything at all. You didn't know when you proposed marriage. I won't fault you for walking away." She looked up into his eyes. "Just say *something.*"

He searched her face for a moment, and then shrugged. "Did you like being a boy?"

"I—well." It was not a question she'd ever been asked, and it startled her out of her fear. "It was all I really knew at first. The deception started when I was so young. I didn't think anything of it." She sighed. "I hated lying, though. All the pretenses to avoid removing clothing around others. I hated that a great deal. And when I was twelve, I started to fancy one of my friends. That was…deeply awkward."

"I should say." He blinked at her. "This explains a great deal about you."

"I had to learn to be a girl again, afterward. How to walk. How to talk. So many little things to do wrong. It was just…easier to be small and quiet. I couldn't make any mistakes that way."

"It makes me think I should have a very long talk with you about the appropriate subjects for female education," he said with a sudden smile. "After we're married."

"You're not being serious. Your Grace, I'm a scandal waiting to happen."

"Minnie, I want to abolish the peerage. I write radical pamphlets in secret. I am not going to shriek, 'Oh, no! A scandal!' and run away. I don't mind scandal."

Minnie looked him in the eyes. "But I do, Your Grace. I do."

The door rattled once, then again. A few moments later, after some more extremely loud fumbling with the handle, Lydia opened the door. She came in carrying a pitcher of water.

"That," Minnie said, "must be water fetched all the way from Bath. Did you walk there yourself or take the train?"

Lydia gave her a cheeky grin. "Well? Is everything settled?"

"My question exactly." Robert raised an eyebrow.

And Minnie found she couldn't answer. She wanted him. She *liked* him. If he'd been any other man, she'd have taken him. But marrying him would put her in front of not just a few people, but the entire country. And with him at her side, they would all be looking. She felt ill just thinking about it.

She looked away. "I need more time."

"Time? Time for what?" Lydia demanded.

But Robert held up his hand. "Then have it," he said. "Think it through from all angles. Consider your strategies, if you must, and advance your supply lines. Whatever it is you must do to feel secure." He flashed her a smile, a confident smile. A smile that said he knew she wouldn't turn him down.

"Take your time," he said, stepping closer to her and leaning in. "And in the end, Minnie, take me."

Chapter Sixteen

ROBERT SHOULD HAVE GUESSED what the gossip would bring, but the next morning's visitor still came as a surprise. He was on the verge of going out—had just stepped outside his door, in fact—when a carriage drew up in front of the house. A servant leaped from the back and placed a stool on the pavement.

The door opened, and his mother disembarked. Her eyes landed on Robert. She didn't frown. She didn't squint. In fact, the duchess did not show any emotion at all. Instead, she simply stepped onto the pavement and floated up the steps.

"Clermont," she said in greeting.

He inclined his head a half inch. "Duchess."

She swept in the open door as if he were holding it for her. Without asking permission, she accosted a passing maid and ordered tea. He followed in bemusement. Two minutes later, she'd seated herself in his front parlor. She waved her own maid away and faced him.

"I take it," she said, "that you haven't made a general practice of debauching genteel young women of the middle class."

She said the words *middle class* as if they smelled of rotten eggs.

"You are referring to the events of last night?" he said, matching her tone. "I make it a habit to ruin a pair before tea. I find the anticipation makes the morning hours pass with delightful alacrity."

She sniffed. "That is the sort of joke your father would have made."

Robert's hand clenched in his glove. "No," he said. "That is the sort of thing my father would have *done*. He would never have joked about it, not in mixed company."

She waved a hand in acknowledgment. "This is not the first I have heard your name coupled with that of Miss Pursling. Tell me you are not considering anything untoward."

"I don't see why you should care. You never have."

The Duchess of Clermont simply shrugged. "Your actions, such as they are, reflect on me."

Of course. She wasn't taking an interest in him; she never had. She was simply seeing to her own reputation, worrying about the difficulties that he might cause her. He'd waited his entire life for her to notice him.

He'd studied hard when he first went to school, earning praise from all his tutors. He'd written her in excitement, hoping that she'd read his letter, that he would have done enough to make her proud.

But his first letter had received no response. So he'd tried harder. If he was not just good, but *great*... Surely then his mother would be proud of him. So he'd studied harder, tried more, achieved even more. He'd written her again after four months, shyly placing his accomplishments before her.

The post had brought an endless round of nothing.

Undaunted, he'd tried harder. He'd sent his third letter at the end of the year, informing her that he'd been first in his class. For a week that summer, he'd held his breath every day when the post arrived. For a week, he'd been disappointed.

And then, one day, he'd received a one-line response.

Tell your father that this strategy won't work, either.

It had been a matter of principle to continue on as he had before—to prove that all that effort hadn't been for *her*. Even so, it had taken him years to break the habit of hoping.

"Well?" she said, studying him now. "What is it that you intend with the girl?"

Robert stared across the room. "I believe," he said slowly, "that a son ought to defer to his mother. To answer her queries, because he owes her respect for the years of care she has given."

Her whole form tensed.

"I'm feeling generous. I shall answer one question for every month you spent in my company as a child."

He looked over at her. Her lips thinned. Her fingers tapped an angry rhythm against her saucer.

Robert stood up. "As you are no doubt aware," he said, "that leaves you with no questions at all. This interview is done."

And so saying, he stood and left the room.

⌘ ⌘ ⌘

A PROPOSAL OF MARRIAGE, MINNIE REALIZED, shouldn't make her feel ill. Especially when she actually liked the man. But she couldn't argue with the truth of her body. Her stomach cramped just thinking about what marriage to him would mean. It wasn't a falsehood when she told her great-aunts the next morning that she needed to lie down.

She'd promised to consider the advantages of his proposal, but all attempts to do so were swept away by visions of angry faces surrounding her. "Fraud!" they yelled, and "Devil's spawn!" Duchesses attracted crowds. Duchesses attended parties. Duchesses didn't faint when too many people looked at them. If they did, they'd always be collapsing.

She could imagine the private portion of their relationship all too well. Her skin burned with the hope of that. They had too many kisses between them now for her to pretend she didn't want him. But while she might have done well as Robert's lover, the thought of being a duke's wife made her feel ill. And eventually, any private understanding they might have would be overshadowed by the inevitable public disaster.

Her reverie was interrupted in the afternoon by the clatter of wheels on the drive. She propped herself up on one elbow so that she could see out the window and watched in bemusement as four matching dark horses drew up in front of her great-aunts' cottage. A servant jumped off the back, opening the carriage door, setting down a stool upholstered in bright colors. And the Duchess of Clermont stepped out. She looked around in every direction, her nose upturned. No doubt taking in the cabbage fields beyond the house, the paint peeling off the barn to the left, the rust on the hinges…all the signs of poverty waiting just on the edge of vision.

She wore a pale pink gown, frothed with lace at the cuffs and hems as if she were a fancy cake in a baker's window. The duchess shook her head as if to dispel the commonplace sight of the house before her and swept up the walk. One of her servants glided before her and sounded the knocker.

It was starting already. The crowds. The dubious looks. The recrimination.

Minnie was hardly surprised when Great-Aunt Caro came to see her a few minutes later.

"Minnie," she said in awed tones, "I know you're feeling poorly, but the Duchess of Clermont most particularly wishes to see you. Shall I send her away?"

Obviously, the duchess had heard the news from her son.

"No," Minnie said. "I had better see her."

Caro helped her lace her dress and smoothed her hair into a bun. She didn't say anything as she worked. She didn't ask why the Duchess of Clermont would call, nor did she question Minnie's illness. Minnie could fault her great-aunts for a great many things, but they let her be and trusted her to make her own decisions.

"Minnie," she finally said, when she'd put down the brush and pronounced her gown presentable, "if you needed anything—anything at all—you would tell me, wouldn't you?"

Her great-aunt was wearing a dress she'd turned for the fifth time. Half the lines in her face were likely Minnie's fault. If anything happened to Eliza, Caro would have nowhere to go. And still she trusted Minnie.

It didn't matter what would happen if Minnie became a duchess. It didn't matter that she would be terrible at the endeavor. The choices had all been whittled away, one by one, and there were worse things than feeling obligated to marry a man that she liked.

"No," Minnie said. "I wouldn't tell you. It's long past the time when I should be depending on you. *You* should be able to trust in me."

Her great-aunt's eyes grew shadowed.

"Oh, Minnie," she said in a choked voice.

Minnie squeezed her hand. "Don't worry about me." She drew a deep breath and went down to do battle.

Up close, the duchess's gown was even more stunning. Four layers of the finest lace ringed her hands. The fabric was a print of delicate flowers, tucked and embroidered and layered upon itself with cunning stitchery far beyond Minnie's own skill. She could see no hint of Robert in the woman's face. Her nose was small and turned up, and her mouth seemed set in an eternal grimace.

Minnie ducked her head and curtseyed low in the doorway, all too conscious of her own well-worn frock: a plain, serviceable gray with black cuffs that had been turned once to hide the fraying. The duchess surveyed her in silence, no doubt cataloging her every deficiency. She didn't need to say a word. That raised eyebrow, that slight widening of the eyes in surprise—they all said the same thing. *How dare you think you can marry my son?*

No matter what Minnie's decision might be, she wouldn't cower before this woman. She met the other woman's gaze straight on, refusing to look away.

"Well," the duchess finally said. "I understand what he sees in you."

The words were so surprising that Minnie forgot her resolve. "You do?"

The duchess stood up and strode over to Minnie. "Poor," she said, tapping the worn cuffs of Minnie's sleeves. "Scarred." She indicated her cheek. "No bearing, no deportment, no sense of proper manners. You're his charity project."

After the turmoil of the past day, it was a relief to feel cold, simple anger. Minnie's chin lifted. "And yet he has not offered me a single pound."

"Marriage to him would be worth more than a few guineas."

Minnie set one hand on her hip. "If you think your son's interest in me extends to mere charity, you don't know him very well. There are surely more deserving victims than I."

The duchess shook her head. "I know my son," she said with a low growl. "He looks so much like his father that it took me years to realize the truth. He's far too much like me."

"Like *you?*" Minnie looked at the woman again. Other than the pale color of her hair, there was nothing of her in her son. She could not have been more than fifty years of age, but already frowns had burrowed harsh lines in her forehead. Her mouth was set in an expression of permanent dislike. "He's nothing like you."

Pearls slid on the duchess's wrist as she waved her hand dismissively. "Like I used to be," she said. "Soft. Yielding." Her lips became even harder. "Gullible. He's an utter romantic—don't deny it. He has to be, asking a woman like you to marry him."

"A woman like me." Minnie felt her own mouth curling in distaste. "What do you mean, a woman like me?"

"For the rest of his life, everyone will be looking at him and wondering why he married *you,* whispering about how terribly the Blaisdell family name has been besmirched."

"I should think that would be his lookout, not yours."

The other woman's eyes flashed. "Do you know how much I gave up so that my child would be born with every advantage? For years I suffered through marriage to his cretinous, adulterous lump of a father. I had his bastard thrown in my face. I had to—" She cut herself off and shook her head. "It doesn't matter. I gave up everything so that my son could have this life. *Everything.* You cannot conceive what I had to bear. I did not make a sacrifice of my entire life so that he could throw himself away on a *nobody.*"

From that Minnie surmised that Robert's mother didn't know about his hope to abolish the peerage.

But the duchess's tirade went on. "You bring nothing to the match— no family, no money, no land, no power."

"I am aware of my assets, Your Grace."

"And you're going to marry him anyway," the duchess said scornfully. "I know my son. He's likely caring about *right* and *wrong,* wanting so desperately to belong to something. He'll hurl himself at whatever cause he so blindly chooses, heedless of the harm to himself."

Perhaps the duchess knew Robert better than Minnie had initially supposed.

The duchess sniffed. "He probably thinks he's saving you from a life of drudgery."

Minnie's cheeks flushed as the other woman once again took in her too-simple gown. The duchess's gaze traveled down to Minnie's gloves, up again to the simple knot Caro had made with her hair. Minnie stood straight, staring right back at her.

"He *is* saving you from a life of drudgery," the duchess concluded. "I can't blame you for letting him do it."

"Who said I'm letting him?" Minnie snapped. "I'd not want to find myself in your shoes. Not for any one of your ridiculously indulgent gowns."

Surprisingly, that brought a smile—one that warmed the other woman's face, making her appear decades younger. "Really? Then you may have an iota of sense." The woman set a beaded reticule on the table. "I know I sound harsh, but he is my only child. Such as we are." She let out a sigh. "I am not entirely unfeeling. I once found myself in your position." Her lips curled up, but there was no smile to the expression, only snarl. "It turns your head, to be courted by a duke. A young, handsome duke. I knew Robert's father had a black reputation, but I was certain I could cure him of all that ailed him. He'd stop gambling and drinking to excess, and if he had me…why, he'd never look at another woman again."

The duchess removed a single glove and folded it before meeting Minnie's eyes.

"I had all my romantic notions beat out of me by the time I was twenty. But it wasn't just the duke who was responsible. It was everyone I encountered. All of high society saw me as nothing more than a purse for the Duke of Clermont. I was told every day for years and years and years, in whispers that were not quite behind my back, that I was not my husband's equal. It didn't matter that he had no sense and no money. I was beneath him, and the fact that I dared to oppose him… Nothing my husband did ever caused a whisper, but my insistence that I be treated with respect? *That* was a scandal. When he visited whores, it was nothing to society. He struck me because I insisted on marital fidelity, but the only thing the *ton* found outrageous in *that* was that I dared to question him." The duchess's voice shook. "At least I had money. What do you think it will be like for you?"

Minnie swallowed. "Robert isn't like that."

The duchess's hands compressed around her solitary glove. "I have read *Pride and Prejudice*. I know precisely what role you're casting me in—the officious Lady Catherine, foolish meddler, who believes that Darcy must marry her miserable daughter." Her lips pinched. "Maybe that is my place. I should sit here and shriek at you, 'Are the shades of Clermont House to be thus polluted?'"

Minnie blinked in surprise, and the woman smiled.

"I did tell you I was once a romantic," she said. "So maybe I am to be Lady Catherine. But I see so much of my foolish, younger self in him—that gallantry, that certainty of love, that hope for the future. I would not wish my life on anyone."

This conversation had not gone as Minnie had first imagined. Instead of enraging her, the duchess's words brought a sort of cold clarity to the situation.

"You must love your son very much," she said.

"No," the other woman said softly. "I suppose I could have, once. But there's only so often a boy can be used as a knife to your heart before you stop feeling anything at all. I hadn't any choice about it, and..." She shrugged. "I haven't the emotion to browbeat you much further, or to beg. I will just ask, as nicely as I can." She looked into Minnie's eyes. "Please don't do this to my son."

The duchess, Minnie concluded, was an odd woman. Extremely odd. She felt a twinge of compassion for her.

"He's a gentler boy than his father was." Her lips pinched. "When he sees how they treat you, he'll be miserable. He never could stand for mistreatment."

"All very well," Minnie said. "If I were a better person, I suppose I would agree and refuse his suit for his own good. But you said it yourself. I have no fortune, no family, no future." She smiled awkwardly. "You've already heard rumors connecting me with your son. How do you suppose my reputation will fare in his absence?"

The duchess's eyes narrowed. "Has he..."

"I'm not ruined," Minnie continued. "And the gossip thus far is only outraged. But even a hint of a dark spot is all I need. Nicety of principle is a luxury for the wealthy. I can't afford it." She shook her head. "I know how utterly disastrous it would be to marry him. More than you could imagine."

The thought of being the duchess—of fielding those whispers, feeling the weight of everyone's stare everywhere she went—made Minnie feel dizzy. But she had the opportunity to provide for herself, for her great-aunts, for good. She shook her head. "I know it would be a disaster. But I have no choice. I must do it."

She looked up to find that the duchess was actually smiling at her. "How refreshing," the other woman said. "Here I thought you would wail and beat your breast amidst protestations of love. But you're singularly unromantic."

Minnie gave a sharp jerk of her head in denial. "I can imagine castles and dukes as much as any woman." But she would never have imagined Robert. He was better than any prince. She could see the gleam in his eye as he told her he wanted the peerage abolished. If it were just the two of them, she might have fallen in love with him. It was a miracle, given her past, that she'd met someone she could come to love—and who seemed to return her regard in some form. Rejecting that felt dangerous. Some gifts might not come around a second time.

And yet proclaiming herself a duke's wife? That was the kind of pride that went before not a mere fall, but a tumble off a steep cliff.

She could see every jagged stone waiting at the bottom.

She was well and truly caught between hope and hubris.

"I could be romantic," she said softly. "But romance is also a luxury I can't afford."

"How ironic." The other woman stared at her. "I actually think you'd be good for him, if only you were someone else entirely."

Minnie laughed and shut her eyes.

The duchess leaned forward. "So let us see how your principles fare when you have a choice. I'll give you five thousand pounds."

Minnie's eyes jerked open. She looked at the woman—she was sure she had to be joking. But the duchess watched her with all seriousness.

"You will," Minnie said, dazedly. Five thousand pounds—it seemed an impossible amount. Enough to live on. Enough to assure her great-aunts' future. Enough to form a reasonable dowry, if that's what she wanted, or for her to move to the continent. It was too much money.

But then she considered the gown the duchess was wearing—all that fabric, yards and yards of lace, the careful stitchery. That gown itself probably cost more than a hundred pounds.

"I'll have to refuse him for it, I suppose."

The duchess shrugged. "I can't pretend that I can offer you enough to compensate you for marrying him. He would probably settle more on you in marriage than a mere five thousand. But... I told you, I know him. He's rather too persistent for a bare refusal." The woman looked off into the distance, as if remembering something. Her lips compressed in distaste. "He tries, and he tries, and he tries again. With Robert, he won't give up until you slap him in the face as hard as you can. Betray him once, and he'll never look your way again."

The duchess had said she didn't love her son. But she was an odd woman—cold and angular one moment, fragile the next. She was a shard of stained glass, casting colors about the room, and yet capable of slicing everything she touched. In one moment, she seemed to care about her son. In the next...

"You can't actually want me to hurt Robert," she said. "You cannot be asking me to do that."

The duchess shrugged. "It would be good for him, I think. He's too romantic as it is. Too trusting." She looked up at Minnie and shrugged without an ounce of apology.

A strange, hard woman. Maybe Robert could be made into a creature like her...

"I don't know that I can do that," Minnie said hoarsely. "Hurt him so badly that he..."

But she was already envisioning how it might be done.

"You seem a capable woman," the duchess said with a frown.

Minnie's own secrets had once been thrown wide to the world. How could she do it to someone else? How could she do it to *him*?

But how could she marry him?

Minnie met her gaze. "I don't know," she repeated, "that I can do that."

After the duchess left, after Minnie fended off Caro and Eliza's well-meaning questions, she went up to her bedroom. The house on the farm was not large; Minnie had a small chamber in the front, just above the ground-floor parlor. From here, she could see the acres of cabbage fields, picked over in preparation for winter, waiting to be plowed under. But her view was mostly occluded by the barn. On cold days, the heat from the cattle would release steam when the doors were opened. Today, only little wisps of white escaped the barn, scarcely visible through the rain that had begun.

The property had once been a hunting box with some attached acreage. Caro and Elizabeth had made it into a farm. They'd pooled what little money they had been between them, had hired men to lay the fields and plow the ground, year after year. Even with all that work, though, the land wasn't truly theirs. Caro had been left the hunting box for her lifetime only. After she passed away, the property would go to some distant cousin.

With five thousand pounds, Minnie might purchase her great-aunts' farm when the time came.

With five thousand pounds, she could do that and go very far away. Wilhelmina Pursling might disappear. She could go where nobody had ever heard of her. Somewhere where she wouldn't have to make herself small to try and please a man. All she would have to do to get that safety was precisely what she'd promised Robert in the first place. She would have to be his enemy.

But the alternative…

She could simply tell the duchess no. For all the woman talked about knowing her son, Minnie didn't believe she had any notion of who he was. Robert wouldn't be happy with some proper peer's daughter. She'd seen the light that came into his eyes when he talked about his plans for the future. If she did this, she couldn't pretend it was for his benefit.

It was for hers. Because she would rather betray a man she could come to love than face the crowd again.

She could see her pale reflection in the window glass, superimposed on the farm. She looked herself over—those too-pale cheeks, the scar on her face. Eyes that shifted around, refusing to fix on any one spot. She held up her hand and watched it tremble.

"You're only considering this because you're scared," she told herself.

But that wasn't quite true. It was because she was terrified.

Chapter Seventeen

DUSK CAME, BUT MINNIE HAD NOT YET COME TO A DECISION. She was pacing in her room when she heard a pounding on the door below. There was the noise of scuffling and then a shriek from the entry beneath her feet.

"Minnie! Minnie!" Lydia's voice.

Minnie rushed to her door. A storm had come on since the duchess's visit and rain beat against the windows in sheets.

Minnie didn't stop to put on slippers. She simply threw her bedroom door open and darted toward the stairs. Her friend stood in the entry, dripping water in a puddle. Her hair had fallen from its half-curls to lie in a sodden black mess at her shoulders. Her skirts and petticoats were bedraggled.

"Minnie," she said again, before Minnie could descend the stairs to her. "Stevens is back, and you would not believe what he is saying to Papa. He's saying—"

Minnie held a finger to her lips. "Shh." She tilted her head to where the maid stood, watching in confusion. *Don't say anything. They might gossip.*

"He's saying," Lydia said in hushed tones, coming up the staircase, "that *you're* the author of those handbills."

Minnie's heart pounded in her chest. "Is he? Has he any proof?"

"He's saying that you are a liar and a cheat—that he has proof that your mother never married, not ever, that you're a child of sin. He's saying your real name is Minerva Lane—"

Minnie set her hand over Lydia's mouth. "Shh," she repeated softly. "I know what he's saying. No need to repeat it. Who does he think Minerva Lane is?"

Lydia frowned at the question. "Just—just some other woman. Stevens thought it was the name you were given to hide the truth of your illegitimacy."

So. Stevens had discovered her real name—she *had* lived in Manchester when she was a tiny child, and someone must have remembered the connection. But he hadn't traced her family history, or figured out why she'd taken on a new name. If he'd been looking in Manchester, he might well have missed the reason. After all, the scandal had broken in London.

"You have to come sort it all out. Stevens is talking about a warrant for your arrest."

"For my arrest?" Minnie gasped.

"For criminal sedition. Papa has known you all these years. I don't know how it could have happened, how he could think anything so impossible. I heard it all through the door. Minnie, you must come. Maybe if you send for the duke…"

Thunder rattled the windows, so loud that Minnie flinched.

"No," she said swiftly. "Not him. Not him. He can't save me."

Stevens might not know why Minerva Lane had changed her name, but he would soon. Once that name was uttered in public, there would be no hiding her past. If Minnie married Robert, exposure would not just be a possibility. It would be a certainty. She would never be able to escape this noose around her neck. She could feel it tightening about her now.

Another clap of thunder came, long and low, vibrating through the air. Her hands trembled with it, and in the end, fear made the decision for her. She had a heartbeat to choose between ruin and betrayal, between the possibility of love and the certainty of defeat. And when it came down to it, love had served her poorly before.

"We have to leave now," Lydia insisted. "I know you can put things right. You always do."

Minnie knew what she had to do. She could see it already, a nightmare vision stripped of color.

"Have a horse saddled," Minnie said to the housemaid, who still waited in the entry below.

There was only one path out of this mess, and it was going to break Minnie's heart.

"Come, come." Lydia tugged on her sleeve.

"Dry off a little." Not that it would do any good, what with them venturing out again. "I need…five minutes. Five minutes to gather some papers." Five minutes to slay two birds with one single betrayal.

She walked into her room in a daze. Slowly, she pulled out the stash of papers she'd built up. Evidence, painstakingly collected. Including the letter he'd written her.

Minnie looked straight ahead. Her heart thumped heavily, but she bundled it all up without trembling.

⌘　⌘　⌘

IT TOOK NEARLY THREE-QUARTERS OF AN HOUR for Minnie to make her way to the Charingfords' house in the storm. By the time she arrived, Minnie's skirts were dripping and her hair was no doubt a tangled, sodden mess. But there was no time to waste with anything so frivolous as drying. As soon as Lydia escorted her inside, she threw the parlor doors open and walked inside.

"Miss Pursling!" Mr. Charingford exclaimed, jumping to his feet.

Stevens slowly stood, folding his arms in disapproval. His eyes slid over Minnie, fell on Lydia behind her, and then shifted away. "Miss Charingford," he said icily. His gaze shifted back to Minnie.

"Tell them," Lydia said behind her. "Tell them the truth."

Stevens shifted to look at Minnie. "You, I presume, are Miss Minerva Lane."

She had known it was coming. Her stomach lurched, even so, at hearing her old name spoken aloud, seeing the look in Stevens's eyes. Lights flashed in front of her vision.

It is nothing. You are nothing. It can't touch you here.

"Correct," Minnie said.

Behind her, Lydia let out a gasp. But Minnie couldn't look back. She couldn't bear to see her friend's face now.

"So, you're a bastard. What else have you been hiding?"

Minnie held up a hand. "I am a great many things," she said quietly. "But there is one accusation that will not hold. I am not, nor have I ever been, a writer of seditious handbills."

"Lies," Stevens growled.

Minnie met Mr. Charingford's eyes. "I have never been involved—and all the proof points to another man."

Stevens shook a finger at her. "More lies."

But Mr. Charingford stepped forward. "Are you sure?" he asked. "Because, Minnie, as little as I would like to think of you in this way, I know what you can do."

He didn't look at his daughter as he spoke, but Minnie knew he was thinking of that long-ago afternoon when she'd explained what needed to be done to safeguard Lydia's reputation.

She ignored him. "I shall prove it."

All her emotions seemed distant—a light stuffed away under a metal hood, shining brightly where nobody could see it. She was dark and calm. She was nothing inside.

"Who do you claim is responsible?" Charingford asked. "Grantham? Peters?"

She opened the fabric sack at her side. She'd wrapped the contents first in waxed paper, then in oilcloth; they were only a little damp when she pulled them out.

"These," she said, separating out the first sheaf of pages, "are the papers that our dear friend *De minimis* has produced thus far. The following can be observed under a jeweler's lens. First, the type that produced these has an *e* with a defect: it has a hairline crack. Right here." Facts. That was all she was: a collection of facts, and no more. She pointed, and then flipped a page. "And on this one. And this next one here. It's quite distinctive."

She spread another sheaf of papers in front of her. "These are the sort of papers that can be purchased in large quantity here in Leicester."

Stevens started forward.

Minnie held up a hand. "They are all made locally. You'll note that I've marked their origin in the corner; even if you do not trust me, you can ascertain the truth of what I'm saying with a morning's inquiry. Use that same jeweler's lens on this paper, and you'll discover something that will hardly seem surprising. All the paper that is made in Leicester takes advantage of local materials. The three mills here all incorporate waste products from the textile industry into their papers: rags, bits of cotton, wool. Paper from Leicester, when closely examined, has characteristic threads of fibers throughout, no matter what the grade. This—" she tapped Robert's handbills "—this has none."

"What are you trying to say?"

She ignored Stevens. She was an encyclopedia, a dictionary, telling truths and nothing more.

"Here are samples of printing from the local presses. I have cataloged the defects in the type personally; once again, I assure you that a little time spent on your part would verify this assertion. You will note that there are no hairline fractures in any *e* that is the size shown in the handbill."

"Come to the point, *Miss Lane*." Stevens sneered. "We already knew that whoever was producing the handbill was not acting alone. This only tells me that you had help from abroad. A national organization, perhaps?"

She wouldn't let him fluster her. Mr. Charingford was watching her more closely. Deliberately, she picked up another few pieces of paper. "Now, this paper was purchased in London. You'll note that I have paper of several different grades in this pile. This one—" she plucked the piece from the bottom "—this one here, you'll discover is a precise match in content for the paper on which the handbills are printed. Do keep the rest of the paper in mind, however. Who do you suppose the manufacturer is?"

"I'm in no mood to play guessing games. You've already said it's from London."

"It's from Graydon Mills. Do you know anything about Graydon Mills?"

"I tell you, *Miss Lane,* if you do not come to a conclusion—"

"Let her finish," Charingford growled.

Minnie nodded. "Graydon Mills was founded sixty-seven years ago by a Mr. Hansworth Graydon, a farmer who made his first fortune in sheep, and his second, third, and fourth fortunes in manufacturing. He owned quite an empire. His wealth was so extensive that he was able to marry his daughter well. When Mr. Hansworth Graydon died, he left the bulk of his properties to his grandson. You know him as Robert Alan Graydon Blaisdell, the ninth Duke of Clermont."

This was met with silence, then a snort of derision.

"You have to be mad," Stevens sneered. "You think to escape your rightful punishment by exploiting so far-fetched a coincidence?"

Mr. Charingford said nothing, just motioned for Minnie to continue.

"His Grace uses paper from Graydon Mills for all his personal correspondence as well," Minnie said. "A premium grade, to be sure."

"I don't care if he does!" Stevens's face was turning red. "I've heard enough innuendo. Charingford, if you will—"

Slowly, Minnie drew out the letter he'd handed her on the train.

"This," she said, "is personal correspondence from His Grace." Her voice was trembling now. Her hands were, too. She smoothed the paper against the table and gripped the edge. "I will point out that he uses the highest quality of Graydon Mills paper that there is—there's the watermark. His signature, too, can be authenticated." She pointed. "But I rather think you will find the contents more interesting than the source."

Stevens snatched the paper from her hand.

"Don't know what I'm doing…" he muttered, reading. And then he stopped and looked up at her.

"I write handbills," he read slowly. He read it again, and then a third time, his eyes moving more slowly across the paper with each successive reading. Over his shoulder, Charingford perused the words with a growing frown. He moved away, shaking his head.

"I don't believe this," Stevens said. But his words were not the words of a man who doubted the letter. They were an attempt to deny reality.

"Minnie," Charingford said, "this letter…the tone of it is intimate. The salutation. The words he uses. Even the way the letter is signed. How is it that you came to be in possession of this letter?"

Robert might possibly have forgiven Minnie for revealing the truth under the circumstances. The duchess had said that she'd needed to betray him, to earn his scorn.

If she had been playing a game, this was the moment when she would have kissed her chess piece. Once she made this move, there would be no going back.

Minnie lifted one eyebrow. "The Duchess of Clermont approached me," she said, quite distinctly. "She wants her son to give up his ideals. She offered me five thousand pounds if I could stop him."

The truth. Not the full truth, and said as it was, it conveyed an impression that was entirely false. Her hands were shaking.

"Tell him that I said that," she said, her voice surprisingly steady. "Show him, and he won't deny his involvement."

There was no longer any turning back. If she'd read the relationship correctly, telling the duke she had been in league with his mother would end any esteem he had for her.

But then, the moment Stevens had connected her with the name Minerva Lane, all chance at a happy marriage with the duke had ended.

"He's a duke," Stevens said dully. "How could a *duke* do this?"

"Ask him." She dropped her head. "I wouldn't know what a duke does or why he does it."

"And how am I to bring him to account, even if he did?" Stevens was still staring at the paper. "He's riled the town near to boiling with his handbills and his assertions. Next you know, you'll have workers marching, refusing to come to work. How am I to keep peace if the citizens of the town think the law can be broken with impunity?"

Minnie reached for the letter—but Stevens yanked it away from her. He shuffled angrily through the papers, looking at them.

"Someone," he said. "Someone must pay."

She had paid once, and she would pay again. But for now... Now, she'd earned her money. She'd have enough to leave, enough to escape Minerva Lane for good. So why did she feel like weeping?

"Get out," Stevens said. "Just—get out. I'll deal with you later."

Minnie slowly left the room.

Lydia had waited, pressed against the wall the entire time. But as Minnie went by, she followed her out into the front room.

"Lydia." Minnie's voice was shaking.

"What was that?" Lydia asked. "It couldn't have been the truth. The Duchess of Clermont paying you? Minnie, she only arrived in town a few days ago, and this thing with the duke has been going on much longer than that. Telling them your name is really Minerva Lane? If you were really named Minerva Lane, you would have told me. I know you would have."

Minnie flinched. "Lydia."

"You *would* have told me," Lydia repeated. "You are like a sister to me. You can't be anyone else."

"My name really is Minerva Lane." She dropped her eyes. Somehow, this story should have been easier on the second retelling, but it was even harder with her friend's eyes on her.

"No." Lydia shook her head more fiercely. "It can't be. You would have told me."

"In a way, Minerva Lane never existed," Minnie said. "When I was very young, my father dressed me as a boy and brought me around Europe, showing me off. He called me Maximilian. The truth came out." She swallowed. "I was ruined. You can only imagine how I was ruined. I changed my name to escape his legacy."

"But…" Lydia was shaking her head. "But how could that be true? If it were true, *you would have told me.*" She was becoming more vehement with every repetition of the phrase.

"No," Minnie said. "I wouldn't have."

Lydia drew up her chin. "You knew everything—absolutely *everything* about me. How could you not tell me?"

Lydia's ragged breath, her clenched fists, felt worse even than that moment when the crowd had surrounded her, when they'd gathered around her…

"Lydia. I couldn't. If I told you—"

"I wouldn't have said anything. Not ever."

Minnie's scar felt tight. Her whole head burned. Her stomach churned. "I can barely bring myself to speak of it. When I do, my whole body starts to shake. I stop being able to breathe. I couldn't have you looking at me while I said it. I couldn't."

"God forbid," Lydia said, "that you should have showed me a weakness. Why, I might have thought you a mere mortal."

Minnie closed her eyes. "I still love you. Lydia?"

"How can you?" Lydia said coldly. "The person who was my friend— she wasn't even real. She was a construct."

"No. It was…it was real." But her voice was quiet now, so hard to marshal, and Lydia wasn't even looking at her.

"Get out," Lydia said. "I can't even look at you right now. Get out."

Minnie stumbled to the door. It was still raining hard, and the rumble of thunder sounded like the stomp of feet, the roar of a crowd. Lightning flashed, searing across her vision.

"Here," Lydia said, shoving an umbrella into her hand. "Take this. No, you ninny, I don't care what happens to you. I just want you out of my sight. Go!"

Minnie wasn't sure how she staggered down the steps to the pavement. She could scarcely even see through her tears. When she opened her eyes, she saw three men across the way. They looked at her curiously. Perhaps it was not every day they saw a woman stumble out of a house. Just three, but it was enough.

It's nothing. It's nothing. You're nothing.

But she wasn't nothing, and she couldn't pretend that the events of today had happened to anyone but her. She bent over double and was noisily, violently ill on the pavement.

When her stomach settled, she stood. She was still shaking, but it felt as if that wave of nausea had carried everything away. Not just the physical shakes, but her fear, her timidity, twelve years of lies. Everything that had made her Wilhelmina Pursling, the shy, retiring wallflower who stuck to the corners, had been washed away.

She glanced at the Charingfords' house over her shoulder. Wilhelmina Pursling was gone, and with her had gone a decade of friendship.

Bravo, Minnie. Bravo.

Sighing, she opened the umbrella and started toward the mews where she'd left her horse.

Chapter Eighteen

IT WAS ODD, ROBERT THOUGHT, THAT HIS OUTLOOK could change so completely in twenty-four hours. Two days ago, he'd made an offer of marriage. He'd been full of hope and desire and longing. And today...

"So, you see, Your Grace, we are at an impasse."

Robert was seated in his parlor. Captain Stevens stood before him, a sheaf of papers laid out on his table.

"I cannot announce that it is *you* who authored the handbills," Stevens said. "To give such sentiments the imprimatur of a duke would leave the rabble with no reason to hold back at all."

Robert could scarcely listen. His mind was still fixed on that letter. It was a good thing he'd been sitting when Stevens had brought it out and told him that his own mother had paid Minnie to obtain it, or he might actually have stumbled.

She could have just said no.

"You, yourself, will likely face no consequences." Stevens frowned. "But if I detect your *sincerity* correctly... For every handbill that you author, I will have one suspect arrested and imprisoned."

"Without proof? Knowing that they are not involved?" Robert's voice was quiet.

"It's all of a piece," Stevens said. "Someone must pay. If nobody does, we all will. I cannot—the *law* cannot—be flouted in this manner."

Even through the roaring in Robert's ears, he recognized what Stevens was doing—threatening him by threatening others. He'd known that someone was behind the convictions for criminal sedition—convictions that should never have happened. He'd wanted to draw out whoever it was that had perverted the law.

At least he'd succeeded in that. He made a mental note to have Stevens removed from office. Just as soon as he had a chance to gather his wits.

"I see," Robert said. "Well, thank you for your time."

"But—"

Robert was already standing, leaving the room without so much as a glance back.

He paced in his library, waiting for his emotions to catch up with him.

But in the end, what triumphed was a surprising sense of calm—as if he'd been through a sandstorm, and it had scoured away the excess, unreliable flesh of his emotion, leaving only his bones behind. Bones didn't yearn. Bones didn't wish. Thank God for that.

He didn't feel the slightest bit of anger as he asked his staff to have a horse readied for him. The road to her great-aunts' farm was long, but he didn't feel a sense of annoyance at the minutes ticking by. He didn't feel anything at all.

He didn't feel anything when he threw his reins over a hitching post. Not one twitch from his chest as he knocked on the door. It seemed as if he were wrapped in muffling cotton, as if the entire world had gone mute around him. The door opened soundlessly, and he could scarcely hear himself request to see her.

The drawing room where he was shown might have been devoid of all furniture, for all that he noticed it. He didn't sit. He didn't look. He only waited, knowing what might come.

She opened the door.

Perhaps, deep down, he'd feared that when he saw Minnie once more, he'd be so overcome by his feelings that he would forgive what she had done. He'd built up an image of her, expanding on things she hadn't said, words she'd never spoken, until he'd imagined himself enamored of a woman who didn't exist. But when she walked in, he didn't feel anything.

She was small, and she drew in on herself. All the magic had gone from her. He felt nothing but a dull ache where she had once been.

He was safe, thank God. Safe from himself.

"Your Grace," she said simply.

He inclined his head to her.

It was the first time in all of their acquaintance where she had treated him like a duke. It was the first time that he'd wanted to be treated as one. Dukes didn't need to explain. They didn't need to beg. They just *did,* and nobody ever questioned their actions.

"You must know why I'm here," he said.

She bowed her head. Distantly, he noticed that she looked miserable. There were dark circles under her eyes. And that light he'd seen in them— that beautiful light that had seemed to fill the room—was utterly extinguished.

He didn't care. He didn't care about anything any longer.

"Your Grace. I owe you an explanation."

"I don't want an explanation." Ice didn't listen.

"But—"

"I don't care why you did it," he said. His words seemed to ring out with a hollow, staccato sound. "I don't care how much my mother paid you. I don't care about you at all."

She flinched. "Then let me assure you—"

"I have even less wish for your assurances." Not, he realized, that she'd ever given him any. He'd been the only one providing them. He'd fooled himself into thinking that if only she knew him, if only he could explain to her, that she might…what?

That she might care about him, too. Just a little. She'd known who he was, what he wanted. He'd told her his dreams, his secret wishes. He'd offered her everything.

And he hadn't been enough.

His own delusion, once again. His own foolish daydream, built up around someone who scarcely noticed him.

The difference was that this time, he wasn't going to be the one watching someone else walk away. He wouldn't be the one waiting hopelessly for letters that never arrived.

He made himself breathe evenly, until that sense of benumbed calm returned. Swathed in cotton? No, cotton was too light to hold the entirety of him. He was buried in sand, each grain a weight pressing against his chest, so heavy that all other sensation was blocked. He didn't feel anything at all, and he liked it.

She must have seen something of what he didn't feel flit across his face, because she bowed her head. "I'm so sorry, Your Grace."

"I don't want an apology," he snapped.

"Then why are you here?"

"Simple," he said. He wished that he'd been sitting down, only so that he might stand at this moment. "I'm here to say good-bye." He strode to the door and then turned. She was gaping at him. "And now I've said it."

And on those words, he strode out.

It seemed to take ages to traverse the hall back to the entry and another age to get his hat and cloak. He could hear his heart racing in his chest.

This time, Minnie would run after him. She would throw herself at his feet and beg for clemency, and he—why, he would take great satisfaction in not even glancing down. He would brush her off his shoes like so much dust.

He wouldn't forgive her. To forgive her, he would have to care, and to care, he would have to let himself feel.

But she didn't come, and so he never had to decide what to do.

⌘ ⌘ ⌘

BREAKFAST WITH HIS MOTHER the next morning suited Robert's dark mood all too well. The clink of her teaspoon as she stirred in sugar interrupted a silence that seemed weighted down by a hundred conversations they'd never had. Today, he was in a mood to be irritated.

The duchess set her cup down with the finality of a builder slapping bricks in mortar, finally, and looked at him.

"I suppose," she said, tilting her chin in the air, "that you agreed to see me because you're angry about what I did."

He simply folded his arms and looked at her.

"I didn't tell her what to do, mind," she said. "That, your Miss Pursling decided on her own. But yes, I admit it freely. I *did* pay Miss Pursling five thousand pounds to refuse your offer in as ungracious a manner as she could."

His mind blanked. It took every ounce of will that he had to keep his arms folded, to keep staring at her. But this time, his silence didn't produce any comment. She simply took another sip of tea, leaving him to make sense of the confusion he felt.

"You paid her to refuse me," he said.

She nodded.

Stevens had said—he had said most distinctly—that Miss Pursling had been paid to find out his secrets. He'd thought she intended to entrap him. He'd thought that the attraction had been all on his side. He'd remembered, with chagrin, the way she'd pretended to be withdrawn and shy, and wondered how it was that he hadn't noticed this element of untrustworthiness.

"Why, Mother," he finally drawled. "I didn't know you cared."

For all the sarcastic cast of his words, there was a good deal of truth to them. She'd never done anything that could be termed remotely motherly. Interfering in his marital prospects was almost as good as a kiss on the cheek from her. It was…touching. Infuriating, too. Wrong. High-handed. But…touching.

She sniffed and looked away. "It was just money. Don't make anything of it."

"On the contrary. I am excessively grateful. If she can be bought off so cheaply, it's best that I know it now."

She watched him for a few moments, as if she didn't believe that he could be so calm, so unruffled.

"I told her," his mother said, "that if her betrayal was bad enough, you'd never think of her again. It turns out I was right."

She seemed to take no joy in her victory. She didn't smile. There was no hint of gloating in her voice.

"You are too forgiving," she said, "until you don't forgive at all. So tell me. At what point did you finally give up on me?"

He sucked in his breath. "What an odious assumption. I never had any hope of you." He couldn't look at her as he spoke, though. She'd had too many letters from him to believe that.

"It was your father's funeral, wasn't it?"

He did not even allow himself to blink.

"You wrote me beforehand, asking me to come. Now that he was gone, you said—"

He slammed his fist on the table. Tea splashed everywhere. "Asked you to come?" Now he looked at her, glaring. She didn't shrink back from him. She didn't glower in return. She simply looked at him calmly, as unruffled as she always was. She might have been a china doll for all the response in her eyes.

"I didn't ask you to come," he said quietly. "I begged. Did you know, I honestly believed that you would take me back with you? I had convinced myself that the only reason you put off knowing me better was that you could not abide my father's presence. That once he was gone, we might have a chance. When you weren't at the service, I told myself you would come after it was finished. When you didn't come then, I convinced myself that you'd wait until everyone else had departed. Finally, I said that once it was dark and nobody would know, you'd come and get me. Until that day, I believed—I don't know how, as I had no evidence of it—that it was only my father that kept us apart. But it wasn't that. You didn't care."

"No," she said softly. "I didn't."

"Did you ever? Or do you hate me as much as you hated him?"

"As much?" She frowned. "I would say that I hated you in a different way."

He wished he could find that imperturbable calm he'd had just a few moments ago. Even though he'd known it had to be true—even though he'd suspected that his mother disliked him—to hear it spoken out loud made it real. Even after all these years, after all that time he'd spent making himself indifferent to her, it still cut.

"Those first months," she said, "when your father took you from me—I thought I'd never breathe again. But I could not let him know how important you were. If I had, God knows what he might have threatened you with. So I woke every morning and dressed and went in company. I laughed when things were funny and expressed sympathy when they were not, all the while feeling as if a cavern had been made of my chest."

She didn't look as if she'd ever had anything inside her chest, so smoothly did she speak.

"By the time you were three, you were a trap for my heart. Every word that came to me of you, every short visit your father grudgingly allowed, was like a wall closing in around me. The more adorable you became, the more certain your father was of my return—and the more he'd threaten me. I had to pretend not to care. After a while, I became so good at pretending that…that perhaps I stopped caring in truth. And yes, I resented you every time you made me feel anything." She shrugged, nonchalantly. "But what was I to do? Stay with him? I tried it. But by that time, he was impossible. After that last time, when you were nine… I spent an evening barricaded in my room, with him bellowing and pounding on the door, threatening to…" She gave him another sidelong look. "I believe if he had not been quite so drunk, matters would have become exceedingly ugly. I couldn't stay. And legally, you were his. What was I to do, except stop caring?"

Robert shook his head. "Every time you left, he used to tell me it was my fault. That I had failed to captivate you. That I should have been more—"

More lovable, although his father had never used that word.

She looked at him. "When your father died, I assumed he'd made you over in his image. By the time I realized it wasn't so…" She shrugged again. "By then, it was too late to salvage anything of mother and child. Luckily, by then, I didn't care. I didn't feel anything at all. So now, knowing I'm far too late to do anything, now…"

She looked up at him.

"Now," she said, "I find I still don't care." Her eyes glistened momentarily, and she looked away, her jaw squaring as she clamped her lips together.

"I see," he said in puzzlement.

"I really don't care. I can't. I don't know how anymore." So saying, she took out a lace-edged handkerchief and dabbed at her eyes.

"Are you…"

"No. I never cry." She met his eyes fiercely.

"I see," he repeated.

And he actually thought that he did. This trip—her visit out here, her ham-handed pronunciations, her foolish interference—maybe she didn't care. Maybe, after all these years, she'd forgotten how to care about him.

But she was trying to. She made him think of a foal just-born, struggling up onto spindly legs, attempting to stand and falling down flat.

She sniffed again. "By the time I figure it out," she said, "you'll have given up on me entirely. It seems a fitting punishment."

She set down her handkerchief and glared at him, daring him to contradict her.

Once, when he was young, she'd come for a visit. He'd run out to meet her at the carriage. He didn't know how old he had been at the time, but he remembered hugging her knees, as high as he could reach.

She hadn't touched him back, hadn't even bent to pat his head. She'd simply glanced at him, told him to show some decorum, and kept walking.

So he didn't move to touch her now. He didn't think she would like it, and he felt too raw to risk a rebuff.

"Well, then," he said briskly. "Thank you for taking time from your indifference to meddle in my marriage prospects. I thought she was made of sterner stuff. Apparently."

"Oh, no," the duchess said. "I approve of her. Find another girl just like her, but a marquess's daughter this time."

"You know," he said, "I have no idea who her people really are. Pursling isn't even her real name."

"No?"

"She was born Minerva Lane."

At that, his mother gasped aloud. "Minerva *Lane?*"

"You know who she is?" He looked at her in surprise. "She told me it would be a scandal."

"Scandal? Her? No." She shook her head violently. "*Scandal* is what happens when girls are too easy with their favors—a simple matter to overcome, one that can be papered over, if not forgotten, by a good marriage and enough money. Miss Lane wasn't ruined, Robert. She was destroyed. Utterly destroyed."

Chapter Nineteen

Minnie hadn't been able to speak to her great-aunts on the prior evening.

But there was no putting off the conversation when the Duchess of Clermont sent over a draught from her bank. She brought them into the front room and sat them down.

"There is something you both should know," she said. "Yesterday, when Lydia came to get me, it was because Stevens had gone to Manchester. He knows that there is no Miss Wilhelmina Pursling. That I'm an imposter. He knows I was born Minerva Lane."

The two women gasped and then looked at each other. "Do they know what—"

Minnie shook her head. "They don't know everything."

"Don't scare me like that," Caro said, putting her hand over her heart. "But what are we to do? With Gardley gone..."

Minnie looked away. "As it turns out, I've come into some money. Five thousand pounds."

Her great-aunts stared at her. The women looked so different, and yet the shocked expressions on their faces were mirrors for each other.

"Dear," Eliza finally said. "We know that this is a difficult time. But five thousand pounds is a great deal of money, and we would hate it if, ah, if..."

They really thought she might have come into it by unsavory means. If they thought that, they might wonder...

"No," Minnie said bitterly. "I *earned* this, fair and square." Well, maybe it hadn't been fair. And maybe it hadn't been precisely square. Still, she'd earned it legally. Legally and...rectangularly. That would have to do.

"How?"

"I had an offer of marriage. His mother didn't want me to accept." Minnie looked away. "I didn't." Two words, and still they broke her heart.

But she'd long since given up any desire to wish that things were different. Wishes were stupid, foolish things.

"An offer of marriage?" Caro echoed. "But from whom? I cannot imagine—" She cut herself off as the downstairs maid entered.

"Miss," she said, nodding to Minnie. "Misses. There's someone here to speak with Miss Pursling."

"Who is it?" Eliza asked.

Lydia. Lydia had come. Minnie would be able to explain everything, make everything right—

But the maid ducked her head, suddenly self-conscious, and Minnie knew with a sense of great foreboding who it was.

"His Grace," she said, "the Duke of Clermont."

Her stomach turned to ice, but her hands seemed too warm. She didn't know whether to laugh or cry, whether to run into his arms or to clamber out the window to escape. She simply stared ahead of her, the draught for five thousand pounds folded in her pocket in silent accusation.

"Oh," Eliza said.

"I had heard rumors." Caro rubbed her head. "But it sounded so improbable. You would have told us if there was anything to it. Wouldn't you have?"

Minnie couldn't make herself meet their eyes.

"I—maybe we should discuss this later. Later."

Caro nodded. Eliza came to her feet, leaning heavily on the cane she used indoors. "Minnie," she said softly. "If you don't want to marry him, you don't have to. We'll never force you to do it. No matter what has happened—what you've said, what you've done. No matter what you choose. We love you."

When he was shown in a few moments later, Minnie was fighting tears. She couldn't even turn to look at him. She could only mark the sound of his boots against the floor, coming close, stopping a few feet behind her.

He stood, perhaps waiting for her to acknowledge him. But she couldn't. If she turned around now...

"I thought of climbing up to your window," he said, his voice grave, "but I'd have to take off my boots to attempt brick, and besides, the window I thought was yours looked suspiciously narrow. Now I know why Juliet had a balcony. So I decided on the remarkably unromantic route—I knocked on the front door."

She let out a shuddering laugh. "Romeo was also sixteen." She took another deep breath, schooled her face to calmness, and then turned around. "I thought you'd said your farewells already. What are you doing here?"

In answer, he reached for her hand. While her back had been turned, he'd removed his gloves and laid them on the table. She should have pulled away, but she was still too raw to resist. His fingers entwined with hers. His hands were soft and strong against hers.

"All right," he said. "I'm just going to come out with this. I ruined everything."

"You ruined everything," Minnie repeated. "*You* ruined everything." She stared at him, wondering if he'd somehow lost his mind overnight. He nodded in response to that, though, and she gestured to a seat. Her head was spinning.

"You told me," he said, sitting down, "that you couldn't be a duchess. I waved off your concerns."

She blinked and then sat in a chair opposite him.

"It didn't start coming together until my mother told me that she'd paid you to refuse me, not to expose me. And that didn't make sense either, once I thought about it. My income is a minimum of ten thousand pounds a year—something everyone knows. Given a choice between five thousand pounds and marriage to me, any rational person would choose me. If you were as coldly calculating as I thought, we'd be married, not glaring at each other across two feet of space."

She shook her head.

"Besides, if my mother had paid you to stop me, you would have used my letter right away. You wouldn't have waited. And how would she have even known what I was doing? That you were the one person who might find out about it? The story doesn't hold together, Minnie." He glanced over at her. "I have never been so thankful to realize that I have been lied to."

Her throat hurt. All that effort to try to push him away—and still he wouldn't go.

"I didn't listen to what you were telling me." He looked at her. "I didn't listen to what you *weren't* telling me. Everything I heard was all about me. I heard that you didn't want me. That you couldn't care for me. I heard that you were anxious about attention, but I didn't listen." He steepled his fingers. "So let me tell you what I should have heard. Your father was one of the world's foremost chess—"

Minnie jumped out of her seat. "You *know*." Her heart was pounding in great, unforgiving thumps. Her breath came in ever-smaller gasps of air. The air around her seemed to shimmer. But of course he knew. She'd told him her name. Everything beyond that was a matter of research. She took one wild step backward and tripped on her chair.

But before she could fall in a bruising heap against the bookcase, Robert stepped forward and caught her. His arms were solid and warm about her. "Shh," he breathed. "It's just me. I'm not going to hurt you. I'm never going to hurt you, Minnie."

She looked up into his eyes. Her pulse was racing, but there was no crowd nearby, no shouting.

It was just him.

This time, when he sat, he pulled her on top of him. They fit against one another like two pieces of a puzzle, her head falling automatically to his shoulder, his hand going to her hair. She shouldn't be leaning against him. This shouldn't be happening. It had broken her heart to push him away once; how could she do it again?

"Let's try this again," he said softly, clasping his hands around her. "I've found out only the bare details. Your father was one of the world's foremost chess players. What happened then?"

Minnie's stomach was still fluttering. But his arms were around her—and he knew. He knew, and he wasn't throwing things at her. He waited patiently for her to be ready.

Safe was the last thing she felt when she had to think of those dark times—but at least for the moment, she didn't feel like vomiting.

She took a deep breath. "My father was actually a baronet's fifth son. High standing—although not by your standards—but utterly impoverished. He made his way in the world by trading on his skill at chess. He was gregarious, open, and everyone liked him. His personal fortune was almost nonexistent, but he was so likable that it never mattered. He always had an invitation to stay somewhere."

Sometimes they had been invitations in England, other times offers to visit Europe, to spend months with men who wanted to study chess with a bright, taking young man. Once, on one of those sea voyages she'd taken with him, a sailor had told her to look at the coast when she felt seasick, and the nausea would go away. Now, she watched the bookcase and was surprised to find that her world steadied.

"My parents were married only a few years before my mother died in childbirth. I don't remember much before the age of five, except for my father's visits. My first memories are of him teaching me to play chess. I knew how pieces moved before I knew the alphabet. I looked forward to his visits above all else. And one day, when I was very, very young, he asked me if I wanted to go with him the next time he went abroad."

Minnie let out a shaky breath. Robert didn't say anything. He just pulled her closer.

"Of course, a young girl couldn't travel the Continent with only her father—not and stay with the sorts of people we were staying with. I would have needed a nurse, a governess, and by that time finances were too tight to allow such a thing. It was a very simple thing, my father said. He would introduce me as Maximilian Lane, his son. He asked me if I would mind." She shut her eyes. "I was five. I didn't know what to think. He said it would be great fun, and I agreed."

The fluttering in her belly had begun to calm.

"I don't think I understood, in those early years, what a curiosity I was. I remember people posing me chess problems. Sometimes I solved them. Sometimes I didn't." She shrugged. "As I grew older, I solved more of them."

"The one account I read of Maximilian Lane," Robert put in, "said he was quiet and solemn and quite, quite brilliant. You'd play with adults who had years of experience and beat them handily—and then, when they praised you for it, you'd put the board back fifteen moves and explain, just as earnestly, what they should have done to win."

"Yes," Minnie breathed, shutting her eyes. "I remember that. Winning all the time—it had the most extraordinary effect on me. I thought I would always win. I didn't understand the concept of risk."

She hadn't understood the concept of loss, either.

"The rest, I've had to guess at after the fact. By the time I was twelve, my father was deeply in debt. He made promises to people, claimed that he had made fabulous investments in Russian industry. To bolster those claims and attract further investors, he paid out results from his own limited funds. Then he paid the next round of investors with funds gleaned from his newest dupes. But there were no investments, and unless he found some money quickly, he would have been found out."

Minnie looked down. She'd only known back then that he became more erratic—wildly happy one moment, enraged the next.

"I wasn't invited to the first international chess tournament in London. My father was. A few days before, however, he claimed to have taken suddenly ill and offered me up to take his place. Nobody objected."

She couldn't help it. Little tremors were going through her body.

"He needed a great deal of money, and the odds were favoring me. So he had one of his friends bet every penny he owned against me. Then he ordered me to throw the game."

He hadn't told her why. They'd shouted at one another that day.

"Lanes can do anything," she'd thrown in his face. He'd looked at her so strangely when she'd said that. It wasn't until later that Minnie realized that he had never expected her to use his own words to defy him.

Robert's arms were warm against her ribs, his chest moving in time with her breath. The silence of the room enfolded them. There was nothing around, nobody near. Just her and the memories.

"As a child, there's a curious blindness you have to the faults of your parents. My father was my dearest friend. We were always together. He taught me everything I knew. He'd never had a harsh word for me. I absolutely *worshipped* him. He used to say that if we only believed hard enough, everything would turn out all right. That if you'd just think and wait, you'd find a way. When I refused to throw the game, he found his way." She took another deep breath. "He told the scandal sheets that I was a girl. In the middle of the tournament."

She could still see the board in the final round. She'd just kissed her rook and set it on the board. She had been four moves from mate.

"The officials interrupted me. They disqualified me. They tossed me out on my ear, and it was all over the London papers the next few days. Everything I had been, *everything*—all the people who I thought were my friends, all the things that I'd accomplished—were wiped away. I had masqueraded as a boy, and I'd scandalized everyone."

"Amazing it lasted as long as it did," he said.

"I was twelve. Had it been one more year… Then I would have grown my bosom, and there would have been no hiding the truth at all." She shook her head. "I don't know what would have happened in the ordinary course of events. But now that the truth had come out, people began to ask questions of my father. There were thousands of pounds at stake in his business, and his stories didn't stand up to inquiry. His trial was a very public affair. I attended—twelve years old, wearing skirts for the first time in years, awkward and uncertain. It was there I first heard my father's defense. He claimed he was driven to do it. By me. He said that *I* told him to dress me as a boy and take me with him. I came up with the scheme involving faked Russian industry. I caused his ruin. I did it all."

Robert put his arm around her. "You were *five* when it started."

"I was an unnatural child. That's what he said—over and over. I was an unnatural child. And who could disagree? I was demonstrably odd. Able to beat grown men at chess, some of the best in the world. I was so quiet, always watching. It didn't help that everyone could see me at the trial, could see how strange I was. I had no idea how to move like a girl. My hair was short. I'd spent the years of my childhood with dissolute men. I didn't know the first thing about proper behavior.

"My father always said if you believed a thing hard enough, reality would have no choice but to make it true. When he testified on the stand, he'd convinced himself. He called me devil's spawn in front of all of London."

She had thought things couldn't get any worse than that frozen horror in the courtroom—seeing the man she'd loved, the man who had never had a harsh word for her, point at her and denounce her. Seeing the frightening light in his eyes that said he believed it. He had been all she had in the world—and he'd left her suddenly, publicly alone.

"He was a charismatic, convincing man. They convicted him, not of theft, but of petty fraud—enough to give him two years' hard labor, but no more. But the people who had been there were convinced that he'd been wronged. When I left the courtroom, completely unsure of myself, I was surrounded by a mob. They shouted. They spat. I don't know who threw the first rock. I don't know how many they threw." She looked over at him. "I fainted by the time they were pulled off me, but I've never forgotten it. Ever since then, I can't bear crowds. I think of them, and I start to shake. I just utterly panic."

"Have you never had anyone to stand by you?" he asked. His voice was low and hoarse.

"My great-aunts. Lydia, until—" She nearly choked saying those words. But even then, she'd not been able to trust in them. Her great-aunts would pass away. She'd always known that someday, Lydia would find out the truth and take a disgust to her. "Up until the end, I would never have guessed that my father would do that. I like to think that maybe he was ill. That he didn't know what he was doing when he betrayed me." Her eyes glistened. "He passed away in prison, so maybe it was true. I have to believe that, because no matter how I try, I can't stop loving him. He taught me everything I knew. He was my entire life. And I don't know how to hate him as much as he deserves. So you see, Your Grace, I can't marry you. I can't even think of it without shaking. London society would tear me apart."

"No," he said quietly. "It won't."

She turned to him. "How can you say that?"

"It won't," he promised, "because I won't let that happen." He turned her chin so that she looked him in the eyes. "Once, you told me I was lucky because I could look wherever I wished without fear. I don't think I really began to understand what you meant until I found out..." His arms closed around her more tightly. "I knew you were upset. You told me you were frightened. Lucky me, that I could not understand what you meant— how terrified you were."

She was shaking.

"I give you my word that if you marry me, I will protect you. I will stand by your side and never do harm to you. I've already spoken with Stevens and Charingford, and they'll keep their mouths shut. I promise you on all that I keep sacred that I will do my utmost to keep your past secret, and that if I should fail in that, I will use everything in my power to keep you safe. You will never again need to fear if you marry me."

"And what will I have to give you in return?"

"Your allegiance." He held her close. "For as long as we can stand one another's presence, your body would be nice, too. I don't expect love. I don't expect you'll want me forever. But I think that we could make a good go of it."

"You don't expect love." She shook her head in confusion. "This is the second time you've said that. Is this going to be like one of those dreadful novels where you warn me not to fall in love with you, and if I do, then you'll turn into Bluebeard and try to lop my head off? You're handsome. You have all your teeth." She looked into his eyes and lightly touched her hand to his cheek. He grew very still. "I can offer you no promises. If you're any good in bed, I might fall in love with you. If that is going to be anathema…"

"No," he said swiftly. He looked away from her, and when he spoke again, there was a slight rasp to his words. "No. That would be perfectly…unobjectionable."

From his words, she might have thought him uncaring. But that catch in his voice and the way he tilted his head toward her again, gave the lie to his indifference. He looked at her like a thirsty man gazing on an oasis, trying to decide if it were an illusion brought on by the heat.

It made a sudden, impossible sense of everything. *He doesn't want a loveless marriage. He's just resigned himself to one.*

His mother had said that Robert had the heart of a romantic. Minnie had been overwhelmed by other worries at the time, but perhaps the duchess had the right of it. He championed those who had no voice of their own. And for some reason, he had long since convinced himself that he would never be loved.

She was so close to falling in love with him that she almost opened her mouth and told him so. But that light in his eyes—the way he'd looked at her when he said it would be unobjectionable—it would be cruel to say it before it was true.

It will be true soon enough, she thought.

Ever since her father's betrayal, she'd scolded herself, saying that she'd brought what happened on herself for wanting too much. For daring to think that at twelve—as a girl—she could challenge grown men and walk away unscathed.

But maybe her mistake had been not trying hard enough.

"There is a great deal," he said, "that a duchess can do that a young, unmarried lady cannot. Come be lucky with me, Minnie."

The moment to open her wings was when she plummeted to the ground. If she didn't try, it would be no surprise that the ground rose up and struck her.

For so long, she'd told herself that it was stupid to hope. But maybe it wasn't. She couldn't see how her future would work out. But she could hope for love and safety, and maybe, *maybe* she'd not be slapped down for reaching for it with trembling hands.

"Oh, God," she said, her voice shaking. "I'm really going to do this."

He let out a shaky breath of relief. "Good. Good." His arm tightened around her, crushing her to him. He held her close and whispered in her ear. "I hope I'm good in bed."

It was as close as he'd come to admitting that he wanted her to love him. Minnie smiled and kissed him. He tasted like salt spray from the sea. Her heart fluttered in her chest like the wings of a flock of birds.

"I hope you are, too," she said shyly. And then she kissed him again, their hands locking together. She kissed him until the afternoon sun filled the room, until she grew light-headed from the feel. She held him and kissed him until Great-Aunt Caro stood by the door and cleared her throat.

Minnie blushed, but he stood.

"You must be one of Minnie's great-aunts," he said smoothly. "I'm Robert Blaisdell, the Duke of Clermont, and I should very much like to marry your niece."

Chapter Twenty

ROBERT RETURNED TO HIS HOME and found his brother and his cousin both present, sorting through sheaves of foolscap, scribbled over. Part of Sebastian's upcoming paper, from the notations on them.

They didn't see him enter the room.

"So here's another thing," Sebastian was saying. "Why is it that tortoise-shell-and-white cats are nearly always female? Short of running a massive cat breeding program—"

He looked up as Robert came to stand by him.

"You're going to become a purveyor of cats?" Robert asked with a smile.

Sebastian gestured widely. "I was just telling Oliver about my collection of curiosities. You know, things that I've observed that I can't yet explain. There's an eighty-year-old woman in London who starts every morning by feeding stray cats in an alley. I had her make sketches of the cats, along with descriptions—weight, sex, eye color, number of toes. All that interesting information. I thought something might come of it." He cocked his head at Robert. "You look different."

"I do?" He *felt* different. It was a newfound sense of wonder, a pleased confidence.

"You do," Oliver said. "To be perfectly frank, over the last few days you've looked…"

"Like something that the cat dragged in," Sebastian put in. "A six-toed cat. Did you know that six-toed cats have seventeen percent more claw?"

Oliver shrugged. "Like something that was dragged in by all of Sebastian's strays. And *then* there was the staring off into space."

"And the distressed sighs." Sebastian demonstrated, heaving mightily and then deflating into a sad, stricken ball.

"Distressed sighs!" Robert protested. "Not once did I stoop to distressed sighs! I might have emitted a manly huff of oppression." He demonstrated, folding his arms firmly and pressing his lips together with a half-grunt.

"Oh? Then what did you call this?" Sebastian stared off into the distance, a look of misery on his face. He gave a little sniffle and then let out his breath in a long, drawn-out sigh.

"I call that exaggeration. I call it perfidy! Death to any man who says such things!"

Oliver laughed. "You are feeling better, I see. So what brings on the change of mood? Did she agree to marry you after all?"

Robert blinked. "How...? But I didn't even tell you I had asked."

Oliver's smile widened. "Ten pounds, Malheur."

Sebastian gave what could best be termed a *distressed sigh.*

"Yes," Robert said quietly. "She agreed to marry me. The ceremony will be in four days. I've only to get the license and handle the settlements. I'm glad I found you together, because I wanted to tell you two first. I don't know if you'll understand, but..." He trailed off.

Neither of them said anything, and that companionable silence explained the matter more fluently than Robert could have. Sebastian could make a joke out of anything. Oliver was more than willing to mock him. But they knew when to do it and when to stop.

"If I have a family," Robert said, his voice a little rough, "it's you two. I was hoping the both of you might stand up for me at my wedding. Sign as witnesses. That sort of thing."

"Of course," Oliver said.

Sebastian shrugged. "I am precisely the person I would choose for such an honor, were I you. I applaud your good sense."

Robert didn't bother to try to work out what Sebastian meant by that. There was a moment—a very short moment—when Robert felt he might have hugged the two of them. He almost wanted to do it—to reach out and grab them and hold them close. They'd been there for him through the hardest moments in his life—his father's funeral, the days that followed as he went through his father's effects and discovered that the man had been even worse than he'd imagined...

In lieu of an embrace, he simply folded his arms. "It would mean a great deal to me."

"Of course," Sebastian said, turning away from Robert, "you know what this means, Oliver. The two of us must now organize a wild, debauched party for Robert on the eve of his leg-shackling." He rubbed his hands together in glee.

Oliver met his gaze calmly. "Wild," he repeated. "Debauched. I am in complete agreement."

Robert felt a hint of apprehension. "You know," he said, "this is very kind, but not necessary."

They ignored him, facing one another.

"Well, you know. Fit the punishment to the criminal, and all that sort of thing. It *is* Robert, after all." Sebastian ran his hand through his hair, mussing it. "Now what will we do for women?"

"Really," Robert said a little more forcefully. "I know I've not yet said my wedding vows, but I must insist that…"

But they weren't paying him any attention. "I know just the thing," Oliver said, brightening. "Mary Wollstonecraft. I have a copy of *A Vindication of the Rights of Women* in my room—I'll be sure to bring that."

"Excellent," Sebastian said, rubbing his hands together. "And there's this letter I received by this curious woman from the United States—one Antoinette Brown. She wrote the most extraordinary things about evolution and women's rights. I'll bring that."

"I have a pamphlet by Emily Davies."

Robert's lips twisted upward despite himself.

"I was thinking I could bring a copy of Thomas Payne," Oliver said, "but that would make our numbers uneven."

"Violet," Sebastian said, with a wave of his hand. "She can be surprisingly handy in an argument."

"Ah, I suppose she'll do in a pinch." Oliver stood, and set his hand on Robert's shoulder. "Let nobody say that the Brothers Sinister have no idea how to be depraved."

"There shall be brandy!" Sebastian stood. "And we shall even drink it, although Robert will stop after two glasses because he always does."

"There will be food!" Oliver declaimed, mirroring Sebastian's stance. "And we shan't drink that, because then we would choke."

Sebastian grinned. "On the eve of your wedding, Robert, we shall offer you the sorts of female delights that you have always lusted after. Philosophical tracts upon philosophical tracts, all of them advocating political change that would result in an upheaval of the current social order. We shall set forth their essays, and then…" He paused, as if for dramatic emphasis. "Then, my friends, we shall argue about them!"

Robert smiled and looked away. "You two will be the death of me. I don't know what I'd do without you. I'm not *that* bad."

"Speaking of which," Oliver said. His face went momentarily solemn. "Your wedding. Your father is no longer with us, and your mother does not…ah, does not always know her duties. I thought perhaps we might offer to help."

Beside him, Sebastian nodded.

And here Robert thought that he'd considered everything already. He'd already decided on a wedding gift. He'd sent to London for attorneys to manage the settlements. But it wouldn't have surprised him if he had missed something. There was so much about the notion of family that he simply didn't know. "Help with…?"

Oliver leaned forward. "It's about the wedding night," he said earnestly. "About what happens on it. You need to know." He lowered his voice dramatically. "When a man and a woman love each other, they come together in a very special way."

Robert jabbed his brother with an elbow. "You," he said, "are terrible." But he was smiling, and he couldn't stop.

⌘ ⌘ ⌘

"So."

Minnie looked up from her breakfast the next morning, just in time to see the Duchess of Clermont in the doorway.

Great-Aunt Caro began to struggle to her feet; Eliza had already jumped up. A maid trailed the other woman, wringing her hands ineffectually and trying to convey silent apologies for the intrusion.

But the duchess didn't look at those other women. Her gaze fixed on Minnie.

"You're marrying my son in three days. You know it will be a complete disaster."

This woman, Minnie reminded herself, was going to be her mother-in-law for decades. It wouldn't do to have her as an enemy.

It also wouldn't do to have the duchess think her cowed. Minnie gave her the barest nod, as between equals. "Are you here to dissuade me? Demand a return of your five thousand pounds?" She lifted her chin and returned her attention to the toast on her plate. "I shall rip up your bank draught."

The duchess snorted, sweeping into the room. She pulled back a chair for herself before the maid could jump to attention and then sat at the table expectantly.

"Well?" she demanded. "Pour the tea."

Minnie did and then, at the duchess's direction, added sugar.

As she did, her great-aunts stole looks back and forth, as if silently arguing with one another about whether they should intervene. But the duchess paid them no mind. She took a piece of toast—slightly burnt— and set it on her plate.

Minnie handed her the cup and saucer. She took a sip and then set it down, as if by so doing she'd satisfied the demands of good manners. "And here I thought you had some sense, Miss Pursling."

"I do. Are you here to browbeat me again?"

The duchess shook her head. "Only the most deluded, romantic woman who found herself in my position would suppose that throwing a tantrum at her son's bride-to-be would alter the outcome. You know the risks. My son knows the truth. I made my best offer and it wasn't enough. The world rarely cares for my inclinations. When matters don't go my way, there's only one thing to do." So saying, she lifted the toast and took a dainty bite.

"What is that?" Minnie asked.

The duchess swallowed her bite with a small frown, set down the toast, and then stirred her tea. "Do you like cats, Miss Pursling?"

Minnie blinked at this turn to the conversation. "I am fond of them, although I wish Pouncer would stop leaving mouse livers on my bed."

The duchess waved away rodent innards with one lace glove. "Have you ever seen a cat apologize, or admit it was in the wrong?"

"Cats don't talk," Caro put in, her first words for the morning.

The duchess looked up, glaring at her. "A woman capable of keeping her infamous grand-niece in safety for a decade can surely bring herself to understand a little figurative speech." She turned back to Minnie. "Have you ever seen a cat attempt to pounce on a target, and miss?"

"Of course."

"And what does the cat do?" She didn't wait for an answer. "It acts as if it *intended* to miss. 'Yes,' it says, 'I let that one go as a warning to all the others. Now I shall lick my paws for the next five minutes, precisely as I had planned.'"

"It *says* that?" Minnie asked innocently.

"Figuratively speaking. My point is, be the cat. Everyone respects a cat."

"Well, actually," Eliza said, "in the time of the Black Plague—"

The duchess extended a hand. "Do not pollute my perfectly acceptable figurative speech with irrelevant facts!" she thundered. "There is no need for those." She focused on Minnie once more. "Now, I have decided that you and my son must honeymoon in Paris."

This abrupt change of subject had Minnie shaking her head. "That seems...*romantic*. Are you sure?"

"Exactly," the duchess said. "It *seems* romantic, and as little as I approve of the actual existence of romance, I am well aware that you will need the *appearance* of it very badly." She pursed her lips and then looked at the wall.

If Minnie hadn't known better, she would have thought that the woman looked embarrassed. She finally spoke again—for the first time, not looking directly at Minnie.

"Second," she said, "you might consider not consummating the marriage."

"What? Why? So it can be annulled?"

The duchess rolled her eyes. "That is a horrid myth. You cannot annul a marriage for simple lack of consummation. Trust me; I have consulted every lawyer in London as to the ways in which one might end a marriage. I know the law to an inch. I merely think it best if your first child did not come until at least ten or eleven months after the marriage. Let nobody think that you married because you were pregnant. They *will* talk, otherwise. For decades."

"Is that more of your figurative speech again?" Caro put in.

"Experience," the duchess said grimly. "Robert was an eight-month baby."

Minnie choked and shut her eyes, trying to expunge the implications from her mind.

"He was early," the duchess said calmly. "First children often are. I have said so every day for the last twenty-eight years, and so it must be true." She fixed Minnie with a glare. "So you'll refrain from marital relations for a good two months."

"I will not," Minnie said. "I have no inclination to refrain from something I want to do merely because people I have never met might assume the worst about me. Besides, given my past, it's rather like a murderer worrying that he might go to hell for saying unkind things about a friend's horse."

"Hmm." The duchess frowned and then shrugged. "Well. I was only testing you. I had to make sure that with your background, you took an interest in men. Better to find out such things now."

She looked certain. She sounded certain. And yet Minnie had the distinct impression of a cat licking its paws. *I didn't really want that mouse.*

"Speaking of which, the most important reason to go to Paris." The duchess pointed at Minnie. "You need a new wardrobe. You cannot do with just *acceptable*. You must be brilliant. So tell me, girl, do you prefer to dress like a drab little peasant, or do you wear stomach-turning garb simply because your impoverished great-aunts force you to it?"

On the other side of the table, Caro and Eliza gasped in unison. Minnie coughed. "Absolutely. Nothing pleases me more than turning a gown for the fourth time! If my cuffs aren't falling apart, I don't feel truly at home." She glared at the other woman. "I'll thank you not to insult the women who gave me a home when they were not obligated to do so. Insult me all you wish, but leave Caro and Eliza out of it."

The duchess didn't blink an eye at this. "What do you think of my style of dress?"

"Too fussy, too conservative," Minnie said without blinking. "It does very well for you, I suppose, but for me——"

"Excellent. What would you pick out for yourself? What sort of duchess would you be?"

Years of looking over fashion plates with Lydia hit her with a sharp sense of loss, one that seemed like a staggering blow. She should have been picking out her wedding trousseau with Lydia, who would have been crowing that she was *right...*

"Well," Minnie said, "I won't pretend to be a conventional duchess. I don't like those layers of lace, no matter how popular they are now. I'd feel positively buried in them. I'd want clean lines, bright fabrics." She let out a breath, imagining. "Lots of fabric. No more skimping."

"And you'll need to learn to cover your scar. My girl will be able to——"

Minnie turned to the other woman and gave her a repressive look. "This?" she said, touching her cheek. "Oh, no. I *intended* to get that. I consider it a beauty scar."

The duchess gave a crack of laughter and stood abruptly.

Minnie stared at her.

"Well?" the other woman said crossly. "We haven't got all day. I've all the fashion magazines at my hotel. If we wire your measurements to my people in France, they can do the final fittings the hour you arrive. And there's still a good deal that can be purchased here."

"You...came all the way here solely to take me *shopping?*" Minnie asked.

"Once you are the Duchess of Clermont," the other woman said, not acknowledging her question, "never let anyone know you could be anything else. If you don't hear what they say about you, it can't possibly be true. By the time society discovers your existence, you'll have to already be a duchess."

Chapter Twenty-one

THE DAYS UNTIL ROBERT'S WEDDING sped by all too quickly. Robert didn't know whether to be excited or apprehensive. He felt both. For one, his mother had taken Minnie under her wing and had sent for a seamstress from London to provide what she said were "basic essentials."

When he asked, she brushed him off with a tart, "If you're going to throw the girl to the wolves, it's only appropriate to outfit her with a red cloak."

Then there were those moments they stole together. He'd had a few kisses to whet his appetite—if you could call it *just* a kiss when he'd pushed her against the wall and unbuttoned her gown half down her front. By the morning of his wedding, his appetite was sharp indeed.

In one sense, it was lucky that their ceremony was early. In reality, the extremely early hour had been chosen specifically so that they would be able to make the journey to Paris by the end of the day. If that early-morning mail train was not late into London, if the steamer made it across the Channel in good time…

But he couldn't think of any of that as he looked in her eyes and spoke his vows. It wasn't just physical desire that had him so on edge. When she promised to love him, to comfort him, he felt an electric thrill that ran down his whole body. And when he promised the same, it seemed to seal them together, to bridge the distance between them in a way that even the kiss that followed could not.

He knew that many of his compatriots avoided marriage at all costs. They saw matrimony as an annoyance, a wife as another person who would nag and prod. But when he repeated his vows, he heard "as long as we both shall live" and he hoped.

After the ceremony, they separated briefly. Minnie went with her great-aunts to gather up a few things; Robert oversaw the loading of baggage. It was only half an hour later that they met again at the train station. They had no chance to speak as they boarded. Robert shook his brother's hand and then his cousin's. Violet gave him an embrace, and his mother… She inclined her head to him. They waved from the window of the car until the station disappeared into the countryside.

"Whose idea was it," Robert whispered in her ear, "to put a sixteen-hour journey between the ceremony and the consummation of the marriage?"

"Mine. I think." She half-turned to him, and he caught a glimpse of her face. She didn't look eager for what was to come; she looked unhappy. She glanced back out the window almost longingly, at the silhouettes of the town receding in the distance. All the buildings blurred together into gray stone and a forest of brick chimneys. Not so much to miss, that.

And then Robert recalled that she had two great-aunts who loved her, and that he was taking her away from them.

"Give me a moment," she said. "I'll be right as rain in a little while. I just thought—I really thought that Lydia would come to my wedding."

It took him a moment to remember who *Lydia* must be—Miss Charingford, the friend who had always been at her side.

"I sent her a letter telling her everything, absolutely everything about me. I asked her to come. I thought she'd see me off at least," she said. "But she didn't even send a note."

He'd been about to suggest that they spend the journey readying themselves for their hotel bed in Paris. But there was no place for cheerful lewdness here. Instead, he touched her hand gently, afraid to say anything that might worsen her mood.

But she hadn't been lying when she said she'd need only a while to recover. By the time they reached London, she was smiling again. "You know," she said, "the last time I was in Paris, I was eight. Back then, travel to the Continent took days." She shook her head. "Days to get anywhere at all."

"I didn't go to the Continent until I reached my majority," Robert said. "So I've only known the days when train and steamer took us everywhere."

They reached London by ten thirty, Southampton just after noon, and stood on French soil by three that afternoon. True to Minnie's word, all hint of her unhappiness had vanished. She watched everything with interest, smiled as if nothing was wrong…and, when they got into the final train car for the day, leaned her head against his shoulder in a display of idle affection that had him holding his breath and thinking of very cold icicles applied directly to his thigh.

Good thing that he hadn't suggested they try more. Just the feeling of her hand entwined in his had him wondering if he was going to ravish his wife for the first time while hurtling down the tracks.

No. He was going to ravish her in a hotel room. On a bed. And it was going to be incredible.

It was going to be incredible, he repeated to himself when they arrived in Paris.

He repeated it again, with gritted teeth, when he found out that his mother had arranged a fitting for Minnie upon her arrival—an hour-long delay at nine in the bloody evening, before dinner, on the night of his marriage.

By the time they found themselves seated at an intimate meal together, Minnie in a heavily brocaded robe that covered her from neck to toe, it was eleven at night. He picked moodily at his food; she did the same. They dismissed the servants after the second course; Minnie claimed not to be hungry and set down her silverware.

She stood.

It was almost midnight. They'd been traveling most of the day; for most of the day, he'd been on edge thinking of what he would get to do tonight. And now, tonight was here.

"Minnie," he said slowly. "After today's tiring journey, I thought we might—"

She undid the tie of her robe and let it fall to the ground, and the remainder of his sentence vanished.

"You thought we might?" she inquired, smiling at him.

God, that voice. God, that body. She was wearing a gown of sheer white fabric, embroidered in white scrollwork that twined suggestively from her hips to her breasts. Which were unbound. All too visible through the fabric. There was a bit of openwork by her legs; she took a step toward him, and the fabric swirled around her, giving him flashes of bare skin, long legs.

Had he actually been going to suggest that they put off their wedding night until they'd had some rest?

"I thought," he said as his blood rushed south, "that I'd spend the remainder of the evening ravishing you."

She smiled. "That's what I thought you were going to say."

"Look at you." And he could, now. He stood up from the table and circled her. "Just look at you."

The fabric molded to the peaks of her nipples. Dreams and fevered imaginings paled before reality. A dream conjured up a perfect half-moon of a breast, but it missed the light smattering of freckles. He might imagine smooth, pale skin. This close, he could see that her skin was pebbled with cold. And it was a smattering of colors—a light overlay of pink, where her blood pounded beneath the skin, hints of tan and white. He could even make out a pale white line along one rib that could have been a scar.

Those minor imperfections riveted him. This was no painter's imagination, no unreal fantasy displayed in his mind. This was Minnie, and she was here, real and breathing.

Red ribbon bows held the gown together at her shoulders. The one over her right arm was loose, and it seemed to taunt him, that half-made knot, not quite pulled firmly together, threatening to loose itself and let the sheer fabric slide down her skin.

"Do you remember that fundamental physiological flaw?" he muttered.

"Remember it? I'd hoped to exploit it."

"Oh." He reached for her. "Good. Then assume I said something brilliant."

He took hold of her shoulders and pulled her in for a kiss. It wasn't just a kiss, lips on lips. It wasn't even just his body, pressing against hers. He could feel her breaths speed up, unbound by a corset. His hands slid up her body. Her breasts were round and firm; her nipples hardened as his fingers brushed them. This was the beginning of *everything*.

"Assume I said something bloody brilliant," he muttered.

From her breast, it was only a short way to that loose ribbon, only a twist of his fingers to undo it and draw the silk down. He found her breast again, this time uncovered. The texture of female skin—so warm and vibrant, soft to the touch and yet firm when caressed—enthralled him.

But she was even less shy than he. She slid her hands under his coat, around his waist. She kissed him long and slow.

"Are you afraid?" he whispered, drawing her closer to the bed.

"I know I'm supposed to be…but no. No." He'd always found her voice sensual, but now it was downright erotic.

She sat on the bed and crooked her finger. "I'm not feeling particularly clever myself. I want you."

Any hope he'd had of restraining himself evaporated at that. He shed his coat while she undid the buttons of his waistcoat. They pulled off his shirt together, both of them laughing when his hand got stuck in one cuff and she had to turn it inside out on his wrist to pull it off. Her fingers explored his chest, setting him to shivering while he undid his trousers.

When he'd shed trousers and smallclothes in a great mass on the floor, she pulled him back on the bed and kissed him again. This kiss was even better—skin against skin, her hands brushing his thighs, then gently exploring his organ. He fumbled the other ribbon tie off her shoulder as their tongues met. They were chest to chest, then, as he clumsily extricated her from her gown, bare legs to bare legs. He took hold of her hands in his and pressed them together full-length.

Her mouth was hot against his. His cock was hard against her hip. They kissed, his pelvis grinding into hers, and all his dreams, all his most sordid imaginings, paled before reality. He was going to have her. He was finally, really, truly going to have her. He spread her legs and got on his knees between them.

When faced with the pretty pink folds of her sex, it was impossible not to touch her. She let out a little gasp when he touched her there—not of shock, but encouragement. She strained against his fingers. Fingers weren't enough. He came on top of her, careful, so careful with his weight. She moaned when he rubbed the head of his erection against the opening of her passage.

"Oh, God," she said, in that so-arousing voice. "Robert…"

"God. I want you so badly."

He pushed an inch inside of her.

She inhaled and set her hand against his chest—not a caress, but a slight pressure pushing him away, and he stopped. His biceps ached subtly, frozen as he was above her.

"Does it hurt?" he asked.

"No…" She smiled weakly and then said, in direct contradiction, "Only a little."

It wasn't much, but it was enough to pop the bubble of unthinking lust that had taken him so thoroughly. He was making a hash of things. He was forcing himself on her with scarcely a kiss and a fumble to ready her.

"Don't stop," she said, but when he thrust deeper inside, her entire body tensed. The pleasure he felt only magnified his unease. She closed around him—soft and warm, tight, so tight. She felt good. But he could feel her muscles, tense and unyielding beneath his body. Her fingers clenched in the bed sheets. Her jaw was set, as if she managed to grit her teeth only through strength of effort.

"I'm sorry." He tried to kiss her. "I'm sorry."

She lifted one hand and touched his cheek. "Stop *worrying*, Robert. I'll tell you if it becomes unbearable."

Bearable. This was *bearable* for her, when it was good for him.

Only good.

Somehow, he had had some notion that sexual intercourse with her would be different. That the complexity of what he felt for Minnie, their rapport… He had imagined that all of that would make this moment different in some way. That somehow, he would slide into her and his world would catch fire.

Knowing that it was just bearable for her robbed the act of anything but physical pleasure. This was his wedding night. It was supposed to be magical, as stupid and naïve as that sounded.

When he thrust inside her, it was supposed to feel different. He yearned for something magic to come out of her flesh—some secret thing that would transport them. Something that would make this more than *good* for him, more than bearable for her. As it was—he tried to suppress the terrible thought with her body so wary under his, but couldn't quite—he'd have preferred his left fist to this.

No matter how he took her, whether slow or swift, no matter whether he curled his hands in her hair or set them next to her shoulders, there was no magic in the act. When one made love to a woman one really cared for, it was *supposed* to feel different.

If you're any good in bed, I might fall in love with you.

She'd said it with a smile, but he hadn't realized how much he wanted her to love him. He yearned for it, and he felt the possibility drift away with every thrust that was merely bearable.

He shut his eyes and thought of England, concentrated on the smaller pleasures of the act—the pleasant hum of his body as he slid inside her, the slow burn of his pleasure, gathering at the base of his spine.

"God, Minnie," he said, and drove harder into her. It *was* good. Good was enough. She was enough—her body, tightening around his, her hips, her breasts brushing against his chest with every last thrust. And then it was very good, in those final ragged moments. He came hard inside her, his release catching him up in a moment that was almost as sweet as what he'd wished for.

When he was finished he disengaged from her and lay down, trailing his fingers along her ribs.

So. One more romantic, idealized dream, fallen prey to reality. No sense crying over that. And…and it couldn't always be like that for her, could it? He hoped not. He almost wished he *had* asked Oliver for advice.

Beside him, Minnie turned to him. He still couldn't look her in the eyes. Slowly, she set her hand on his arm. "I don't wish to alarm you." Her voice was a little cool; he tipped his head to one side and looked at her as best as he could in the failing light.

"What is it?"

"I think we were doing it wrong."

His whole body grew tense. If she hadn't said it, they could have pretended. He pushed subtly away from her. "The first time, I hear, is the worst. For women. It will get…better." It had to.

"No," she repeated more gravely. "We were doing it wrong. I know what it's supposed to feel like, at the end. And what happened for you? It didn't happen for me."

"I know," he snapped. "God. You don't have to tell me that. You could barely tolerate the act. You don't need to rub in the fact that I couldn't bring my wife to orgasm. I'm well aware of the truth."

This outburst was met with silence, and Robert let out a shaky breath.

"I'm not trying to criticize," she finally said. She sounded astoundingly reasonable, under the circumstances, and that made him want to snap at her more. "It's just—the way we were doing it, it wasn't ever going to happen for me. And…well, I had rather hoped that it would."

"What do you mean, it wasn't going to happen? How would you know?"

She simply looked at him, and he realized he was snapping at his wife because he'd not brought her to ecstasy. Because he'd had a better time of it than she had.

Excellent work, Robert.

"I'm sorry." He let out a sigh. "I shouldn't yell at you. It's not your fault." He took a deep breath.

Minnie took his arm. "We're intelligent. We'll figure it out. We have ten days in Paris to get it right."

Hell. Ten nights like this one? He really would beg off first.

"Nine," he corrected. "One down."

"This one isn't over." Minnie bit her lip. "I have no experience with men, but… Do you want me to show you?"

"Show me?"

Her cheeks went slightly pink. "You know. Show you what I would do on my own."

After the debacle he'd made of the night, it was impossible that he should want her again. And yet those words set in motion a tickle at the back of his mind, a hint of interest. He cleared his throat. "I don't have anything else planned for the evening."

She let out a little laugh. "I suppose. It starts here." Her hand crept between her thighs.

"I started there."

"A little higher up." She did something with her hand—something he couldn't see until he sat up and focused on her fingers. They slid, not into her passage, but higher, focusing on the glistening nub between her legs. Her strokes were light and swift. Her breath caught once and then evened out.

So did his. "What are you thinking about?"

She met his eyes. "You. Do you remember when you threw the paste at me?"

"Mmm."

"That night, I went home and thought of you taking off my gown."

He'd just spilled his seed in her. He shouldn't have been capable of an erection for a good long while. But blood was flowing to his cock. "Funny," he said hoarsely. "I thought something similar that night."

"I thought about you a lot at night," Minnie said. "It was...embarrassing."

"There was a point, there, where I thought my left hand had your name branded on it. All I had to do was touch my cock and think of you..."

Her body was spread before him, her hair a great mass on the pillow.

He nudged her knees apart so he could see what she was doing. As he did, his throat grew dry. Her skin appeared to soften as she touched herself. She was a deep pink between her legs, her nether lips unfolding like a flower in the rosy lamplight. That dark rose beckoned him in, inviting his touch.

Her hands pressed into her flesh in a smooth, practiced motion, and he could see her passage glisten. He could smell the difference in the air—the scent of her growing arousal.

"All I had to do," he said fiercely, "was think of you, and I'd be hard as a rock. God, Minnie, keep doing that." He'd never thought of her doing this—pleasuring herself—but it was by far more arousing than any of the scenarios he'd dreamed up.

"I need a little more." Her eyelashes fluttered. "Would you like to help?"

His throat was dry. "I'd love to. How?"

"Touch me." She curved her hand around one breast. "Here."

He leaned down and cupped her breast, slid his finger along the curve of it.

"More. Harder," she urged him.

So he took the coral bud of her nipple in his mouth. She let out a little moan as he did so, her whole body arching next to his. That moan—that brought his arousal roaring back to life. His cock went from mildly interested to fully engaged.

"Yes," she moaned. "Please. Just like that."

He licked her first and then nibbled lightly at her. Her moans grew louder.

He set his other hand over hers, on her sex. He could feel her touching herself, could feel the bed swaying with the rhythm of her fingers. She'd been lightly moist when he entered her; she was wildly slick now. Slick and glorious. Her fingers were pushing harder; harder; his own played alongside hers, glorying in the smooth silkiness.

"Do you want to know the first time I thought about you?" he asked. "That first night we met. God, that encounter played out so differently when I imagined it again. A woman with a voice like yours, a figure like yours, encounters me alone behind a davenport? I thought about you on your knees, fastening those clever lips of yours around my cock. And I wanted you."

She came with a fevered cry. Her whole body shuddered in waves of pleasure. For a moment, it felt as if those waves were traveling through him, too. When she was done, he could hardly think. His entire body screamed in demand. He didn't ask. He didn't talk. He simply spread her legs farther apart and pushed inside her.

This time, he sank into her depths in one solid thrust. This time, he could feel the difference in her body. The little shuddering waves that still traveled through her clutched at his cock. She was slick from want.

He pressed her hand back into place. "Don't stop," he said hoarsely. "Keep doing that."

Her hips rose to his. Her hand continued its motion, an added stimulation at the base of his cock. He could feel her pleasure all around him, first ebbing, and then gathering again as he took her. And as if the dam had been broken to bits with her first orgasm, this time she came quickly—in scarcely a minute, her release a scalding hot wash of pure lust that had her clamping down on him.

He couldn't have enough of her. He pounded into her again and again, each thrust better than the last, each one building, building to a crescendo that washed over him in fierce waves. It was almost painful, his second release. It was messy and slippery and wrong, and it felt so, so damned right.

He'd had no intention of taking his virgin wife twice in one night—especially not after that disastrous first time. He'd lost all control the moment he'd watch her touch herself between the legs. There had been something about that, something that had touched a deep and primal urge inside him. He'd stopped thinking altogether.

The second time had been everything he'd hoped for and more.

Afterward, he kissed her and she kissed him back. She was all softness around him, melting into him. This was what he'd wanted—this joining.

"Robert," she said eventually, "I had rather assumed that...being what you were, that you were fairly experienced. Are you?"

"It depends what you mean by experience," he said carefully.

She didn't say anything.

"By the time I was old enough to get experience, I had some notion what my father was like. I didn't want to be like him. So I had to be certain—absolutely certain—that I wasn't forcing anyone into anything." He felt his face burn. "And then I also had to be sure that I wasn't like my father, led only by my cock. Lust makes me stupid. I had to be sure it wouldn't make me selfish, too."

Still she didn't say anything.

"There were a few house parties where…matters were quite close, and would have come to the point, had I allowed things to run their natural course. But I always came up with a reason not to. She was interested in my fortune, not myself. She thought she might get an offer of marriage out of it. It never seemed honest, to take a woman who wanted a duke, when I was just *me.*"

He looked up at the ceiling, felt her hand on his body, and shrugged.

"I think," he said carefully, "that given the amount of use I put my left hand to, I really shouldn't qualify as a virgin. I've had scores of sexual experiences. Just…not with other people. I wasn't saving myself for marriage."

Just for you.

He didn't say it. It seemed too raw, too close to the heat of intercourse to share.

Sex with Minnie wasn't what he had imagined intercourse would be like in his romantic daydreams. That had been too much of flowers and moonbeams, cold and perfect and clean.

This…this was warm and messy, and he wanted it again and again and again with a ferocity that he couldn't quite comprehend.

"Did we do it right that time?"

She snuggled against him. "Oh, yes," she said dreamily. "Very right."

He made a note: If she yawned in his arms afterward, he'd done a good job. A nice goal to have, wearing out his wife. Her eyelids drooped, and he felt a fierce sense of pride wash over him.

He'd told her that he had no expectation of love.

It wasn't that he didn't believe in love. The thought of love was like water in the desert. Now *there* was a stupid cliché, one that made him think of a man in ragged clothing staggering through the Sahara, searching for an oasis among the sand dunes.

But the Antarctic was a desert, too—a cold desert, one made dry because water there turned to ice the instant it hit the air.

So he believed in love. He'd always believed in love. He'd been surrounded by water all his life; it had simply been frozen solid. He'd loved as hard as he dared and watched it freeze before his face. It was no surprise now when he checked his feelings and discovered that he loved her. The surprise was that this time, when he dared to take a sip, he found water instead of ice.

He could have wept.

"That," he said to Minnie, "was really…honestly…the most awe-inspiring event that I have ever taken part in. And I want to do it again."

"Tomorrow," she murmured. "We have nine more days, after all."

Chapter Twenty-two

BEFORE THE SUN FOUND THE HORIZON, Minnie woke to feel her husband's lips against her neck, his arms around her. She'd slept the sleep of sated exhaustion; vaguely, she was aware that she was still tired. But it didn't matter. If she was tired, it was a good sort of tired, the kind that took delight in the feel of his body against hers, his hands running down her ribs with possessive intent. It felt more like a dream than a waking. She was warm and his touch was sweet.

If last night had been a discovery, this morning was about exploration—about fitting her hands into the curve of his back, about running her hands down his chest and then up again, noting the sensitive spots. The heady, insistent eagerness of the wedding night had been replaced with a sense of quiet wonder.

She was ready by the time he slid inside her. This morning, his thrusts were a gentle rocking, a full-body kiss, one that coaxed her orgasm from her in stages, rather than wresting it from her by force.

When he'd finished, he leaned his forehead against hers. "Good morning."

The sky was beginning to turn pink. She couldn't have had a full night's sleep, but she didn't want to drift back into dreams. She wanted to capture this moment and stretch it forever.

"Good morning."

He hadn't let go of her.

"You know," he said, "I'm absolutely ravenous. If I'm remembering right from my last trip, there's a little bakery down the street that should have something out even now."

By the time they'd dressed, the light of morning had flooded the streets below. The hotel they were in—some fancy affair; on the previous night, the name had been the last thing on her mind—let out onto a wide avenue. A park, ringed by a metal fence, stood on one side. Stone buildings with cunning façades marched down the other. Robert led her down a side street past the park. His little bakery was, in fact, a café that overlooked the River Seine. Not just the Seine; their hotel was in the heart of the city, steps from the *Île de la Cité*.

A few months ago, she would have never imagined coming to Paris with a husband. She wouldn't have dreamed of a hotel that was scarcely a quarter mile from the Notre Dame cathedral. This was grander than even Lydia's wildest imaginings—but no. Thinking of her friend gave Minnie a pain deep inside.

Instead, she concentrated on everything old and beautiful, everything bright and new. The colored awnings; the elegant buildings; the small flock of pigeons that came to roost near them as they ate, cocking their heads in interest at the croissants that Robert obtained from the baker.

The pastries were so good, warm and buttery and flaky, that Minnie almost didn't want to share with the birds.

But as they were throwing the remnants of their breakfast to the cooing pigeons—trying to make sure that the intrepid little brown birds on the side got a few crumbs as well—a small boy with a crutch limped up. A beaver cap was pulled over his head, not big enough to cover too-large ears.

He should have been too young to have that calculating look in his eyes. But age had nothing to do with the necessity for cunning. He took a limping step toward them, leaning heavily on his crutch. The wobble in his stride was too exaggerated to be real. Some things, one didn't need to translate.

Minnie's fingers closed over the bracelet at her wrist.

His eyes flashed in calculation once more. If he'd been planning to pick their pockets while they tossed bread, he switched to another strategy just as swiftly.

"A few centimes, Monsieur," said the boy in passable English. He took off his cap and swept it toward Robert. "A few centimes for the cripple."

How he'd pegged them for English... Well, she supposed it wasn't hard to figure out. They'd been talking to each other, after all.

Minnie had rather expected Robert to brush the urchin off, but he stopped and pulled out a purse. Without saying a word, he reached in and took out a coin. She saw the glint of gold as he flipped it toward the boy.

The boy's fingers flashed; he grabbed the coin from the air in reflex. But his mouth dropped open when he looked at what he'd caught. His crutch fell from his grasp; unheeding, he stood staring.

Robert let go of Minnie's arm and took two steps forward. He bent down and picked up the crutch.

"Next time," he said in his English-accented French, "don't drop your stick. Another man might not have understood this was an act and would be less forgiving."

"M'sieur." The boy looked again at the coin in his hand before taking the crutch from Robert and scampering away without any sign of disability.

"You knew he was faking the limp?" Minnie asked.

Robert shrugged. "It seemed likely."

"And you gave him—what did you give him anyway?"

"A twenty-franc coin. I doubt he's ever seen one in his life."

Twenty francs. That was worth almost a pound. For a street urchin, that sort of bounty was worth months and months of begging.

"Why, when you knew he was lying?"

He gave her a little smile. "Frauds need a helping hand as much as anyone else. I know all about that." He glanced toward the street where the boy had vanished. "*Especially* when it's done like that."

"You know about telling lies for money?" Minnie felt a smile come over her. She stood, brushed the crumbs off her gown, and strode over to him.

"Indeed. Some of my first memories are about lying for money." He tucked her hand into the crook of his arm and they began to walk. On the left, a wrought iron rail separated their path from the Seine. The river drifted by. Minnie refused to believe its waters could be brown and dingy.

"Really?" She huffed in disbelief. "What trinket did you want to buy?"

"No trinkets." He flashed her a smile and patted her arm. "It's rather an amusing story. You see, my parents married under...odd circumstances. My father convinced my mother he loved her. She believed him; my father could be most convincing when he put his mind to it. But *her* father knew a bit more of the world, and he suspected that dukes didn't fall into passionate, life-altering love with wool-merchants' daughters who had enormous dowries. Not on a few weeks' acquaintance, at any rate. So instead of handing over a vast sum of money to my father upon their marriage, he put it all in trust, to be paid out so long as my mother was happy."

Robert had retrieved an extra bag from the baker. He opened it now and passed her a bun—crisp and golden and warm—and took out one for himself. This he began to apportion into pieces, tossing them over the iron rail for the ducks.

"This does not sound like the beginning to an amusing story," Minnie said dubiously.

"Well, the background information isn't very funny, I suppose." Robert frowned and broke off a piece of crust. "But the rest of it is, I promise. In any event, to summarize: my father hadn't any real money of his own, and my mother controlled the rest. So when she came to visit—"

"Your *mother* would *visit?* Was she not living with you?"

"No, most of the time she was not. I don't think I saw her for the first three years of my life." He scratched his chin. "If she'd been living with my father, the trust would have paid out—those were the terms. My mother controlled the money by her presence. She didn't want my father to get a penny, and so when he told her that she would have to live with him in order to see me, she told him to go to hell."

Minnie thought back over her conversations with his mother. She'd said all sorts of things, but not this. It explained a great deal, though. Far too much, in fact. This was not turning out to be anything like an amusing story. Minnie blinked at her husband, but he had a little smile on his face, as if this were all part of some joke. He tossed bread blithely in the air and grinned when the ducks squabbled for it.

"So, in any event—"

"Wait just one moment. Your father didn't let your mother see you for the first three years of your life?"

"Correct." He frowned and broke off another bit of crust from his bun. "He didn't have any control over the money under the terms of the trust, but legally he did control me. So…" He shrugged again, as if this were perfectly normal. "One can't blame him for trying."

One couldn't? Minnie could.

But Robert simply threw bread into the water and kept talking.

"By the time I was four," he continued, "they'd worked out an arrangement. My mother's father gave a handful of factories to my father so he could keep his worst creditors at bay." He glanced at Minnie. "Graydon Boots was one of those. In return, my mother was allowed to see me for a few days twice a year. I would desperately try to be good when she came—so good that this time, she wouldn't leave. My father, naturally, supported me in these endeavors. When I was six years old, his brilliant plan was this: I would pretend that I couldn't read, presumably because in my father's straitened circumstances, he could not afford a tutor. He was sure that would break her down."

Minnie cleared her throat, which seemed strangely tight. "Did it?"

"Almost. I played the most pitiful urchin ever. I pretended not to know my letters. I stared blankly at pages and shrugged. I started to recite my alphabet, but skipped letters L through P. I counted to one hundred for her and transposed the sixties with the seventies. I added five and six and came up with thirteen." He grinned at her. "And my father was right—it almost worked. After a few days, she dashed off a letter to her father, ordering him to send another trunk with her things. She ordered a primer from a local shop. And every afternoon, she would take me in her parlor, and she'd sit me down and we would go through the alphabet. She was very severe about it—regimented, even. We were on a strict schedule."

"You did…" She couldn't contemplate a duke's son not knowing how to read at that age, but then, she couldn't contemplate a duke growing up and never seeing his mother, either. "You did already know your letters, didn't you?"

He gave her a nonchalant shrug. "Naturally. There wasn't much else for me to do besides read. After three days of pretending ignorance, I was already chafing at the bit, wondering when I could get back to finishing Robinson Crusoe. But it was working—she hadn't left yet. When we got to M-is-for-Mouse, I changed it to M-is-for-Mama. She gave me this look—this stern look with her lips pressed together—and demanded to know why I'd said that. I told her it was because I didn't want any mice about, but I liked having her there."

How he could smile, when Minnie's heart was breaking, she didn't know.

But he shook his head in what looked like quiet amusement.

"Apparently, that was slathering on the need for pity a little too thickly, because she shook her head and then said that today, we would not be learning the alphabet any longer; she had some very important, very private letters to write, and I was going to have to play quietly by myself. She handed me some paper and a pencil, and told me to amuse myself drawing."

"I can't believe that didn't melt her heart."

"Oh, no. By that time, my mother was a hardened soul. And she knew just how to appeal to me. Very important, very private letters—she repeated that twice. Naturally, I could not resist the urge to get a peek at them. She wrote them sitting next to me, while I pretended to sketch birds. Her very important, private letter said, over and over again, 'Clermont should go bugger himself.'"

He grinned at that memory—of his mother writing profanity about his father—while Minnie looked on aghast.

"Of course I asked her, 'What is a bugger?' Thus was my childish attempt at fraud revealed. I had just proven that I could read. She didn't say a word. She simply stood up and left the room. She and my father had the most frightful row after that. I believe that she actually threw things at him that time around. And I didn't see her again for almost eighteen months."

Minnie didn't know what to say. He stood there, smiling, as if he'd just related a funny little story—like the anecdote Minnie might have told about the time she got lost when she was seven and put her hand in another man's pocket, thinking he was her father.

"God," he said, "I can't believe what an unworthy little cad I was."

How could he smile about his father conscripting him at the age of six, using him as a weapon against his own mother? How could he laugh about his mother walking away from him? How could he pretend there was anything amusing about the fact that his father took a newborn babe away from its mother in order to get more money out of her?

"You know, Robert," she said, choking on the words, "there is really nothing funny about that story. Nothing."

Slowly, the smile on his face faded. "You didn't think so? But…" He frowned and rubbed his chin. "Not the first part, I understand that. And…and I suppose it's not precisely a story that ends happily. I hadn't thought of that, but I'm so used to the ending that I think nothing of it. But the middle bits—surely those were funny. Weren't they?"

"When you changed the primer to M-is-for-Mama, did you mean it?"

For one second, there wasn't the slightest hint of amusement in his eyes. He looked so old, the tiny lines at the corner of his mouth gathering as his lips pinched together. And yet he also looked young—impossibly young, as if his six-year-old self were still looking out from behind his eyes, watching his mother walk away.

"Maybe." He looked away from her, and then looked back. That urbane amusement was back on his face now, but it looked lopsided on him—as if he were trying to wear a hat that didn't quite fit.

"That's why it's not funny."

"There are funny elements to it," he protested. "Adding five and six and getting thirteen?"

His hand had cinched itself more tightly about her elbow. He didn't throw the next piece of bread to the ducks so much as hurl it so hard that one of them quacked in surprise and darted away before realizing that it was fleeing food. And perhaps that was when she realized how much it meant to him. It had to be a funny story to him. This little tale about telling lies at his father's behest and wanting, so desperately, for his mother to stay—this was a story about the breaking of his child's heart.

This was the man who had understood that marriage to the expected noble's daughter would end in regret and recrimination if it came out that he intended to abolish the peerage. He knew in his bones what it meant to have a wife walk away from him, and he'd rejected the possibility—rejected it, even though it would mean gossip and scandal, even though it would certainly mean that the highest sticklers in society would never accept his family.

He didn't look at her. "That bit about skipping portions of the alphabet? Surely that's at least a little amusing?"

This was a man who wanted his wife to love him, but who would not even allow himself to hope for it. And that was when Minnie realized that she had something he'd never had. She'd been loved. Her father had adored her up until the moment when his pending conviction had broken his spirit. She had happy memories, years of them, with him. After he'd disappeared, her great-aunts had swept in. She might not agree with everything they'd told her, but they'd loved her. They'd treated her as if she mattered. She took love for granted.

Lucky her.

He had to laugh at what had happened. If he didn't laugh, he would cry. She couldn't have understood it until just that moment—because at that moment, she knew that she had to laugh, too, or burst into tears on his behalf. He looked at her with such urgency that she could not bear to force the issue.

"Yes," she said quietly, entwining her fingers with his. "I do see that, now. It *is* funny."

⌘ ⌘ ⌘

THOSE FIRST DAYS IN PARIS seemed like jewels to Robert. As if he'd lived all his life behind clouds and the sun had come out in blinding force.

They woke. They walked. They visited museums and places of interest; they found their way back to their rooms in the afternoon and made love. Boxes at the opera went unused in favor of more time in bed.

"You said you thought of me on my knees," she said one afternoon. "How on earth would that work?"

So he'd explained. And then she'd insisted on trying it—and after a little instruction, trying had turned into his cock hard in her mouth, his hands on her shoulders. He' gasped as she took his length until he spilled. After that, it had only seemed fair to return the favor. It had taken him a little longer to grasp the gist of it, but it was worth the effort.

If you're good in bed, I might fall in love with you.

He was determined to become good, and he had years of fantasies to explore.

Sometimes, the things they imagined proved anatomically impossible, and they ended up collapsed in a laughing heap on the floor. Sometimes—like the time he bent her over the desk—it was very, very good.

On their fourth night in Paris, he put rubies around her neck—just rubies, after he'd taken everything else off—and had his way with her.

Afterward, she fingered the gems around her neck. "Are these supposed to be a bribe?" she asked. "You should realize by now that you don't have to offer me anything to get me in your bed."

"I *would* realize that," he said cheerfully, "but luckily for you, lust makes me stupid. You get rubies."

She had only smiled.

But she'd been right. They *had* been a bribe. Not for her favors; he didn't like the idea of paying for sex as a married man any more than he had as a bachelor. But by this point, he wanted her to love him. He wanted it with a deep yearning that he couldn't have explained. He almost told her himself that night, that he loved her. But they had nearly a week left. There was time for love to come. No need to rush at all.

He fell asleep with his arm around her and woke the next morning in the same position. The rubies at her throat winked at him in the early light, a blood-red portent of things to come.

He stared at them and shook his head to clear it of such a strange, unsettling thought.

And that's when someone pounded on the door.

⌘ ⌘ ⌘

MINNIE WOKE TO A COLD DRAFT and the memory of a ruckus. She opened her eyes; their bedchamber was empty. She blinked and looked around. It was only then that she heard the murmur of voices in the main salon. She got up, found a robe, and made her way to the door between the rooms.

There was a garçon standing there. He handed Robert, who was also encased in a dressing gown, a plain brown envelope. Robert slipped him a coin. "Wait outside in case there's a need for an immediate reply."

He shut the door.

"A telegram?" Minnie asked. "I hope it's not bad news." The rubies he'd put on her last night seemed heavy on her throat, out of place while she was garbed in nothing but an embroidered outer covering.

Robert slid his index finger under the flap to break the seal. "I'm going to guess it's from Carter, my business manager. It can wait until after—" He spoke carelessly, flipped open the envelope, and glanced at the paper inside.

Minnie watched all the color wash from his face. He stared at the message, his lips moving softly. Finally he looked up.

"It's from Sebastian."

"Mr. Malheur? Your cousin, the scientist?"

His breath hissed in, snake-like. "That very man."

"Robert, what is it?"

He was still staring at the page. His face seemed hewn from marble—hard and white. "Tell Rogers to pack my things." He spoke in cold, clipped tones. "He can have them on the next train." He pulled a watch from his pocket, frowned at it, and then opened the door to the waiting garçon. "Send a reply: 'I'll be there immediately.'" He tossed another coin to the man, who disappeared.

Robert still hadn't met Minnie's eyes, but he turned around. "I must be on the nine-thirty express. That gives me almost an hour. I haven't time to—"

"What's wrong?"

She had to follow after him into the dressing room, trotting to keep up with his long strides.

The snarl on his lips softened momentarily as he looked down at her. "You stay," he said more gently. "You've shopping to do, and there's no need—"

She put her hand on his chest. "No need but the fact that I gave you my vows just days ago. Through better or worse, Robert. Do you think you'll be running off on me already, leaving me here to guess what has happened? If you're leaving, I'm coming."

She had thought he might argue, but he simply shook his head and rang for his valet.

"What is it?" she asked again.

"It turns out they've charged a suspect with criminal sedition for distribution of my handbills," Robert said. "Found—ha. Arrested. Indicted."

"What? They've charged you in your absence?"

"No. Not me." His lips curled even more. "The man they have is innocent, but that won't stop them from pursuing the matter. Perhaps they think to embarrass me, without thinking that they're destroying the life of a man who is, and always has been, my superior."

"Who? Who is it?"

His face contorted, and his hands gripped hers. "Oliver Marshall," he said. "My brother."

Chapter Twenty-three

ON THE EXPRESS TRAIN FROM PARIS TO BOULOUGNE, Robert booked an entire first-class compartment. Not for luxury; he would hardly have noticed at this point. It was simple self-preservation. If he had to make polite conversation about his journey, he would never survive. Instead, he stared at the passing countryside as the sun climbed in the sky. The hours passed.

He didn't sit in any of the comfortable seats, didn't partake of any of the charming fruit-and-cream-laden pastries that Minnie must have ordered for him. He tried a biscuit at her urging, but it tasted like ash in his mouth, and he laid it aside after one bite. He stood near the front of the compartment, one hand on the wall, the other holding a cigarillo out the open window.

He'd long since realized that he used cigarillos as an excuse to avoid company. Now, the trickle of smoke that escaped into the compartment made another barrier, a hazy wall built between him and his wife. He took a drag on it anyway, and the smoke was acrid and harsh in his lungs, a more fitting punishment for what he'd allowed than his own guilt.

He'd known that Stevens wanted a culprit. He'd *known,* and in the haste—and lust—of his wedding, he'd put the matter off for his return. He thought he had time enough to deal with it.

The miles clacked past, marked only by his watch and the passing villages. Long hours slipped by, punctuated only by the shriek of the brakes and the whistle of the train for the few stops that the express made. First Beauvais, then Amiens, was left behind. It was only when the train skirted the silver-barked beeches of the Forest of Crécy that his wife braved the forbidding looks he gave her and crossed to him.

"You know," she said, coming to stand by him near the farthest wall, "pushing won't make it go faster."

"No?" He tapped the end of his cigarillo out the window and watched embers fly away, pulsing briefly in the wind. "Doesn't slow it down, either. Not that I can see."

She looked away. Her fingers tapped against the window; her jaw squared.

A third punishment, that slight withdrawal, one that stung more than the smoke he'd inhaled.

But this way, you're punishing her, too. His fist clenched and he shook his head.

She didn't say anything. The train went around a curve; she put one hand against the wall to steady herself. The protest of the metal couplings, bending in place, surrounded them. The sound of the train, clack-clacking along at something just above thirty miles an hour, swallowed up any other response she might have given.

Not even one week married, and he was already fouling everything up. He'd wanted…so much. Not just a wife in name, but a family in truth. Someone who *chose* him.

Stupid bloody dream, that. At this particular moment, he wouldn't have chosen himself, either. He gave the cigarillo another flick and watched orange sparks fly.

And that was when he felt her arm close around him from behind. She didn't say anything at all, just pressed against him, holding him tight. She squeezed until it was clear that she wasn't letting go, no matter how foul his mood. His breath rasped in his lungs, and this time not from the smoke.

"Oh, Minnie," he heard himself say. "What am I going to do?"

"Everything you can. When is the trial?"

He shook his head. "I don't know."

"You're a duke. There must be something you can do." She paused. "Legal matters… I know almost nothing about them. But cannot trials be quashed?"

"This one, it's intended to embarrass me," Robert said. "Retaliation, I think."

His face grew grim.

"There's been something odd afoot in Leicester. I started looking into it because I discovered what my father had done with Graydon Boots. Those charges of criminal sedition always arose just when matters between workers and masters had come to a head. They're grudges, not a proper application of the law."

"All the easier to have it quashed, then," Minnie said.

"Not that simple." Robert tapped the cigarillo against the window frame once again. "Sebastian said they've already had a few reporters come in from London to cover the matter. It's being reported that a man in my household committed a crime. Stevens no doubt thinks he has an easy conviction, that with me out of the country, I won't be able to respond. He thinks the damage will be done by the time I come back. I'll be embarrassed, and Oliver—a guest of my house and a known associate—will be branded a criminal."

"But that won't happen," Minnie said.

Robert was silent a little longer. "I could bring enough pressure to bear that the case would be dropped."

Her arms tightened around him.

"But I can't stop the talk that would result if I quashed the inquiry. My brother…he's worked hard, so damned hard, to build up a store of respect for himself. He's beginning to have a reputation as an intelligent, fair-minded man. If I quashed the inquiry—even if we won, eventually, on the grounds that the papers weren't even seditious—the idea that he had written such radical sentiments under an assumed name would destroy everything he's worked for. So, yes, I could stop the legal trial. But my brother doesn't just need a favorable verdict. He needs to be publicly exonerated of the charge."

"And you'll see it done."

She said it so confidently, so sweetly, that for a moment he almost believed her.

"I'll do anything." His voice broke. "My brother told me once that family was a matter of choice. If I were to turn my back on him now, what kind of brother would I be to him?" He let the cigarillo go; it swirled in the eddies alongside the train and disappeared around the bend before he saw it land. The forest passed by, receding in the distance. Now there was only rolling pastureland.

He counted three fences before he spoke again. "My father raped his mother."

She sucked in her breath.

"That's the claim I have on him—that an unwilling woman was once forced to my father's will. That my family was so powerful that justice was subverted."

"It wasn't you."

"It was the Duke of Clermont. I bear his name, his face." His hands tightened into fists. "His responsibility. I suppose in some ways it was the height of selfishness for me to even claim him as a brother. But I can't let go. If family is a matter of choice, I'll choose him. And I will, over and over, until—"

The thought was a crushing weight against his chest. He almost staggered with it. He did stagger, when the train shifted direction once more. But Minnie leaned into his shoulder, steadying him, and then guided him to sit on one of the cushioned benches.

"You'll choose him until what?" she asked.

"Until the stars fall from the sky," he said. "Because he chose me first."

It was such a damning thing to admit, that vulnerability. He felt like a turtle, stripped of its shell, being readied for soup.

But she didn't lift a brow at that. Instead, she stood before him, her skirts spilling around his knees. Her fingers traced his eyebrows, pressing against his temples before running back along the furrows of his forehead. It felt…lovely. As if she could coax the tense guilt from his features.

"My great-aunts used to do this for each other," she said. "When things did not go well."

He brushed her hands away. "I don't need *comforting.*"

He didn't deserve it.

But before he could stand up and turn away, she grabbed hold of his hands. Her grip wasn't firm, but it was sure.

"If family is a matter of choice," she said softly, "I've chosen you."

He let out a long breath.

"And I will," she said, "again and again."

He lifted his head. Her eyes were wide and gray and guileless, and she was saying words that he'd longed to hear for years. On a breath, he stood, reaching for her. His hands closed on her hips; a scant few moments later, his mouth captured hers. There was no thought, no calculation in that kiss. She was simply achingly present.

"Minnie," he murmured against the heat of her lips, and then again, "Minnie."

Tonight would be the fifth night of their marriage. He'd had her while she laughed. He'd taken her while she moaned for him. He'd never taken her feeling as he did now—dark and uncertain.

He didn't ask this time, or whisper to her what he wanted to try. He didn't ready her with kisses. He pushed her against the wall of the train car, and before she had a chance to struggle or cry out, captured her skirts in his fists, gathering up petticoats and crinoline. He had only to free his erection. One thrust—one push inside her, and he'd be as bad as his father, taking a woman because she was there and he wanted to feel her. One thrust, and he'd punish himself even more.

Her head was down, bowed before him. He towered over her. There was nobody around, no way she could call for help. He'd probably frightened her to death.

He let her skirts fall and stepped away. "I'm sorry," he said. "I'm in a filthy, filthy mood. You'd best walk away while you still can."

She looked up at him then. Her eyes were pale gray and absolutely lovely. But she didn't twitch a muscle.

Shadows from a passing tree flickered over them, painting their faces in a shifting palette of light and darkness. His body shivered with need.

"I mean it, Minnie," he said quietly. "Walk away. If you could see what I was thinking now, you'd be scared half to death. Do you know what I could do to you?"

"No." Her voice was almost placid. "Tell me."

"I shoved you against the wall." He set his hands on either side of her head. "I might have had my way with you."

"Had your way with me," she mused, shaking her head. "Which way is your way, again?"

He narrowed his eyes. "You know what I mean."

"I'm afraid I don't have any idea."

He took a step forward, trapping her against the wall. "Must I spell everything out?"

"Please."

"I could plunge my cock inside you." His hips ground into hers. "No preamble. No nothing."

Her eyes widened. The corner of her mouth tilted. "Oh, no," she said. A dimple popped out on her cheek. "Not your cock. Anything but your cock."

He found himself smiling in spite of everything. "God damn it, Minnie. Can't you take my bad mood seriously?"

She ignored him. "And here I was, feeling so…so empty. Why, if you were to slide inside of me, it might give me the most curious feelings." As she spoke, she undid his trousers. Her fingers played down the length of him, stroking his erection.

"But there's no worry of that," she said. "You're so massive, I don't think you would fit." She gave the head of his penis a squeeze as he spoke, and he let out a gasping laugh.

"God, Minnie. I can't see straight."

"It's a good thing you have hold of your urges," she said, more quietly, "because I'm so wet now, and it would be dreadfully embarrassing if you were to—"

He lifted her against the wall, wrapped her legs around him, and slid inside her. She was wet, so wet, and hot. The pleasure of her body, clasped around him, was so intense that it almost hurt. The light rhythmic sway of the car rocked him into her.

He braced them against the wall, his muscles straining.

"That's right, Robert." Her arms came around him. "That's right. Just like that."

He moved inside her, sliding, straining, until sweat popped out on his brow. He let his lust get the better of him, let his instinct take over until there was nothing but her, her around him, her breasts beneath his hands, her pulse pounding in time with his thrusts.

She came around him, tightening in waves of pulsating heat around his cock. And he pounded into her, hard at first, and then even harder, until his own climax came. In the moment when he spilled his seed, he imagined them connected by far more than the scrape of his teeth against her jaw, the tangle of their hands, the clamp of her legs still wrapped around him. It was more than just the physical act of burying himself in her body.

In that moment, for the first time in his life, Robert believed that there was someone for him. Someone who would be there for him through the hardest times. More than a lover, a friend, an ally. A wife—for better or worse, richer or poorer. In sickness and in health. In laughter and in tears.

He stood, breathing heavily, humbled by the gift he'd been given. He could only touch her cheek in awe.

"Minerva, mine," he whispered.

He felt as if he were discovering her anew. As if, amidst all the turmoil of the day, he'd finally been granted his heart's desire. And now that he had her, he didn't want to let her go.

She set her head against his shoulder. "That's better," she said.

It was so new, this thing he felt between them. New and unfamiliar, and so welcome that he was almost afraid to acknowledge it, lest it disappear. And yet if he said nothing…

"Somewhere," he said, "someone is saying that I made a dreadful mistake in marrying you."

She pulled her head from his shoulder and looked up at him, her eyes wide.

"They're wrong." He put his arms around her. "All of them, wherever they are. You are the best choice I have ever made."

There was a light in her gray eyes when she looked at him, one that made him feel a thousand feet tall. He could have conquered an entire army with her at his side. Whatever it was that had gone wrong would come out right.

It was almost too much to believe.

And so instead, he dipped his head and kissed her again.

⌘ ⌘ ⌘

BY THE TIME ROBERT ARRIVED IN LEICESTER, he'd been traveling the better part of the day. His wedding night, the slow, timeless memory of waking next to Minnie the next morning, followed by days of languorously making love to her...all those things had been washed away by the harsh, rhythmic clack of express trains, the vibration of steamers.

He gave himself no time to eat or wash when their train finally arrived in Leicester in the late evening. It was dark, and the moon was already high overhead. He put Minnie in a carriage and proceeded immediately on foot to the center of town.

The evening was dark and windy, but not quite cold. Sebastian's telegram had told him where Oliver was held—in the Guildhall itself, just beneath the library where he'd first met his wife, mere steps from the hearing room where they'd first been introduced.

And indeed, when he came up on the building in the dark of night, it seemed as if it might have been the evening that they met. Some sort of event was going on in the Great Hall. He knocked on the side door instead, waited, and then knocked louder still, until the man who passed for gaoler came.

"No visiting." He frowned at Robert. "Not at this hour."

Robert slipped the man a heavy coin. "I'm not a visitor."

The man didn't even blink. "Right this way, sir," he said.

Paris and the croissants seemed very far away. The memory belonged to some other man, someone happily married, shyly delighted with the future that was slowly unveiling itself. All that happiness was taken over by a hollow feeling in his gut as he was led to the holding room. The gaoler unearthed a hooded lantern that showed grimy walls and wooden doors. He unlocked the main doors and then went up to one of the cells. Wood scraped against wood.

Robert aimed the light forward. The man hadn't opened the door to the cell. Instead, he'd moved a panel, one that covered a fixed slot at eye level, a few inches high and maybe half a foot long.

The gaoler took a few steps back and motioned Robert forward.

Robert stepped close, lifting the lantern as he did. The rays didn't reach into the pitch-black interior of the cell behind that slot.

"Oliver?" His voice was low.

"Robert?" He heard a rustle. "God, that's bright. I can't see a thing."

The light from the lantern was anemic at best, not even enough to show the dimensions of the cell his brother was in. For Oliver to think it bright... he must have been sitting in darkness for hours. All the time

Robert had spent in his first-class compartment, his brother had been in here. He shivered.

"Do you have blankets?" Robert demanded. "Food?"

"What are you doing here?" Oliver replied in an unnaturally cheerful voice. "You're on your honeymoon now. You're supposed to be in Paris."

"This is my fault." Robert set the lantern down and stepped forward, dropping his voice. "I wrote those goddamned handbills. I never wanted you involved at all. It's my fault you're in that stinking cell." Not a figure of speech, that. He'd come close enough to scent the air wafting from that little slot. *Stinking* was putting it mildly.

"Well, I surmised you were the author," Oliver said after a short pause. "They sound like you, if you know what I mean. It was fascinating reading. Why didn't you tell me?"

"I knew someone was obtaining false convictions for criminal sedition," Robert huffed; his breath was white in the cold of the room. "I wanted to find out who it was. I'm the one person they couldn't charge. If I'd told you, you might be considered an accomplice."

"Ah. Clever."

"Not clever enough, obviously. I'm shocked that I arrived in town in time. I imagined they would have rushed you through to conviction."

"Apparently not." Oliver sighed. "They're waiting for a witness to arrive. Do you remember Lord Green, from our Cambridge days?"

"Lord Green? Yes, I remember him—but what the devil is he going to say? Have you seen him more recently than I have?"

"No, not since the time we had that last wager over the chess game, three years back. But they've called him to testify, and I have no idea what the devil he's going to say."

Chess again. It couldn't be a coincidence. What it all meant, though… Robert shook his head.

"Well, you've a witness, too. I'd like to see a jury vote to convict you when the Duke of Clermont attests that he did it himself. That you knew nothing of it."

He brought his hand up to the slot. But instead of being able to grasp his brother's hand, or clap him on the shoulder, his fingers met a cold metal grate, the bars spaced too closely to allow more than his smallest finger through. He could only brush his brother's fingertips.

"Here now," the gaoler called. "None of that—passing of knives and the like where I can't see it."

Robert dropped his hand in frustration.

"I'll be back in the morning," Robert promised. "We'll work everything out then. I'll order a bottle of champagne in anticipation of your release."

"Better make it a gallon of carbon oil."

"Carbon oil?"

"This cell has lice."

Robert winced. Dark, smelly, louse-ridden—he'd done this to his brother. The self-recrimination boiled up inside him. But if Oliver could manage good cheer…

"Good thing, then, that I couldn't slap your shoulder," he said.

"Ha."

He turned to go. "I give you my word. I won't let them convict you."

But as he turned, he realized that a second figure had joined them in the dark—someone shorter than Robert and wider. In the darkness, he caught only a suggestion of hard muscle and imposing strength.

"No," the man said, looking at Robert. "You won't. I'll hold you to that, Your Grace."

The figure took another step forward, and the light from the lantern caught his face.

"I give my word, Mr. Marshall," Robert repeated.

Oliver's father looked at him. Simply looked, but he projected a quiet menace without saying a word.

"Father," Oliver said behind them. "Stop glowering. You're embarrassing me."

"Hmm." Mr. Marshall stepped forward. "We came as soon as we heard. Your mother is seeing to a place to stay. She should be here in a few minutes, once she gets past the gaoler's wife."

That, Robert decided, was his cue to vanish. He had to be gone before the rest of Oliver's family appeared.

"I'll see you tomorrow," he promised and slipped out before he could burden Mrs. Marshall more than he already had.

There was a cabstand in the square down the street. He was on his way there when soft feet pounded up behind him.

"Wait," a woman's voice called. "Your Grace."

Robert blinked in surprise and turned. A cloaked figure raced toward him and threw back her hood.

"Miss Charingford," Robert said in surprise.

"Listen to me," the woman said urgently, "and listen well. Stevens threw Mr. Marshall in gaol to embarrass you."

"He succeeded. In that and more."

"He thinks you'll be in Paris throughout the trial. That he'll have your man of business—"

"He's not my man of business," Robert spat.

"Whatever he is. Stevens thinks he can prove that the man was involved, that he can insinuate that he worked on your orders."

Robert looked at her. "He can't prove that," he finally said. "It isn't true, and I should know. He can't prove it unless he's suborned testimony from someone."

Miss Charingford shook her head. "He can prove that Mr. Marshall was involved," she said. "At least, he's going to try."

"He can't possibly do any such thing," Robert repeated.

Miss Charingford blinked. "I know," she finally said, more quietly. "But you…you need to know how he's planning to prove it. There's a phrase in one of those pamphlets, a quote from some book on obscure chess strategy. It's well known that you take no interest in the game. But there's a witness coming who will testify that he discussed strategy with Marshall, that he loaned him the volume in question."

"Oh." Robert let out a drawn-out breath, recalling Minnie's anger the next day. "I know…I know exactly which phrase you are referring to. I know exactly how I knew it, too."

Dread rose up in him. He remembered how angry Minnie had been at him for using her words, how sure she had been that they would cast blame on her. He felt sick to his stomach.

"Precisely," Miss Charingford said. "Minnie sent me a letter explaining everything. I had to let you know. Stevens doesn't know about her past. Just her name." She shook her head. "He thinks there's nothing to her but a name. It never occurred to him to ask what she might have done."

"How did you find out what they planned?"

She was silent for a moment, then sighed. "My father told me. He was the magistrate who swore out the warrant for Marshall's arrest. He didn't have any choice, you see."

"Didn't he?" Robert asked dangerously.

"No," she replied. "Stevens is *good* at breaking strikes. The best there is. But he helps those who help him, and since I refused him, he's insisted that my father must do more."

"I see," Robert said quietly. And he did. No matter what happened with Oliver, Stevens would not continue to serve the militia. "Do you suppose your father would talk with me, if I came by?"

She gave him a short nod and then turned to go.

"Wait, Miss Charingford. There's one last thing."

She hadn't come to their wedding. He remembered those few hours on the train from Leicester to London, when Minnie had looked almost lost for mourning this woman.

He looked her in the eyes. "Minnie misses you."

As if she could hear the accusation in his words, Miss Charingford shrank away. "I miss her, too," she whispered. "No. I don't. I don't know. I'm still angry with her. It doesn't mean I want her hurt." She shook her head. "I had better go, before someone realizes I've gone out. I just—I had to tell someone, and I can't face her yet. Please don't tell her it was me. Not until I'm ready."

So saying, she turned away.

They were going to present proof that Oliver was involved. Robert started walking again, but this time, he passed the square where a solitary cabriolet driver nodded off with his hands on the reins.

He could do his best to quash the investigation—and leave his brother under a cloud of suspicion. Or he could speak. When speaking had entailed taking all the scandal on himself, there had been no question. But now he would have to explain how it was that His Grace, the Duke of Clermont, came to quote from an obscure volume of chess strategy.

He'd promised Minnie that he would protect her secrets. He'd promised his brother that he would see him free and clear. He could not do both those things.

Some devil in him made him imagine precisely how Minnie would react to hearing him admit the truth. It was even worse than anything he could imagine doing to her—putting her in a courtroom, watching someone she cared for give her up without hesitation. He couldn't do that to her. He couldn't.

But Oliver... Oliver was his brother. The man who had accepted him without question, despite the fact that his father had done nothing but harm to his family. He was his brother. His *brother*, the only thing he had known of family for years.

That image in his head of the courtroom—of Minnie turning white as he betrayed her—played itself over and over in his mind. The worse it was for her, the more it would strengthen the public belief that he spoke the truth. It made Robert feel ill to think of it. It would utterly destroy their marriage. She really *would* leave him—and he wouldn't even be able to voice a protest.

Because she would be right. He would deserve it.

Robert walked on the streets a very long time, until his feet ached and his hands turned to ice, until he could scarcely think for the turmoil in his head. He walked, and he decided.

Chapter Twenty-four

WHEN HE FINALLY RETURNED TO HIS HOME, he was sure Minnie would see what he intended to do. She'd seen everything else about him so easily. But she was waiting for him with tea and a late supper, and whatever she saw in his expression, she must have attributed to unhappiness over his brother's situation.

"I don't think a conviction will stick," Robert told her over a warm cup.

"That sounds like good news."

He held his hand out, let it wobble from side to side. "It's not the worst news. There's not enough evidence to convict him, but there...there may not be enough to vindicate him, either. Not unless I explain my involvement."

"And will you do it?"

He paused and looked her in the eyes. "This no longer just involves me."

She looked up at him. When had she begun to trust him? Why had he let her?

"Who else does it involve?" she asked.

"My mother, for one." He shut his eyes, not able to look at her as he told the first lie. "If I explain everything, I must publicly disclose my relation to Oliver. The truth would embarrass my mother—he was conceived scarcely a few months after her marriage—and it would humiliate Oliver's parents. Oliver himself...well, it wouldn't hurt him to be known as a duke's son."

"I see," she said slowly.

"It's worse than you think. You see, it's no longer about the trial itself, but the public account of it. If I just asserted that he was my brother, some people would always believe that I said it just to save him from the conviction for the sake of friendship. He'd not be exonerated. But...imagine that, for the sake of verisimilitude, I was to announce the truth of his parentage with my mother in the room. How do you suppose she might react?"

"I... Well. The duchess—dowager duchess, I mean—she's strong as flint. But just as brittle."

"She would probably turn white. She might stand up and leave. And that reaction, more than anything, would give the assertion the stamp of veracity. I could drive her into reacting." He looked over at her. "It would humiliate her, but it might save my brother."

"Perhaps, if she knows it's coming—"

"When she knows what is coming, she can steel herself not to react. If she knew it was coming, likely she wouldn't even attend." He looked at her. "I am sure that I can convincingly make the case for Oliver's innocence. But to do it, I might have to sacrifice—forever—any peace I might make with my mother. Tell me, Minnie. Is it worth it?"

She was silent for a long time, looking in his eyes. He buried the truth deep, deep, so that she would not hear what he had not said.

"And you'd do that?" she finally asked. "Lose all hope of your mother, for your brother's sake?"

"My father—" The words came out hoarsely. He shut his eyes. It was his only chance to explain it to her, even if she did not yet know what she was hearing.

"No," she said. "You don't have to answer. On the scale of things, we are weighing your mother's humiliation against your brother's future. Your brother must come first."

She put her arms around him. Her touch burned. He didn't deserve it. He didn't deserve *her*. He shrugged her off, stood, and went to stand a few paces away.

"It's more than that," he said softly. "It isn't just the fact that my father forced himself on his mother. It isn't that he tried to have her sent off, that he refused to acknowledge the child, that he failed to provide anything except the barest modicum of support. It isn't just that my actions put him in a stinking cell tonight." He clenched his fists. "I've tried to choose everything my father was not. And so I can't. I can't leave my brother alone in this. I can't risk his conviction, and I won't stand by while I have breath to save him."

"No, Robert," she said. "Of course you won't." She ran her hand along his cheek. "You have too much to do to waste your energy on regrets now. Do what you must."

There was no way to escape his regrets, looking down at her. It didn't make it any better, that he'd received her tacit approval. In some ways, it made that knotting in his gut feel worse.

She smiled up at him. "Now, what can I do to help?"

His heart almost broke as he looked down at her.

"You can make sure my mother is in the courtroom on the day of the trial," he said slowly. "Sit with her, and make sure she is there when I speak."

Because if Minnie brought the duchess…she would be there herself.

No time for regrets now.

Still, he felt them piercing his skin like silent splinters as she smiled at him. "You can trust me," she promised.

And he'd done it. He'd fooled his wife.

⌘   ⌘   ⌘

ROBERT RETURNED TO HIS BROTHER'S CELL at ten the next morning. The money that he'd handed the gaoler the night before had already made a difference. The top half of the cell door had been opened, showing heavy iron bars behind. The cell itself had been scrubbed out, and Oliver had been given water to wash with.

There was still an unmistakable stench to the holding room, but at least now it was only toe-curling and not enough to actually trigger gagging.

"I had a good talk with the lawyers this morning," Oliver said cheerfully. "My parents are out having breakfast, but they'll be back soon."

"Then I won't take long," Robert said.

A hint of confusion flashed over his brother's face, but Robert bulled ahead and told him what he'd learned on the previous night—about the substance of Lord Green's testimony, about the quote from a volume of chess strategy.

Oliver leaned back against the cell wall. "Come to think of it," he said, "that *is* a good point. I didn't recognize the quote. Where did you ever hear the term *discovered attack?* You never played chess."

Robert drew a deep breath. "Do you know who Minerva Lane is? Or Maximilian Lane, I suppose."

Oliver gave a surprised little huff and leaned forward. "Maximilian Lane? Of course I know who he—who *she* is. She's famous in the annals of chess. Or infamous, I suppose. I've studied her games, you know. They were recorded during…" He broke off and looked Robert in the eye. "You're joking," he said. "Never tell me that your Minnie is Minerva Lane."

"Uh." Robert shrugged. "As it happens…yes."

"That's how you knew."

Another nod. "Stevens knows her real name, but he hasn't uncovered her past."

"I see." Oliver took two paces to the edge of his cell and turned around. "Of course she's hiding who she is. She'd be ruined if everyone knew." He didn't say anything—didn't ask whether Robert would expose his wife's past. He didn't beg him to do it. Oliver would never ask for such a thing. But he took hold of the bars of his cell and squeezed until his knuckles turned white. "What a mess."

"Not a mess." Robert stepped closer. "Between you and me, I got everything—the title, the fortune. I've made up the difference as best I can. The least I can do is make sure you have a little freedom."

Oliver cocked his head and looked at him. His nose wrinkled again, this time in confusion. "That's what you think? You think that between the two of us, you got the better deal, that I was left with nothing?"

It wasn't an opinion. It was a fact. He'd given his brother as much as the other man would take, but Oliver was still fighting to secure his position in society.

"Never mind," Robert said.

"No, I won't brush it off with a *never mind*. You really think that you were born with more than I was?"

"I know I was."

Oliver turned away, his shoulders stiff. "Think again, Robert. Think again. I wouldn't trade what I have—cell, lice, and all—for all your fortune."

"And what is it you have that is so valuable?"

"I have a family that loves me."

Those words hit Robert hard. He'd just begun to hope for the possibility of happiness, only to have it wrested from him. He couldn't seem to draw breath. He felt as if he'd been struck in the stomach, struck hard enough to send his lungs into spasms.

He looked up at his brother standing before him, his face in half-profile. What little light there was glinted off his glasses, illuminated his bright hair.

It wasn't just Oliver he saw behind those cold iron bars, but everyone who cared about him—gruff, menacing Mr. Marshall, the stately Mrs. Marshall, three sisters, an aunt, two nephews… and reflected in the light of his spectacles, a brother.

A brother he'd found at twelve, one who had adopted him with a cheerful happiness that had shocked Robert. Oliver had taught him everything he knew about being part of a family.

"Yes," Robert said, his voice a little hoarse. "Well. As it turns out, I have a family that loves me, too. And I'm not about to abandon him."

He put his hand up to the iron bars.

"I have lice," Oliver reminded him.

"Shut up and take my hand."

It was an awkward handclasp they shared, an iron bar between their palms, but Robert wouldn't have traded it for the world.

"Let me do this for you," he said. "Because when we met at Eton, you could have knocked me down and kicked me in the ribs, and instead you chose to be my brother."

"Also," Oliver said brightly, "your latest source of contagion."

Robert laughed. "I have two gallons of carbon oil waiting for you already. I can spare a pint to douse my fingers, if necessary."

A throat cleared behind him, and Robert turned. What little humor he'd found turned to ash.

He didn't know how long the woman had been standing there. He'd seen her once before, more than a decade ago, but that one time had been enough. She was burned on his memory.

Mrs. Marshall was far shorter than her son. Her chestnut hair had a little more white in it than when last he'd seen her, but it only made her seem all the more regal. They looked at each other across the room, like two gazelles scenting each other across a meadow—watching, watching, watching, hoping that nothing would hunt them down.

"I'm sorry," Robert said. "I'm going now." He slid past her, giving her as wide a berth as he could without actually flattening himself against the wall. He went out the door into the courtyard. Plaster and timber rose two stories above him, shielding them from the late autumn sun. It was cold; he drew on gloves, pulled his hat down over his ears.

And just as he was readying himself to go, footsteps sounded again, and Mrs. Marshall came out of the holding room. Their eyes met again across the courtyard; Robert dropped his.

Ever so slowly, she crossed the paving stones to him.

"Mrs. Marshall." He could scarcely breathe. "I'm so sorry."

"Your Grace." She looked at him and then immediately looked away.

"No honorifics." He folded himself onto a bench at the edge of the courtyard. It was wet from last night's rain; he could feel the damp seeping through his trousers. But he didn't want to tower over her. Bad enough that he'd encountered her at all during this time and brought to her mind those other memories. "You, of all people, shouldn't be *Your Grace*-ing me."

She turned to him. He studied the paving stones beneath his feet.

"After what the collective dukes of Clermont have done to you and yours," he said quietly, "we don't deserve the respect. All I can say is that I'm sorry. I'm so, so sorry that Oliver—"

"It's not your fault."

"It most certainly is. My brother is awaiting trial for an act that I committed, for no reason except that they can't get at me. If that isn't my fault, I don't know what is." He contemplated the walls. "But I promise you, I won't let anything happen to him. I won't."

She stood before him a few moments longer. He kept his head down, aware of her every breath.

And then, very slowly, she brushed her skirts to the side and sat gingerly on the stone bench next to him. Six inches away, but still next to him. "You've been a good friend to my son."

"I've been his *brother.*" He still didn't look at her.

"He talked about you all the time when he was home from school. You and Sebastian Malheur—but especially you. Needless to say, Mr. Marshall and I found it rather alarming. But he didn't talk about a boy who seemed like a younger version of your father. You sounded thoughtful and quiet, two things that the Duke of Clermont never managed to be. I always wished I had been better prepared all those years ago. When Oliver spoke of you, you sounded so sweet that I had envisioned a completely different boy. To walk in the room and see you looking at me—with his eyes, and his nose, and his mouth—I don't know what came over me. I didn't even really come back to myself until I was half a mile away."

"There's no need to explain. I know what my father did. If I were you, I wouldn't be able to look at me, either."

"Oliver said after, he thought I'd hurt your feelings."

Robert shook his head. "There is no room for my feelings in this. You were wronged. It's not your responsibility to extend the olive branch, but mine, to get out of your way. To give to you what little comfort you can find."

"Maybe," she said slowly. "Maybe. But what I can't help thinking is this."

The sky was blue overhead, without a single cloud in it. It seemed impossible at this time of year, and yet there it was. Robert tilted his head back and shut his eyes.

"We told Oliver the truth about his birth when he was quite young. Or, I should say, Hugo told him. Not everything, you understand, but a child's version. There was a bad man. He hurt me. Some people might say that other man was his father, but we loved him, and it wasn't true. I didn't want to say anything at all, but Hugo convinced me." She sighed.

Robert tried to imagine what it would be like to have parents who actually considered what to tell their children, who cared about these details. Who assured him that they loved him.

I want to be that kind of parent. His fists clenched.

"Hugo was very matter-of-fact about it, and so Oliver took it in stride. Until he found out about you. Then he had nightmares."

"About me?" Robert repeated.

"Yes. He woke up crying one night, and wouldn't stop. When I asked what was wrong, he said that the bad man had his brother, and we had to go get him."

Robert felt a lump form in his throat. "Ah," he managed carefully.

"I thought it was sweet, actually, and that stage passed. But..." She turned to look at him directly. "But now, it has been almost thirty years since I saw your father. What he did to me took all of ten minutes, and I still remember it." She paused and then reached over and tapped him on the knee.

He looked over into her eyes. This time, she didn't flinch from him.

"You," she said quietly, "you grew up with him. That must have been awful."

For a second, Robert saw his father looming over him, so much taller back then, so much bigger.

What kind of a son are you? He'd thrown up his hands in aggravation. *Any other boy, and things would be so much better. Even your mother doesn't want you enough to stay.*

"Oh," Robert said quietly. "It wasn't so bad. Most of the time, my father didn't even remember I was there."

And perhaps Mrs. Marshall heard that tiny catch in his voice, because ever so slowly, she put her arm around him.

"You poor, poor boy," she said.

⌘ ⌘ ⌘

Robert's duty for the afternoon did not promise to be so enlightening as his morning.

"I have no idea what to think of you, Your Grace."

Robert stood in the entry to the Charingfords' home. It seemed a comfortable enough place, papered in cream and blue, the entry itself bright and cheerful. But Mr. Charingford, who stood across from him, looked neither bright nor happy. His hair was graying and thin, and he'd folded his arms over his chest.

"I've agreed to this," the other man said, "because you showed good sense on precisely one occasion."

"One occasion?" Robert raised an eyebrow. "When was that?"

"When you married Miss Pur—I suppose I cannot call her that now, can I?" Charingford tilted his head and almost smiled. "When you married your wife. I tried to convince my son to have a look at her, but he never could get past that scar. Her friendship with my daughter... We spent four months together in Cornwall on a journey, and I think I know her better than anyone in town besides her great-aunts. She was a good choice."

She had been. Robert ached to think of what would come tomorrow.

"I can only hope that some of her sense has begun to seep into your consciousness. I cannot know what you were thinking to write those handbills. To come here and try to convince people like me to support voting reform." Charingford gave him a look under lowered eyebrows.

"If you know I wrote those handbills," Robert asked, "why did you indict Mr. Marshall?"

Charingford's eyes dropped. "There was enough evidence to support his involvement. And..."

"And Stevens asked you," Robert filled in.

Charingford bit his lip. "You know about that?"

"Don't lecture me on sense," Robert said. "I asked to see your factory, and you agreed to show me. Let's get on with it."

Charingford gestured and a footman opened the front door. As he did, the dull vibration that came from the factory across the street accelerated to a roar.

"If you will," he said grimly. "Your Grace."

The clatter of the machinery was almost overwhelming as they crossed the cobblestones of the street. The factory doors had been newly painted a gleaming green, standing out against the coal-streaked brick of the walls. The noise surrounded them, a cacophony of shrieking and shaking. Mr. Charingford ushered him inside with a series of gestures and then, when they'd made their way up a small staircase to stand on a metal platform that overlooked the operation, turned to face him.

"This is the main room," he shouted, straining to be heard over the clatter of the machines below. "Here's where the yarn is knitted into hose."

He pointed down into the factory below. A woman, her white-streaked hair tied back in a careless bun, operated a machine that wound yarn onto metal bobbins on one side of the room. A handful of men strolled from one circular frame to the next, moving pieces when necessary, replacing bobbins, handing the products off to boys who scampered with them into an adjacent room. They moved with an economy of motion that seemed to spring more from weariness than expertise.

"Each machine can produce two pairs of stockings in nine minutes," Charingford shouted. "And the men are needed only to take the work off the stitch hooks at the end and to reset the cylinder that guides the shape of the stocking. Look at them, Your Grace. They don't even have to make decisions in their daily work. How could we trust them to decide the future of our country? To understand the workings of industry?"

Robert simply tilted his head, listening over the racket of the machines. "They're singing," he said. "Why are they singing?"

Mr. Charingford paused and put one hand to his ear, listening. "They're happy to be at work, Your Grace. They're singing a hymn— praise to God."

Robert was a man looking down on a factory floor from above. All he had to do was *look,* while the workers below turned and wound and cut.

Lucky you, he could hear Minnie say, *that you can consider the future without terror.* He didn't think he could even understand what it meant to stand down there, to toil in this unrelenting noise for day after day. All he knew was that it wasn't as simple as gratitude and hymns.

Over the short course of their marriage, he'd never been farther from Minnie than he was at this moment. He'd lied to her, and tomorrow he was going to break his promise to her and hurt her. And yet he could hear her right now over the thunder of the machinery.

"I don't pretend to understand what it means to be a working man, Mr. Charingford, but I am a factory owner. I inherited a good bit of industry from my grandfather. And when I look at your factory floor, I don't see men who are happy to be at work."

A woman on the floor looked up at them as he spoke. There was no hatred in her eyes, no contempt. Just a soft look around the edge of her eyes—a quiet yearning.

Perhaps she had once been a genteel young lady who failed to marry. Maybe she'd had no choice but to take on work until her hair grayed before her time and her skin turned to leather. Still, she looked up. Like everyone else, her lips moved in song.

"Well?" Mr. Charingford said. "What is it that you see instead?"

"I see Minnie." His voice caught. "I see who she might have been in ten years, when her great-aunts' health faded away."

Mr. Charingford drew in a sharp breath.

"I see your daughter if the market for hosiery should vanish."

"Not Lydia," Charingford said in shocked tones. "Surely not..." But he trailed away unhappily.

"I see who my brother might have been if another man hadn't stepped in to raise him. I see my childhood cook, if I hadn't pensioned her off. The only person I don't see is myself." He let his hands trail over the catwalk. "I have never been there, and I never will. The only thing I understand now is that I cannot comprehend what it is like to stand on a factory floor and look up and sing."

Mr. Charingford tilted his head and looked at him, really listening now.

"I've a goodly share of faults. I rush in, where I should tread carefully. I speak, where I should listen. But when I hear them sing, I don't just hear a hymn. They're singing to God because they haven't found anyone else who will listen."

Charingford spoke cautiously. "Stevens says that if we listen once, we'll only stir the workers on to greater unreasonableness."

"Have you found that Stevens becomes more reasonable the more you give in to his demands?"

Charingford looked away.

"How much has he asked of you, Charingford? You're a magistrate. Has he said he won't help you if you don't do as he says? Has he asked for money? Or did he simply demand that he be awarded the hand of your beautiful daughter in exchange for his efforts?"

Charingford's hands closed on the metal rail in front of him. He closed his eyes. "That," he said. "He did—all of that."

"I have found," Robert said, "that in the long run, paying my workers enough that they do not consider the future with terror costs far less than employing men to terrorize them."

"You sound like Minnie," Charingford muttered. It sounded like a complaint.

Robert simply smiled and shook his head. It was, perhaps, the sweetest compliment he'd been given.

A young boy darted across the floor below, conveying a full bobbin to a man who had turned to one of the machines.

"If you don't look carefully," Robert said, "the men and women on the floor fade into indistinguishable browns and grays. You don't have to see them as anything except the working arms of the machines, flesh and blood instead of steel and iron. Drawing wages, instead of being purchased upfront. But machines don't sing. Machines don't hope. And Charingford, I don't think we could stop them, not with a thousand copies of Captain Stevens. I don't intend to try."

"You're a radical." There was no heat in the accusation. Charingford looked out over the factory. But now, his gaze stopped here and there— on women who bound the hose up in paper, on men who worked the machines.

"I know," Robert said.

"If you'd talked to me when first you arrived, instead of writing handbills…"

"I'm growing up. And my wife, it appears, is having some effect on me." Robert shrugged. "You never know. By the time I'm thirty, I might actually start making a difference."

Chapter Twenty-five

IT WAS LATE WHEN MINNIE'S HUSBAND returned home—so late that all the servants except one solitary footman had gone to bed. Minnie heard the front door open and then close behind Robert. She could imagine him taking off his things—greatcoat, frock coat—and handing them to the footman. She waited to hear his footsteps on the stairs, but as the minutes ticked by, they didn't come.

Minnie slowly stood and tiptoed out of their room. The house below had been doused in darkness. The only reason she could find her footing on the great staircase that led to the entrance was that a hint of light was coming from some room in the back. She followed that path of golden light down the hallway.

The door at the end was ajar. Robert sat at the table, a plate in front of him filled with the cold remains from dinner. He wasn't eating; he simply held his fork in one hand, staring blankly off into nothingness. His head was bowed a fraction, as if he were supplicating the beef before him for some great thing. While she watched, his hand crept to the corner of his eye and brushed against it—almost as if he were swiping away a tear.

He wasn't crying. He didn't reach for a handkerchief. But his hand stayed there, next to his eye, as if to ward off any other emotion.

Her own breath caught.

She retreated down the hallway, cursing her soft silk slippers. He hadn't even heard her coming. Loudly, she opened the door to the parlor and retrieved the package that she'd obtained earlier that day. Even more loudly, she slammed the parlor door shut.

It was impossible to scuff slippers against carpet, but she did her best. By the time she got to the door, he'd set his hand down. That look of intense bleakness had faded, and he even managed to manufacture a little smile for her.

"Minnie," he said. "I didn't think you would be awake."

As if she would have been able to sleep, thinking of him and worrying about his brother. The trial was scheduled for tomorrow. She could see the toll the strain had taken on him. There were dark circles under his eyes, worry lines grooved on his forehead.

"I had a hard time sleeping without you," she answered. She set the package on the table near him.

He picked up a chunk of beef on his fork. "No time for supper," he said, almost apologetically, before putting it in his mouth. "And I find I'm starving."

She sat next to him. "I'm a little hungry, myself."

They were probably both lying. They probably both knew it.

Still, Minnie took a roll to keep him company, and while he ate, she shredded it on her plate. If nothing else, her presence spurred him on to do justice to the food before him. He ate mechanically—peas and turnips and carrots, as well as the beef in a sauce that had congealed. It turned her stomach to think of it, but he didn't seem to taste anything he put in his mouth. He seemed surprised when his fork found nothing on the plate.

"Long day," he said. "I—I think I'll be going straight to bed." But he didn't stand.

Minnie took that as an invitation to walk over to the sideboard and pour a glass of sherry. She brought it to him; their fingers touched as she passed it over.

"Will everything be all right?" she asked.

In response, he put his head in his hands. Minnie put her fingers over his. His skin was warm to the touch; she could almost feel his temples throbbing. Slowly, she rubbed his forehead; he made a little noise and then leaned into the pressure.

"I don't know," he said quietly. "I'm not..." He turned his head sideways to meet her eyes and then quickly looked away. "I'm not certain." His fingers drummed against the table. "But I'll do everything I can to make it so. My brother..." He drew in another deep breath. "My father didn't care. He didn't help. Oliver grew up with none of the advantages I had, and to have him so publicly take the blame for something that I have done—Minnie, I can't abide it. I feel on the brink of madness just contemplating it. You must know that."

"I know." She rubbed his forehead. "But you're doing everything you can."

"Yes." His voice was bleak, so bleak. "Still, I can see no way that this can turn out well."

"Maybe not. But whatever happens, we'll face this together."

He took in another long breath. "Minnie... Tomorrow there's going to be a crowd at the courthouse. Someone notified the London newspapers that I would be testifying, and now there are not just two reporters present, but twenty."

"Are you asking if I can manage with a crowd? I can be in crowds. They make me uneasy, but so long as everyone's not looking at me, I can make do."

If anything, that intensified the bleakness in his eyes. He seemed to deflate right there at the table. "I…Minnie. I don't know what to say."

She shook her head. "I have to be there," she said. "There is no other way. So I will." She'd work out the details later.

He shook his head. "At least one good thing has come of this. I came to Leicester to stop the misuse of criminal sedition as a tool to end strikes. Now I know who's behind it." He gave her a sharp smile. "I had the most interesting talk with…with a magistrate about what Stevens has asked for in order to help him keep the peace. Justice *will* be done."

"Good," Minnie said. "Excellent. I have something else for you, and I hope it's good, too. I got you something." She indicated the object wrapped in brown paper that she had brought in with her.

He eyed the oblong package warily, then took hold of one corner and pulled it to him. "What is this?"

"A gift."

"It's not my birthday." He glanced up at her. "It's not Christmas, not for over a month."

"It's not a gift for any occasion." She could feel her heart pounding in her chest. "It's just one where I saw it and wanted you to have it."

Like those rubies he'd given her, now packed away in a box for a happier occasion.

"It's heavy," he said, feeling the edges. "A book? An atlas?"

"I'm not going to tell you," she said. "You have to open it and find out."

He tugged on the twine, and, when the rough bow came undone, dropped the string to the floor. The paper crinkled as he unfolded it.

The volume was bound up in soft cream-colored leather, embossed in a subtle pattern. There was no title on the front, nor, when he tilted it, was there one on the spine. She held her breath as he pulled back the cover and flipped through the first creamy pages.

This book had come off no printing press. It had been lovingly, perfectly, illustrated by hand. She thought that the illustrations were watercolors, but if they were, they were astonishingly vibrant—layers and layers of paint ghosted on top of one another until the reds were as deep as dying leaves in autumn and the blues as real as a summer sky. The first illustration—a giant letter A—stood on the crest of a hill. The letter itself was composed of myriad smaller pictures. An apple tree, bending in the wind, formed one side of the letter. At the very height of its branches, an albatross stood, stretching its wings to the sky. An alpaca stretched to eat an apple, its neck forming the other side. An adder curled at its feet, but instead of threatening any of the other creatures, it appeared to be busily munching on an apricot. The entire illustration was composed of things that started with A.

He stared at it before turning the page to letter B—bees, birches, and buttercups. "You got me a primer?" He looked bemused.

"I thought—" She swallowed. "You said you wanted to have lots of children. I thought I would get you a primer that didn't have any words printed in it. That way, you might make up anything that you wanted for each letter. And you wouldn't be wrong."

He looked at the pages. He touched the edge of one, and she wondered if he was thinking about the M—which, indeed, had both mice and the figure of a mother, holding her child's hand entwined in the moonlight, with moths and magpies flying around a mulberry bush at the dead of midnight. But he didn't flip to that letter. Instead, he turned to look at her.

"You got this for me," he said.

She nodded.

"Because…"

"Because I was thinking about you."

He stood. She couldn't read his expression at all.

But then he put his hands on her shoulders, and, when she looked up at him, he kissed her. He kissed her with no finesse, no gentleness. He kissed her with all the emotion that he hadn't shown since he'd walked in the door—fiercely, savagely, as if he'd returned from an absence of ten years and needed to remind her of everything that had happened. His arms came around her, wrapping her to him as tightly as chains. He was a scorching heat against her. He took kiss after kiss after kiss, scarcely allowing her to draw breath before wrapping her in another one. He pulled her to him so tightly that she scarcely noticed when he lifted her up and set her on the table in front of him. He left her mouth long enough to suck on her chin, her neck. Little spots of pleasure bloomed in the wake of his kisses, and still he went further down—until he undid the buttons at the neck of her nightgown, enough to pull it down over her breasts.

His mouth closed over her nipple and she gave herself over to him. There was nothing but the heat of his tongue against her, the savagery of his hands on her hips. Her back met the hard wood of the table.

"God, Minnie," he breathed. "What will I do without you?"

"Why would you ever have to know? I'm not going anywhere."

He didn't seem to hear her. He let go of her long enough to undo his trousers and then captured her wrists in his hands, holding them to her side. He didn't look in her eyes, though.

"I'm here," she said. "You don't have to hold me down. I'm not going anywhere."

He didn't let go. Instead, he let out a growl and pushed inside her. Her body was slick to receive him. He'd not even bothered to remove his trousers all the way, and when he buried himself inside of her, she felt the fabric against her thighs. Somehow that fact—that he'd been so desperate for her that he'd not even disrobed, that he'd pushed her on a table—only heightened her desire all the more. The glorious slide of his body into hers seemed even more delicious, even more forbidden.

There wasn't anything pristine and proper about his lovemaking. It was something far more feral, an elemental force that she'd never experienced before. His thrusts were hard and steady; his hair curled around his forehead, dripping sweat.

"God," he groaned.

She clenched him tightly, and he growled once more. "I want you," he said fiercely. "God, I want you. Why can't I have you?"

"You can. You do."

But he didn't speak in response. Instead, he took her harder. He seemed almost in a frenzy. He growled one final time and then came. He let go of her wrists as he did—but only so he could take hold of her face and kiss her.

As his climax passed, his kiss faded from savage to sweet. He gently pulled away, took in a shuddering breath, and looked around, as if to verify that he had just had his way with her on top of the table.

Well-constructed, that table. It had scarcely even budged, no matter how he'd taken her.

He disengaged from her and slid off to stand on the floor. She sat up gingerly.

"Minnie," he breathed.

"If you say one word other than 'Lord, that was magnificent,' I will bite you," she said.

He let out a laugh. "God." He fingered the side of her face. "You are magnificent."

But there was still a shadow on his face, a curtain pulled over his expression. He stepped back from her and she could feel him withdraw.

And Minnie knew. She could see it in the tilt of his head, the way his eyes didn't meet hers. There was something he wasn't telling her.

She smiled wanly and tapped his wrist.

"I don't want you to father all our children atop a wooden table, but this once...this wasn't so bad."

"I just...I just needed to know you were still mine." His hand hovered near her shoulder and then dropped down to his side. "I don't know what came over me."

She reached out and took hold of his hand and entwined it with hers. "You know, it has always been one of my dearest wishes to drive a man to distraction. It was simply glorious to do it." She touched her finger to his lips. "I know how difficult today must have been for you—how hard these last days must have been. You told me when we married that you wanted an ally, someone who always saw *you* rather than a duke." She pulled him close. "And here I am."

"Here you are," he breathed. His voice was raspy. His hands closed on her hair. "Here you are."

⌘ ⌘ ⌘

AT THREE IN THE MORNING, Robert's dreaming mind took over. He saw himself on the stand and Minnie—a younger, more vulnerable version of herself—in the audience.

"She's an unnatural child," he heard himself say. "The spawn of the devil himself. She made me do it."

She watched him, her eyes wide and hurt—and then she shattered in a fountain of gray glass. He reached for her, but the shards only cut his hands to ribbons.

He woke gulping air, reaching for her, with the realization fresh on his mind. Oh, God. He was going to do *that* to her—to betray her on the stand in front of everyone, just as her father had done.

She was curled on her side next to him. In her sleep, her hand rested on his hip; her head leaned against his shoulder. Even in her sleep, she trusted him.

He couldn't do it. He couldn't do this to her.

He dragged himself out of bed instead. By the light of a flickering candle, he wrote her a letter telling her everything—what he'd planned, why he'd wanted it.

I have to tell the truth about you, he finally wrote. *I can't see my way around that. But don't come to the trial today. I'm sorry about what must be said—but don't come to the trial.*

I love you.

His hand hovered, wanting desperately to write one last sentence.

Please forgive me.

But he didn't know how she could. He wasn't even sure if he could make himself ask.

Before he left to meet Oliver's lawyers, he roused her maid and put the letter in her hands.

"Here," he said, gesturing to a chair just outside their bedroom. "Sit here. Make sure that whatever you do, she reads this letter as soon as she awakes, and not one instant later. It is urgent."

The rest of the morning passed in a blur. He seemed to wait forever for the trial to start, but once it did, the prosecution's evidence bled together into a meaningless stream of testimony and examination. Robert's sense of unease grew.

All around them, reporters made industrious notes in shorthand. The defense started their case. This was the moment when Minnie would have appeared in the room, his mother in tow. But she didn't arrive. Thank God.

Robert was finally called to the stand, and everything else seemed to disappear—the courtroom, the jurors, the reporters watching in avid interest. There was nobody but him and the barrister conducting the examination.

The questions were simple at first—his name, his title, his age, the last time he'd sat in Parliament. And then…

"Do you know who wrote the handbills that are at the heart of the prosecution's case?" asked the barrister.

"Yes," Robert answered. "I did."

A surprised murmur rose up from the crowd.

"Did anyone assist you with them?"

"I had them distributed by a man who could not read, had them printed more than a hundred miles away. Nobody in the household I set up here in Leicester knew the first thing about them. I made sure of that."

"Nobody? What about Mr. Marshall?"

"*Especially* not Mr. Marshall," Robert said emphatically. "You see, I wrote those because it had come to my attention that there has been a rash of criminal sedition convictions in town—ones that did not appear to be properly charged under the law. I wanted to draw out those who were involved in the scheme. I wrote the handbills because I could not be tried, but wouldn't have involved another person in the jurisdiction of Leicester. I wouldn't have wanted to put anyone at risk."

"What would you care about Mr. Marshall?" asked the barrister. "He was only a paid employee, was he not?"

"He was not," Robert said forcefully. "I have never paid him—I settled funds on him. And even if I didn't care about the wellbeing of my employees, he is my brother." Gasps and a second murmur arose. Robert had been so concentrated on the questions that he hadn't looked out at the courtroom. He did now. For one moment, the reporters in the front row looked at him in shock. Then they grinned in delight as they realized that the story here was even more interesting than they'd supposed. To a man, their pencils began working feverishly. He smiled, looking out over them—until his eyes fell on the back of the room.

There, seated in the last row, was Minnie. She must have come in while he was speaking. Next to her sat his mother.

Had she not received his message? What was she *doing* here?

"Your Grace." The barrister's voice seemed slow, so slow, and yet Robert could not outrun it. He couldn't even move from his seat. "Do you play chess?"

Minnie's eyes burned into his.

"No." He couldn't turn away from her.

"Have you ever played chess?"

"A few times, when I was young. Enough to know the rules of the game. But I know very little."

"Can you explain how you came to write about a 'discovered attack' in your handbills—and how you did so in terms that closely parallel words in an obscure handbook of chess strategy?"

"Yes," Robert said. "I can."

The entire courtroom became quiet.

"As it happens, when I wrote that, I had been talking with someone who is an expert at chess. Not Mr. Marshall."

"And who was this person?"

Minnie would know what was happening now. She would understand why he'd asked her to come to the courtroom. She'd know that he'd trapped her, betrayed her in public, done everything to her that he'd promised not to do. He should have shaken her awake this morning and told her himself.

She was watching him with a curious look on her face. And then, oddly enough, she touched two fingers to her lips and held them up to him.

I'm sorry, Minnie.

"In 1851," Robert heard himself say, "a twelve-year-old girl by the name of Minerva Lane almost won the first international chess tournament."

In 1851, Minerva Lane was betrayed and ruined by her father. And now, Robert was doing it again.

"Are you acquainted with Minerva Lane?"

He made himself look Minnie in the eyes when he drove the knife in. Her face was gray, her eyes wide. Slowly, ever so slowly, she lowered the fingers that she had kissed.

The words felt like shards of glass in his mouth, but he formed them anyway. "I'm married to her."

Chapter Twenty-six

KNOWING WHAT WAS GOING TO HAPPEN DIDN'T HELP. Minnie couldn't even feel her heart beating, so thick was her anxiety. As Robert spoke, her whole body turned to ice. And when everyone turned to see who he was looking at—when all their eyes landed on her, dark with accusation—a wild, ragged panic took her. The murmurs grew to a crashing swell.

"That's her," someone said.

She couldn't remember how to breathe. Her lungs caught in airless spasms. She shoved to her feet, but the crowd was all around her. Shouting. Screaming. Her vision swam with dark spots that grew ever larger. The last thing she saw was Robert standing up from the witness stand and vaulting over the edge. And then everything went dark.

She wasn't sure when she came back to consciousness. It returned slowly, like a piece of a dream gradually coming to life. There was the gentle sway of the carriage, her husband's arms around her, his breath against her neck. His hands. He was whispering words of encouragement, but she couldn't open her eyes.

Awareness came in flashes. Being carried up the stairs. Softness surrounding her. And his voice—Robert's voice—was there, even in the middle of restless dreams. It made a muffled murmur in her ear until the disquiet fell away and she drifted off.

When she awoke, it was afternoon. She was lying in bed. Not, she realized, their bed. This was *her* bed—the bed that had been set up in the duchess's quarters. It was the first time that she'd been on this mattress, and she didn't like it.

Someone had taken off her blue silk day gown and her corset, petticoats, and drawers, leaving her in her shift. She wasn't surrounded by a crowd—but yes, she really had fainted again. In public. Other memories followed swiftly on the heels of that. The courtroom. Robert, sitting up front. Robert, looking directly at Minnie as he spilled all her secrets to everyone.

She wasn't angry so much as curiously hollow. Minnie sighed and sat up.

She could remember falling. But the most curious thing—she couldn't remember hitting the ground. Slowly, gingerly, she poked one toe out of bed. Her feet found the floor; she tested her weight on them, and they held.

And that was when her eyes fell on a figure in a chair across the room—a female figure.

"Lydia," she gasped. "What are you doing here?"

Lydia stood. "Your husband sent for me." Her face seemed shadowed. "I heard what happened. He said you needed me, so I…I came."

"But…"

"I'm so sorry," Lydia said in a rush, moving to her side. "For the longest time, I could only think that you had lied to me, that I couldn't trust you. That you didn't trust me." Lydia sat down next to her. "I said you didn't tell me anything, but I knew. I knew you had these spells, that you hated crowds. This isn't the first time I've seen you collapse in front of everyone. If I had thought, I would have realized. I've been so hateful."

Minnie looked at her friend. "Don't say that."

"How can I not? It wasn't a lie when you found out I was pregnant and you told me that everything would be all right. It wasn't a lie when I miscarried and you read to me for hours while I lay in bed fearing that I, too, would die. I wish you had told me, but…" Her voice grew quiet. "Nothing between us has ever been a lie. And I should have been here for you, as you were for me, long before now."

Lydia gave her a fierce hug, one so tight that Minnie didn't think she would ever let go. She didn't want her to.

"I'm also sorry," Lydia said in a more prosaic tone of voice, "because it means I never had a chance to say I told you so."

They looked at each other and laughed. "You did. And you were right. It's been—" Minnie frowned. "What's that noise?"

Lydia turned around. "That? That's just your husband talking to people in his chamber."

His chamber? That was *their* bedchamber. They'd never used separate rooms thus far. Even during her husband's dark moods these last days, they'd shared a bed. This room had gone entirely unused.

She could hear him talking—not loud enough to make out the words, but at just the volume where she might hear the cadences of his speech, the rhythm of clipped orders being delivered.

"Lydia," she asked, "where is my husband?"

She would have sworn that he'd carried her home. He'd sent for Lydia. The last time she'd collapsed, he'd been there when she awoke, even knowing that the blow to her reputation would require him to offer marriage. Why was he not here?

Lydia shook her head. "In the other room."

"He should be here. He *was* here." She pulled on a dressing gown from her wardrobe. Then she tottered a few steps to the door that separated them. The handle turned under her weight and the door swung in.

There were three servants in his room—his valet and two footmen—and several trunks. Robert was sitting with his back to her, watching them bustle about. One footman had just emerged from his dressing room, arms loaded with a stack of colored silk waistcoats. He placed these in a trunk, and Minnie's world came to a standstill.

"Robert, what on earth are you doing?" Minnie asked.

He froze, his back turned to her. The servants all looked away and started packing more swiftly, more silently. Only their sidelong glances showed their interest.

"You recuperated rather swiftly," he said, his spine still to her. "I had thought I would be gone by the time you were up and about."

"Gone? But where are you going?"

Finally, he rose and turned. But even though his body was generally pointed in her direction, still he didn't look at her. "Away."

She'd panicked when he'd spoken in front of all those people. They'd looked at her; her old terror had risen up. But as awful as fainting was, it was *easy*. Once you did it, you no longer had to deal with the situation at hand. There was no escape from this. This…this just hurt.

"Away? Where away? For how long?"

"I made you a promise," he said at last. "And I broke it into more pieces than anyone would have thought possible. I can only imagine how furious you must be with me." His jaw squared. "I won't hold on to you. I won't beg." He gave her a wintry smile. "I'm making things easier for you."

Her head was ringing. "Just like that?"

"No scenes. No arguments. No need to throw anything." He finally looked up and gave her a tired smile. "You'll have anything you want; just ask for it."

If anything, the footmen had begun to pack faster, as if to prove that their ears could not hear what was being said.

Minnie walked slowly into the room to stand before him. "I don't understand. Are you saying—"

"I know what happened out there. You only married me because I told you that I would protect you. And I just—"

"One moment, Robert." Minnie waved her hand at the servants. "I think you'd all best go now. In fact, I think it would be best if you could clear the wing for the next hour or so."

A pause. One footman looked at the cravats he carried. Another glanced at the duke, who squared his jaw and said nothing.

Minnie clapped her hands. "Leave everything and go." They scattered.

Minnie turned around. Lydia was still standing in the doorway connecting their two rooms, watching with wide eyes. She held up her hands. "I am already gone," she said. "Come see me later, Minnie."

She cast Robert a hard glance and then she, too, disappeared.

They waited, listening, until the retreating footsteps faded into the distance.

And then Minnie set her hands on his chest, and gave him a hard shove. "Robert, you idiot, what in blazes are you thinking?"

"I had to." He stared at her. "I had to. He was my brother, and I had to—"

"Oh, you stupid man." She gave him another shove, and he stumbled back, his legs hitting the bed. "That is not what I'm talking about."

"I left a note," he said. "This morning. I should have talked to you about it sooner. I should have woken you up. It took me that long to come to my senses. I feel sick, thinking that you were exposed to that simply because—"

"I got your note," Minnie said. "I read it. I decided you were right."

"You did…you did what?" He blinked at her stupidly.

"I got your note," Minnie repeated. "I read it. I decided your initial impulse was right. There was no hiding the truth of my identity. It was going to come out no matter what we did. That meant the only thing on the line for me was a little humiliation. Compared to your brother's life, what would that mean?"

"Minnie!" He sounded horrified. "But you—"

She put her hand on his shoulder. "You had to tell everyone the truth of my past to save your brother from being ostracized. Do you imagine that I would have insisted on your silence, with that at stake? Yes, that scene was awful. Yes, I never want to do anything like it again. I don't like it when people look at me. I can't breathe. I can't see straight." She looked at him. "It was awful, but it was not the end of the world. And you think it means the end of our marriage?"

He blinked. "It…isn't?" Finally, he looked her in the eyes. He looked surprised, stunned even. "But you're angry with me. I can see it."

"Of course I'm angry."

He shook his head. "Then… Aren't you going to leave?"

"Of course I'm angry," she repeated. "Because I thought I meant something to you. And you're willing to walk away simply because you can't be bothered to patch things up."

"Can't be bothered…" he repeated in a stunned voice. He looked at her. He turned and looked at the half-packed trunks, at the pile of cravats the footman had abandoned on a chest of drawers.

"I just…" His voice was soft and tired. "I don't understand. I hurt you. I knew I was going to do it, and I did it anyway. How can I make that right? I can't tell you not to be angry. You should be angry. You deserve to be angry."

This was the man whose mother had walked away from him as a child. This was the man whose father had seen him as nothing more than a tool to extract money from other pockets. Robert had forgiven Minnie for her earlier deception. But he had so little expectation of forgiveness for himself that he couldn't even ask for it.

Minnie reached out and took his hand. "Do you know why I am furious? Because you would rather leave than try to make our marriage work."

He searched her eyes. "I…"

"I know. You don't want to fight. But fights don't destroy a marriage. Not making up does."

He swallowed. "You *want* to fight?"

"Yes. And I want you to say that you were terribly, desperately, sordidly wrong."

He flinched. "I was. I know I was."

"I want to believe you when you apologize. I want to know in my soul that you would never do anything to hurt me. I want you to promise me that next time this happens, you'll come talk to me first, and we'll decide what to do together."

He was looking at her, his head cocked.

"And then, when you've done all that, I want to forgive you." Her eyes filled with tears.

"But why do you want to do all that?"

"Because I love you," she said. "I love you. I love you."

He let out a deep breath. "You're certain?" he said quietly.

She nodded.

"I see," he said. And then, without saying another word, he walked out of the room.

Chapter Twenty-seven

MINNIE STARED AT THE DOOR where Robert had exited, her mind a whirl of confusion. Why had he left? Where was he going? What was she to do?

She went to the window to see if he was leaving the house entirely, took one look outside, and stepped back with a gasp. There was a small crowd encamped on their doorstep, a throng of hats in shades of brown and black forming a half circle almost three deep. One man looked up, saw her, pointed—

Minnie jumped back, her heart pounding.

If he'd gone out, she wouldn't even be able to follow after him.

She turned back to his room. A newspaper lay on a chest of drawers. She unfolded it curiously and discovered that it had been printed this afternoon. It couldn't have been more than a half hour old.

Duke of Clermont Authors Handbills, the headline proclaimed. In smaller type underneath, the subtitle read: *Duchess Is Former Chess Champion.*

She read that again, shaking her head at how bland it felt. "Well," she finally murmured. "I suppose 'Duchess is former fraud who dressed as boy and deceived hundreds' wouldn't fit. Three cheers for restricted paper size."

The article itself was surprisingly evenhanded. The worst accusations she'd weathered in the past—monster, cheat, unnatural devil's spawn—were absent. Her past was summarized in a short, factual paragraph. It was shocking, no doubt, but time had blunted the power and charisma of her father's words.

Mr. Lane claimed the entire scheme was his daughter's idea, but no evidence was ever found to support the assertion that a twelve-year-old child had been involved in the fraudulent endeavor.

She felt as if she'd opened a door on what she believed was a towering monster, only to find it five inches tall. There were things one might say about the child of a criminal. One didn't say those things about a duke's wife.

The account of today's trial seemed equally strange.

Reading about her own collapse was a decidedly odd experience. It felt as if she were observing her emotions from a distance. She could hear the gasps of those around her in the courtroom, but now she understood them as surprise, not condemnation. She could see herself go pale, without her own skin going clammy, her breath cycling dangerously swiftly.

It allowed her to see what happened afterward, too. She'd fallen into a dead faint. A man near her had spat at her—and when he had, the dowager duchess had smacked him over the head with her umbrella. She'd glared at everyone else who threatened to close in, keeping them at bay.

Robert had leaped over three benches—surely that had to be an exaggeration—to reach her.

When the duke brought his wife out of the courtroom, he deigned to answer a few questions. He affirmed that he was aware of his wife's identity on their marriage—a claim that seems unassailable in light of the marriage registry, which names his wife as Minerva Lane. His Grace explained his choice of bride as follows: "Why would I take a conventional wife, when I could have an extraordinary one?"

Minnie set the paper down and shut her eyes. Her eyes stung with prickling tears. She could hear him in that quote—could imagine the roll of his eyes, the look of annoyance he'd cast at them. Her body had the memory of being held, even if her mind did not.

She wasn't sure what any of it meant, but she was sure of one thing.

He was coming back.

She read on in the paper. The article was only a few columns long. A related note mentioned that after the trial, Captain George Stevens had been taken into custody and charged with accepting bribes in exchange for performing his official duty. Minnie smiled wanly. Good.

The door opened. Robert stood in the hall, a book clutched to his chest. He met her eyes, his expression wary.

"You'll have to excuse me if I make a hash of this," he said quietly. "But I've never done it before."

"What are you doing?"

In answer, he walked into the room and laid the leather-bound volume on the chest of drawers near her.

It was the primer she'd bought him the other day. "I..." He looked down and then looked up at her. "I decided what these letters stood for," he told her. "I thought I might tell you."

It took her a moment to realize that he was nervous. He glanced at her sidelong and opened the book to the first page.

"A," he said, "is for all the ways I love you."

That fierce prickle of tears stung her eyes with renewed force. She blinked, unwilling to let them cloud her vision. She wanted to *see* him, to make out the details of his pale, tousled hair, the way he bit his lip.

He looked away. "This is stupid," he muttered, reaching for the corner of the cover. He'd almost slammed it shut before Minnie realized what he was doing and insinuated her hand between the open pages.

"No!" she protested. "It's not."

His hand hovered over hers. He swallowed.

"There is nothing stupid about your telling me you love me. *Ever.*"

"Oh," he said quietly. He seemed to take a few moments to absorb that before he opened the primer again. "A is for 'All the ways I love you.' There are more than twenty-six, but as this is the alphabet we have, I'm going to have to restrict myself. At least for now."

He turned the page to a brilliant scarlet B, illuminated the way one might see in a medieval manuscript. Beech trees made up one side of the letter, and a butterfly perched on the top of the curve of the B. "B is for 'But I am going to make mistakes.' Something I am sure does not come as a surprise to you." He looked at her and turned the page. "C is for Confession. I don't know how to do this. I don't know how to be a husband. I don't know how to be a father. All I learned from my father is how *not* to do it—and that is rarely any guide. But…" Another turn of the page. "D is for Determination." Another page-flip. "E is for Eternity, because that's how long it will take before I give up again. F—that's for Forgiveness, because I think I'll need a great deal of that, before I start to get things right."

"You are getting things right at this very moment," Minnie said with a smile. "Keep on."

He nodded and turned the page. "G is for… G is for… G is for 'Good heavens, I should have written these down.' I've forgotten."

Minnie found the corners of her mouth twitching.

He frowned in perplexity. "Really. I have no idea what comes next. I puzzled them all out in my head, and they were going to be utterly brilliant, and when I was finished, you were going to leap in my arms and everything would be better."

Minnie leaned over and flipped a few pages over until she found the letter M. This was the page that had been on display in the bookshop when she purchased it. M was done in blues and blacks with hints of gold, the silhouettes of mulberry bushes making the dark shape of the letter against a moonlit sky. This M, perhaps, evoked midnight.

"This is the most important one," she said. "M is for Me. I'm yours, even when you make mistakes." She tapped it.

He stepped forward and slowly, slowly pulled her into his arms. "Minnie," he said, "my Minerva. What would I ever do without you?"

"There's only one other letter that we need to talk about." She turned back one page. "L is for love. Because I love you, Robert. I love you for the kindness of your heart. I love you for your honesty. I love you because you want to abolish the peerage. I love you, Robert." She pulled him close. "I'm not going to toss you out for one mistake."

"But I—"

She shook her head. "We'll get into that later. For now, Robert... There are other things that demand our attention."

"Yes," he said slowly.

"There is a crowd of reporters downstairs," she said, "and we've just told everyone who I really am."

"I'll get rid of them." He stood.

She held up one hand. "No," she said slowly. "I don't think that will be necessary."

⌘　⌘　⌘

"DO YOU EXPECT TO INTRODUCE THE DUCHESS in society?"

"What does the Dowager Duchess of Clermont think of all this?"

"Why did you write those handbills? Is it part of a parliamentary ploy?"

As Robert stepped into his front parlor a few hours later, the shouted questions overwhelmed him, rising atop one another, adding up to indistinguishable cacophony. The sun had set by now; the oil lamps burned brightly, and the bodies packed in the room had brought the temperature up above the level of comfort.

The newspapermen had been invited in fifteen minutes earlier, and apparently they'd made themselves comfortable enough to scream inside his private residence.

He waited until Oliver had entered the room behind him before he raised his hand. The shouted questions continued, but as Robert gave no answer—and instead stared the men down—eventually the hubbub subsided.

"Gentlemen," he said, when everyone had quieted down. "Let me explain what is going to happen. I have invited you into my home. I have offered you tea and sweet biscuits."

More than one hand surreptitiously brushed crumbs off of coats at that comment.

"If you abide by the rules I set, all your questions will be answered and then some. But the man who raises his voice above a pleasant, conversational tone—that man will get tossed out on his ear. The man who speaks out of turn, he will be shown the door. If you behave like a mob, you will be treated as one. If, however, you act as civilized people, we will entertain all questions."

"Your Grace," a man shouted from the back, "why the rules? Is there something in particular you fear?"

Robert shook his head gravely. "Oliver." He gestured behind him. "Please show the shouting gentleman to the door."

"Wait! I didn't—"

Robert ignored the man's protests, letting the others watch him be escorted out of the room. When the door closed on his babbled explanation, he turned to the remaining crowd. There were maybe twenty of them, perched on chairs raided from the other rooms. They all had their notebooks out. Forty eyes watched him warily.

"There are no second chances, you see," Robert said. He heard the door open once again behind him. "Oliver, if you would please demonstrate the proper way to ask a question?"

His brother went to stand next to the nearest newspaperman and then raised his hand quietly.

Robert gestured at him. "I acknowledge the gentleman on the side."

"Your Grace," Oliver asked in a normal speaking voice, "why have you set these rules? Are you afraid of something?"

"An excellent question," Robert said. "I have established these rules because, in a few moments, my duchess will be joining me, and I have no intention of exposing her to a howling mob."

The men sat up straighter at that, leaning forward.

"You see," Robert said, "it is the *manner* of asking that I care about. All questions will be entertained—although those that are too personal, we may decline to answer. Would anyone like to start?"

Glances were exchanged among the men, as if they were all afraid to get it wrong. After a few moments, a man in the back diffidently raised his hand. Robert nodded to him.

"Your Grace," the man asked, "why did you marry Minerva Lane?"

"I wanted a duchess who was beautiful, clever, and brave more than I wanted one who was well-born. I didn't need money. The fact that I was also in love with her was a welcome bonus." Robert indicated another man. "You're next."

"*Does* she wear the trousers in your marriage?"

It was a question Robert suspected he'd hear again and again, over and over, until he answered it to everyone's satisfaction.

"Do you want to know the first thing she did with my money?" Robert asked. "She visited a *modiste* in Paris."

That brought a chuckle.

"Trust me," Robert said, "anyone who looks as lovely as my wife does in skirts and a corset has no intention of wearing trousers."

Heads bent, scribbling down those words.

Minnie had been right. *They have a pattern in their mind for what a woman should be,* she'd said. *On the one hand, it's a pack of lies. But you can use those lies against them. Show them that I match the pattern in one respect, and they'll not question whether I am different in another.* She had smiled. *In my case, it's quite simple. I like pretty clothing. If we can make them see that, they'll not ask about anything else.*

"This is all well and good," another man said when Robert called on him, "but do you believe that the young Minerva Lane induced her father to defraud others, that she was the cause of his conviction and untimely death? And if so, has she repented of it?"

Robert gritted his teeth, felt his temper rise, but he forced himself to calmness. "No," he said. "Her father opened the false accounts. Her father told lies to his compatriots when she was not present. Common sense suggests that when he was caught and faced the gallows, he was willing to tell another lie to save himself, no matter who it harmed.

"The Duchess of Clermont has suffered enough for her father's falsehoods," he said. "In this, I must claim the right of husband." He smiled tightly. "And so I'll beat the stuffing out of anyone who suggests otherwise."

His pronouncement was met by the sound of a dozen pens scratching against paper.

If you say that, Minnie had said, *you know you'll have to do it. At least once.*

He was looking forward to it.

"Speaking of whom," Robert said, "I do believe it's time for me to fetch her."

He turned around, aware of the soft susurrus that arose behind him. He opened the side door and stepped through.

Minnie was waiting in the adjacent room, hands clasped, pacing from side to side.

He stopped at the sight of her. She was wearing a gown he'd never seen before—one that had, no doubt, been commissioned in Paris between bouts of lovemaking. It was a brilliant crimson in color, the kind of gown that would draw every eye. She was laced tightly, emphasizing her curves. And she was wearing the rubies he'd given her.

She had a black lace shawl looped over her arms, which were otherwise bare, and flowers in her hair. But to all this, she'd added something he'd only seen in paintings from the last century. She'd added a simple black beauty patch at the corner of her mouth. It drew the eye to her scar, made that web of white across her cheek seem like a purposeful decoration instead of a reminder of a senseless act of violence. The very modernity of her gown, coupled with that antique fashion, made her seem like a creature from no century at all.

He realized that he'd stopped dead, staring.

"You know, Minnie," he said, slightly hoarse, "you're ravishing."

"Am I? Your mother hates the patch," she said. "Are there many of them?"

He went to her. "Almost twenty. But I've done my best to frighten them into civility. Are you sure you want to do this?"

She drew in breath; that diamond shuddered on her bosom. "Positive."

He took her hand. "Because I'm willing to send them to the devil..."

Her palm was cold, clammy, her breath a little rapid.

"...and I'll be here by your side the entire time," he said. "Nobody will come close. I promise."

"I know." She squeezed his hand and then, together, they walked back to the front parlor. She paused in the entrance. He wasn't even sure if it was nerves that stopped her or if she simply wanted to make an impression.

In any event, it was clear that she had. The men let out little gasps of disbelief—as if they expected, somehow, that she would have shown up at the door in coat and trousers. And then they scrambled to their feet.

Minnie smiled. Robert, holding her hand, could feel her pulse racing in her wrist, could feel her fingers digging into his palm as all those eyes fell on her. He knew how much that smile cost her. He also knew that if they'd shouted at that moment, if they'd made any noise at all like a mob, she might have passed out right then. Instead, the men were silent as death, not wanting to be tossed out.

He conveyed her to the divan at the head of the room, seated her, and then sat himself.

The divan was on a little bit of a raised platform.

Minnie looked around, taking them all in. "Well," she said. "I suppose this is as close as I'll come to a throne."

That drew a surprised laugh from the crowd.

"You'll have to excuse me, gentlemen." Her voice was quiet, so quiet that everyone strained forward to hear her. "I've asked for silence. My voice is not loud, and I am nervous."

A hand went up at that. "Are you afraid of what truths we might uncover?"

A bold question to pose to her face. Minnie didn't flinch.

"No," she responded simply. "My fear is more primal in origin. When I was twelve..." She paused, took a measured breath, and continued. "Well, I believe you all know what happened when I was twelve, from my father's statement in the courtroom to the mob that surrounded me afterward. They left me with this scar." She touched her cheek. "Ever since then, large groups have made me faint of breath. I cannot bear to have so many eyes looking at me without remembering that time. In fact, I'm grateful for you all taking shorthand. It's far better than having you stare at me en masse." She said it with a deprecating smile, but her fingers were still tightly clenched around Robert's.

Pens scribbled away at that. They wouldn't detect what Robert could see so clearly—the pallor of her cheeks, the light pink of lips that were usually rose.

"Even now," Minnie said, "all these years after, thinking about it makes my hands tremble." She disentangled her hand from Robert's and held it up in proof. "If there were ten more of you, I am not sure I could do this. And if you were shouting, I might actually pass out." She gave them another smile. "That *is* what happened in the courtroom today."

"How will you attend balls, parties—the sort of gatherings where duchesses are obligated to make appearances?"

"I am sure," Minnie said, "that I will receive many kind invitations from my peers for precisely those events."

They'd discussed that exact question, going over it again and again, until each word was perfect.

"I am also sure," she said, "that everyone will understand that when I refuse those invitations, no malice is intended. Over the course of the next few years, however, my husband and I will be hosting a series of smaller events. I will be overseeing a number of my husband's charitable concerns, and I feel confident that I will come to know many of my peers that way."

"And you're not afraid that you'll be shunned for your prior history?"

"I'm sure there are some who will not wish to know me. But my situation no doubt means that my circle of acquaintances will be, by necessity, exclusive. If any woman wishes to withdraw herself from contention for a place there, she is more than welcome to do so." She smiled at the gathered men.

As she spoke, they transcribed her words in shorthand. They would appear verbatim in half the papers around the nation. But while they all wrote, a few men lifted their heads to look at her.

She looked undoubtedly feminine; she'd shown them a weakness and put them at ease. But the gray-haired reporter on the side—Parret, Robert thought he was—was giving Minnie an interested look. He'd been covering London gossip and politics for longer than either of them had been alive, and he was perhaps recognizing what Robert already knew. The Duchess of Clermont had just issued a challenge to the ladies of London. She wasn't going to beg for their company or grovel for their good opinion. Her friendship was a singular, original honor, and she would bestow it with care.

Parret raised his hand. "Your Grace," he said, "was your talent for chess a...childhood fluke? A fraud?"

A little smile played across her face, this time genuine. "No," she said simply. "It wasn't."

He raised an eyebrow and contemplated her. "You said you were nervous. You don't look nervous."

"When I used to feel anxious, I would once tell myself that I felt nothing. It helped, a little, until I could get away by myself." Her hand folded around Robert's. "Now I know I'm not alone. And that helps even more."

Not alone.

It wasn't just her hand in his, their bodies side by side on the divan. It was a sense that they were facing not just this trial together, but a life. It wouldn't be easy. It wouldn't even always be fun. But even at the worst times, it would be better for her by his side.

Not alone. It filled him, that certainty. To their side, Oliver was smiling faintly. Minnie set her other hand atop Robert's, and for a second, he looked into her eyes. When this was finished—when they'd sent these men running to tell the world that the Duke and Duchess of Clermont were a force to be reckoned with—he'd show her how not-alone she was.

He'd leave the necklace on, he decided. Everything else...

"Your Grace," someone asked, interrupting his reverie, "if we could talk about those handbills? What was your intention with them?"

"Ah, yes," Robert said. "It's quite simple. I'm a duke. As such, I consider myself responsible for not just my own welfare, but that of the entire country." He smiled, met his brother's eyes, and leaned forward. "If we silence those who wish to speak, how can I do my job? Captain Stevens's arrest was just the beginning."

Now Minnie's hands tightened around his.

"I don't know how much I'll achieve in my lifetime," he said, "but this is just the beginning."

Epilogue

Four years later.

IT MIGHT HAVE LOOKED LIKE ANY OTHER DAY to anyone else, but Robert knew better. The tension in the air was thick; a gentleman beside him clenched his fist and leaned forward. Beside him, Oliver and his father sat, looking on. Lydia and her husband were perched on chairs across the room. Lydia knew little of chess, but still she watched with her hand on her mouth. Three others made those present eight, not counting the two people in the middle of the room.

But eight was no longer enough to make Minnie nervous. Indeed, she looked to have forgotten everything. She sat at the small table that had been set up in the middle of the room, and she appeared to be the only one in the room who felt no nerves at all.

She had taken London by storm—which was to say, as with any good storm, some people stayed indoors when they saw her coming. But by and large, the people who mattered hadn't shunned her. There had been more curiosity regarding the Duchess of Clermont than there had been ill feelings. She'd given salons—exclusive salons, limited in number—and people had come. Important people.

Gradually, she'd relaxed into the role. She still wouldn't go to large parties; she still tried to avoid people watching her on the streets. But in settings like this… In settings like this, everyone could see her for who she really was. She was dressed in a gorgeous blue silk gown, and she didn't seem to be put out at all, even though the man across from her had begun to sweat.

Finally, he picked up his piece. He held it in his hand and then set it down. Gustav Hernst, who had ended up as the winner of the first International Chess Tournament in London some fifteen years earlier, played his piece.

Minnie studied the board casually. She picked up a piece after a moment's contemplation and then, with everyone watching, gave it a kiss.

Hernst shook his head and toppled his king on the board. He slumped in his chair. "You are still very good," he said. "Too good. You should have won the last time we played." His German accent was barely noticeable. "But I could not resist."

Minnie stood and held out her hand. "A good game," she said.

"An excellent game. I am glad your husband invited me. What happened all those years ago…it should never have taken place. The game should not have been stopped, most particularly not when you were about to win. It always rankled. It is my pleasure to make things right."

At that, Minnie looked over at Robert. After all these years, the warmth he felt when looking into her eyes hadn't faded. It had grown deeper still, familiarity lending him a knowledge of her moods. She smiled at him and held out her hand.

"Come," she said. "There's a little refreshment laid out in the main hall."

But when everyone left the room, they let Oliver serve as guide. Minnie and Robert lingered behind, and once everyone had disappeared down the corridor, they opened the door across the way.

The Dowager Duchess of Clermont had refused to watch what she termed the spectacle, claiming that it was improper and foolish. But Robert had suspected an ulterior motive on her part.

And indeed, young Evan, scarcely three years old, sat on her knee, staring at the primer. "Goose!" he proclaimed happily.

"What else is G for?"

"Grandmama," Evan said.

The woman snorted. "Flatterer. Choose another word, if you please."

Evan frowned. "Gray," he finally said. "You have gray hair. Did you know that?"

"Now *that* is calumny of the worst sort," his mother said calmly. But her arms curled around her grandson, and she leaned in, breathing in his scent.

"Mama," Robert said, "refreshments are being served in the main salon."

She looked up. "Oh," she said with a small frown. "I'm…busy." Her head bent again, and a small smile touched her lips. "I'm very busy."

Thank you!

Thanks for reading *The Duchess War*. I hope you enjoyed it!

- Would you like to know when my next book is available? You can sign up for my new release e-mail list at www.courtneymilan.com, follow me on twitter at @courtneymilan, or like my Facebook page at http://facebook.com/courtneymilanauthor.
- Reviews help other readers find books. I appreciate all reviews, whether positive or negative.
- You've just read the first full-length book in the Brothers Sinister series. The books in the series are *The Governess Affair*, a prequel novella about Oliver's parents, *The Duchess War*, *A Kiss for Midwinter*, *The Heiress Effect*, *The Countess Conspiracy* (out late 2013), and *The Mistress Rebellion* (out sometime in 2014). I hope you enjoy them all!

If you'd like to read an excerpt from *The Heiress Effect*, Oliver Marshall's story, and *A Kiss for Midwinter*, Lydia Charingford's story, please turn the page.

The Brothers Sinister: Excerpts

Excerpt from *The Heiress Effect*:

Miss Jane Fairfield can't do anything right. When she's in company, she always says the wrong thing--and rather too much of it. No matter how costly they are, her gowns fall on the unfortunate side of fashion. Even her immense dowry can't save her from being an object of derision.

And that's precisely what she wants. She'll do anything, even risk humiliation, if it means she can stay unmarried and keep her sister safe.

Mr. Oliver Marshall has to do everything right. He's the bastard son of a duke, raised in humble circumstances—and he intends to give voice and power to the common people. If he makes one false step, he'll never get the chance to accomplish anything. He doesn't need to come to the rescue of the wrong woman. He certainly doesn't need to fall in love with her. But there's something about the lovely, courageous Jane that he can't resist…even though it could mean the ruin of them both.

Cambridgeshire, England, January 1867

MOST OF THE NUMBERS THAT Miss Jane Victoria Fairfield had encountered in her life had proven harmless. For instance, the seamstress fitting her gown had poked her seven times while placing forty-three straight pins—but the pain had vanished quickly enough. The twelve holes in Jane's corset were an evil, true, but a necessary one; without them, she would never have reduced her waist from its unfashionable thirty-seven inch span down to the still unfashionable girth of thirty-one inches.

Two was not a terrible numeral, even when it described the number of Johnson sisters that stood behind her, watching the seamstress pin the gown against her less-than-fashionable form.

Not even when said sisters had tittered no fewer than six times in the past half hour. These numbers were annoyances—mere flies that could be waved away with one gilt-covered fan.

No, all Jane's problems could be blamed on two numbers. *One hundred thousand* was the first one, and it was absolute poison.

Jane took as deep a breath as she could manage in her corset and inclined her head to Miss Geraldine and Miss Genevieve Johnson. The two young ladies could do no wrong in the eyes of society. They wore almost identical day gowns—one of pale blue muslin, the other of pale green. They wielded identical fans, both covered with painted scenes of bucolic idleness. They were both beautiful in the most clichéd, china-doll fashion: Wedgwood-blue eyes and pale blond hair that curled in fat, shining ringlets. Their waists came in well under twenty inches. The only way to distinguish between the sisters was that Geraldine Johnson had a perfectly placed, perfectly natural beauty mark on her right cheek, while Genevieve had an equally perfect mark on her left.

They had been kind to Jane the first few weeks they'd known her.

She suspected they were actually pleasant when they were not pushed to their extreme limits. Jane, as it turned out, had a talent for pushing even very nice girls into unkindness.

The seamstress placed one last pin. "There," the woman said. "Now take a look in the mirror and tell me if you want me to change anything out—move some of the lace, mayhap, or use less of it."

Poor Mrs. Sandeston. She said those words the way a man scheduled to be hanged this afternoon might talk about the weather on the morrow—wistfully, as if the thought of less lace were a luxury, something that would be experienced only by an extraordinary and unlikely act of executive clemency.

Jane sashayed forward and took in the effect of her new gown. She didn't even have to pretend to smile—the expression spread across her face like melted butter on warm bread. God, the gown was hideous. So *utterly* hideous. Never before had so much money been put in the service of so little taste. She batted her eyes at the mirror in glee; her reflection flirted back with her: dark-haired, dark-eyed, coquettish and mysterious.

"What do you ladies think?" she asked, turning about. "Ought I have more lace?"

At her feet, the beleaguered Mrs. Sandeston let out a whimper.

As well she should. The gown already overflowed with three different kinds of lace. Thick waves of blue *point de gaze* had been wrapped, yard after obnoxiously expensive yard, around the skirt. A filmy piece of *duchesse* lace from Belgium marked her décolletage, and a black Chantilly in a clashing flowered pattern made dark slashes down the sleeves of her gown. The fabric was a lovely patterned silk. Not that anyone would be able to see it under its burden of lace frosting.

This gown was an abomination of lace, and Jane loved it.

A real friend, Jane supposed, would have told her to get rid of the lace, all of it.

Genevieve nodded. "More lace. I definitely think it needs more lace. A fourth kind, perhaps?"

Good God. Where she was to put more lace, she didn't know.

"A cunning belt, worked of lace?" Geraldine offered.

It was a curious sort of friendship, the one she shared with the Johnson twins. They were known for their unerring taste; consequently, they never failed to steer Jane wrong. But they did it so nicely, it was almost a pleasure to be laughed at by them.

As Jane wanted to be steered astray, she welcomed their efforts.

They lied to her; she lied to them. Since Jane wanted to be an object of ridicule, it worked out delightfully for all concerned.

Sometimes, Jane wondered what it would be like if they were ever honest with each other. If maybe the Johnsons might have become real friends instead of lovely, polite enemies.

Geraldine eyed Jane's gown and gave a decisive nod. "I absolutely support the notion of a lace belt. It would give this gown that certain air of indefinable dignity that it currently lacks."

Mrs. Sandeston made a strangled sound.

It was only sometimes that Jane wondered if they could have been friends. Usually, she remembered the reasons she couldn't *have* real friends. All one hundred thousand of them.

So she simply nodded at the Johnsons' horrific suggestions. "What think you two of that clever strip of Maltese that we saw earlier—the gold one, the one with the rosettes?"

"Absolutely," Geraldine said, nodding her head. "The Maltese."

The sisters cast each other looks above their fans—an exchange of sly smiles saying, clear as day: *Let's see what we can get the Feather Heiress to do today.*

"Miss Fairfield." Mrs. Sandeston put her hands together in an unthinking imitation of prayer. "I beg you. Keep in mind that one can achieve a far superior effect by employing fewer furbelows. A lovely piece of lace, now, that's the centerpiece of a beautiful gown, dazzling in its simplicity. Too much, and..." She trailed off with a suggestive twirl of her finger.

"Too *little,*" Genevieve said calmly, "and nobody will know what you have to offer. Geraldine and I—well, we have only a mere ten thousand apiece, so our gowns must reflect that."

Geraldine gripped her fan. "Alas," she intoned.

"But you—Miss Fairfield, *you* have a dowry of one hundred thousand pounds. You have to make sure that people know it. Nothing says wealth like lace."

"And nothing says lace like...more lace," Geraldine added.

They exchanged another set of looks.

Jane smiled. "Thank you," she said. "I don't know what I would do without the two of you. You've been so good to me, tutoring me in all things. I have no notion of what's fashionable, nor of what message my clothing sends. Without you to guide me, who knows how I might blunder?"

Mrs. Sandeston made a choking noise in her throat, but said nothing more.

One hundred thousand pounds. One of the reasons Jane was here, watching these lovely, perfect women exchange wicked smiles that they didn't think Jane could understand. They leaned toward one another and whispered—mouths hidden demurely behind fans—and then, glancing her way, let out a collective giggle. They thought her a complete buffoon, devoid of taste and sense and reason.

It didn't hurt, not one bit.

It didn't hurt to know that they called her friend to her face and sought to expose her foolishness to everyone they saw. It didn't hurt that they egged her on to more—more lace, more jewels, more beads—simply so they might fuel their amusement. It didn't hurt that the entire population of Cambridge laughed at her.

It couldn't hurt. After all, Jane had chosen this for herself.

She smiled at them as if their giggles were the sincerest token of friendship. "The Maltese it is."

One hundred thousand pounds. There were more crushing burdens than the weight of one hundred thousand pounds.

"You'll want to be wearing that gown Wednesday next," Geraldine suggested. "You've been invited to the Marquess of Bradenton's dinner party, have you not? We insisted." Those fans worked their way up and down, up and down.

Jane smiled. "Of course. I wouldn't miss it, not for the world."

"There will be a new fellow there. A duke's son. Born on the other side of the blanket, unfortunately—but acknowledged nonetheless. Almost as good as the real thing."

Damn. Jane hated meeting new men, and a duke's bastard sounded like the most dangerous kind of all. He would have a high opinion of himself and a low opinion of his pocketbook. It was precisely that sort of man who would see Jane's one hundred thousand pounds and decide that he might be able to overlook the lace dripping off her. That kind of man would overlook a great many defects if it would put her dowry in his bank account.

"Oh?" she said noncommittally.

"Mr. Oliver Marshall," Genevieve said. "I saw him on the street. He doesn't—"

Her sister gave her a gentle nudge, and Genevieve cleared her throat.

"I mean, he looks quite elegant. His spectacles are very distinguished. And his hair is quite…bright and…coppery."

Jane could just imagine this specimen of thwarted dukehood in her mind's eye. He would be paunchy. He would wear ridiculous waistcoats, and he'd have a fob watch that he checked incessantly. He'd be proud of his prerogatives and bitter of a world that had led him to be born outside of wedlock.

"He would be utterly perfect for you, Jane," Geraldine said. "Of course, with our lesser dowries, he would find us quite…uninteresting."

Jane made herself smile. "I don't know what I would do without you two," she said, quite sincerely. "If I didn't have you to look out for me, why, I might…"

If she didn't have them trying to set her up as a laughingstock, she might one day—despite her best efforts—manage to impress a man. And *that* would be a disaster.

"I feel that you two are like my sisters, given the care you take for me," she said. Maybe like stepsisters in a blood-curdling fairy tale.

"We feel the same," Geraldine smiled at her. "As if you were our sister."

There were almost as many smiles in that room as there was lace on her gown. Jane offered up a silent apology for her lie.

These women were *nothing* like her sister. To say as much was to insult the name of sisterhood, and if anything was sacred to Jane, it was that. She had a sister—a sister she would do anything for. For Emily, she would lie, cheat, buy a dress with four different kinds of lace…

One hundred thousand pounds was not much of a burden to carry. But if a young lady wanted to remain unmarried—if she *needed* to stay with her sister until said sister was of age and could leave their guardian's home—that same number became an impossibility.

Almost as impossible as four hundred and eighty—the number of days that Jane had to stay unmarried.

Four hundred and eighty days until her sister attained her majority. In four hundred and eighty days, her sister could leave their guardian, and Jane—Jane who was allowed to stay in the household on the condition that she marry the first eligible man who offered—would be able to dispense with all this pretending. She and Emily would finally be free.

Jane would smile, wear ells of lace, and call Napoleon Bonaparte himself her sister if it would keep Emily safe.

Instead, all she had to do for the next four hundred and eighty days was to look for a husband—to look assiduously, and not marry.

Four hundred and eighty days in which she dared not marry, and one hundred thousand pounds to the man who would marry her.

Those two numbers described the dimensions of her prison.

And so Jane smiled at Geraldine once again, grateful for her advice, grateful to be steered wrong once again. She smiled, and she even meant it.

⌘ ⌘ ⌘

Excerpt from *A Kiss for Midwinter*:

Doctor Jonas Grantham doesn't believe in optimism, good cheer, or holiday spirits. But he does believe in love—and it's just his luck that the woman he adores, the vibrantly beautiful Miss Lydia Charingford, wants nothing to do with him. This winter, though, he's vowed to let her know how he feels. Even though he suspects it means that she'll never speak to him again…

AS SHE SPOKE, LYDIA GATHERED UP HER THINGS and placed them carefully in her satchel, securing the container of ink in a side-pocket so that it wouldn't be jostled about. She was aware that she was humming as she did so—a rendition of *Good King Wenceslas*.

Christmas was almost on them, and she couldn't have been happier. The air smelled of cinnamon and ginger. Pine boughs decorated lintels, even here at the Nag's Head. It was a time for wassail and cheer and—

"Happen we all miss your Miss Pursling—that is, the Duchess of Clermont," Crawford said softly. "Yes, my Willa would love your company."

The smile froze on Lydia's face.

Wassail, cheer, and the slight, selfish emptiness she experienced when she remembered that her best friend was no longer a mere hour's journey away, but a hundred miles distant.

But she forced her lips into a wider grin. "La, silly," she said. "I'll see her again next autumn, just as soon as Parliament lets out. How could I miss her?" If she smiled wide enough, it might fill that space in her heart. She pulled on her gloves. "Happy Christmas, Marybeth."

Lydia had her own idea for a Christmas for Marybeth Peters—something far better than a basket. She only needed her father to agree.

The group scattered in a shower of holiday greetings. Lydia waited until they were all gone, waving cheerfully, wishing everyone the best for the holidays.

Almost everyone. Her cheeks ached from smiling, but she would *not* look to her left. She wouldn't give him the satisfaction.

"Well," a dark voice said to her side as the door closed on Marybeth, "you are chock-full of holiday spirit, Miss Charingford."

Lydia looked pointedly in front of her at the ivy-and-pine centerpiece on the table. "Why, yes," she said. "I suppose I am. Happy Christmas, Doctor Grantham."

He didn't thank her for the sentiment. He surely didn't return a polite greeting of his own. Instead, Doctor Grantham laughed softly and her spine prickled.

Lydia turned to him. He was tall—so very much taller than her that she had to tilt her neck at an unnatural angle to stare him down. His eyes sparkled with a dark intensity, and his mouth curled up at one corner, as if he nursed his own private amusement. He was handsome in a brooding sort of way, with those eyes, that strong, jagged nose. All the other girls giggled when he looked their way. But Grantham made Lydia remember things she didn't like to think about.

He particularly made her remember them now. He looked at her down his nose and gave her a faint, mocking smile, as if she'd made a terrible error by offering him holiday greetings.

Lydia straightened. "Happy Christmas," she repeated, her voice tight. "You're allowed to say it back even if you don't *really* wish the other person happy. It's a polite nothing. I won't imagine you mean anything by it—just as you know that I don't truly care whether you're happy."

"I didn't think you were wishing me happy," Grantham responded. "I thought you were simply describing events as you saw them. Tell me, Miss Charingford, is it *really* a happy Christmas for you?"

Lydia flushed. Christmas memories were not always fond. In fact, Christmas brought to mind the worst moments in her life. Leaving home with her mother and her best friend six years earlier. A dingy house let in Cornwall, and that awful, awful night when the cramps had come...

"Yes," she said forcefully. "Yes, it is. Christmas is a time for happiness."

He laughed again softly—mockingly, she thought, as if he knew not only the secret that she kept from all of Leicester, but the one she held hidden in her heart. He laughed as if he'd been there on that dreadful night that had seemed the absolute opposite of Christmas—an evening when a girl who was very much not a virgin had miscarried. There'd been blood and tears rather than heavenly choirs.

"You," he said to her, "you of all people…you should relent from this incessant well-wishing." He shrugged. "You *do* know that it doesn't make any difference, whether you wish me well or I wish you happy."

Lydia's eyebrows rose. "Me, of all people?" He'd so closely echoed her thoughts. Sometimes, it seemed as if he knew precisely what she was thinking—and when he spoke, it was designed to make her feel badly. Lydia bared her teeth at him in a smile. "What do you mean by that? Have I less of a right to good cheer than the average person?"

"Less of a right? No. Less of a reason, however…"

"I couldn't know what you intend by such veiled assertions."

His eyes met hers, and he raised one sardonic eyebrow. "Then let me unveil them. I am, of course, referring to the man who got you with child while you were one yourself."

She gasped.

"I am always astonished, Miss Charingford, when you manage to have a happy word for any member of my sex. That you do—and do it often— never ceases to amaze me."

The room was empty but for them, and he stood two feet from her. He'd spoken so quietly there wasn't the least danger of their being overheard. It didn't matter. Lydia balled her hands into fists. The smile she'd scarcely been able to form moments before was forgotten entirely.

"How dare you!" she hissed. "A *gentleman* would do his best to forget that he knew such a thing."

He didn't seem concerned at all with her assertion. "But you see, Miss Charingford, I must be a doctor before I allow myself to be a gentleman. I do not recall such a thing in order to hold you up for moral condemnation. I state it as a simple medical fact, one that would be relevant to further treatment. Certain female complaints, for instance—"

Lydia bristled. "Put it out of your mind. You will never treat me as a patient. *Ever.*"

Doctor Grantham did not look put out by this. Instead, he shook his head at her slowly, and gave her a smile that felt…wicked. "So be it. When you're trampled by a runaway stallion, I shall be sure to express my wholehearted regrets to your parents. 'No, no,' I will say. 'I couldn't possibly stop your daughter from bleeding to death on the pavement—my professional ethics forbid me to treat anyone who has unequivocally refused me consent.'"

He was laughing at her again. Well, technically, he wasn't *actually* laughing. But he was looking at her as if he wanted to, as if he couldn't wait for her to scramble and reverse her prior edict. Lydia gave him a firm

nod instead. "Good. I would rather bleed to death than have your hands
on me." She tucked her gloves under her arm, and reached for her shawl.

He was still smiling at her. "I'll pay my respects at your funeral."

"I don't want you there. If you dare come, I'll haunt you in your
sleep."

But that only sparked a wicked gleam in his eye. He took a step closer,
forcing her to tilt her head up all at an unnatural angle. He leaned over her,
bending his neck. And then he whispered.

"Why, Miss Charingford." That smile of his tilted, stretching. "There's
no need to wait until you're *dead* to visit my bed. In fact, I'm available right
now, so long as we finish before—"

She didn't think. She pulled back her arm and slapped him as hard as
she could—slapped him so hard that she could feel the blow reverberating
all the way back to her shoulder.

He rubbed his cheek and straightened. "I suppose I deserved that," he
said, somewhat ruefully. "Your pardon, Miss Charingford. I was in the
wrong. I should never have spoken of that way." He looked down. "In my
defense—and I know this is a weak defense—we were talking about death,
and that always brings out the worst of my humor. Which, as you have no
doubt discovered, is abominable to begin with. I pray that I do not one
day watch you bleed to death on the streets." His voice was solemn, and
for once, that twinkle vanished from his eyes. "I hope it is not you. But it
will be someone, and the only thing I can do about it is laugh."

For a moment, she almost felt a tug of sympathy. To deal with death
every day, to have only humor to keep the specter of darkness at arm's
length… But then she remembered everything he had said to her—those
pointed reminders that she was a fallen woman. She remembered his all-
too-knowing eyes, following her across the room whenever she
encountered him. She might have been able to forget her mistake for
months on end were it not for him.

She wound her scarf around her neck. "Now you've made me regret
striking you."

"Truly?" That eyebrow raised again.

He stood close, so close that when she picked up her coat, he was
able to intervene and hold it out for her. Nice of him to act the gentleman
now, now when it meant that she sensed the warmth of his hands against
hers, his bare fingers brushing her wrist. His touch should have been cold,
like his depraved, shriveled heart. Instead, a jolt of heat traveled through
her.

"Truly." She set her hat on her head and adjusted the cuffs of her coat
to cover her gloves. "You see, I interrupted you before you told me how

long you were giving yourself to finish the deed. I'd not have given you above thirty seconds, myself."

His crack of laughter followed her out the door. She could hear it echoing in her mind—laughter that sounded jolly and fun, without a hint of meanness to it, the kind of laughter she would expect to hear next to the sprightly ring of Christmas bells. It wasn't fair that Doctor Jonas Grantham of all people could laugh like that. Still, she heard it playing in her mind—saw him, his head thrown back, delighted—until the wind-swept streets swallowed up the sound of his merriment.

Other Books by Courtney

The Brothers Sinister Series
The Governess Affair
The Duchess War
A Kiss for Midwinter
The Heiress Effect
The Countess Conspiracy — December 2013
The Mistress Rebellion — 2014

Not in any series
What Happened at Midnight
The Lady Always Wins

The Turner Series
Unveiled
Unlocked
Unclaimed
Unraveled

The Carhart Series
This Wicked Gift
Proof by Seduction
Trial by Desire

Author's Note

I GIVE ALL MY BOOKS CODE NAMES, which I usually reveal on my website. This one was called "Chess Champion," and as the name was a spoiler, I didn't want to include it there. But now you know.

Every piece of historical fiction alters history in at least some tiny regard. For this book, I had to shift history in several instances, and I wanted to acknowledge those areas upfront.

First, and most obviously, the first international chess tournament—which did take place in London in 1851—was won by Adolf Anderssen rather than Gustav Hernst, and there were no shenanigans involved in the running of the tournament, nor were there twelve-year-old children of any gender involved.

The description about what happened to Minnie when people discovered she was a girl—and her father betrayed her—was taken from a newspaper clipping that I read years ago. It described a man who was discovered to be a woman. A crowd formed, and the woman was beaten up. Gender roles were very strictly policed back then.

My largest departure, and one that would change the world that followed, is the scientific discoveries that Sebastian lectures about here. I wanted Sebastian to be an infamous scientist and a follower of Darwin, but I also wanted him to be able to put forth discoveries of his own that were just as revolutionary. Those who follow the history of science know that in our world the science of genetics was first discovered by Gregor Mendel, in a paper that was presented in 1866, which went absolutely nowhere. Nobody made the connection between Mendel's discovery and the theory of evolution, even though what Mendel set forth was essentially a theory for the transfer of genes from one generation to the next. It wasn't until early in the twentieth century that Mendel's work was rediscovered and given its due.

In my world, I have claimed Mendel's work for Sebastian. These are discoveries he *could* have made at the time. But the discovery of genetics by someone who had direct contact with Charles Darwin would radically change the pace of scientific advancement. In that sense, the world I have written would have to necessarily diverge from the world we live in after the time of these books.

(Actually, Sebastian's work started with the color of snapdragons, which, unlike Mendel's peas, are incompletely dominant to each other.)

In a fourth departure, the Leicester of 1863 really didn't need a duke to write handbills and radicalize the populace. It was fairly radical on its own. For instance, by 1863, workers in Leicester had started a food cooperative. Today, the idea of a food co-op seems more commonplace. At the time, it was a huge stride forward. Workers were paid by factory owners, who also owned most of the shops nearby.

A food cooperative—one where workers pooled their money and used it to bring in fruits and vegetables at reasonable prices—was in fact a huge advance in factory towns. It allowed workers to pay less and get more, and Leicester's food cooperative was one of the first—and one of the most successful—to be put in place. Stevens refers to it as a "radical" item, and in point of fact, it would have seemed so to some factory owners. Anything that reduced the dependence that workers had on their masters was "radical."

Another subject of civil unrest was the question of vaccination. Vaccinations first became mandatory in England in 1853, and many people absolutely hated it. It was the subject of a great deal of civil disobedience. The reasons given at that time were *very* different from those that are given by those who dislike vaccines today. (For one thing, vaccinating people before the germ theory of disease was understood led to all sorts of complications that we don't face today. Think of the diseases that are spread today by reusing needles.) and the inclusion of that tiny part of the historical debate is meant only to represent the times, not to say anything about the modern issue.

Whether a duke in 1863 might, in fact, work for the abolition of the peerage is not something I can know. In any event, I don't know if Robert would have been happy with the pace of improvement in England. Today, British peers are no longer tried by the House of Lords; they no longer have veto power over bills passed by the House of Commons. And hey, it only took a small handful of centuries to get to that point.

Oliver asks for "carbon oil" when he is imprisoned. Referring to the substance he wanted as "carbon oil" is a little bit of a stretch on my part. In the United States, we'd call it "kerosene." In the UK, it's referred to as "paraffin." Using the latter term proved confusing for early readers who associated paraffin with the waxy stuff that's used in manicures these days. In the early 1860s, paraffin/kerosene/carbon oil was new enough that usage hadn't been nailed down. "Carbon oil" *was* used to describe the substance. In this instance, I decided to take a little liberty and go with a name that it could have been called by at that time, one that wouldn't confuse anyone.

Acknowledgments

I NEVER KNOW WHERE TO START with acknowledgments, because there are so many people who must be acknowledged. At best, I hope to remember people in large groups, crossing my fingers that I don't forget anyone important. Invariably, I forget almost everyone. First and foremost, my family—my parents and my many sisters and few brothers—I'm always grateful for you, for understanding things that don't make sense to anyone else. Mr. Milan, for preferring cantankerousness generally. And I'm especially grateful for Pele and Silver, which makes no sense at all because they do nothing but demand attention and toss mice around.

This book wasn't easy to write or edit. Tessa, Carey, and Leigh, I don't know what I would do without you. Peeners—ditto. Sherry and Tessa once again helped me write back cover copy, because seriously, I suck at that. Robin Harders always pushes me to think about things I'd rather not think about; Martha Trachtenberg catches all the many ways I spell people's names, because seriously, I suck at that, too. Nick Ambrose is fast and reliable, and without Anne Victory, I'd be saying "Oops!" a lot more.

But mostly, I want to thank my readers. Every difficult book reaches a point where I want to kick it and scream and run around in circles. If I didn't know that you were waiting for this, I might have huddled in a little shivering ball on my bed instead of taking a deep breath and going back to writing. You make it worth it for me, and I hope I returned the favor.

CPSIA information can be obtained
at www.ICGtesting.com
Printed in the USA
LVOW12s2329220316

480330LV00003B/198/P